**“I am to … nt for you,” I…**



“What are the…

“Seven years’ house arrest here in Haslam.”

“Seven *years*?”

“Or I take you as my wife.”

“That’s not funny. Not even remotely funny.”

“It’s not a joke. I either marry you, or leave you here in Haslam to begin your house arrest.”

He saw Jemma recoil and her face turn white.

“I warned you that Sheikh Azizzi would not be lenient. He is not a Copeland fan either. He knows what your father did to my mother, and he wants to send a message that Saidia will not tolerate crime or immorality.”

“But seven years!” She reached for the edge of the table to steady herself. “That’s…that’s…so long.”

“Seven years or marriage,” he corrected.

“No. *No.* Marriage isn’t an option. I won’t marry you. I would never marry you. I *could* never marry you.”

# THE DISGRACED COPELANDS

***A family in the headlines—for all the wrong reasons!***

For the Copeland family each day brings another tabloid scandal. Their world was one of unrivalled luxury and glittering social events. Now their privileged life is nothing but a distant memory…

Staring the taunting paparazzi straight in the eye, the Copeland heirs seek to start new lives—with no one to rely on but themselves. At least that's what they think…!

*It seems fame and riches can't buy happiness—but they make it fun trying!*

Read Morgan Copeland's story in:
*The Fallen Greek Bride*

Read Jemma Copeland's story in:
*His Defiant Desert Queen*

Look out for more scandalous stories about

***The Disgraced Copelands***

by Jane Porter

*Coming soon!*

# HIS DEFIANT DESERT QUEEN

BY

JANE PORTER

MILLS & BOON

Published in Great Britain 2015
by Mills & Boon, an imprint of Harlequin (UK) Limited,
Eton House, 18-24 Paradise Road, Richmond, Surrey, TW9 1SR



ISBN: 978-0-263-25054-1

Harlequin (UK) Limited's policy is to use papers that are natural, renewable and recyclable products and made from wood grown in sustainable forests. The logging and manufacturing processes conform to the legal environmental regulations of the country of origin.

Printed and bound in Spain
by CPI, Barcelona

*New York Times* and *USA TODAY* bestselling author **Jane Porter** has written forty romances and eleven women's fiction novels since her first sale to Mills & Boon® Modern™ Romance in 2000. A five-time RITA® finalist, Jane is known for her passionate, emotional and sensual novels, and loves nothing more than alpha heroes, exotic locations and happy-ever-afters. Today Jane lives in sunny San Clemente, California, with her surfer husband and three sons. Visit www.janeporter.com

**Books by Jane Porter**

***The Disgraced Copelands***

*The Fallen Greek Bride*

***A Royal Scandal***

*His Majesty's Mistake*
*Not Fit for a King?*

***The Desert Kings***

*King of the Desert, Captive Bride*
*The Sheikh's Chosen Queen*

***Greek Tycoons***

*At the Greek Boss's Bidding*

***Ruthless***

*Hollywood Husband, Contract Wife*

***Desert Brides***

*The Sheikh's Disobedient Bride*

*A Dark Sicilian Secret*
*Duty, Desire and the Desert King*

**Visit the author profile page at**
**www.millsandboon.co.uk for more titles**

For Lee Hyat,
who has been there every step of the way since reading *The Italian Groom*! Thank you for being my first reader and a most loyal and cherished friend.

# PROLOGUE

SEETHING, SHEIKH MIKAEL KARIM, King of Saidia, watched the high fashion photo shoot taking place in the desert—his desert—wondering how anyone could think it was okay to enter a foreign country under a false identity and think he, or *she*, as it happened to be in this case, could get away with it.

Apparently the world was filled with fools.

Fools by the name of *Copeland.*

Jaw tight, temper barely leashed, Mikael waited for the right moment to intervene.

He'd been pushed too far, challenged directly, and he'd meet that challenge with swift retribution.

A king didn't negotiate. A king never begged, and a king refused to curry favor.

Saidia might be a small kingdom, but it was powerful. And the government of Saidia might tolerate the West, but Westerners couldn't enter Saidia, flaunt Saidia law, and think there would be no repercussions.

Jemma Copeland was a foolish woman. So like her father, thumbing her nose at the law, believing she was above it.

Perhaps Daniel Copeland had got away with his crimes. But his daughter would not be so lucky. Miss Jemma Copeland was going to pay.

# CHAPTER ONE

NECESSITY HAD TAUGHT Jemma Copeland to shut out distractions.

She'd learned to ignore the things she didn't want to think about, to enable her to do what needed to be done.

So for the past two hours she'd ignored the scorching heat of the Sahara. The insistent, hollow ache in her stomach. The stigma of being a Copeland, and what it meant back home in the United States.

She'd blocked out heat, hunger, and shame, but she couldn't block out the tall, white-robed man standing just a foot behind the photographer, watching her through dark, unsmiling eyes while a half dozen robed men stood behind him.

She knew who thc man was. How could she not? He'd attended her sister's wedding five years ago in Greenwich and every woman with a pulse had noticed Sheikh Mikael Karim. He was tall, he was impossibly, darkly handsome, and he was a billionaire as well as the new king of Saidia.

But Mikael Karim wasn't supposed to be on set today. He was supposed to be in Buenos Aires this week and his sudden appearance, arriving in a parade of glossy black luxury SUVs with tinted windows, had sent ripples of unease throughout the entire crew.

It was obvious he wasn't happy.

Jemma's gut told her something ugly could happen soon. She prayed she was wrong. She just wanted to get through the rest of the shoot and fly out tomorrow morning as planned.

At least he hadn't shown up yesterday. Yesterday had been

grueling, a very long day, with multiple shots in multiple locations, and the heat had been intense. But she hadn't complained. She wouldn't. She needed the job too much to be anything but grateful for the chance to still work.

It still boggled her mind how much things had changed. Just a year ago she had been one of America's golden girls, envied for her beauty, her wealth, her status as an It Girl. Her family was powerful, affluent. The Copelands had homes scattered across the world, and she and her gorgeous, privileged sisters were constantly photographed and discussed. But even the powerful can fall, and the Copeland family tumbled off their pedestal with the revelation that Daniel, her father, was the number two man in the biggest Ponzi scheme in America in the past century.

Overnight the Copelands became the most hated family in America.

Now Jemma could barely make ends meet. The fallout from her father's arrest, and the blitz of media interest surrounding the case, had destroyed her career. The fact that she worked, and had supported herself since she was eighteen, meant nothing to the public. She was still Daniel Copeland's daughter. Hated. Loathed. Resented.

*Ridiculed.*

Today, she was lucky to get work, and her once brilliant career now barely paid the bills. When her agency came to her with this assignment, a three day shoot with two travel days, meaning she'd be paid for five work days, she'd jumped at the opportunity to come to Saidia, the independent desert kingdom tucked underneath Southern Morocco, and nestled between the Western Sahara and the Atlantic Ocean. She'd continued to fight for the opportunity even when the Saidia consulate denied her visa request.

It wasn't legal, but desperate times called for desperate measures so she'd reapplied for a new visa as her sister, using Morgan's passport bearing Morgan's married name, Xanthos. This time she'd received the needed travel visa.

Yes, she was taking a huge risk, coming here under a false name, but she needed money. Without this paycheck, she wouldn't be able to pay her next month's mortgage.

So here she was, dressed in a long fox fur and thigh high boots, sweltering beneath the blazing sun.

So what if she was naked beneath the coat?

She was working. She was surviving. And one day, she'd thrive again, too.

So let them look.

Let them *all* look—the disapproving sheikh and his travel guard—because she wouldn't be crushed. She refused to be crushed. The clothes were beautiful. Life was exciting. She didn't have a care in the world.

Despite her fierce resolve, perspiration beaded beneath her full breasts and slid down her bare abdomen.

Not uncomfortable, she thought. *Sexy.*

And with sexy firmly in mind, she drew a breath, jutted her hip, and struck a bold pose.

Keith, the Australian photographer, let out an appreciative whistle. "That's beautiful, baby! More of that, please."

She felt a rush of pleasure, which was quickly dashed by the sight of Mikael Karim moving closer to Keith.

The sheikh was tall, so tall he towered over Keith, and his shoulders were broad, dwarfing the slender Australian.

Jemma had forgotten just how intensely handsome Mikael Karim was. She'd modeled in other countries and had met many different sheikhs, and most had been short, heavyset men with flirty eyes and thickening jowls.

But Sheikh Mikael Karim was young, and lean, and fierce. His white robes only accentuated the width of his shoulders as well as his height, and his angular jaw jutted, black eyebrows flat over those intense, dark eyes.

Now Sheikh Karim looked over Keith's head, his dark gaze piercing her, holding her attention. She couldn't look away. He seemed to be telling her something, warning her of something. She went hot, then cold, shivering despite the heat.

Her stomach rose, fell. An alarm sounded in her head. He was dangerous.

She tugged on the edges of the coat, pulling it closer to her body, suddenly very conscious of the fact that she was naked beneath.

Sighing with frustration, Keith lowered his camera a fraction. "You just lost all your energy. Give me sexy, baby."

Jemma glanced at the sheikh from beneath her lashes. The man oozed tension, a lethal tension that made her legs turn to jelly and the hair prickle on the back of her neck. Something was wrong. Something was very wrong.

But Keith couldn't read Sheikh Karim's expression and his irritation grew. "Come on, focus. We need to wrap this up, baby."

Keith was right. They did need to wrap this shot. And she was here to do a job. She had to deliver, or she'd never work again.

Jemma gulped a breath, squared her shoulders, and lifted her chin to the sun, feeling her long hair spill down her back as she let the heavy fur drop off her shoulder, exposing more skin.

"Nice." Keith lifted his camera, motioned for his assistant to step closer with the white reflective screen, and began snapping away. "I like that. More of that."

Jemma shook her head, letting her thick hair tease the small of her spine even as the fur fell lower on her breasts.

"Perfect," Keith crooned. "That's hot. Love it. Don't stop. You're on fire now."

Yes, she was, she thought, arching her shoulders back, breasts thrust high, the nipples now just exposed to the kiss of the sun. In Sheikh Karim's world she was probably going to burn in the flames of hell, but there was nothing she could do about it. This was her job. She had to deliver. And so she pushed all other thoughts from mind, except for giving the image they wanted.

Her shoulders twisted and the coat slid lower on her arm, the fur tickling the back of her bare thighs.

"Lovely, baby." Keith was snapping away. "So beautiful. Keep doing what you're doing. You're a goddess. Every man's dream."

She wasn't a goddess, or a dream, but she could pretend to be. She could pretend anything for a short period of time. Pretending gave her distance, allowing her to breathe, escape, escaping the reality of what was happening at home. *Home.* A sinking sensation filled her. *What a nightmare.*

Battling back the sadness, Jemma shifted, lifting her chin, thrusting her hip out, dropping the coat altogether, exposing her breasts, nipples jutting proudly.

Keith whistled softly. "Give me more."

"*No,*" Sheikh Mikael Karim ground out. It was just one word, but it echoed like a crack of thunder, immediately silencing the murmur of stylists, make-up artist, and lighting assistants.

All heads turned toward the sheikh.

Jemma stared at him, her stomach churning all over again.

The sheikh's expression was beyond fierce. His lips curled, his dark eyes burned as he pushed the camera in Keith's hands down. "That's enough," he gritted. "I've had enough, from all of you." His narrowed gaze swept the tents and crew. "You are done here."

And then his head turned again and he stared straight at Jemma. "And you, Miss *Copeland.* Cover yourself, and then go inside the tent. I will be in to deal with you shortly."

She covered herself, but didn't move.

The sheikh had called her *Miss Copeland*, not Mrs. Xanthis, the name she'd used on the visa, but Copeland.

Panic flooded her veins. Her heart surged. Sheikh Karim knew who she was. He'd recognized her after all these years. The realization shocked her. He, who knew so many, remembered her.

Hands shaking, she tugged the coat closer to her body, suddenly icy cold despite the dazzling heat. "What's happening?" she whispered, even though in a dim part of her brain, she knew.

She'd been found out. Her true identity had been discovered. How, she didn't know, but she was in trouble. Grave trouble. She could feel the severity of the situation all the way down to her toes.

"I think you know," Sheikh Karim said flatly. "Now go inside the tent and wait."

Her knees knocked. She wasn't sure her legs could support her. "For what?"

"To be informed of the charges being brought against you."

"I've done nothing wrong."

His dark eyes narrowed. His jaw hardened as his gaze swept over her, from the top of her head to the boots on her feet. "You've done *everything* wrong, Miss *Copeland.* You're in serious trouble. So go to the tent, now, and if you have half a brain, you'll obey."

Jemma had more than half a brain. She actually had a very good brain. And a very good imagination, which made the walk to the tent excruciating.

What was going to happen to her? What were the official charges? And what would the punishment be?

She tried to calm herself. She focused on her breathing, and clamped down on her wild thoughts. It wouldn't help her to panic. She knew she'd entered the country illegally. She'd willingly agreed to work on a shoot that hadn't been condoned by the government. *And* she'd shown her breasts in public, which was also against Saidia's law.

And she'd done it all because she hadn't taken money from her family since she was eighteen and she wasn't about to start now.

She was an adult. A successful, capable woman. And she'd been determined to make it without going to her family begging for a handout.

In hindsight, perhaps begging for a handout would have been wiser.

In the wardrobe tent, Jemma shrugged off the heavy fur coat, and slipped a light pink cotton kimono over her shoulders, tying the sash at her waist. As she sat down at the stool before the make-up mirror, she could hear the sheikh's voice echo in her head.

*You've done everything wrong...*

*Everything wrong...*

He was right. She had done everything wrong. She prayed he'd accept her apology, allow her to make amends. She hadn't meant to insult him, or disrespect his country or his culture in any way.

Jemma straightened, hearing voices outside her tent. The voices were pitched low, speaking quickly, urgently. Male voices. A single female voice. Jemma recognized the woman as Mary Leed, *Catwalk*'s editorial director. Mary was usually unflappable but she sounded absolutely panicked now.

Jemma's heart fell all over again. Bad. This was bad.

She swallowed hard, her stomach churning, nerves threatening to get the better of her.

She shouldn't have come.

She shouldn't have taken such risks.

But what was she to do otherwise? Crumble? Shatter? End up on the streets, destitute, homeless, helpless?

*No.*

She wouldn't be helpless, and she wouldn't be pitied, or mocked, either.

She'd suffered enough at the hands of her father. He'd betrayed them all; his clients, his business partners, his friends, even his family. He might be selfish and ruthless and destructive, but the rest of the Copelands weren't. Copelands were good people.

Good people, she silently insisted, stretching out one leg to unzip the thigh-high boot. Her hand was trembling so badly that it made it difficult to get the zipper down. The boots were outrageous to start with. They were the stuff of fantasy, a very high heel projecting a kinky twist, just like the fashion layout itself.

They would have been smarter doing this feature in Palm Springs instead of Saidia with Saidia's strict laws of moral conduct. Saidia might be stable and tolerant, but it wasn't a democracy, nor did it cater to the wealthy Westerners like some other nations. It remained conservative and up until two generations ago, marriages weren't just arranged, they were forced.

The tribal leaders kidnapped their brides from neighboring tribes.

Unthinkable to the modern Western mind, but acceptable here.

Jemma was tugging the zipper down on the second boot when the tent flap parted and Mary entered with Sheikh Karim. Two members of the sheikh's guard stood at the entrance.

Jemma slowly sat up, and looked from Mary to the sheikh and back.

Mary's face was pale, her lips pressed thin. "We've a problem," she said.

Silence followed. Jemma curled her fingers into her lap.

Mary wouldn't meet Jemma's gaze, looking past her shoulder instead. "We're wrapping up the shoot and returning to the capitol immediately. We are facing some legal charges and fines, which we are hoping to take care of quickly so the crew and company can return to England tomorrow, or the next day." She hesitated for a long moment, before adding even more quietly, "At least most of us should be able to return to England tomorrow or the next day. Jemma, I'm afraid you won't be going with us."

Jemma started to rise, but remembered her boot and sat back down. "Why not?"

"The charges against you are different," Mary said, still avoiding Jemma's gaze. "We are in trouble for using you, but you, you're in trouble for…" Her voice faded away. She didn't finish the sentence.

She didn't have to.

Jemma knew why she was in trouble. What she didn't know was what she'd be charged with. "I'm sorry." She drew a quick, shallow breath and looked from Mary to Sheikh Karim. "I am sorry. Truly—"

"Not interested," he said curtly.

Jemma's stomach flipped. "I made a mistake—"

"A mistake is pairing a black shoe and a blue shoe. A mistake is forgetting to charge one's phone. A mistake is *not* entering the country illegally, under false pretenses, with a false identity. You had no work permit. No visa. Nothing." Sheikh Karim's voice crackled with contempt and fury. "What you did was deliberate, and a felony, Miss Copeland."

Jemma put a hand to her belly, praying she wouldn't throw up here, now. She hadn't eaten much today. She never did on days she worked, knowing she photographed better with a very flat stomach. "What can I do to make this right?"

Mary shot Sheikh Karim a stricken glance.

He shook his head, once. "There is nothing. The magazine staff must appear in court, and pay their fines. You will face a different judge, and be sentenced accordingly."

Jemma sat very still. "So I'm to be separated from everyone?"

"Yes." The sheikh gestured to Mary. "You and the rest of the crew, are to leave immediately. My men will accompany you to ensure your safety." He glanced at Jemma. "And you will come with me."

Mary nodded and left. Heart thudding, Jemma watched Mary's silent, abrupt departure then looked to Sheikh Karim.

He was angry. Very, very angry.

Three years ago she might have crumbled. Two years ago she might have cried. But that was the old Jemma, the girl who'd grown up pampered, protected by a big brother and three opinionated, but loving, sisters.

She wasn't that girl anymore. In fact, she wasn't a girl at all anymore. She'd been put to the fire and she'd come out fierce. Strong.

"So where *do* felons go, Sheikh Karim?" she asked quietly, meeting the sheikh's hard narrowed gaze.

"To prison."

"I'm going to prison?"

"If you were to go to court tomorrow, and appear before our judicial tribunal, yes. But you're not being seen by our judicial tribunal. You're being seen by my tribe's elder, and he will act as judge."

"Why a different court and judge than Mary and the magazine crew?"

"Because they are charged with crimes against Saidia. You—" he broke off, studying her lovely face in the mirror, wondering how she'd react to his news, "You are charged with crimes against the Karims, my family. Saidia's royal family. You will be escorted to a judge who is of my tribe. He will hear the charges brought against you, and then pass judgment."

She didn't say anything. Her brow creased and she looked utterly bewildered. "I don't understand. What have I done to your family?"

"You stole from my family. Shamed them."

"But I haven't. I don't even know your family."

"Your father does."

Jemma grew still. Everything seemed to slow, stop. Would the trail of devastation left by her father's action never end? She stared at Mikael suddenly afraid of what he'd say next. "But I'm not my father."

"Not physically, no, but you represent him."

"I don't."

"You do." His jaw hardened. "In Arabic society, one is always connected to one's family. You represent your family throughout your life, which is why it's so important to always bring honor to one's family. But your father stole from the

Karims, shamed the Karims, dishonoring my family, and in so doing, he dishonored all of Saidia."

She swallowed hard. "But I'm nothing like my father."

"You are his daughter, and you are here, unlawfully. It is time to right the wrong. You will make atonement for your disrespect, and your father's, too."

"I don't even have a relationship with my father. I haven't seen him in years—"

"This is not the time. We have a long trip ahead of us. I suggest you finish changing so we can get on the road."

Her fingers bent, nails pressing to the dressing table. "*Please.*"

"It's not up to me."

"But you are the king."

"And kings must insist on obedience, submission, and respect. Even from our foreign visitors."

She looked at him, seeing him, but not seeing him, too overwhelmed by his words and the implication of what he was saying to focus on any one thing. It didn't help that her pulse raced, making her head feel dizzy and light.

The grim security guard at Tagadir International Airport had warned them. Had said that His Highness Sheikh Karim was all powerful in Saidia. As king he owned this massive expanse of desert and the sand dunes rolling in every direction, and as their translator had whispered on leaving the airport, "*His Highness, Sheikh Karim, isn't just head of the country, he is the country.*"

Jemma exhaled slowly, trying to clear the fog and panic from her brain. She should have taken the warnings seriously. She should have been logical, not desperate.

Desperate was a dangerous state of mind.

Desperate fueled chaos.

What she needed to do was remain calm. Think this through. There had to be a way to reach him, reason with him. Surely he didn't make a habit of locking up American and British girls?

"I'd like to make amends," she said quietly, glancing up at Sheikh Karim from beneath her lashes, taking in his height, the width of his shoulders, and his hard, chiseled features. Nothing in his expression was kind. There was not even a hint of softness at his mouth.

"You will," he said. "You must."

She winced at the harshness in his voice. Sheikh Mikael Karim might be as handsome as any Hollywood leading man, but there was no warmth in his eyes.

He was a cold man, and she knew all too well that cold men were dangerous. Men without hearts destroyed, and if she were not very careful, and very smart, she could be ruined.

"Can I pay a fine? A penalty?"

"You're in no position to buy yourself out of trouble, Miss Copeland. Your family is bankrupt."

"I could try Drakon—"

"You're not calling anyone," he interrupted sharply. "And I won't have Drakon bailing you out. He might be your sister's ex-husband, but he was my friend from university and from what I understand, he lost virtually his entire fortune thanks to your father. I think Drakon has paid a high enough price for being associated with you Copelands. It's time you and your family stopped expecting others to clean up your messes and instead assumed responsibility for your mistakes."

"That might be, but Drakon isn't cruel. He wouldn't approve of you…of you…" Her voice failed her as she met Mikael's dark gaze. The sheikh's anger burned in his eyes, scorching her.

"Of what, Miss Copeland?" he asked softly, a hint of menace in his deep voice.

"What won't he approve of?" he persisted.

Jemma couldn't answer. Her heart beat wildly, a painful staccato that made her chest ache.

She had to be careful. She couldn't afford to alienate the sheikh. Not when she needed him and his protection.

She needed to win him over. She needed him to care. Somehow she had to get him to see her, the real her, *Jemma.* The person. The woman. Not the daughter of Daniel Copeland.

It was vital she didn't antagonize him, but reached him. Otherwise it would be far too easy for Sheikh Karim to snap his fingers and destroy her. He was that powerful, that ruthless.

Her eyes burned and her lip trembled and she bit down hard, teeth digging into her lip to keep from making a sound.

Fear washed through her but she would not crack, or cry. Would not disintegrate, either.

"He wouldn't approve of me flaunting your laws," she said lowly, fighting to maintain control, and cling to whatever dignity she had left. "He wouldn't approve of me using my sister's passport, either. He would be angry," she added, lifting her chin to meet Sheikh Karim's gaze. "And disappointed."

Mikael Karim arched a brow.

"In me," she added. "He'd be disappointed in me."

And then wrapping herself in courage, and hanging on to that fragile cloak, she removed her boot, placing it on the floor next to its mate, and turned to her dressing table to begin removing her make-up.

# CHAPTER TWO

MIKAEL SAW JEMMA'S lower lip quiver before she clamped her jaw, biting down in an effort to remain silent, as she turned back to her dressing table.

He was surprised at how calm she was. He'd expected tears. Hysteria. Instead she was quiet. Thoughtful. Respectful.

He'd planned on defiance. He'd come prepared for theatrics. She'd almost gone there. Almost, but then thought better of it.

Perhaps she wasn't as silly as he'd thought.

Perhaps she might have a brain in her pretty head after all.

He was glad she wasn't going to dissolve into tears and hysteria. And glad she might be starting to understand the gravity of her situation.

But even then, he was still deeply furious with her for knowingly, willfully flaunting every international law by entering a foreign country with a false identity, and then practically stripping in public.

It wasn't done.

It wasn't acceptable.

It wouldn't even be allowed in San Francisco or New York City.

So how could she think it would be okay here?

His brow lowered as his narrowed gaze swept over her. She looked so soft and contrite now as she removed her makeup. It was an act. He was certain she was playing him. Just as her father had played his mother…before bankrupting her, breaking her.

His mother would be alive today if Daniel Copeland hadn't lied to her and stolen from her, taking not just her financial security, but her self-respect.

Thank goodness Mikael was not his mother.

He knew better than to allow himself to be manipulated by yet another Copeland con artist.

Mikael refused to pity Jemma. He didn't care if she was sorry. Had Daniel Copeland shown his mother mercy? No. Had Daniel Copeland shown any of his clients concern…compassion? *No.* So why should his daughter receive preferential treatment?

"Will I have a lawyer present?" she asked, breaking the silence.

"No," he said.

"Will I have any legal representation?"

"No."

She hesitated, brow furrowing, lips compressing, somehow even more lovely troubled than when posed on the desert sand in the fur and thigh high boots.

Yes, she was beautiful. And yes, she'd inherited her mother's famous bone structure, and yes, even in this dim, stifling tent she still glowed like a jewel—glossy dark hair, brilliant green eyes, luminous skin, pink lips—but that didn't change the fact that she was a criminal.

"Neither of us have lawyers," he added, hating that he was even aware of her beauty. He shouldn't notice, or care. He shouldn't feel any attraction at all. "There is just the case itself, presented by me, and then the judge passes the sentence."

"You represent yourself?"

"I represent my tribe, the Karim family, and the laws of this country."

She turned slowly on the stool to face him, her hands resting on her thighs, the pink kimono gaping slightly above the knotted sash, revealing the slope of her full breast. "What you're saying is that it will be you testifying against me."

He shouldn't know that her nipple was small and pink and that her belly was flat above firm, rounded hips.

Or at the very least, he shouldn't remember. He shouldn't want to remember. "I present the facts. I do not pass judgment."

"Will the *facts* be presented in English?"

"No."

"So you could say anything."

"But why would I?" he countered sharply. "You've broken numerous laws. Important laws. Laws created to protect our borders and the safety and security of my people. There is no need to add weight or severity. What you've done is quite serious. The punishment will be appropriately serious."

He saw a flash in her eyes, and he didn't know if it was anger or fear but she didn't speak. She bit down, holding back the quick retort.

Seconds ticked by, one after the other.

For almost a minute there was only silence, a tense silence weighted with all the words she refrained from speaking.

"How serious?" she finally asked.

"There will be jail time."

"How long?"

He was uncomfortable with all the questions. "Do you really want to do this now?"

"Absolutely. Far better to be prepared than to walk in blind."

"The minimum sentence is somewhere between five to ten years. The maximum, upward of twenty."

She went white, and her lips parted, but she made no sound. She simply stared at him, incredulous, before slowly turning back to face her dressing table mirror.

She was trying not to cry.

Her shoulders were straight, and her head was high but he saw the welling of tears in her eyes. He felt her shock, and sadness.

He should leave but his feet wouldn't move. His chest felt tight.

It was her own damned fault.

But he could still see her five years ago in the periwinkle blue bridesmaid dress at Morgan's wedding.

He could hear her gurgle of laughter as she'd made a toast to her big sister at the reception after.

"We will leave as soon as you're dressed," he said tersely, ignoring Jemma's pallor and the trembling of her hands where they rested on the dressing table.

"I will need five or ten minutes," she said.

"Of course." He turned to leave but from the corner of his eye he saw her lean toward the mirror to try to remove the strip of false eyelashes on her right eye, her hands still shaking so much she couldn't lift the edge.

It wasn't his problem. He didn't care if her hands shook violently or not. But he couldn't stop watching her. He couldn't help noticing that she was struggling. Tears spilled from the corners of her eyes as she battled to get the eyelashes off.

It was her fault.

He wasn't responsible for her situation.

And yet her struggle unsettled him, awakening emotions and memories he didn't want to feel.

Mikael didn't believe in feeling. Feelings were best left to others. He, on the other hand, preferred logic. Structure. Rules. Order.

He wouldn't be moved by tears. Not even the tears of a young foreign woman that he'd met many years ago at the wedding of Drakon Xanthis, his close friend from university. Just because Drakon had married Jemma's older sister, Morgan, didn't mean that Mikael had to make allowances. Why make allowances when Daniel Copeland had made none for his mother?

"Stop," he ordered, unable to watch her struggle any longer. "You're about to take out your eye."

"I have to get them off."

"Not like that."

"I can do it."

"You're making a mess of it." He crossed the distance, gestured for her to turn on her stool. "Face me, and hold still. Look down. Don't move."

Jemma held her breath as she felt his fingers against her temple. His touch was warm, his hand steady as he used the tip of his finger to lift the edge of the strip and then he slowly, carefully peeled the lashes from her lid. "One down," he said, putting the crescent of lashes in her hand. "One to go."

He made quick work on the second set.

"You've done this before," she said, as he took a step back, putting distance between them, but not enough distance. He was so big, so intimidating, that she found his nearness overwhelming.

"I haven't, but I've watched enough girlfriends put on make up to know how it's done."

She looked at him for a long moment, her gaze searching his. "And you have *no* say in the sentencing?" she asked.

"I have plenty of say," he answered. "I am the king. I can make new laws, pass laws, break laws…but breaking laws wouldn't make me a good king or a proper leader for my people. So I, too, observe the laws of Saidia, and am committed to upholding them."

"Could you ask the judge to be lenient with me?"

"I could."

"But you won't?"

He didn't answer right away, which was telling, she thought.

"Would you ask for leniency for another woman?"

His broad shoulders shifted. "It would depend on who she was, and what she'd done."

"So your relationship with her would influence your decision?"

"Absolutely."

"I see."

"As her *character* would influence my decision."

And he didn't approve of her character.

Jemma understood then that he wouldn't help her in any way. He didn't like her. He didn't approve of her. And he felt no pity or compassion because she was a Copeland and it was a Copeland, her father, who had wronged his family.

In his mind, she had so many strikes against her she wasn't worth saving.

For a moment she couldn't breathe. The pain was so sharp and hard it cut her to the quick.

It was almost like the pain when Damien ended their engagement. He'd said he'd loved her. He'd said he wanted to spend his life with her. But then when he began losing jobs, he backed away from her. Far better to lose her, than his career.

Throat aching, eyes burning, Jemma turned back to the mirror.

She reached for a brush and ran it slowly through her long dark hair, making the glossy waves ripple down her back, telling herself not to think, not to feel, and most definitely, not to cry.

"You expect your tribal elder to sentence me to prison, for at least five years?" she asked, drawing the brush through her long hair.

Silence stretched. After a long moment, Sheikh Karim answered, "I don't expect Sheikh Azizzi to give you a minimum sentence, no."

She nodded once. "Thank you for at least being honest."

And then she reached for the bottle of make-up remover and a cotton ball to remove what was left of her eye make-up.

He walked out then. Thank goodness. She'd barely kept it together there, at the end.

She was scared, so scared.

Would she really be going to prison?

Would he really allow the judge to have her locked away for years?

She couldn't believe this was happening. Had to be a bad dream. But the sweltering heat inside the tent felt far too real to be a dream.

Jemma left her make-up table and went to her purse to retrieve her phone. Mary had informed the crew this morning as they left the hotel that they'd get no signal here in the desert, and checking her phone now she saw that Mary was right. She couldn't call anyone. Couldn't alert anyone to her situation. As Jemma put her phone away, she could only pray that Mary would make some calls on her behalf once she returned to London.

Jemma changed quickly into her street clothes, a gray short linen skirt, white knit top and gray blazer.

Drawing a breath, she left the tent, stepping out into the last lingering ray of light. Two of the sheikh's men guarded the tent, but they didn't acknowledge her.

The desert glowed with amber, ruby and golden colors. The convoy of cars that had descended on the shoot two hours ago was half the number it'd been when Jemma had disappeared into the tent.

Sheikh Karim stepped from the back of one of the black vehicles. He gestured to her. "Come. We leave now."

She shouldered her purse, pretending the sheikh wasn't watching her walk toward him, pretending his guards weren't there behind her, watching her walk away from them. She pretended she was strong and calm, that nothing threatened her.

It was all she'd been doing since her father's downfall.

Pretending. Faking. Fighting.

"Ready?" Sheikh Karim asked as she reached his side.

"Yes."

"You have no suitcase, no clothes?"

"I have a few traveling pieces here, but the rest is in my suitcase." She clasped her oversized purse closer to her body. "Can we go get my luggage?"

"No."

"Will you send for it?"

"You won't need it where you are going."

Her eyes widened and her lips parted to protest but his grim expression silenced her.

He held open the door. The car was already running.

"It's time to go," he said firmly.

Swallowing, Jemma slid onto the black leather seat, terrified to leave this scorching desert, not knowing where she'd go next.

Sheikh Karim joined her on the seat, his large body filling the back of the car. Jemma scooted as far over as she could before settling her blazer over her thighs, hiding her bare skin. But even sitting near the door, he was far too close, and warm, so warm that she fixed her attention on the desert beyond the car window determined to block out everything until she was calm.

She stared hard at the landscape, imagining that she was someone else, somewhere else and it soothed her. The sun was lower in the sky and the colors were changing, darkening, deepening and it made her heart hurt. In any other situation she would've been overcome by the beauty of the sunset. As it was now, she felt bereft.

She'd come to Saidia to save what was left of her world, and instead she'd shattered it completely.

The car was moving. Her stomach lurched. She gripped the handle on the door and drew a deep breath and then another to calm herself.

*It was going to be okay.*

*Everything would be okay.*

*Everything would be fine.*

"It's beautiful," she whispered, blinking back tears.

He said nothing.

She blinked again, clearing her vision, determined to find her center…a place of peace, and calm. She had to keep her head. There was no other way she'd survive whatever came next if she didn't stay focused.

"Where does this elder, Sheikh Azizzi, live?" she asked, keeping her gaze fixed on a distant dune. The sun was dropping more quickly, painting the sky a wash of rose and red that reflected crimson against the sand.

"Haslam," he said.

"Is it far?"

"Two hours by car. If there is no sandstorm."

"Do you expect one?" she asked, glancing briefly in his direction.

"Not tonight, but it's not unusual as you approach the mountains. The wind races through the valley and whips the sand dunes. It's impressive if you're not trying to drive through, and maddening if you are."

He sounded so cavalier. She wondered just how dangerous a sandstorm really was. "The storm won't hurt us?"

The sheikh shrugged. "Not if we stay on the road, turn off the engine and close the vents. But I don't expect a sandstorm tonight. So far there appears to be little wind. I think it will be a quiet night in the desert."

She tried to picture the still crimson desert as a whirling sea of sand. She'd seen it in movies, but it seemed impossible now. "And so when do we see the judge?"

"Tonight."

"Tonight?" she echoed, and when he nodded, she added, "But we won't be there for hours."

"We are expected."

His answer unleashed a thousand butterflies inside her middle. "And will we know his verdict tonight?"

"Yes." Sheikh Karim's jaw hardened. "It will be a long night."

"Justice moves swiftly in Saidia," she said under her breath.

"You have no one to blame but yourself."

She flinched at his harsh tone, and held her tongue.

But the sheikh wasn't satisfied with her silence. "Why did you do it?" he demanded, his voice almost savage. "You've had a successful career. Surely you could have been happy with less?"

"I'm broke. I needed the work. I would have lost my flat."

"You'll lose it anyway, now. There is no way for you to pay bills from prison."

She hadn't thought that far. She gave her head a bemused shake. "Maybe someone will be able to—" she broke off as she saw his expression. "Yes, I know. You don't think I deserve help, but you're wrong. I'm not who you think I am. I'm not this selfish, horrible woman you make me out to be."

"Then why did you enter Saidia with your sister's passport? I can't imagine she gave her passport to you."

"She didn't."

"I didn't think so," he ground out.

Jemma bit down on the inside of her lip, chewing her lip to keep from making a sound.

"I *know* Morgan," he added ruthlessly. "Drakon was one of my best friends. And you probably don't remember, or were too young to notice, but I attended Morgan and Drakon's wedding five years ago in Greenwich. Yes, you and Morgan might both be brunettes, but you don't look anything alike. It was beyond stupid to try to pass yourself off as her."

Fatigue and fear and dread made her heartsick, and his words drilled into her, like a hammer in her head, making her headache feel worse. She pressed her fingers to her temple to ease the pain. "How did you find out I was here?"

He shot her a cool look. "You had a very chatty stylist on the shoot. She sat in a bar two nights ago drinking and talking about the layout, the models, and you. Apparently your name was mentioned oh...a dozen times. *Jemma Copeland. That Jemma Copeland. Jemma Copeland, daughter of Daniel Copeland.* In today's age of technology and social media, it just took a couple Tweets and it went viral. One minute I was in Buenos Aires, thinking everything was fine at home, and then the next I was boarding my jet to return home to deal with *you*."

He shifted, extending his long legs out, and she sucked in an uneasy breath. He was so big, and his legs were so long, she felt positively suffocated, trapped here in the back of the car with him.

"I wish you had just let me go. We were leaving tomorrow morning anyway," she said softly. "You were out of the country. You didn't have to rush home to have me arrested."

"No. I could have allowed the police to come for you. They were going to arrest you. They wouldn't have been as polite, or patient, as I've been. They would have handcuffed you and put you in the back of an armored truck and taken you to a jail where you'd languish for a few days, maybe a week, until you were seen by our tribunal, and then you would have been sentenced to five, ten, fifteen years…or longer…in our state run prison. It wouldn't have been pleasant. It wouldn't have been nice at all." His expression was fierce, his gaze held hers, critical, condemning. "You don't realize it, but I've done you a favor. I have intervened on your behalf, and yes, you will still serve time, but it will be in a smaller place, in a private home. My assistance allows you to serve your time under house arrest rather than a large state run prison. So you can thank your stars I found out."

"I'm amazed you'd intervene since you hate the Copelands so much."

His dark gaze met hers. "So am I."

# CHAPTER THREE

For several minutes they traveled in silence.

"So why *did* you rush home from Buenos Aires since you despise the Copelands?" she asked, unable to stifle the question, genuinely curious about his motives.

He didn't answer immediately, and when he did, his answer was short, brusque. "Drakon."

She picked her next words with care. "You must know he won't approve of you locking me up, for six months or six years. I'm his sister-in-law."

"His ex-sister-in-law. Morgan and Drakon are divorced, or separated, or something of that nature."

"But he likes me. He has a soft spot for me."

Mikael's lips compressed. "Perhaps, but you're a felon. Even as protective as he is, he will still have to come to terms with the fact that you broke the law, and there are consequences. There must be consequences. Saidia cannot be lawless. Nor can I govern at whim." His head turned, and his dark eyes met hers. For a long moment there was just silence, and then he shrugged. "And at last, the Copelands will be held accountable for their crimes."

Her stomach flipped. Her heart lurched. "You want to see me suffer," she whispered.

"Your father should have accepted responsibility and answered for his actions. Instead he ran away."

"I hate what he did, Sheikh Karim. I hate that he betrayed his customers and clients…friends. His choices sicken me—"

"There was a reason your visa was denied. The refusal was a warning. The refusal should have protected you. You should not have come."

She turned her head and swiftly wiped away tears before they could fall.

No, she shouldn't have come to Saidia. She shouldn't have broken laws.

But she had.

And now she'd pay. And pay dearly.

She felt Mikael's gaze. She knew he was watching her. His close, critical scrutiny made her pulse race. She felt cornered. Trapped.

She hated the feeling. It was suffocating. Jemma's fingers wrapped around the door handle and gripped it tight. If only she could jump from the car. Fling herself into the desert. Hide. Disappear.

But of course it wouldn't work like that.

Her father had tried to evade arrest and he'd taken off in his yacht, setting across the ocean in hopes of finding some bit of paradise somewhere.

Instead his yacht had been commandeered off the coast of Africa and he'd been taken hostage and held for ransom. No one had paid. He'd been hostage for months now and the public loved it. They loved his shame and pain.

Jemma flinched and pressed her hands together, fingers lacing. She didn't like thinking about him, and especially didn't like to think of him helpless in some African coastal village.

If only he hadn't run.

If only he hadn't stolen his clients' money.

If only…

"The doors are locked," Mikael said flatly. "There is no escape."

Her eyes burned. She swallowed around the lump in her throat. "No," she murmured, "there isn't, is there?"

She turned her head away again, trembling inwardly. It had been such a bad, bad year. She still felt wrecked. Trashed. Devastated by her father's duplicity and deceit. And then heartbroken by Damien's rejection.

To have your own father destroy so many people's lives, and then to have the love of your life abruptly cast you off…

She couldn't have imagined that her life would derail so completely. One day everything was normal and then the next, absolute chaos and mayhem.

The media had converged on her immediately in London, camping outside her flat, the journalists three rows deep, each with cameras and microphones and questions they shouted at her every time she opened her front door.

*"Jemma, how does it feel to know that your father is one of the biggest con artists in American history?"*

*"Do you or your family have any plans to pay all these bankrupt people back?"*

*"Where is all the money, Jemma?"*

*"Did your father use stolen money to pay for this flat?"*

It had been difficult enduring the constant barrage of questions, but she came and went, determined to work, to keep life as normal as possible.

But within a week, the jobs disappeared.

She was no longer just Jemma, the face of Farrinelli, but that American, that Jemma *Copeland.*

Every major magazine and fashion house she'd been booked to work for had cancelled on her in quick succession.

It was bad enough that six months of work was lost, but then Damien had started losing jobs, too.

Damien couldn't get work.

Farrinelli cancelled Jemma's contract as the face of Farrinelli Fragrance. Damien didn't wait for Farrinelli to replace him too. He left Jemma, their flat, their life.

Jemma understood. She was bad for his career. Bad for business. For Damien. Farrinelli. Everyone.

Heartsick, miserable, she opened her eyes to discover Sheikh Karim watching her.

Tears filled her eyes. She was ashamed of the tears, ashamed for being weak. How could she cry or feel sorry for herself? She was better off than most people. Certainly better off than the thousands of people her father had impoverished.

But she never spoke about her father, or what he did. She didn't openly acknowledge the shame, either. There were no words for it. No way to ever make amends, either.

"Please don't think this is a challenge, nor is it meant to be disrespectful," she said quietly, swiftly dashing away tears before they could fall. "But I did not come here on a lark. I am not a rebel schoolgirl. I came to Saidia because I desperately needed the work. I had thought I'd fly in, work, fly out, and no one would be the wiser. Clearly, I was wrong, and for that, I am very sorry."

Mikael listened to the apology in silence. The apology meant nothing to him. Words were easy. They slipped from the tongue and lips with ease.

Actions, now those were difficult.

Action, and consequence, those required effort. Pain. Sweat. Sacrifice.

It crossed his mind that Jemma had no idea what was coming once they reached Haslam. Sheikh Azizzi, the judge, was not a soft touch. Sheikh Azizzi was old world, old school, and determined to preserve as much of the tribal customs as possible.

He was also Mikael's godfather and intimate with Karim family history, including Mikael's parents' drawn-out divorce, and his mother's subsequent banishment from Saidia.

Sheikh Azizzi had not been a fan of his mother, but the divorce had horrified Sheikh Azizzi and all of the country. Divorce was rare in Saidia, and in a thousand years of Karim rule, there had never been a divorce in the Karim royal family, and the drama and the endless publicity around it—the news in the international papers, not Saidia's—had alienated the Saidia public.

No, Mikael's father had not been a good king. If he hadn't died when he did, there might have been an uprising.

There *would* have been an uprising.

Which is why ever since Mikael had inherited the throne, he'd vowed to be a true leader to the Saidia people. A good king. A fair king. He'd vowed to represent his country properly, and he'd promised to protect the desert kingdom's culture, and preserve ancient Saidia customs.

Thus, the trip to Haslam to see Sheikh Azizzi.

Sheikh Azizzi was both a political and spiritual figure. He was a simple man, a village elder, but brave and wise. He and Mikael's father had grown up together, both from the same village. Sheikh Azizzi's father has served as a counselor and advisor to the royal Karim family, but Sheikh Azizzi himself did not want to serve in a royal capacity. He was a teacher, a thinker, a farmer, preferring the quiet life in ancient Haslam, a town founded hundreds of years ago at the base of the Tekti Mountains.

But when a neighboring country had sought to invade Saidia fifty some years ago, Sheikh Azizzi was one of the first to volunteer to defend his country and people. He'd spent nearly two years on the front line. Halfway through, he was wounded in battle, and yet he refused to leave his fellow soldiers, inspiring the dispirited Saidia troops to fight on.

After the war ended, Sheikh Azizzi returned home, refusing all gifts, and accolades, wanting no financial reward. He wasn't interested in being a popular figure. He didn't want attention, didn't feel he deserved the attention. What he wanted was truth, peace, and stability for all Saidia people.

"I will ask Sheikh Azizzi to be fair. I cannot ask for him to be compassionate," Mikael said suddenly, his voice deep and rough in the quiet of the car. "Compassion is too much like weakness. Compassion lacks muscle, and conviction."

"Does he know about my father, and what he did to your family?"

"Yes."

"So he won't be fair."

"Fair, according to our laws. Perhaps not fair according to yours."

For two hours the convoy of cars traveled across the wide stretch of desert, before turning southeast toward the foothills and then on to the Tekti mountain range. They traveled up a narrow winding road, through the steep mountain pass, before beginning their descent into the valley below.

Finally they were slowing, the cars leaving the main road for the walled town built at the foot of the mountains.

Jemma was very glad the cars were slowing. She needed fresh air. She needed water. She needed a chance to stretch her legs.

"Haslam," the sheikh announced.

She craned her head to get a better look at the town. Twenty-foot-tall walls surrounded it. Turrets and parapets peeked above the walls. The vehicles' headlights illuminated huge wooden gates. Slowly the massive gates opened and the convoy pulled into the village.

They drove a short way before the cars parked in front of a two-story building that looked almost identical to the buildings on either side.

Jemma frowned at the narrow house. It didn't look like a courthouse or official city building. It seemed very much like an ordinary home.

The driver came around the side of the car to open the back passenger door. "We will go in for tea and conversation, but no one here will speak English," Mikael said, adding bluntly, "and they won't understand you. Or your short skirt." He leaned from the car, spoke to the driver and the driver nodded, and disappeared.

"I'm getting you a robe," Mikael said turning back to her. "It won't help you to go before Sheikh Azizzi dressed like that. I am sure you know this already, but be quiet, polite. Respectful. You are the outsider here. You need to make a good impression."

"Sheikh Azizzi is here?"

"Yes."

"I'm meeting him *now*?"

"Yes."

Fresh panic washed through her. "I thought we were going in for tea and conversation!"

"We are. This is the judicial process. It's not in a court with many observers. It's more intimate…personal. We sit at a table, have tea, and talk. Sheikh Azizzi will either come to a decision during the discussion, or he will leave and make a decision and then return to tell us what he has chosen to do."

"And it really all rests with him?"

"Yes."

"Could you not override his decision? You are the king."

Mikael studied her impassively. "I could, but I doubt I would."

"Why?"

"He is a tribal judge, and the highest in my tribe. As Bedouin, we honor our tribal elders, and he is the most respected man from my tribe."

The driver returned with a dark blue folded cotton garment and handed it to Mikael. Mikael shook out the robe and told her to slip it over her head. "This is more conservative, and should make him feel more comfortable."

She reached up and touched her hair. "Shouldn't I have a headscarf too?"

"He knows you're American, knows your father was Daniel Copeland. No need to pretend to be someone you're not."

"But I also have no wish to further offend him."

"Then perhaps braid your hair and tie it with an elastic. But your hair is not going to protect you from judgment. Nothing will. This is fate. Karma."

Jemma swiftly braided her hair and then stepped from the car, following Mikael. *Fate. Karma.* The words rang through her head as she walked behind the sheikh toward the house.

Robed men and women lined the small dirt road, bowing

deeply. Mikael paused to greet them, speaking briefly and then waving to some children who peeked from windows upstairs before leading her to the arched door of the house. The door opened and they were ushered inside.

Candles and sconces on the wall illuminated the interior. The whitewashed walls were simple and unadorned. Dark beams covered the ceiling in the entry, but the beams had been painted cream and pale gold in the living room.

As Mikael and Jemma were taken to a low table in the living room, Jemma spotted more children peeking from behind a curtain before being drawn away.

"Sit here," Mikael instructed, pointing to a pillow on the floor in front of the low square table. "To my right. Sheikh Azizzi will sit across from me, and speak to me, but this way he can see you easily."

Jemma sank onto the pillow, curling her legs under her. "He's not going to ask me anything?"

"No. Over tea I will give him the facts. He will consider the facts and then make his decision."

"Is this how you handle all tribal crimes?"

"If it's not a violent crime, why should the sentencing be chaotic and violent?"

She smoothed the soft thin cotton fabric over her knees. "But your country has a long history of aggression. Tribal warring, kidnapped brides, forced marriages." She quickly glanced at him. "I'm not trying to be sarcastic. I ask the question sincerely. How does one balance your ideal of civility in sentencing, with what we Westerners would view as barbaric tribal customs?"

"You mean, kidnapped brides?"

Her eyes widened. "No. I was referring to arranged marriages."

He said nothing. She stared at him aghast. The seconds ticked by.

Jemma pressed her hands to her stomach, trying to calm the wild butterflies. "Do you really kidnap your brides?"

"If you are a member of one of the royal families, yes."

"You're serious?"

"Yes."

"*Why*?"

He shrugged. "It's how one protects the tribe, by forging new ties through forced marriage with other tribes."

"It's barbaric."

"It settles a score."

"You sound so cavalier about a very violent act."

"The marriage might be forced, but the sex is generally consensual." His dark gaze held hers. "One takes a bride to settle a debt, but the captive bride becomes a royal wife. The marriage must be satisfying for both."

"I sincerely doubt a forced marriage can ever be satisfying!"

"A forced marriage isn't that different from an arranged marriage, and that is also foreign to your Western way of thinking, so perhaps it's better if you do not judge."

A shadow filled the doorway and an older, robed man entered the living room.

Mikael rose, and hugged the older man. They clasped each other's arm and spoke in Arabic. After a moment both Mikael and Sheikh Azizzi sat down at the table, still deep in conversation.

Sheikh Azizzi hadn't even looked at her yet. Mikael didn't glance her way either.

Their conversation was grave. No laughter, no joking. They took turns speaking, first one, and then the other. The mood in the room was somber. Intense.

They were interrupted after fifteen minutes or so by a male servant carrying a tea tray. Sheikh Azizzi and Mikael ignored the man with the tray but Jemma was grateful to see the tea and biscuits and dried fruit arrive. She was hungry, and thirsty. She eyed the teacup placed in front of her and the plate of biscuits and fruit but didn't touch either one, waiting for a signal from Mikael, or Sheikh Azizzi. But neither glanced her way.

She longed for a sip but waited instead.

They talked for at least another fifteen minutes after the tea tray was brought in. The servant came back, carried away the now cold tea on the tray, and returned five minutes later with a fresh steaming pot.

Jemma's stomach growled. She wanted to nibble on one of the biscuits. She didn't even care what the tea tasted like. She just wanted a cup.

But she sat still, and practiced breathing as if she were in her yoga class in London. Instead of getting upset, she'd meditate.

Jemma closed her eyes, and focused on clearing her mind, and her breathing. She wouldn't think about anything, wouldn't worry…

"Drink your tea, Jemma," Mikael said abruptly.

She opened her eyes, looked at him, startled to hear him use her first name, and somewhat uneasy with his tone. It hadn't been a request. It'd been a command.

He expected her to obey.

Nervous, she reached for her tea, and sipped from the cup. The tea was lukewarm. It tasted bitter. But it wet her throat and she sipped the drink slowly, as the men continued talking.

Sheikh Azizzi was speaking now. His voice was deep and low. His delivery was measured, the pace of his words deliberate.

*He's sentencing me*, she thought, stomach cramping. *He's giving the judgment now.* She looked quickly at Mikael, trying to gauge his reaction.

But Mikael's expression was blank. He sipped his tea, and then again. After what felt like an endless silence, he answered. His answer wasn't very long. It didn't sound very complicated, but it did sound terse. He wasn't happy.

Jemma didn't know how she knew. She just knew.

Both men were silent. Sheikh Azizzi ate a dried apricot. They sipped more tea. There wasn't any conversation at this point.

Mikael placed his cup on the table and spoke at last. His voice was quiet, and even, but there was a firmness in his tone that hadn't been there earlier. Sheikh Azizzi replied to Mikael. A very short reply.

A small muscle pulled in Mikael Karim's jaw. His lips thinned. He spoke. It sound like a one syllable reply. A fierce one syllable reply.

She glanced from Azizzi to Mikael and back. The two men stared at each other, neither face revealing any expression. After a moment, Sheikh Azizzi murmured something and rose, exiting the room and leaving Mikael and Jemma alone.

# CHAPTER FOUR

*THAT DID NOT go well.*

Aware that Jemma was looking at him, aware that she'd been waiting patiently, exceptionally patiently for the past hour to know her fate, Mikael finally glanced at her.

Shadows danced on the walls, stretching tall across the tiled floor. He didn't like her. Didn't admire her. Didn't feel anything positive for her.

But even in the dim lighting, he recognized her great beauty.

She wasn't merely pretty, she was stunning. Her face was all hauntingly beautiful planes and angles with her high regal brow, the prominent cheekbones, a firm chin below full, generous lips.

She was pale with fatigue and fear, and her pallor made her eyes appear even greener, as if brilliant emeralds against the ivory satin of her skin.

Sitting so close to her, he could feel her fatigue. It was clear to him she was stretched thin, perhaps even to breaking.

He told himself he didn't care, but her beauty moved him. His mother had been a beautiful woman, too, just as Mikael's father's second and third wives were both exquisite. A king could have any woman. Why shouldn't she be a rare jewel?

Jemma was a rare jewel.

But she was also a rare jewel set in a tarnished, defective setting.

He now had a choice. To save the jewel, or to toss it away? It was up to him. Sheikh Azizzi had given Mikael the decision.

"Well?" Jemma whispered, breaking the tense silence. "What did he say?"

Mikael continued to study her, his thoughts random and scattered. He didn't need her. He didn't like her. He'd never love her.

But he did desire her.

It wouldn't be difficult to bed her.

He wondered how she'd respond in bed. He wondered if she'd be sweet and hot or icy and frigid.

His gut told him she'd be hot and sweet. But first, all the Copeland taint would have to be washed away. "I am to decide your punishment for you," he said finally. "I've been given a choice of two sentences and I must pick one."

"Why?"

"Because Sheikh Azizzi knows me, and he knows I wish to do what is right, but what is right isn't always what is popular."

"I don't understand."

"I am to decide if I should follow ancient law, and tribal custom, or choose a modern punishment for you."

"And have you made up your mind?"

"No."

"What are the choices given to you?"

"Seven years house arrest here in Haslam—"

"*Seven* years?"

"Or I take you as my wife."

"That's not funny. Not even remotely funny."

"It's not a joke. It's one of the two choices presented to me. Marry you, or leave you here in Haslam to begin your house arrest." He saw her recoil and her face turn white. "I warned you that Sheikh Azizzi would not be lenient. He is not a Copeland fan either. He knows what your father did to my mother, and he wanted to send a message that Saidia will not tolerate crime or immorality."

"But seven years!" She reached for the edge of the table to steady herself. "That's…that's…so long."

"Seven years, *or* marriage," he corrected.

"No. No. Marriage isn't an option. I won't marry you. I would never marry you. I could never marry you—"

"You'd rather be locked up for seven years?"

"*Yes.* Absolutely!"

Mikael leaned back, studying her pale face and bright eyes. She was biting down, pressing her teeth into her lip. "I don't believe you."

"Not my problem."

"I'm a king. I can provide a lavish lifestyle."

"Not interested." Her eyes burned at him, hot, bright. "Seven years of house arrest is infinitely better than a lifetime with you."

He should have been offended by her response. Instead he felt vaguely amused. Women craved his attention. They fought for his affections. Ever since he'd left university, he'd enjoyed considerable female company, company he'd turned into girlfriends and mistresses.

Mikael enjoyed women. He was quite comfortable with girlfriends and mistresses. But he was not at all open to taking a wife, despite the fact that as king it was his duty to marry and produce heirs.

Something he was sure Sheikh Azizzi knew. But Sheikh Azizzi, like much of Saidia, was eager for the country's king to marry as quickly as possible.

Sheikh Azizzi also knew that nothing would pain the Copeland family more than having the youngest daughter forced into a marriage against her will.

It was fitting punishment for a family that believed itself to be above the law.

But in truth Mikael didn't want a wife. He didn't want children. He didn't want entanglements of any kind. It's why he kept mistresses. He provided for them materially and in return they'd always be available to him, without making any demands. Mikael was torn between his duty and his desires.

He studied Jemma now, trying to imagine *her* as his wife. Without her make-up he could see purple smudges beneath her eyes and her naturally long black eye lashes. She had a heart-shaped face. Clear green eyes. Full pink lips.

The same pink as her nipples.

His body hardened, remembering her earlier, modeling, and naked beneath the fur coat.

She had an incredible body.

He would enjoy her body. But he'd never like her. Never admire her. She wasn't a woman he wanted for anything beyond sex and pleasure.

He pictured her naked again. He'd certainly find pleasure in her curves and breasts and that private place between her legs.

"So it's house arrest," Jemma said. "Seven years. Would the sentence start tonight? Tomorrow?"

"I haven't made up my mind," he answered.

Her green eyes widened. Her lips parted and for a moment no sound came out and then she shook her head, a frantic shake that left no doubt as to her feelings. "I will not marry you. I will not!"

"It's not up to you. It's my choice."

"You can't force me."

"I can." And silently he added, *I could.*

Just like that, the idea took root.

He could marry her. He could force her to his will. He could avenge his mother's shame. He could exact revenge.

For a moment there was just silence. It was thick and heavy and he imagined she must hate it. She must find the silence stifling because she was completely powerless. She had no say. He would decide her fate. She would have to accept whatever he chose for her.

He found the thought pleasing.

He liked knowing that whatever he chose, she would have to submit.

She with the lovely eyes and soft lips and full, pink tipped breasts.

"But you do not wish to marry me," she whispered. "You hate me. You wouldn't be able to look at me or touch me."

"I could touch you," he corrected. "And I could look at you. But I wouldn't love you, no."

"Don't do that to me. Don't use me."

"Why not? Your father used my mother to bring shame on my family name."

"I'm not my father and you're not your mother and we both deserve better. We both deserve good marriages, proper marriages, marriages based on love and respect."

"That sounds quite nice except for the fact that I don't love. I won't take a wife out of love. I will take her out of duty. I will marry as it is my responsibility. A king must have heirs."

"But I want love. And by forcing me to marry you, you deprive me of love."

"Your father deprived my mother of life. I'm Arabic. A life for a life. A woman for a woman. He took her. I *should* take you."

"No."

"Saidia requires a prince. You'd give me beautiful children."

"I'd never be willing in bed, and you said even in a forced marriage, the sex is consensual."

"You'd consent."

"I wouldn't."

"You'd beg me to take you."

"Never."

The corner of his mouth lifted. "You're wrong. And I will prove you wrong, and when I do, what shall you give me in return?"

Jemma rose from the table, and went to the doorway. "I want to go. I want to go now."

"I don't think that's one of my options."

Jemma didn't know where to look. Her heart raced and her eyes burned and she felt so sick inside.

This wasn't what she'd thought would happen. This wasn't how she'd imagined this would go. Jail was bad. Seven years under house arrest boggled the mind. But *marriage*?

The idea of Sheikh Karim forcing her to marry him made everything inside her shrink, collapse.

She'd thought the last year had been horrific, being shunned as Daniel Copeland's daughter, but to be married against her will?

Her eyes stung, growing hotter and grittier. She pressed her nails into her palms, determined not to cry, even as she wondered how far she'd get if she bolted from the house and ran.

Marrying Mikael Karim would break her. It would. She'd been so lonely this past year, so deeply hurt by Damien's rejection and the constant shaming by the media, as well as endless public hatred. She couldn't face a cold marriage. She needed to live, to move, to breathe, to feel, to love…

*To love.*

It was tragic but she needed love. Needed to love and be loved. Needed connection and contact and warmth.

"Please," she choked, the tears she didn't want filling her eyes, "please don't marry me. Please just leave me here in Haslam. I don't want to spend seven years here, but at least in seven years I could be free and go home and marry and have children with someone who wants me, and needs me, and loves me—" She broke off as Sheikh Azizzi entered the room behind her.

The village elder was accompanied by two robed men.

Jemma pressed her hands together in prayer, pleading with Mikael. "Let me stay here. Please. *Please.*"

"And what would you do here for seven years?" he retorted, ignoring the others.

"I'd learn the language, and learn to cook and I'd find ways to occupy myself."

Mikael looked at her, his dark gaze holding for an endless moment and then he turned to Sheikh Azizzi and spoke to him. Sheikh Azizzi nodded once and the men walked out.

"It's done," Mikael said.

"What's done?"

"I've claimed you. I've made you mine."

She backed up so rapidly she bumped into the wall. "*No.*"

"But I have. I told Sheikh Azizzi I've claimed you as my wife, and it's done."

"That doesn't make us married. I have to agree, I have to speak, I have to consent somehow..." Her voice trailed off. She stared at Mikael, bewildered. "Don't I?"

"No. You don't have to speak at all. It's done."

"Just like that?"

"Just like that." He rose and stalked toward her. "And like this," he added, sweeping her into his arms and carrying her out of the house, into the night.

Outside, the convoy of vehicles were gone. Villagers clustered near a kneeling camel.

"Who is that for?" Jemma choked, struggling in Mikael's arms.

He tightened his grip. "Settle down," he said shortly. "Or I'll tie you to the camel."

"You wouldn't!"

"You don't think so?" he challenged, stepping through the crowd to set her in the camel's saddle.

The leather saddle was wide and hard and Jemma struggled to climb back off but Mikael had taken a leather strip from a pouch on the camel and was swiftly tying her hands together at the wrist, and then binding her wrists to the saddle's pommel.

The crowd cheered as he tethered her in place.

"Why are they cheering?" she asked, face burning, anger rolling through her as she strained to free herself.

"They know I've taken you as my wife. They know you aren't happy. They know you are ashamed. It pleases them."

"My shame pleases them?"

"Your shame and struggles are part of your atonement. *That* pleases them."

"I don't like your culture."

"And I do not like yours." He scooted her forward in the saddle, and then took a seat behind her, his big body filling the space, pressing tightly against her. "Now lean back a little."

"No."

"You'll be more comfortable."

"I can assure you, I would not be comfortable leaning against you."

"We are going to be traveling for several hours."

She shook her head, lips compressed as she fought tears. "I hate you," she whispered.

"I wouldn't have it any other way." He gave a tug on the reigns and the camel lurched to its feet.

The villagers cheered again and Mikael lifted a hand, and then they were off, heading for the gates and the desert beyond.

# CHAPTER FIVE

THEY RODE FOR what felt like hours through an immense desert of undulating dunes beneath a three quarter moon. The moon's bright light illuminated the desert, painting the dunes a ghostly white.

Jemma tried to hold herself stiff and straight to avoid touching Sheikh Karim but it was impossible as time wore on, just as it was impossible to ignore his warmth stealing into her body.

A half hour into the journey she broke the silence. "Where are we going?"

"My Kasbah. My home," he said. "One of my homes," he corrected.

"Why this one?"

"It is where all Karims spend their honeymoon."

She didn't know what to say to that. She didn't know what to think, or feel. So much had happened in the past few hours that she felt numb and overwhelmed.

Part of her brain whispered she was in trouble, and yet another part hadn't accepted any of this.

It didn't make sense, this forced marriage. She kept thinking any moment she'd wake up and discover it a strange dream.

Her captor was big and solid, his chest muscular, his arms strong, biceps taut as he held her steady in the saddle, his broad back protecting her from the cold.

He struck her as powerful but not brutal. Fierce and yet not insensitive.

In a different situation she might even like him. In a different situation she might like the spicy exotic fragrance he wore. In a different situation she might find him darkly beautiful.

But it wasn't a different situation. There was no way she could find him attractive, or appealing. She wasn't attracted to him, or the hard planes of his chest, or even aware of the way his muscular thighs cradled her, pinning her between his hips and the saddle's pommel.

They lapsed back into a silence neither tried to break. But an hour later, Mikael, shifted, drawing her closer to him. "There," he said. "My home."

Jemma stared hard into the dark, but could see nothing. "Where?"

"Straight in front of us."

But there was nothing in front of them. Just sand. "I don't see—"

"Watch."

The brilliant moonlight rippled across the desert, bathing all in ghostly white.

And then little by little the desert revealed a long wall, and then a bit later she was able to see shapes behind the wall. The shapes became shadowy clay buildings.

In the middle of the night, in the glow of moonlight, it looked like a lost world. As if they'd traveled back in time.

She sucked in a nervous breath as they approached massive wooden gates cut into the towering clay walls. Two enormous gas lanterns hung on either side of the dark wooden gate, and Mikael shouted out in Arabic as they reached them, and just like that, the gates split, and slowly opened, revealing square turrets and towers within.

Robed people poured into the courtyard as the gates were shut and locked behind them.

They were lining up before the first building with its immense keyhole doorway, bowing repeatedly.

"What's happening?" she whispered.

"We're being welcomed by my people. They have heard I've brought home my bride."

The camel stopped moving. Robed men moved forward. Mikael threw the reins and one of the men took it, and commanded the camel to kneel.

Sheikh Karim jumped off the camel, and then turned to look at her. His gaze held hers, his expression fierce. “What we have just done is life changing. But we’ve made a commitment, and we shall honor that commitment.”

Then he swung her into his arms and carried her through the tall door of his Kasbah, into a soaring entrance hall, its high white plaster ceiling inset with blue and gold mosaic tile.

He set her on her feet, and added, “Welcome, my wife, to your new home.”

A slender robed female servant led Jemma through the Kasbah’s labyrinth of empty halls. The maid was silent. Jemma was grateful for the silence, exhausted from the long day and hours of travel. The last time she’d glanced at her watch it had been just after midnight, and that had to be at least an hour ago now.

The silent maid led Jemma down one hallway to another, until they reached a white high ceilinged room with walls covered in delicate ivory latticework. The bed’s silk coverlet was also white and stitched with threads of the palest gold and silver, while silver and white silk curtains hung on either side of the tall French doors which opened to a courtyard of ivory stone and planters filled with palms, gardenias and white hibiscus.

The room wasn’t huge but it was opulent, elegant, and blissfully serene, an inviting, soothing oasis after a grueling and frightening day.

“Tea? Refreshment, Your Highness?” the maid asked in polite, accented English.

*Your Highness?*

Jemma glanced behind her, expecting Mikael to be there. But no one stood behind Jemma. The room was empty.

And then it hit her. The maid was speaking to her. They

all knew she'd married Mikael, then. They all knew she was his bride…

Would he come to her tonight? Did he expect to consummate the marriage tonight?

Jemma sank down on one of the white sofas in the sitting area, no longer sure her legs would support her.

"No, thank you," she said. "I'm fine. I think I just want to sleep."

"Shall I draw you a bath before I leave?"

Still dazed, Jemma nodded. "Yes, please."

A few minutes later the maid had gone and steam wafted from the bathroom, fragrant with lilacs and verbena.

Jemma entered the grand white marble and tiled bathroom with the gleaming gold fixtures, the sunken tub illuminated by a multitude of dazzling crystal chandeliers above.

Awed by the grandeur, she stripped off her dusty robe and gritty clothes and slid into the water for a soak.

The hot scented bath felt so good after the jarring camel ride that Jemma was reluctant to leave the bath until the water began to cool. By the time she finally pulled the plug, she could barely keep her eyes open another moment.

Wrapped in an enormous plush white towel she returned to her bedroom, not at all sure what she'd wear to sleep in, and there on the oversized bed was a simple white cotton nightgown with lace trim at the shoulders and hem.

Jemma slipped the nightgown over her head, gave her long hair another quick towel-dry and then climbed beneath the soft smooth cotton coverlet, desperate to sleep. She didn't even remember trying to fall asleep. She was out within minutes of turning off her bedside lamp.

She was still sleeping deeply when woken by a firm, insistent knock on the outer door.

Opening her eyes, she frowned at the dimly lit room, confused by what she saw. It took her a moment to figure out where she was. Sheikh Karim's Kasbah.

And then she remembered—she'd married him.

Or so he'd said. She didn't feel married. She didn't feel anything at all but sleepy and numb.

Jemma slid her legs from the bed and slipped on the white robe she'd seen draped over a chair before she answered the outer door.

It was Mikael.

"Good afternoon," he said.

She tucked a tangled strand of hair behind her ear. "Afternoon?"

"It's after two."

"Is it? I can't believe it."

"I've ordered coffee to be sent to you, and then you're to join me for a late lunch in the east pavilion. Don't be late." He turned and walked toward the door, but Jemma followed.

"That sounds rather rude, Sheikh Karim," she said, following after him. "Is that how you speak to all your women?"

He glanced at her. "I'm accustomed to being in charge."

"That's fine, but you don't need to be quite so aggressive. A little kindness and courtesy can go a long way."

"I thought I was being kind and courteous by sending coffee to you."

"Yes, but then you ruined it by ordering me to join you, tacking on a warning not to be late. It would have been much nicer if you'd simply asked me to join you in thirty minutes."

"Kings do not ask, Jemma. They command."

"I'm sorry, but I didn't marry a king. I married a man. That is, if we are truly married..."

"We are married. Quite married. As married as one can be in Saidia," he said, cutting her off, and walking back toward her. "But if it takes our consummating the marriage to feel married, then so be it. Tonight I will take you to my bed and there won't be any question in your mind afterwards."

"That's not what I want!"

"How do you know? You've never been in my bed. I think once you are there, you'll like it very much." And then he was gone.

* * *

The next half hour seemed endless to Jemma. He was planning on consummating the marriage tonight?

But she didn't even know him.

She couldn't imagine having sex with him.

He couldn't be serious.

And yet here she was, in the Kasbah, being waited on hand and foot, so she didn't doubt him anymore. He wasn't a man who made jokes. He meant what he said, which meant…

He intended to bed her tonight.

Jemma's clothes from last night had been washed and dried and returned to her. She dressed in the short skirt and blouse, and then slipped her feet into her high wedges. Her hair was wild, a thick tangle of waves from falling asleep with it still wet, and she subdued the waves as best as she could, pulling the long mass into a ponytail and then adding some fat silver bangles to her wrist and simple silver hoops to her ears. Not very fancy but it was the best she could do.

And then the maid knocked on the door. She'd returned to escort Jemma to lunch, leading her through the maze of hallways and halls to a door that led outside to a beautiful walled garden shaded by palms with a tiled fountain in the center of the courtyard.

Mikael was already there, waiting for her.

"I recognize those clothes," he said.

"It's all I have with me."

"I had some gowns put in your wardrobe."

"I didn't see them," she answered, aware that she hadn't looked, either.

He was silent a moment, studying her. "We need to talk, but you also need to eat, so we shall sit, and eat, and talk and hopefully become better acquainted so this wedding night will be more…comfortable…for you."

She made a soft sound of protest. "I don't think eating and talking will make anything about tonight comfortable. I can't believe this is real. Can't believe any of this is happening. I didn't say any vows. I didn't agree to anything."

"You didn't have to. I claimed you and that was all that was needed. My word is law."

"That makes for a very quick and convenient ceremony."

"The ceremony might be quick, but the honeymoon isn't. We will stay together here for sixteen days before we return to my palace in the capitol."

"You don't even like me. How can you contemplate bedding me?"

His lips quirked. It was as close to a smile as she had ever seen from him. "You are not an unattractive woman, Jemma. And I'm sure you are quite aware that a man can desire a woman without engaging one's emotions."

"So when you bed me tonight, it will be without tenderness or passion."

"If you are worried about the act itself, you needn't be. I am a skillful lover. I will take my time and be sure to satisfy your needs. It wouldn't be a proper honeymoon if I didn't."

*A proper honeymoon.*

A proper honeymoon was the trip to Bali with Damien. They'd already booked their air and hotels when he'd broken it off. She'd planned a wedding that hadn't taken place. And now she was married without a wedding and trapped here for a honeymoon she didn't want.

Her eyes burned. Her throat ached. Jemma blinked and looked away, across the courtyard, to the splashing fountain. The water danced and trickled and it amazed her that the water could be so light and tinkling when her heart felt so heavy and broken.

"I don't want to be pleasured," she whispered, reaching up to brush away a tear before it could fall. "I don't want any of this."

"You will become less resistant to the idea as time goes on."

She choked on a hysterical laugh as she glanced at him. "You think?"

He shrugged. "I imagine for you, being from a Western culture, this is terribly strange, but it is not as strange for me. I hadn't ever expected to marry for love. I've known all along that my bride would be from a different tribe. I just didn't expect it to be…yours."

"The despised Copelands."

"Fortunately, you are no longer a Copeland, but a Karim. You've left your family and are now a member of mine. You have a new name. A new start. And new responsibilities. I think it will be good for you." He gestured to the table in the shade. "We can talk more, as we eat. Sit—" he broke off, even as her eyebrows arched.

His lips curved grimly. He gave her a slight bow. "Forgive me," he drawled, not sounding the least bit apologetic. "Let *us* sit. We should try to be comfortable."

She didn't like his tone, and she hated the situation. Nothing about this was right. She would have gladly picked jail or house arrest over being trapped with him. "I can't eat. I'm too upset."

"Then I shall eat, and you can watch, because I am hungry."

"And you wonder why I'm not excited about this honeymoon."

"Yes, I do wonder. By choosing you as my first wife, I've made you a queen. You are wealthy beyond measure. That should please you to no end."

"I've had money. I don't care about money. I care about kindness, and decency. Strength. Compassion. Integrity."

"I have all that, too, so you're in luck. Now, let's eat."

"You are not compassionate."

"I am, for those requiring compassion. But you, my queen, do not need my compassion. You are doing an excellent job feeling sorry for yourself already."

She exhaled in a quick rush. "You lack sensitivity, Sheikh Karim."

"Possibly, as well as patience. Particularly when I am hungry." His dark gaze met hers and held. "But you are only making this more difficult for yourself. Fighting me, fighting the marriage, fighting to accept that we are married and that this marriage is real. I take our vows very seriously."

"What vows? I said none!"

"I claimed you, I've married you," he said, "and so it is done. Now sit. Before I carry you to the table myself."

Reluctantly, unwillingly, Jemma took a seat at the low table inside the shaded pavilion kept cool by overhead fans.

She hadn't thought she could eat, but the first course of chilled soup settled her stomach and she was able to eat some of the grilled meat and vegetables in the second and third courses. She felt better with food, calmer and less jittery. But even then, she was in shock. She thought she'd be in shock for quite some time.

There wasn't much conversation during the meal, which was fine with her. Instead Mikael studied her from across the table as if he were a scientist and she an animal he was observing.

He was the animal, though.

Maybe not an animal. But he was the one that was untamed and unpredictable. The very air around him seemed to snap and crackle with energy and tension, making the soft afternoon light dangerous, mysterious, while her heart raced and her pulse drummed, too thick and quick in her veins.

"Saidia is nothing like your country. Saidia is still essentially tribal in culture," Mikael said, as the last of the dishes were cleared away and he rinsed his fingers in a bowl of hot scented water and dried them on a soft cloth before sending the bowl and towel away. "I expect it will take you time to adjust to our culture, but you must keep an open mind. Our customs will be foreign to you but there is a reason for everything, and value to everything we do."

"And that includes kidnapping one's bride?"

"Most definitely."

"I don't see how kidnapping a woman can ever be justified. Women are not objects, not property."

"Only princes and kings, members of the royal family, kidnap a young woman for marriage."

"That's even worse."

He shook his head. "The custom of kidnapping one's bride goes back a thousand years. It helps protect one's family and society by strengthening tribal relations, forging bonds between rival tribes, protecting one's women and children from nomad tribes that might seek to prey on vulnerable tribes."

"I'm sorry. I still can't wrap my head around the custom."

"Many of Saidia's young people joke about the ancient customs when attending university, but if you asked them if forced marriages and arranged marriages should be banned, not one of them would vote to have them outlawed. It's part of our history. It's a big part of our cultural identity."

"So not all Saidia citizens have an arranged marriage?"

"About half of our young people in the urban areas choose a love marriage. If you move away from the big cities, nearly everyone prefers arranged marriages."

"Why the difference?"

He shrugged. "In the desert, people strongly identify with their tribe and tribal customs. You don't have the influence of technology. Towns are remote. Travel is difficult and change is viewed with suspicion. When you come to Haslam or the other desert communities south of the Takti Mountains, it's like traveling back in time. Haslam isn't the city capitol. The desert isn't urban. And I, as the king, must be sensitive to the new and old faces of my country. I can't alienate the youth in the city, but I must also respect the youth in the desert."

"They don't both want the same thing?"

"They don't want the same thing, nor do they understand each other. It's been a struggle for us, in terms of keeping Saidia connected. When our students are ten, we try to encourage the children to do an exchange; children from the desert leaving home to spend a week in the city with a host family, and the children in the city to go to the desert for a week. It used to be mandated but that became problematic. We still want children to participate, but our city children are bored by the desert and the lack of entertainment, and the children from the desert are overwhelmed by the city noise, pollution, and frenetic activity."

"So what do you do?"

"Try to respect both aspects of the Saidia culture, and be careful not to alienate either."

"It's a balancing act," she said.

"Absolutely." He studied her a long moment, his gaze slowly sweeping from her face down to her shoulders and then breasts. "I don't want to see you in those clothes anymore. I have provided you with a wardrobe, a more suitable wardrobe for the climate, the Kasbah, and our honeymoon."

Jemma had just begun to relax, forgetting her own situation having been pleasantly distracted by the discussion, but suddenly reality came crashing back. She tensed, flushed, angered as well as frustrated. "Is that a request or a command, Your Highness?"

"Both."

"It can't be both. It's either one or the other."

He gave his dark head a shake. "There you go again, making it difficult. You don't need to resist so much."

"Oh, I do. I most certainly do. I'm not a doll, or a mindless puppet. I'm an adult, a woman, and very independent. I've been on my own, and paying my own bills, since I was eighteen. I value my independence, too."

"I appreciate spirit, but there is a difference between spark, stubbornness and plain stupidity." He lifted his hand to stop her before she could speak. "And no, I'm not saying you are stupid. But right now you're stubborn. If the stubbornness continues too much longer, then yes, you've moved into stupidity."

Her cheeks burned. Her temper blazed. "I could say the same for you. You are equally stubborn in your refusal to see me for who I am."

"I see exactly who you are."

"A criminal Copeland!"

"No." He leaned forward, his dark gaze boring into her. "My wife."

Something in his words and fierce, intense gaze stripped her of speech and the ability to think.

For a moment she simply sat there, dazed, and breathless.

"You *are* going to experience culture shock," he said firmly, "but I fully expect you to adjust. We will be here until you adjust. So instead of arguing with me about everything, I think it is time you tried to be more open minded about this, us, and marriage to a Saidia king."

"I'm trying."

"No, I don't think you are, not yet. But I have all day. We have all day. We have all night. We have weeks, actually."

Her lips pressed firm. She glanced away, studying the exotic pink and blue mosaic tile work on the inside of the pavilion. The tiles were beautiful, the colors gorgeous, and unabashedly romantic. The remote Kasbah would have been extremely romantic if she were here, with someone else. Someone like Damien.

She still loved him.

Or maybe, she still loved who she thought he had been. Loving, strong, protective.

Turned out he wasn't so loving. Or protective. His strength was an illusion…all beautiful body and muscle but no core. No spine. No backbone, at least not when it was needed.

"You're not going to cry, are you?" Mikael asked, a hint of roughness in his deep voice.

She shook her head hard. "No."

"You're looking very sad at the moment. Thoroughly crushed. Don't tell me that twelve hours of marriage to me has broken you already."

Jemma jerked her chin up. "Not crushed, or broken. Nor will I be. I won't give any man that kind of power over me."

"Not even that pretty model ex-boyfriend of yours?"

Jemma stifled a gasp. So Mikael had done his research then, and discovered her humiliation at the hands of Damien. She lifted her chin defiantly.

"Especially not him."

"Mmm." But Mikael didn't sound as if he believed her.

"Damien hurt me, but he didn't break me. And my father hurt me, but he didn't break me. And you, Sheikh Karim, might intimidate me, and bully me, but you will not break me, either."

"I do not bully you."

"Oh yes, you do. At least, you try to."

He leaned farther back into the pillows surrounding the low table. The corner of his mouth curved. "You really aren't afraid of me?"

"Why should I be afraid? You're Drakon's friend. You came to his wedding. You saved me from seven years of jail."

He must have heard the ironic note in her voice because the corners of his mouth quirked, and that faint lift of his lips made her heart suddenly do a strange double thump.

The man was extremely intimidating, and yet when he smiled, even this faint half-smile, he became dangerously attractive.

"Ah, yes, I saved you from jail. And you, my queen, are so very grateful."

She didn't miss his sarcasm. "I would have been more grateful if you'd put me on a plane back to London. That would have been nice."

"Indeed, it would have been. But terribly weak on my part. A man must have morals, and principles, and a king even more so."

She stood up and paced restlessly around the pavilion. She knew he watched her. She glanced at him and saw the same, faint smile playing at his lips, eyes gleaming. He seemed amused or entertained. Maybe both. "You're in a good mood," she said, facing him from across the pavilion.

"Would you prefer it if I were in a bad mood?"

Jemma didn't need to think about that one too much. "No, but surely you didn't anticipate taking a Copeland daughter for your wife?"

"That is correct. But you are easy to look at, and I am quite certain, a pleasure to hold."

"That sounds terribly shallow."

His broad shoulders shifted. "It's not a love match. I don't have to like you, or love you. I just need you, as my first wife, to be good, obedient and fertile."

She stiffened and looked at him askance. *First wife*? There would be others? "Multiple wives, Your Highness?"

"Traditional Islamic law allows men four wives, but a man must be able to treat them equally. And not all men choose to have multiple wives. It's really an individual decision."

She couldn't help laughing. It struck her as terribly wrong, and yet also, terribly funny. This wasn't her life. This couldn't be happening. He might as well have plucked her from the photo shoot and locked her in his harem. "Do you intend to take more wives?"

"I haven't thought that far, but my father had four wives. My grandfather, his father, just had two."

But two wives was still one too many.

She shot him a swift glance, trying to decide if he was joking. She hoped he was. Or hoped he'd come to his senses and let her return home. "I thought the practice of polygamy had been outlawed in modern Arab countries," she said, leaning against one of the columns supporting the pavilion arches.

"Tunisia did, yes," he agreed, "But most other countries have focused on reform. In Iraq, a man can take a second wife if he obtains permission from the government, while Morocco and Lebanon have added a clause in the premarital contract, allowing a woman to divorce her husband if he takes a second wife without her consent."

"Were your father's wives happy?"

He reached for a bite of mango from the platter of dried and fresh fruit. "Most of them. He was an excellent provider. But my father was also good to them. Respectful. Tried to please them. Refused to beat them."

Jemma's jaw dropped. "And that constitutes a good husband?"

His dark eyes met hers across the table. He arched a brow. “Don’t you think so?”

*“No.”*

“Marriage in Saidia is a duty. It’s our duty to have children. It is through marriage we gain family, and family is our most cherished institution. Family is everything here. You protect your family at all costs.” He paused for a half second. “Which is how your father failed you. He refused to protect you.”

# CHAPTER SIX

MIKAEL STUDIED JEMMA as she leaned against the column, her face turned away from him, giving him just her profile.

The late afternoon sun dappled her with light and shadows. He was too far away to see the freckles across the bridge of her nose but he imagined them there, as well as the soft pink of her lips.

Looking at her from across the pavilion made him remember her working yesterday, posing for that Australian photographer. She'd been so fierce and determined as the sun beat down on her, baking her inside the fur and thigh-high boots. But she hadn't complained, nor had she as they'd traveled by camel to the Kasbah late last night, her slim warm body against his chest and thighs. He'd felt protective of her last night as they'd crossed the desert. He'd been aware of the dangers in the desert, but even more aware of her.

Last night she'd stirred now and then, restless, and probably uncomfortable, but she hadn't uttered a word. He'd respected her for that.

He had wished she wouldn't wiggle though, as each time she shifted in his arms, her back had rubbed against his chest, and her small, firm backside had pressed against his groin.

He had tried not to think about her firm backside, her rounded hips or her full soft breasts, which he'd seen in all their glory earlier.

And now she was his wife. His bride.

The villagers of Haslam had been happy for him. His people wanted him settled. They wanted him to have children. They wanted to know that there was an heir, and a spare, and then another dozen more. They were also glad he'd taken a bride, following tradition. Tradition was still so very important in Saidia.

Mikael's gaze followed the play of sunlight and shadows over her body. She looked lithe and lovely in her clothes. He was looking forward to getting her out of them. He wondered what she'd be like in bed.

"Do you really hate him?" he asked, reaching for a date and rolling it between his fingers.

"My father?" she asked, clarifying his question.

"Yes."

Her shoulders twisted and she looked away, turning her head so that he could see just the curve of her ear and the line of her smooth jaw. "He did terrible things," she whispered.

Mikael said nothing.

Jemma drew a deep breath, her chest aching, her heart blistered. "But no, I don't hate him. I hate what he did to us. I hate what he did to those who trusted him. But he's my father, the only father I've ever known, and years ago, when I was little, he was like a king. Handsome, and charming and powerful, but also fun. For my fifth birthday, he brought the circus to me. We had a whole circus set up in our front yard with a big top tent, and acrobats and clowns and everything. He organized that. He made it happen." She sighed. "My parents divorced just before I turned six. I didn't see him very much after that."

"So he was a good father when you were little?"

"In a young child's eyes, yes. But during the divorce the battle lines were drawn and I, due to my age, went to Mother. All of us went with Mother, except Morgan, who chose to live with our father."

"Do you know why your parents divorced?"

Jemma hesitated. "I think he wasn't faithful."

"Was the divorce quite bitter?"

"Not as acrimonious as it could have been. They divided up kids and property and went on with their lives."

"But neither married again."

"No. Mother was too upset—she'd loved my father—and he didn't want to lose any more assets."

"This is why love marriages are dangerous. Far better to go in with a contract and no romantic illusions, than enter the marriage with impossible hopes and dreams of a fairy tale relationship that can't exist."

"But in an arranged marriage there is no love."

"Love isn't necessary for a good marriage. In fact, love would just make things more difficult."

"How shall I fulfill…my duties…without love?"

For a moment he was baffled, and then amused. Her point of view was so peculiarly Western. As if only those who had a romantic relationship could find satisfaction in bed. "Love isn't necessary for physical pleasure."

Jemma saw him rise from the cushions and walk around the table. She swallowed hard as he approached her, not knowing where to look, or what to do. Her heart was pounding and her brain felt scrambled.

"Marriage isn't all bad," he added quietly, circling her. "Our marriage will honor you. You are my queen. The first lady in my land. There will be no more public scorn. No more shaming. You will be protected."

His voice was a deep, low rumble, the pitch husky and strangely seductive. Jemma turned her head, watched his mouth. His firm lips suddenly fascinated her. "Until you take your next wife," she said, feeling almost breathless.

"Would you feel differently if you were my only wife?" he asked, reaching out to lift a dark strand of hair from her eyelashes and tuck it carefully behind her ear, his fingertips then caressing the curve of her ear before falling away.

His skin had been so warm, and his touch had been light,

fleeting, and yet she'd felt it all the way through her, a ripple of pleasure.

Aware that she'd never survive, not if she remained this close, Jemma moved away, crossing to the far end of the pavilion where the light was even more dappled. "Are you saying I would be your only wife?" she asked.

"I never planned on taking more than one wife," he answered.

"If you hoped to reassure me, you're not succeeding."

"Do you need reassurance? Is that what this is about?" He was moving toward her again, walking slowly, confidently, relaxed and yet still somehow regal.

Jemma's heart hammered harder as he closed the distance. She didn't feel safe. She didn't feel comfortable or in control.

He didn't stop walking until he was directly in front of her, less than a foot away. "There is always anxiety on a honeymoon," he added, his voice dropping, his tone soothing. "It is natural to feel fear…even reluctance. But you will soon realize there is nothing to be afraid of. You will discover you can trust me. That you are safe with me. Safe to explore your fantasies."

"No!" Her voice spiked as she put a hand out to stop him, unable to imagine exploring any fantasies with him. This was so overwhelming. "This is too much, moving too fast."

She pushed past him to leave the pavilion and step into the sun. She felt his gaze follow her. "You need to give me time," she insisted. "You need to let me come to terms with everything."

"You've had the day."

She spun around. "No, it's not even been a full day. I was asleep until just a couple hours ago. You're not being fair. I need time. Time to accept the changes. Time to accept this new future."

"You will have that time, but you do not need to spend it alone. I think it is essential we spend time together, forming a relationship, and creating the foundation for our future."

She made a soft sound of protest. "How do you expect us

to have a relationship when there is no give or take? When you make the demands and insist on compliance? How can we have anything when you have all the power and control?"

"My power will never be used to hurt you. My power protects you, just as it protected you on the shoot, and then again in Haslam."

"You say you will protect me, but you forget what I'm sacrificing…my independence, my career, my friends, my hopes, my dreams." She shook her head. "But how do I know you will truly protect me? How do I know I can trust you when you use your power to subjugate my will?"

He looked at her, eyebrows lifted. "Because I've given you my word. My word is law."

"In Saidia, maybe. But I'm not Arab or Bedouin. I'm American. And my father said many things, but as we both know, he meant none of them. Damien said more things, promising me love and safety and security, and he didn't mean them, either. So no, I don't trust you. But that's because I don't trust men. How can I? Why should you be any different?"

He didn't speak, but this time he was listening. Carefully. Closely.

"You want a good wife," she said breathlessly. "Well, I want a good husband. I want a kind husband. You say you have integrity and strength. How do I know that? You must allow me to discover the truth myself. You need to allow me to develop trust. And that will take time. You must give me time to prove you are indeed a good man, a strong man, not a liar or a cheat." She pressed her lips together to stop them from trembling. "I understand that my family owes your family something. But I think you owe *me* something."

"You will have my wealth, and more riches than you can imagine."

"I don't want riches! Money doesn't buy happiness." Her fist went to her chest. "And I want happiness. This last year has been awful. Damien didn't break me, but he broke my heart. He hurt me so badly and I'm not ready for more pain."

"So what do you want?"

"Hope," she whispered. "I want hope."

"I don't understand."

"I want to believe that if this…marriage…is not good for me, if you are not good for me, you will set me free."

He said nothing. She could tell she'd surprised him. Caught him off guard.

"I cannot spend my life here in Saidia an unhappy hostage. I can't imagine you'd want such a woman for your wife, either. For that matter, I can't imagine your mother would want you to make your wife so terribly unhappy."

"Do you know anything of my mother?" he asked, his voice sharp.

She shook her head. "No."

"Then maybe it's time you learned who I am, and where I've come from. Follow me."

Jemma trailed after Mikael as he exited the courtyard. They traveled through a maze of hallways. Every time she was sure he'd turn right, he turned left. When she anticipated him turning left, he went right. The Kasbah halls seemed to be circular. It made no sense to her.

Finally he stopped in a spacious hall topped with a skylight and opened the tall door. "This is my personal wing," he said. "It includes a bedroom, office and living room, so I can work when here, should I need to."

She followed him through the tall door into a handsome living room. Wooden panels had been pulled back from the trio of windows and sunlight flooded the room, making the pair of low sapphire velvet couches glow and the gold painted walls shimmer.

They continued through the living room into another room, this one also bright with natural light as one entire wall was made of glass doors.

The room itself was sparsely furnished, the buff stone walls unpainted, and the plush carpet beneath her feet intricately woven of pale gold, faded blue, and a coral pink.

A low couch was on one side of the room while an enormous dark wood desk inlaid with pearl dominated the other side, positioned to face glass doors with the view of a spacious, but Spartan courtyard.

He crossed the floor to the desk, opened a drawer, and drew out a small jeweled picture frame. He held the frame out to her. "This is my mother at twenty-three, just two years younger than you are now."

She took the frame from him. The woman was young and blonde and very beautiful. She had straight bangs and high, elegant cheekbones. Her long hair hid one shoulder and her blue eyes were smiling, laughing, up at the camera.

"She's…so fair," Jemma said, brows tugging as she studied the laughing beautiful girl with straight white-blonde hair.

"She was American."

Jemma's head jerked up. Her gaze met his.

He nodded once. "Your mother was descended from a Mayflower family. So was my mother. She was American as apple pie."

Jemma felt a lump grow in her throat. She looked back down at the photo, noting the girl's swimsuit and cover up and the blue of the sea behind her. "Where was this taken?"

"The Cote d'Azur. My father met her when she was on holiday with friends in Nice. My father swept her off her feet. They were married within months of meeting."

"She's so beautiful."

"She was young and romantic and in love with my father… as well as in love with the idea of becoming Saidia's queen."

Jemma handed the framed photo to him. He put it back in the drawer. "My father betrayed her trust," he said quietly. "And then your father betrayed her trust. Which is why I promise you, I will not betray you. I am a man of my word. And if I vow to provide for you properly, I will. Over time our marriage will hopefully heal the rift between families and countries. It won't be immediate. It might not even happen in our generation, but I hope that it will be better for our children." He studied her, expression fierce, resolute. "We begin our journey as husband and wife tonight, by sharing our first meal together in the Bridal Palace."

Jemma's throat ached. She felt close to tears. "Would your mother approve of what you're doing?"

"Leave her out of this."

"How can I?" she choked. "You don't!"

"One day you will understand the importance of honor. One day when we have our children—"

"No!"

"That is fair. You are right. I will save the talk of children for later. Instead let us focus on tonight, and how we shall retreat to the Bridal Palace, for the first of our eight nights. For the next eight nights, I will pleasure you."

"And what happens after that eighth night?" Jemma asked tartly. "Do you disappear into your suite? Return to Buenos Aires? What happens then?"

"You are in control for the next eight nights. You get to pick a different pleasure each evening, or the same pleasure, or…no pleasure."

She frowned, not understanding.

He saw her expression, correctly reading her confusion. "According to Saidia law, the first eight nights are the groom's. The next eight nights are the bride's. The Saidia bride doesn't have to take her husband into her room, or her bed, for any of the next eight nights, unless she wants to. What happens during the second eight nights is entirely her choice."

"What is the point of that?" Jemma asked.

"It was to teach a randy bridegroom not to be selfish in bed, and provide an incentive for the groom to be patient and tender with his new bride, pleasuring her so thoroughly that she'll hunger for her husband's touch."

Jemma's cheeks were on fire again. Heat coursed through her, her skin prickled, suddenly almost too sensitive.

Mikael's dark eyes met hers. "And I assure you, I intend to

please you so thoroughly you'll beg me to return to your bed for every night of your eight nights."

She drew a slow breath, head spinning. Everything inside of her felt tight, tense.

"I have never heard of any honeymoon being so purely… carnal and erotic."

"It might sound like that, until you remember that most royal brides brought here were innocent virgins, carried here against their will. As I told you, it was customary for the royal groom to kidnap a bride from one of the rival desert tribes. The honeymoon was his chance to win his bride's affection, and loyalty, before he took her home with him. But, if he couldn't win her affections by the end of the sixteen days, then she could leave him without repercussions or shame."

That last bit caught Jemma's attention. "She could choose to go home?"

"If he couldn't make her happy in their sixteen days together." He reached out, stroked the sweep of her cheekbone, making her skin tingle. "I will please you," he said, quietly, decisively. "I promise to satisfy you completely."

She stared at him, wide-eyed, heart pounding. She'd loved Damien and she'd been quite sure Damien had loved her, but he'd never been overly concerned with pleasing her. Pleasuring her.

She couldn't quite get her head around the idea that Mikael was promising to satisfy her completely.

Sexually.

Fulfilling her every fantasy.

"You are making a lot of promises," she said unevenly, her mouth drying.

"They are promises I fully intend to keep."

"I worry that you are…unrealistic."

His hard expression softened. Amusement glimmered in his eyes. "I worry that your expectations are too low." His lips curved faintly. "Perhaps it's time I show you the Kasbah? This is no ordinary desert palace. Its outer walls hide a secret palace."

"A secret palace?" She looked at him, intrigued. "What does that mean? That there's a palace within the palace?"

"Yes. That is exactly what I do mean. Would you like to see? I can take you on a tour of the Bridal Palace now if you're interested."

The Bridal Palace? Was that its real name? Her eyebrows arched. "I'm very interested."

He smiled. "Good. We will start the tour with the rooms near your suite."

## CHAPTER SEVEN

THEY LEFT HIS rooms, and walked through the maze of halls and corridors with Mikael giving her the history of the palace as they returned to her wing. "This Kasbah is known in Saidia as the Bridal Palace. For hundreds of years this is where the king of Saidia brought his new bride after the wedding ceremony. It is where the royal couple honeymoons, and where the king or prince would introduce his virgin bride to the pleasures of the marriage bed."

Mikael pointed down one hall, which led to the entrance of the Kasbah. "The bride would arrive, and pass through the same entrance you passed through last night, and then be escorted by her new maids to this wing. On arrival, the bride would be bathed, massaged with fragrant oils, then robed and taken to the first chamber, the white chamber—a room hidden off your room—which historically has been called the Chamber of Innocence. In the Chamber of Innocence, the groom claims his bride, consummating the marriage. In the morning, the bride is transferred to a different suite.

"Here," he added, walking down another hall to a different corridor and taking a turn to the right. "This is the Emerald Chamber." He opened the only door in the corridor and stepped back to let her have a look. "This is where the bride and groom spend their second day."

Jemma carefully moved past him to glance around the room. The walls were glazed green, the floor was laid with green and white tiles. The bed was gold with green silk covers and a dozen gold lanterns hung from the ceiling.

"There's a courtyard attached," he said. "The garden is fantastic, and the pool looks like a secret grotto."

They stepped out of the room, into the hall. They walked in a circular pattern, continuing right, down another hall to another door. "The Amethyst Room," he said, and it was a room of purple and gold, even more luxurious and exotic than the Emerald Chamber.

"There are eight rooms like these," Mikael said. "In this section of the Kasbah, the rooms have all been laid out in the shape of a large octagon, with a shared garden in the center. Some of the rooms also have a private courtyard, too. Each of the rooms are significant because they represent a different sensual pleasure."

He'd just opened a door to the Ruby Chamber but she didn't even look inside. She stared at Mikael, stunned, and fascinated. "Seriously?"

He nodded. "Each suite has a pleasure attached, and it varies from a form of sex, to a particular position."

Jemma blushed, suddenly very warm. "You're making this up."

"Not at all. Each night for eight consecutive nights, the groom takes his bride to a new room, initiating her into new carnal delights, teaching her, pleasuring her, as well as ensuring she knows how to pleasure him."

Her face burned, hot. It was almost as if a fire had been lit inside of her and she didn't know if it was the things he was saying, or his tone, but his words created erotic pictures in her head, pictures that were so intimate and real that she could scarcely breathe.

He led her around to each of the eight suites, and she marveled at each. The Bridal Palace was beyond fantasy. It was magical. Jemma felt as if she'd entered another world. A world she couldn't have imagined existed anywhere. And yet it did. *Here.*

The exotic perfection was almost too much to take in, each suite more spectacular than the last, the rooms splashed with jeweled color—violet, sapphire, gold, ruby, turquoise, emerald, and silver. The chambers were connected by tall columned corridors, the white and gold tiles shimmering at all hours of the day, while in the very center was a luxurious walled garden featuring pools, fountains, and exotic red, gold and ivory mosaic tiled pavilions.

She'd thought her courtyard was lovely, but the Bridal Palace's secret courtyard was so lavish and sensual it stole her breath, and made her heart hurt.

She didn't know why the Bridal Palace's sensual beauty created pain. She was certain it'd been designed to delight.

"You're very quiet," the sheikh said, turning to look at her.

She passed a small waterfall that tumbled and splashed into a deep bathing pool. "I'm in awe," she said, thinking this was the kind of place you wanted to be on your honeymoon. The low beds covered with the softest cotton and banked with silk cushions. The fragrant garden both hid and revealed the various gleaming pools.

This was a place for passion. Pleasure. Here anything seemed possible…

"I've never seen anything like this before," she added, voice unsteady. "It takes my breath away. These rooms, the gardens, they're pure fantasy. I feel like I'm in a dream."

"I think that's the point," he said, leading her from the central courtyard, through a room shimmering with silver, to the outside hall. "The fantasy element is to help both bride and groom overcome their inhibitions. Here, everything is possible."

The door shut behind them and they were suddenly back in an ordinary hall, in an ordinary world.

She looked at the closed door, amazed by what they'd just left behind. "The rooms…your story…it's a fairy tale for adults."

"But it's not a fairy tale, or a story. It's real. Part of Saidia's culture and tradition. This is where every Saidia king has brought his bride for eight hundred years."

"Your parents came here?"

He nodded. "My father brought my mother here. And now I've brought you."

Jemma's mouth opened, closed. She couldn't think of a single thing to say. It was all too incredible…the exotic beauty, as well as the seductive nature of the Kasbah. Everything in this palace was hedonistic. Indulgent. And he was using the promise of pleasure to cast a spell over her.

"Tonight is the first of our sixteen nights here. For the next eight nights, I shall pick the pleasure, and then on the ninth night, it becomes your choice."

He was walking her back to her suite now, and Jemma was glad he was leading. She felt dazed. Lost. Caught up in the most impossible dream.

"Not tonight," she said as they reached her door. "I'm not ready."

"A kidnapped bride is never ready," he said, and yet he was smiling to soften his words. "I also am not insensitive to the strangeness of our situation. I understand you have fears, and misgivings, but I believe it is better to begin sooner than later. You will be less anxious once we know each other."

"But shouldn't that happen before physical intimacy?"

"The physical intimacy will bind us together. It is the act of physical love that distinguishes the relationship, separating us from others."

Jemma pressed her hands together, fingers locking. "One more day. *Please*."

"But you had one day already. We had today."

"I slept most of it away!"

"Which should mean you are rested and refreshed for tonight." They'd reached the entrance to her suite of rooms. He gestured to her door. "Inside your room you will find several presents from me. You will receive more later. For the next eight days and nights I will shower you with gifts, jewels, and my undivided attention. I think you shall soon discover that these eight days and nights will be everything you ever dreamed…and more."

His gaze met hers and held, even as his words echoed in her head, making her nerves dance.

*Everything you ever dreamed...and more.*

Just like that the night crackled, the air hot and heavy, sultry in the exotic pavilion.

Mikael was so close that he made the hair on her nape rise and her skin prickle. All she could think about was the sheikh stretching his big powerful body out over hers. Blood rushed to her cheeks and she fought to control her breathing.

"You are awfully confident, Your Highness."

"We are married. Don't you think it's time you used my given name?"

"I do not feel married."

"That will change soon."

Jemma disappeared into her room, pulse racing. She turned from the door and nearly tripped over the mountain of trunks stacked just inside the entrance to her sitting room.

The young maid was standing next to the trunks, smiling. "For you," she said. "From His Highness."

Jemma backed away from the trunks, panicked by the tower of gifts.

She didn't want presents. Didn't want to be showered with expensive gifts and jewels.

She wanted the life she had in London. She wanted her friends. Wanted her work. She wanted her own identity and freedom.

The maid watched Jemma, her dark eyes bright, expression cheerful and excited. "Shall I start your bath, Your Highness? We have much to do to prepare."

Jemma shook her head, feeling anything but excited. She couldn't do this. Couldn't go through with this. She wasn't the kind of woman who just gave up, who just gave in. She was not meant to be Mikael's queen. Her future was not here in Saidia, nor did she have any desire to bear the children that would heal the rift between families and countries.

"It is a very big day," the maid added carefully, her confident expression slipping, revealing the first hint of concern. "Much to do. Much tradition."

Jemma sat down on the edge of one of her low white sofas, her hands folding in her lap. "These are not my traditions."

The maid knelt next to Jemma. "Your Highness, do not be frightened. His Highness, Sheikh Karim, is a very good and powerful man. He is very fair. A man of his word. If he tells you something, it is so."

"I think you would say that about all Saidia kings."

"No. I would not say that about the last king, Sheikh Karim's father. The old king was not a good man. He made his first wife very sad. I think His Highness, Sheikh Karim, saw much as a boy. I think he saw things a child should not see. This is why he is different from his father. He has worked very hard to be a good king. The people love him. He honors and respects Saidia people, and Saidia tradition." The maid smiled. "The king will be good to you. You will be happy. I am already happy for you." Her hand indicated the trunks. "Already he has sent many gifts. He tries to show you already he is pleased with you. That you bring him honor."

Jemma shook her head. "He's trying to buy me."

The maid frowned. "Buy you? Like a camel?"

"Yes. But I'm not a thing to be bought."

"His Highness does not buy you. His Highness honors you. Gifts show respect. In Saidia, gifts are good things." She smiled more brightly. "Maybe now you look at your gifts, and then we get ready for tonight."

Jemma struggled to smile. "You open the trunks for me. Show me what is inside."

For the next several minutes, all the maid did was unpack the trunks, starting with the largest leather trunk on the bottom of the stack.

The biggest trunk was filled with clothes. Kaftans, skirts, sarongs, tunics, slinky evening gowns. The medium trunk contained shoes and heels and elegant jeweled sandals. The small trunk held jewelry and accessories.

There was one last trunk, but this one wasn't leather, but silver. The silver box's gleaming surface was embossed with elegant scrollwork and a jeweled handle. Jemma carefully unfastened the latches. Inside the silver box was a white garment bag, white shoes and a small, delicate white silk pouch.

"This is for tonight," the maid said, unzipping the garment bag to remove a long white satin gown that looked like something from a Hollywood movie. "Your bridal gown."

"My wedding gown?" Jemma corrected, thinking maybe she'd misunderstood the girl's English.

"No. The honeymoon gown. For pleasure." The maid smiled, her cheeks pink. "Tonight is the first night. You go to him in white. You meet him in the Chamber of Innocence."

"How do you know all this?"

"I come from the same tribe as Sheikh Karim. My mother and grandmother served the new Karim brides. And now I serve you. It is my job to prepare you for the king's pleasure."

Jemma was neither a virgin nor an innocent and yet she blushed, furiously, feeling ridiculously embarrassed, and shy. "I'm not sure about this."

"You don't need to worry. His Highness will know everything. He will teach you."

Jemma flushed again, her cheeks burning, trying not to feel mortified. The maid must think she was a timid virgin.

"Do you want to try it on?" the maid asking, admiring the long white satin gown.

"No." Jemma turned away from the gown, the fabric soft and begging to be touched, focusing instead on the remaining wedding night gifts and accessories. White satin shoes. Delicate white satin undergarments. And of course, the white silk pouch.

Curious, Jemma loosened the silver strings and emptied

the pouch into her hand. Glittering diamond and pearl earrings spilled into her palm. A small card slid out last, landing on top of the stunning diamond drop earrings.

My first gift to you. Please wear them tonight. I think they will look magnificent on you.

Jemma read the card twice, and then slowly exhaled, her heart hammering.

Was this really happening? Would she really go to him tonight, dressed like a virgin sacrifice, dazzling in diamonds and white?

Jemma slipped the earrings back into the silk pouch, and then placed the pouch and shoes inside the silver trunk before closing the lid and fastening it shut.

Yesterday afternoon she'd been in the middle of a photo shoot when Mikael arrived. She'd known nothing about him, and very little about Saidia, and yet now she was his wife, and being prepared for his bed.

She still couldn't wrap her head around it.

Jemma sat back on her heels and looked at the young maid. "Have you ever heard of a royal groom not satisfying his bride? Have you ever heard your mother or grandmother mention a kidnapped bride returning to her family? Has it happened in Saidia history before?"

The maid nodded. "Yes."

"A long, long time ago, or more recently?"

"During my great-great-grandmother's time, I think. Many, many years ago. And…" The maid chewed her lip, looking unsure of herself. "Maybe my mother's time."

Jemma frowned. "Your mother served my husband's mother."

"Yes."

"Mikael's mother was unhappy?"

"Not at first. Not during the honeymoon, but later."

"Why?"

She shrugged. "I do not know. My mother would never say."

The maid left to start Jemma's bath, and rather than argue with the maid about privacy, Jemma stripped her clothes off and spent the next half hour soaking in the deep marble tub, lost in thought.

The Kasbah was a palace within a palace, and Mikael descended from a line of royal men who'd been taught that it was necessary to know how to please a woman in bed, and even his *duty* to give his woman pleasure. But not just pleasure. He was expected to make her fall in love with him. She needed to want to stay in Saidia. She needed to be happy. And if, during the honeymoon, the Saidia groom couldn't make his bride happy, she could leave him after sixteen days.

The history fascinated Jemma. But it wasn't just history. They were facts. And the facts gave her pause.

If a Saidia man couldn't please his wife, he had to let her go.

Did that mean Mikael would let her go if he couldn't please her?

Out of the bath, the maid set to work rubbing exotic fragrant oils into Jemma's skin, and Jemma provided no resistance, lost in thought.

She'd been brought here as Mikael's first wife. But perhaps now she could force him to free her following their honeymoon. If she wasn't happy after eight days, she'd refuse him the next eight and demand to be allowed to return to her tribe.

While the oil dried, Jemma walked around the courtyard in her cotton kimono, letting the sun's warmth help her skin absorb the oil.

She knelt by the pool in the courtyard, and gazed down into the clear blue water, the bottom of the pool covered in cobalt blue tiles. Her face reflected back at her, her dark hair pulled back from her face, her expression appeared surprisingly serene in the water. Her calmness belied her resolve.

She would leave here.

She would not be charmed.

She would not fall in love.

She would not give him children.

What she'd give him were eight days and nights, and during those days and nights he'd have access to her body. But he'd never have her heart.

The maid fetched Jemma from the courtyard to do her hair.

Jemma's stomach churned as she sat at the silver dressing table, while the maid combed and twisted her hair into place, roping in strands of pearls and clusters of diamonds until Jemma's long dark hair was a glittering, jeweled work of art.

Was Mikael aware that he'd given her a way out? Did he know that she understood her freedom could be won?

But first she'd have to surrender to Mikael for eight days, and eight nights.

Could she do it?

Could she give herself to him totally? Handing over her body, her will, her need for control?

"Shall I help you with your dress now?" the maid asked, Jemma's hairstyle complete.

"No," Jemma said suddenly. She couldn't finish dressing, couldn't slip into the white satin gown, not until she'd seen Mikael. She needed to speak to him. She needed his promise that he'd honor Saidia tradition. "I need to go see His Highness, now. Will you please take me to him?"

The maid opened her mouth as if to protest and then nodded. "Yes, Your Highness. Please, follow me."

The maid knew the palace corridors and they walked swiftly from her wing to his.

The maid knocked on the outer door of Mikael's suite and then stepped back, discretely disappearing into the shadows.

Jemma drew a deep breath as she waited for the outer door to open. It did, and Mikael's valet gestured for Jemma to enter the king's suite.

Jemma glanced up into Mikael's central hall with the soaring ceiling topped by a skylight. She remembered the skylight and the second floor lined with balconies, reminding her of the New Orleans French Quarter.

"Looking for me?" Mikael's deep voice sounded behind her.

Jemma turned, blushing as she spotted Mikael in nothing but a snug white towel wrapped securely around his waist, revealing broad shoulders and muscular torso.

"Yes," she said, forcing her gaze from his impressive body up to his face. His black hair was damp, and glossy, his jaw freshly shaven. His gaze met hers and held.

Handsome, she thought, dazzled by the play of golden light over his bronze features. He was too handsome for his own good. No wonder he was arrogant.

"What can I do for you?" Mikael asked as his valet disappeared.

"We need to talk."

"And I thought you'd come to thank me for my gifts," he answered, smiling faintly.

"They are…lovely," she said hesitantly. "So yes, thank you. But—"

"But you want something else?" he interrupted.

She flushed. "Yes. You could say that."

His eyes, fringed by those endless lashes, narrowed. His gaze swept over her and even from across the courtyard she felt the heat in his eyes, felt the possession.

"What is it?" he asked.

Jemma grew hot. Her pulse quickened. She'd walked quickly the entire way from her room but it didn't explain this new heat in her veins. This was his fault. When he looked at her, he made her head light, made her feel ridiculously dizzy and weak. "I want something that isn't a physical gift."

"You don't care for jewels and clothes?"

"They're fine, but not my favorite gifts."

"I thought every woman loved jewelry and exquisite clothes."

"I am sorry to disappoint you."

He circled her slowly. "You don't disappoint me. You intrigue me. I'm intrigued right now. What it is that you want so badly you'd race to my room just an hour before we are to disappear into the Chamber of Innocence?"

Mikael watched color sweep Jemma's cheeks. She was beautiful in the pink kimono robe, and she sounded breathless and all he could think of was peeling the thin fabric from her shoulders and kissing the pale skin at her collarbone.

She had a beautiful body. He wanted her body. He wanted her.

"Would you care to sit?" he asked her.

"No. I think I'm better standing."

"Does what you need to say require courage?" he asked, wondering if she knew how beautiful she was. He doubted it. She was surprisingly modest. She had no airs or attitude. Someone in her family had done a good job raising her.

"It depends on how you'll take it," she answered.

"Then perhaps let's not talk now. Tonight is special. Tonight is about pleasure."

"Tonight cannot happen without us speaking, Your Highness."

He sighed, an exaggerated sigh. The sigh was purely for show. He was playing with her, enjoying her fire. "*Laeela*, I confess I'm not pleased with the direction our relationship is taking. We do a lot of talking. Or more accurately, you do a lot of talking, and I seem to be doing a great deal of listening."

"You're wrong, Your Highness. You actually never listen."

"I'm sure that's not right. It seems like you talk a great deal."

"That's maybe because you're not used to a woman who has a brain and wants to use it."

"I see." It required effort not to give in to the smile. "That might explain it, but I'm wondering if talking now will maybe interfere with our pleasure tonight? Perhaps we should wait and talk later."

"Most men probably never want to talk, Your Highness, but we must."

"Fine. You talk, and I will listen, provided there is no more of this Your Highness when we are in private. You're my wife, about to come to my bed. I understand you must call me Your Highness in public, but we are alone at the moment, and my name is Mikael."

She blinked and wet her lips, her face awash in rosy color, her eyes a brilliant green in her lovely face, flashing fire.

"Now, what is it you had to say?" he added, reaching out to touch her pink cheek.

She just looked at him with wide green eyes and he savored the moment. "What is it?" he persisted. "Tell me."

She drew a quick breath. "I want you to make me a promise."

She was negotiating with him. Interesting. "Yes?"

"I want you, as the king and leader of the Saidia people, to promise me that you will honor Saidia tradition, and the custom of your tribe."

He could see from the tilt of her chin that she expected him to fight her. She expected a problem. She was preparing to battle.

"I always try to honor Saidia tradition," he said.

"Then promise to honor this tradition."

"Perhaps you need to tell me what it is, first."

She looked into his eyes and then away. She seemed to struggle to find the right words, and then she shrugged, and blurted, "If you cannot make me happy in the first eight days and nights of our honeymoon, I want you to promise to send me home, to my family. My people."

She'd shocked him. For a moment he could think of nothing to say.

"During the tour you explained why the honeymoon is so important," she continued. "It made sense to me, and it made me respect your culture more. I am grateful you come from a culture that believes a woman should be happy, because I, too, believe a woman should be happy. I believe all women should be happy, just as I believe all women should have a say in their marriage, and future." She drew another quick breath. "*I* need to have a say in my future. I need my voice heard. You must give me my voice back."

"But you have your voice. I hear you quite plainly."

"Then give me a gift I will cherish, the gift of your word. Promise me I will be free to return home if you cannot make me happy."

"You doubt me?"

"I won't if you promise me I can trust you."

"I've told you my word is law."

"Then say to me, 'Jemma, if you aren't happy in eight days, I will put you on a plane, and send you back to London.'" Her green eyes held his. "That is all you have to do, and I will believe you, but I need a promise from you, or it is impossible to give you my body, or my heart, if I'm afraid, or full of fear and doubt."

He said nothing.

"Mikael," she added more softly, persuasively, "I need to know that I can trust you. I need to believe you will take care of me. Your promise is the gift of dignity and honor. Your promise means I feel safe and respected, and that gives us the basis for a future. Otherwise, we have nothing. And how can you build a future on nothing?"

She was like a queen, he thought, watching her. Beautiful and regal. Proud, slender, strong. With her dark hair and stunning green eyes, she could easily be one of the great Egyptian queens. Cleopatra. Nefertiti. Ankhesenamun.

If they had met under different circumstances, he would have made her his lover or mistress. He would have enjoyed spoiling her with gifts. He liked to spoil his woman, liked to please her. But he didn't love. He didn't want to love. Love complicated relationships. Love wasn't rational.

He was determined to be rational. He was determined to be a good king.

She reached toward him, her hand outstretched. "Mikael, I need to know you have not just your best interest at heart, but mine, too."

He stiffened. "As king I have all my people's best interests at heart."

"As my *husband,* you must have mine, too."

"I do."

Her hand lightly settled on his chest. "Then promise me, and I can meet you tonight with calm, and confidence, and *hope.*"

He glanced down at her hand where it rested so lightly on his chest, just above his heart.

He captured her hand in his, holding her small fist to his chest. His thumb swept her wrist. He could feel the wild staccato of her pulse. She was afraid. He didn't like her fear. "You've no need to be afraid."

"That is not the same thing as a promise."

"You are still getting to know me, but you will discover I am a man of my word. I do not make rash promises, nor do I break my commitments."

She bit her lip and looked at him from beneath her long dark lashes. "So what does that mean?"

"It means I have eight days to make you happy."

He could see her bite down harder, her pink lip turning white in the center, where her teeth pressed into the tender flesh.

He both envied and pitied the spot.

Once she was completely his, he would suck and lick that poor lip to make amends. His body hardened in anticipation. He would very much like to suck and lick all of her. He would like to feel her tighten beneath him, and then shatter. "But I also understand your mistrust of men. Your father abandoned you, and then your fiancé did the same. You've been surrounded by men who only think of themselves, making rash promises, which is why I can safely give you my word that I *will* make you happy."

"And yet, if you cannot, you will let me return to London?"

His dark gaze raked her, appreciating the jut of breasts and swell of hips beneath the thin kimono. "Yes."

## CHAPTER EIGHT

Back in her room, Jemma couldn't look at herself as she stepped into the beautiful fitted white satin gown. It was too soft and sensual to be a wedding gown, and yet the slinky satin somehow managed to give the impression of a long and Western style bridal gown. The wedding night without the traditional wedding ceremony.

She sucked in a nervous breath as the maid fastened the dozens of tiny hooks in the back of the long dress, and then with shaking hands, she attached the diamond and pearl earrings to her earlobes.

She couldn't believe how her stomach flip-flopped as she stepped into her white-beaded silk shoes. Designer shoes. They fit like a glove.

Jemma glanced at herself in the dressing table mirror. She looked like a bride dressed for the bedroom.

And wasn't that exactly what she was? She was being prepared for her husband's bed. Oiled and scented and bejeweled for his pleasure.

But earlier, in his room, when he'd taken her hand, she hadn't felt fear. She'd actually liked the way his touch made her feel. He was strong and warm and it was such a small thing, this linking of fingers, and yet significant. Touch was powerful. His touch was surprisingly comforting.

And now she was curious about tonight. But not afraid.

Mikael arrived at Jemma's suite of rooms at eight o'clock and he watched her cross the sitting room floor, as she moved toward him, her head high, her eyes wide, the large diamond teardrops swinging from her earlobes, the brilliant cuts in the stone casting tiny dancing lights in every direction. Her gown molded to her body, the delicate straps and cups of the dress revealing smooth shoulders and the swell of her breasts before hugging her flat tummy and the lush curve of her hips and butt.

His narrowed gaze slid over her tall, slender body, appreciating how the satin caressed her, and yet he could also see her without the luscious satin, remembering that stunning glimpse of her when she'd dropped the fur coat during the shoot, and how the full shape of her breasts had been revealed.

The impact of her physical beauty had shocked him. He'd had such a visceral reaction there on the sand dune. He'd been furious—outraged—but he'd also felt a wave of pure possession.

*Mine,* he'd thought.

He'd wanted to cover her. Take her away from everyone. He'd told himself it was duty, responsibility, a response to a wrong.

Now he wondered if it was more than that.

*Mine.*

He held out his hand to her. She gave him her hand. It was shaking. He took her hand, his fingers lacing with hers.

He lifted her hand to his mouth, just as he had earlier, but this time he kissed the back of each finger. "Eight days and nights."

"And it all starts now?"

"Yes."

He swung her into his arms then and carried her down the connecting halls until they reached the entrance to the Bridal Palace.

"We are here," he said, pushing the door open and carrying her inside to a room that glowed with hundreds of white candles.

Jemma spotted the bed, surrounded by more candles, and looked the other way. "Are we going to bed now?"

"No." His deep voice sounded amused. "I'm starving. Haven't eaten since our late lunch. Wouldn't you prefer a bite to eat first?" he asked, setting her on her feet.

"Yes," she said quickly. "Please."

Mikael took her hand and led her past the dozens of candles illuminating the immense bed, to the opposite side of the room, where a door opened to a private courtyard fantastically transformed into a tropical garden with a manmade grotto and splashing waterfall. Dozens of candles lined the walkway, and more candles outlined the steps to the grotto and door.

It was warm in the garden, and fragrant with orchids and lilies and Mikael pulled her close to his side as he led her along the narrow path lined with candles, down an even more narrow stone staircase to a secret room inside the grotto where a table had been set for them among a sea of pale blue silk cushions.

The grotto was made entirely of stone and illuminated with a dozen blue glass lanterns that hung from the pale ivory stone ceiling. Water lapped in a small pool while above them came the sound of rushing water tumbling through over the waterfall.

"This is unbelievable." Jemma breathed, taking a seat among the cushions, very aware of Mikael as he sat down next to her.

He'd come to her tonight not in traditional Saidia robe and head covering, but in black trousers and an elegant dress shirt and once seated at the table, he proceeded to roll the sleeves of his shirt back on his muscular forearms, and then open the shirt another button at the collar, revealing a hint of bronzed skin just below his throat.

"That's better," he said.

She swallowed hard. He'd shocked her earlier in the towel, but it was just as shocking to see him now in Western clothes. He didn't look like a sheikh. He just looked gorgeous.

He looked at her. "You don't think so?"

"No, you look…quite…good," she murmured, thinking good was a total understatement. He looked fantastic.

"Quite good," he repeated, lips curving slightly. "I will take that as a compliment coming from you."

"I'm sure you are complimented all the time. You must know you are very beautiful for a man."

He laughed then. It was the first time she'd ever heard him laugh, really laugh, and the flash of his straight white teeth against his bronzed skin, and the crinkle of his eyes made her heart race.

"I don't get complimented very often," he said.

"No? Why not?"

"I think people might be afraid to pay me compliments."

She arched a brow. "What do you do? Chop off heads?"

"No. But I have a reputation for being no-nonsense."

"I'm sorry to hear that."

His teeth flashed again but he said nothing else, and for the next hour staff came and went, bearing platters of food until the low table was covered. Chicken with tomatoes and honey. Lamb cutlets, tangy beef, coconut rice, a tagine of yam, carrots and prunes.

After the past several days of stress, Jemma was glad to just relax, and eat, and sip her wine. Mikael was his most charming tonight. During dinner he told her stories, amusing stories. "You said earlier you're not a fan of jewels and clothes," he said, leaning against the cushions. "So what do you like? Art? Antiques? Cars?"

"Books." She could see she'd surprised him. "I love to read."

"Fiction?"

"Fiction, non-fiction, everything. Although when I was a girl, I only wanted to read romances. My mother was convinced I'd run off and join the circus or something equally risky and foolish."

"What will she think when she discovers you've married me?"

"She'll be horrified."

He didn't seem to like that. "Why?"

"Because our cultures are too different and she'd be worried that I'd be trapped in a life where I couldn't be myself, and the lack of freedom would make me desperately unhappy."

"That's quite specific."

"Morgan's short, unhappy marriage made quite an impression on all of us."

"And yet the day of her wedding she seemed ecstatic."

"Exactly. But Morgan was so infatuated with Drakon that she didn't ask any hard questions about what her life would be like in Athens, and their marriage was a shock for her. She ended up bitterly unhappy as a new bride in a new city and their relationship quickly fell apart." Jemma smoothed a wrinkle from her satin skirt. "Mother had warned her that life in Greece, as the wife of a Greek shipping tycoon wouldn't be easy, not for an independent American girl who is accustomed to making decisions for herself. And so I'm quite sure my mother would be even more upset if I turned around and married a Saidia sheikh."

Mikael said nothing for a long moment. "Even if it improves your situation?"

It was Jemma's turn to fall silent.

"I'm aware your brother is the only Copeland who has any financial assets left," Mikael added. "And the only reason he does, is because he lives in Europe, and his assets couldn't be seized, but your government will go after him. What he hasn't yet lost due to scandal, will soon be taken by your government."

"Maybe it won't happen," she said, not really believing it herself.

He gave her a skeptical look. "Isn't that the same thing you said about your mother's home? And didn't the government just take that?"

Jemma drew a short breath. It had been one thing losing

the house on St. Bart's and the lodge in Sun Valley, but it was painful losing one's childhood home. Jemma had lived in the Greenwich house from the time she was six until she'd left for London. And maybe she didn't live at home any longer, but it was still her home. It was where she liked to picture her mother, where they all came together to celebrate Christmas or a special occasion.

The government shouldn't have taken the house a month ago. It was her mother's, from the divorce. But apparently her father's name was on the title, too, and that was all they needed to seize it.

"It's not been easy for my mother, no," Jemma said roughly, unable to look at him, the pain fresh and sharp all over again. "But she's lucky she has a few friends who have stood by her. She's relying on their kindness now."

Jemma didn't tell the entire truth.

Yes, a few friends had stood by her mother. But the rest had dropped her. The majority had dropped her. Just like most of Jemma's friends had disappeared, too. It happened to her sisters as well. She had no idea if her brother, Branson, was abandoned. He'd never talked about it, even though he, too, lived in London. But then, Branson never revealed anything personal. He'd always been private and self-contained, so self-contained, that Jemma hadn't been comfortable going to her brother this year and asking for help, or a loan, or even a friendly ear. Instead she'd struggled to handle it all—the shame from her father's duplicity, and the pain of being rejected by the man she loved more than life itself.

She felt Mikael's fingers on her cheek. She stiffened and drew back, then realized he'd touched her because he was wiping away tears. Her tears.

She hadn't even realized she was crying.

"I'm sorry," she whispered, turning away to hide her face.

He turned her face back to him and gently swept his thumb across her right cheek, and then her left. His expression was troubled. Brooding. "Do you cry for your mother?"

"Yes."

"Just your mother? Or, perhaps you are also still hurting from that spineless Englishman who calls himself a model?"

She made a soft, rough sound. "He's a great model."

"But a lousy man."

She smiled despite herself, and then her smile faded. "My sister Logan said he did me a favor. She said it was better that I find out who he is now, before we married, instead of after."

"Your sister is right." His thumb slid across her cheekbone, and then down, along her smooth jaw, his attention fixed now on her mouth. He was going to kiss her. She was sure of it, she could tell by the expression in his eyes, and the way the air sparked and crackled around them, tense, and electric.

She felt raw and emotional. Confused. Everything was changing; the energy between them was different. He'd been so harsh and cold in the beginning but he was different now. He seemed as if he might care.

His head dipped. Her tummy flipped. Her pulse raced. His mouth almost touched hers, but didn't. His breath caressed her lips. "I am sorry that spineless Englishman hurt you. I am also sorry that I add to your pain."

Her heart squeezed. She struggled to catch her breath, feeling bruised.

"But I will make you happy, *laeela.* I promise."

She stared into his eyes, lost, dazzled.

"You will enjoy being my wife." He stroked her cheek again. "You will have riches beyond compare."

Jemma exhaled hard, and sat back, the magic gone.

He didn't understand her. He didn't understand that what she wanted, *needed*, had nothing to do with wealth. "Money does not buy happiness. I've no desire for riches, or wealth. I've had both, and money can buy things, but not what my heart needs."

"What about your body?"

"My *body*?"

His dark eyes gleamed. “What about what your body needs?”

“I don’t understand.”

“Who worships your body?”

Without wanting to, she thought of Damien. They’d had a good relationship, and great sex, but she wouldn’t say Damien ever worshipped her body. She’d never had a boyfriend who’d worshipped her body, and had begun to think after conversations with her girlfriends, that few men did. “No man worships a woman’s body.”

“I fully intend to worship your body.”

“This is incredibly uncomfortable. Perhaps it’s time we discussed your body.”

Mikael grinned. Like his laugh earlier, it was the first time she’d really seen him smile, a real smile and his teeth flashed again, and a tiny dimple appeared on the right side of his mouth. It was astonishing. Not just because he’d smiled, but because of what it did to his face. The smile transformed his hard, fierce features. He looked so approachable, so appealing.

She sucked in a breath, dazzled. “You shouldn’t do that, you know.”

A hint of a smile lingered at the corners of his mouth. “Do what?”

“Smile.”

“Why not?”

“It makes you seem almost human.”

“I *am* almost human.”

“I had no idea,” she retorted, trying to ignore the thumping of her heart and the way he made desire coil inside her.

He smiled again, and his expression was so warm and playful that she suddenly wanted more of him.

Wanted him closer. Wanted him kinder. Wanted him to be good to her.

“I like how fierce you get,” he said.

“You deliberately provoke me.”

The dimple deepened at the corner of his mouth. “Maybe.”

In that moment she saw who he might have been had his life turned out differently. Or perhaps, this is how he might have been with her from the start, had she not been Jemma Copeland.

Maybe he really was warm and sexy, charming and engaging. Maybe.

"And my body is very fine," he said, the smile still lingering in his eyes. "I appreciate your concern."

Suddenly, she very much wanted to know more about him, who he was, and how he lived. Did he have lots of women in his life? Was he the kind of man who serial dated or did he prefer having a long-term relationship?

"Tell me about your body," she said, trying to sound offhand. "Does it see a lot of action?"

"I don't think that's appropriate."

"I'm not asking you to divulge names or numbers. I just want to know you. I'm curious about you. It's the sort of thing a woman wants to know about her man." She held his gaze. "So, are you a player?"

"I used to be a player. I'm not anymore. I haven't been for a couple years."

"Why?"

"Age? Maturity? I just know that around thirty I started to get tired of the chase, and would have just one relationship at a time. How about you?"

"I like having a boyfriend, but don't need to be in a relationship. I'm picky. I would rather be with no one than just anyone."

"A woman with high standards."

"A woman that prefers books to casual sex."

"You might just be the perfect kidnapped bride."

There was silence for a minute and Jemma felt a thousand different things.

But then from the first time she'd met Mikael, he'd made her feel a lot. And here, in this…pleasure palace…she'd begun to feel the whisper of a craving for something. She wasn't sure what it was she wanted, but her dreams last night had stirred something within her and all day she'd felt a restlessness and an ache.

Like a craving for sensation.

Staring into his eyes, she was teased by the possibility. Teased by the suggestion of pleasure. It would feel so good to feel good again. To feel like a woman again. To feel close to someone again.

"If you've finished your dinner," Mikael said rising. "It's time to come with me."

They climbed the stairs from the grotto's secret room to the courtyard of fragrant white lilies and vines clinging to rock. White candles still glimmered against the walls and outlined the walkway. But now in the middle of the courtyard, between the waterfall and door to the Chamber of Innocence stood a narrow table covered in crisp white sheets.

Jemma looked at Mikael, uncertain. "What is that?"

"A massage table. I'm going to give you a massage," he said. "You'll lie there, face down—"

"Why?"

"Most massages start with the back."

"Yes, but why are you giving me the massage?"

"I think you'd enjoy it. And it would help you relax. I want you to relax. I want you to realize that everything that will happen here in the Bridal Palace will feel good. I will never do anything you don't want. And if I do something that does make you uncomfortable, all you have to do is speak up." He drew the top sheet back on the table. "Any questions?"

Jemma tugged on her dress. "Do I wear this?"

"No. You'll take that off—everything off—and then lie down between the sheets, naked."

He'd turned around to give her privacy while she disrobed, but she was on the massage table now, tucked between the sheets.

He looked down at her on the table, her dark glossy hair tumbling over one shoulder.

The massage was for her, not him. He wanted her now. He wanted her naked in his bed now. But she wasn't ready, and he'd meant it when he told her that she had to be comfortable. She had to want him before anything would happen between them.

He placed his hands over the sheet covering her back, letting her feel the pressure of his hands, letting his hands warm her.

After a moment he smoothed his hands over the sheet covering her back.

She felt good. Warm, solid but smooth.

This wasn't going to be a sexual massage. He'd told her that before they started. It was to show her he could be trusted. He wouldn't hurt her, or force her to do anything she didn't want to do.

This massage was simply to help break the ice.

Develop awareness. Create ease between them. Stir the senses, too, so that she'd be comfortable with him physically. You couldn't impose desire. It must come from within.

He concentrated on learning the shape of her back through the sheet, the sheet protecting her, giving her a sense of safety. He had told her that at any point she could stop the massage. If at any point she felt uncomfortable or threatened, she just needed to speak up and the massage would end. But he didn't expect her to stop it.

Moving from her shoulders down, he ran his palms from her spine out, smoothing tension away, relaxing the muscles, letting her continue to warm, encouraging her to breathe more deeply.

After several minutes he drew the sheet down, folded it low on her hips, leaving her lovely back exposed. His eyes followed the line of her body, the narrowing of her waist to the soft swell of her hips. The sheet rested on her bottom, hiding the cleft of her cheeks, but again, he knew it was there. He wanted to see it. Touch it. Touch her.

And he would touch her, but not there, not today.

He drew her long hair into his fist, and quickly braided it, before draping the braid over her shoulder, leaving her back bare.

As he stepped away to reach for the oil he could see her profile. Her eyes were closed, her full lips softly parted. Her pale skin gleamed, and his gaze dropped to the side of her soft breast, and then lower to the gentle curve of hip.

He hardened. He'd wanted her for hours. He felt as if he lived in a constant state of arousal around her.

He'd desired many women, and knew how to pleasure his women, but this one made him ache.

Or maybe it was the fact that he couldn't have her, not today, or tomorrow, or even the day after that made him hurt.

Pouring warm oil into his hands, Mikael rubbed his palms together, spreading the oil, thinning it, and yet the slippery texture was so sensual that he wasn't sure he could do this. It was to tease her, but he was teasing himself and he hated it.

He placed his hands in the middle of her back, where he'd rested them a few moments ago when the sheet still covered her, and then he began to stroke her back, with smooth, firm deliberate strokes to relax her.

She was tense but he was patient, and as he worked on her back, he focused on the satin texture of her skin, the supple muscle beneath the skin, and the long elegant lines of her—shoulder, upper arm, spine, hip, thigh to calf.

For the next two hours he rubbed and kneaded, massaging every muscle group, working on her back, and then massaging her front, her arms, shoulders and the upper planes of her chest. Aware of the stiff peaks of her nipples beneath the loosely draped sheet his own body tightened in response. He wanted her.

He would wait until she gave herself to him. Would wait until she asked—no, begged—for release.

His hands stopped moving. He leaned over her, whispered that he was done, and told her to hold the sheet.

She did, and he scooped her up, carrying her into the Chamber of Innocence where he laid her in the big bed.

"Good night," he said, smoothing the hair back from her forehead. "Sleep well. I will see you in the morning."

He'd carried her into the bedroom and then left her.

Jemma rolled over onto her tummy, and pressed her face into the pillow, her body aching.

She ached for more. Ached to be filled, satisfied.

Hopefully she wouldn't have to lie here like this tomorrow night feeling so…tense. Frustrated. It wasn't a good feeling. Hopefully tomorrow it would be different. Hopefully tomorrow she'd sleep contented. Because wasn't that the sheikh's promise? He was to fulfill her needs, give her pleasure?

Yes, the massage had been nice.

She'd very much enjoyed being rubbed and stroked with warm fragrant oils.

And he'd been a great masseuse, the best she'd ever had. He'd been extremely thorough, taking his time, making the massage last for hours. But that was the trouble.

The massage was supposed to be the start of something. A preliminary to foreplay. She'd expected more. The feel of his fingers working knotted muscles, made her imagine his fingers doing other things…

She'd lay on the massage table knowing that soon he'd touch her, and it wouldn't be just relaxing, but exciting. Stimulating.

She couldn't help daydreaming during the massage, couldn't help fantasizing.

She'd entertained the fantasies, too, because surely she'd need them for the next thing. Sex.

But there had been no next thing.

Just the deliciously long massage by a man who obviously had quite a bit of expertise, and then a good-night.

Most cordial of him. If she'd gone to a spa she'd expect him to be waiting on the other side of the door with a lovely chilled glass of lemon water for hydration purposes. But she wasn't at a spa. She'd expected the massage to…deliver…

It hadn't.

The sheikh knew exactly what he was doing.

Turning her on, leaving her high and dry, leaving her wanting more.

Jemma would have something to say to Mikael Karim in the morning.

# CHAPTER NINE

IT TOOK HER a long time to fall asleep the night before, and when she woke in the morning, it took her a long time to want to leave her bed.

The massage hadn't just stirred her body, it'd somehow stirred her emotions. She woke up feeling unsettled. Undone.

Mikael had promised her that he'd make her happy in their eight days together, but she felt far less comfortable and optimistic now than she had yesterday before he'd carried her across the threshold of the Chamber of Innocence.

But maybe it was this room, she thought, her gaze sweeping the white marble chamber. It was too formal and too cold.

Too lonely, too.

She hadn't imagined that the eight nights of pleasure would start with her sleeping alone. She understood why he'd done it—he was trying to put her at ease—but it was isolating here in this room. The cold marble and silk panels might appeal to someone else, but not to her.

She grabbed her pillow and hugged it. She suddenly missed her family very much and that was saying something because Jemma had been independent for years.

When she'd moved to London at eighteen, her sister Victoria had teased her, saying Jemma would never last in London, and predicted that she would be back within a matter of weeks.

Victoria was wrong. Jemma had never returned, and it had actually been surprisingly easy to leave her family. Maybe it was because as the youngest, she'd grown up watching the others move on and move out. By the time she'd reached her teens, it was just her, and her mom, and her mom was ready for freedom, too.

And London had been a good fit. Once Jemma had moved there, she'd found it easy to embrace her new life, seizing every opportunity, taking every decent job, whether home or abroad. She liked to travel, was comfortable in hotel rooms, didn't mind the long hours, either. Being the youngest, and having to learn to entertain herself, proved beneficial. Jemma was self-reliant. She told herself she needed nothing, and no one.

But that wasn't true, either.

Of course she needed people. She needed good people, loving people, people who wouldn't abandon her the moment things got difficult.

A knock sounded on her door and it opened to reveal Mikael, dressed in casual khaki trousers and a white linen shirt, with a scrap of hot orange fabric in his hands.

"For you," he said, carrying the sheer tunic to her where she lay in bed.

She blinked at him, this new him, still finding it difficult to reconcile the intimidating sheikh with this very sexy man who looked as if he'd be incredibly comfortable without anything on.

Her hands shook as she unfolded the tunic. The neckline was again jeweled and bundled in the center was a tiny blood-orange bikini.

"We're swimming?" she asked, lifting the bikini top, and noting that the silky cups looked very small.

"Only if you feel like it. We're having breakfast outside in the center courtyard, next to the pool. It's already hot today. You might want to swim." He gazed down at her. "You don't have to wear the suit, either. I wasn't sure how comfortable you'd feel swimming naked."

Heat rushed to her face. She grabbed the tiny bikini. "I'll wear the suit, thank you."

* * *

It was a very lazy, self-indulgent day. Jemma felt as if she were on holiday at a luxurious resort. She'd been in and out of the pool a couple times to cool off, but now she stretched out on a plush lounge chair, sunbathing, while Mikael lay on a lounge chair next to her, reading.

She couldn't help sneaking glances at him every now and then, astonished to see him in swim trunks. Astonished by his abs, and his long muscular legs, and the thick biceps. He was nothing like the sheikh she'd met three days ago. He seemed nothing like a sheikh at all.

She looked past him to the pool that sparkled in the sun. She could see one of the staff walking toward them with a tray of fresh chilled towels and more lemon flavored ice water, along with little cups of something.

The little cups contained sorbet, a delicious pineapple sorbet that Jemma ate with a tiny spoon. Mikael didn't eat his. But he sat up to watch her lick the melting sorbet from her spoon.

"You make me hungry," he said, his dark gaze hooded, his deep voice husky.

She blushed and pretended she didn't understand, but it was impossible not to understand what he meant when he stared at her mouth as if it were edible.

"You have a sorbet here," she said. "It's melting quickly, though."

"Perhaps I'll just pour it on you and lick it off."

A wave of heat hit her. She suddenly felt scorching hot. "You wouldn't."

"Don't tempt me."

She sucked the tiny bit of fresh pineapple from the tip of the spoon, assessing. "Where would you pour it?"

"You play with fire, *laeela*."

She squinted up at the sun. "It is hot out."

"Very hot," he agreed, his deep voice now a rumble.

Her tongue flicked at her upper lip, sweeping the sticky juice off. "Maybe you should get into the pool and cool off."

"Maybe you should stop eating your ice as if you were desperate to have sex." He saw her expression and shrugged. "Just a bit of friendly advice."

"You're trying to help me, are you?"

"Protect you."

She sucked hard on the little spoon before looking at him, winged eyebrow arching. "From whom?"

"Maybe from what," he replied, his dark gaze now sweeping her as if he could eat all of her from head to toe.

It was thrilling. Her pulse quickened and Jemma felt a little frisson of excitement race through her. "Which is…?"

"Ravishment."

"Ah." She swallowed hard, and pressed her thighs and knees together, suddenly finding it very hard to breathe normally.

She couldn't remember the last time being ravished sounded appealing. In fact, being ravished had never sounded appealing until now.

It was time something exciting happened. She'd sat here all morning in her tiny blood-orange bikini and wanted his attention. Now that she had it, she wasn't ready to lose it.

"Would it hurt?" she asked. "Being ravished?"

He considered her, his dark gaze raking her. "No," he said at length. "It'd feel very, very good."

Jemma squeezed her knees tighter. "How do I know? You've never even kissed me."

His eyes lit. His hard features shifted, his jaw growing harder even as his mouth curved. He looked dangerous and gorgeous.

She wanted him to pounce on her, devour her.

"Do you want me to kiss you?" he asked, his eyes so dark and hot and intense that she felt like the sorbet, melting into a puddle of sweet sticky juice.

She was almost twitching in her lounge chair. She felt so turned on and strung out at the same time. "Yes. But only if you kiss really, really well."

* * *

Mikeal hadn't planned on liking his new bride. He hadn't even wanted to like her. But she was growing on him. She was by turns smart, funny and fierce, and stunning whether in a formal gown, or a swimsuit by the pool.

She looked incredible right now, as a matter of fact, with her hair still damp from her last swim, her skin flushed and golden from the sun, her amazing body barely covered in that swimsuit which was the color of his desert at sunset.

He'd wanted her all morning but her provocative words threatened to push him over the edge.

She was such a tease. He liked it, though. He liked her fire, wanted to taste her fire. Flame it. Make her burn.

"If you're such a great kisser, why haven't you kissed me?" she asked, tossing her head, sending damp strands of hair over her shoulder to cling to the swell of her breast.

Desire and hunger shot through him. He ached. He hurt. But he would take this so slow that she would be the one begging for him.

His gaze swept over her, admiring the fullness of her breasts, her flat belly, and the bright silky fabric just barely covering her there, between her thighs.

His body tightened with arousal.

"If I start kissing you," he answered, his voice so deep it was almost a growl, "you wouldn't want me to stop."

"You're so conceited," she said, nose in the air, but squirming at the same time.

"I'm honest."

Her cheeks darkened to a dusty pink. "To me, it sounds like a boast. You talk a lot but do very little."

He loved that he could arouse her so easily. He could feel her humming now, wanting, needing. "You love to challenge me," he drawled.

"I was just saying—"

He snapped his fingers, interrupting her, and then pointed to his chair. "Come here."

Her green eyes darkened, widened. She swallowed hard.

"Come, big talker," he said. "Let's see how brave you really are."

And just like that, her courage failed. She ducked her head, bit her lip, uncertain and shy.

He hid his smile. He'd expected as much.

She was a tease. One of those good girls who wanted to be bad.

He stood up, crossed to her chair, and tugged her to her feet. Her green eyes flashed again, worry, excitement, uncertainty.

He held her by the wrist, led her into the red and ivory pavilion behind them, and drew the silk curtains closed, hiding them.

"Sit," he ordered.

She sat down on one of the low couches that wrapped the wall.

He sat down next to her.

"What are we doing?" she whispered.

"Whatever we feel like doing," he answered, his head dipping, dropping low, his mouth so close she could feel the warmth of his breath against her skin.

Jemma held her breath, waiting for the kiss. She felt as if she'd been waiting forever for this moment. But he was taking his time, his lips lightly brushing across her cheek toward her ear.

She turned her head toward him, wanting his mouth on her mouth but his lips were exploring the high curve of her cheekbone, his lips a caress across her sensitive skin. Hot darts of pleasure shot through her. His mouth felt good on her. He smelled good, too. She wanted more of him, not less.

Jemma turned her mouth to his again, inhaling his scent, relishing the rich spicy fragrance of his skin. He'd shaved earlier, this morning, and his jaw was smooth and firm, his mouth full and so very sensual.

Promising pleasure.

Unable to resist, Jemma put her lips to his, and waited. Waited to see what he would do. Waited to see what would happen next.

If he intended to seduce her, she would let him do the work. She was in the mood to be seduced, too. Ready for pleasure, sensation, satisfaction. Exquisite satisfaction.

His hand moved to her chin, fingers trailing across her jaw in a leisurely exploration, and yet every little brush of his fingers made her insides tighten and squirm and her breasts, already aching, feel excruciatingly sensitive.

She wanted him to touch her there, on her nipples, and touch lower, between her thighs. She sighed, growing impatient.

"You're not happy?" he asked, against her mouth.

She squirmed as his fingers played with her earlobe, lightly circling the soft tender skin again and again, making her senses swim and her head spin. "This is a bit frustrating," she answered. "I think it's time you just kissed me."

His lips brushed hers again. "But I am kissing you."

"No," she said, arching as he found the hollow beneath her ear and did something delicious to it, so delicious that she clenched inwardly, craving his hard body filling her, warming her, satisfying her. "A proper kiss," she insisted, no longer caring that she was supposed to resist him. Somehow reality no longer mattered, not when need licked at her veins and Jemma felt starved for sensation.

She reached up to clasp his face, her hands learning the shape of his jaw, the hard angles and planes as she pressed her lips to his, deepening the kiss, focused only on the heat between them.

He drew back after a moment, his eyes almost black in the dark pavilion interior. "Maybe we should stop. I don't want to force you."

"I don't think you're forcing me," she said, giving her head a slight shake, as if to clear her head of the heat and need and intense physical craving to be touched. *Taken.*

She throbbed and pulsed in places that shouldn't throb and pulse. "If anything, I feel as if I'm forcing you."

The corner of his mouth lifted. "I'm not being forced. Trust me."

She stroked her hand over the warm hard plane of his face.

Such a beautiful face. He was using his good looks against her. His charm, too. "You're too good at this."

His laughter was a deep rumble in his chest. "That's better than being bad at this."

"You're making it impossible for me to resist you."

"But you can. All you have to do is say stop, and we are done. I will never force you to do anything."

Then his mouth traveled down her neck, over her collarbone, down her chest, to the swell of her breasts. He lips teased the underside of the breast through the fabric of her bikini, finding nerves in every place he touched. She shivered, gasping as his mouth settled over her taut nibble, sucking the tip through the fabric.

She arched as he sucked harder, the pressure of his mouth making her inner thighs clench together with need.

She was the one to tug the fabric away from her breasts, exposing her nipple, and she was the one to draw his head back down, so his lips covered her bare breast.

She sighed at the feel of his mouth on her hot skin. His lips were warm, the tip of his tongue cool, but once he took the tight bud of her nipple in his mouth, it was his mouth that felt hot, wet, and she gasped, arching into him, her hips lifting, grinding, her body on fire.

She wanted him to take her now. She wanted his hands between her thighs, peeling her bikini bottoms off, wanted him to part her knees and thrust deep into her body, filling her, making the maddening ache inside of her go away.

But he didn't go lower, his hands stayed at her breasts, his mouth fastened to her nipple, sucking and licking, drawing hard on her, whipping her to a frenzy. Throbbing, she rolled away from him, and sat up, stunned that he'd brought her to the verge of an orgasm. She would have climaxed, too, if she hadn't stopped him.

She could barely look at him, excruciatingly shy. The sensations inside her were still so intense. How could she climax without him even touching her between her legs?

Mikael turned her face to him. "Did I scare you?" he asked quietly, his dark eyes searching hers.

She shook her head, but there were tears in her eyes. Her emotions felt wild.

"What then?"

"You're just very good at all…that."

He stroked her cheek with his thumb. "It was too much."

Her eyes burned. Her throat squeezed. "I don't know you." His touch was soothing. It eased some of the tension within her, but not enough. "I don't know you," she repeated. "And for me to feel this way, physically, I think I should."

Jemma always found a way to surprise him.

But it wasn't her words that surprised him now, as much as her emotion. He felt her confusion. She didn't understand what she was feeling.

She wasn't who he thought she was. She was nothing like her father. And her softness and sweetness reminded him of his mother.

Suddenly, he wondered what his mother had been like, as a girl, before she'd married his father. She must have been daring and adventuresome. She was American, after all, and she'd married his father, a sheikh, and although she'd loved the exoticism of her husband's culture, she'd apparently never assimilated into the culture, and Mikael's father hadn't helped her adapt, either. He'd left her to fit in. Left her to sort it out for herself.

A mistake.

But then, their entire marriage had been a mistake. Even he had been a mistake.

His mother had said as much, too.

His chest grew tight, the air bottled inside his lungs.

He did not want his future to be like his past. He did not want his children to grow up with such terrible unhappiness.

He lifted Jemma's hand, kissed her palm, her wrist, feeling the flutter of her pulse against his lips. Her skin felt soft and warm. She was soft and warm and he felt the strongest urge to protect her.

"I have a gift for you," he said, leaning back on the cushions.

"I don't need gifts," she answered, still unsettled, still reserved. "In fact, material things just leave me cold."

"So how can I spoil you?"

"I don't want to be spoiled."

"What can I give you then?"

She studied him for a long moment. "I want to know about you. Tell me something about you."

"Me?"

"Rather than presents, every day tell me something new about *you*."

"Showering you in jewels would be easier."

*"Exactly."* She looked at him, her expression almost fierce. "So if you want to give me something meaningful, give me part of you. Let me know you. That would be a true gift…one *this* bride would treasure."

He smiled faintly. "What shall I tell you? What would you like to know?"

"Tell me more about your mom," she said promptly. "And your dad."

"That's not a very pleasant subject."

"Parents and divorces never are."

"So why would you want to know about them?"

"Because they're important people in our lives. Our parents shape us. For good, and for bad." Her gaze met his. "Were you closer to one than the other?"

He sighed. He didn't want to talk about this, he didn't, but he liked her lying here next to him. She felt good here, and he wanted her to stay. "I don't remember being close to my father," he said after a moment. "But I'm sure he doted on me. Saidia parents tend to spoil their children, especially their sons."

"And your mother?"

"Adored me." It was uncomfortable talking about his mother. "She was a good mother. But then they divorced."

"Do you know why they divorced?"

He looked at her. "Do you know why your parents divorced?"

"My dad was having an affair."

Mikael hated the heaviness in his chest. He reached out and touched a strand of her hair, tugging on it lightly. "My father wanted to take a second wife," he confessed.

"So they divorced?"

"Eventually."

"What does that mean?" Jemma asked, turning onto her side.

"It means it took her nearly five years to successfully divorce him. My father didn't want the divorce, so he contested it."

"He loved her," Jemma said.

"I don't think he loved her. But he didn't want her to shame him. He was the king. How could his wife leave him?"

Jemma was silent a long moment. "Your mother loved him. She didn't want to share him?"

"I don't remember love. I remember fighting. Years of fighting." And crying. Years of crying. But not the tears of Saidia women. His mother only cried quietly, late at night, when she thought no one was listening.

But he had listened. He had heard her weeping. And he had never done anything about it.

Jemma put her hand on his chest, her palm warm against his skin. "She had to know when she married your father that he might take another wife."

"She said he promised her that he would never take another wife. She said he had it added to their wedding contract. But it wasn't there. My father said my mother never added a clause, and that she knew all along there would be other wives. That she was only the first." He hesitated, trying not to remember too much of those years, and how awful it'd been with the endless fighting, and then his mother crying late at night when the servants were asleep. "By the time the divorce was final, he'd taken three more wives."

Mikael looked away from the sympathy in Jemma's eyes,

uncomfortable with it. He focused on the ceiling of the pavilion, and the whirring of the fan blades. "I was eleven when the divorce was finalized."

Her fingers curled against his chest. "Did you go live with her?"

"No. I stayed with my father."

"You wanted to?"

"I didn't have a choice. I had to stay with my father." He glanced at her. "In Saidia, like many Arab countries, mothers do not retain custody of the children in a divorce. The children usually go to the father, or the closest male relative, and the sons always remain with the father."

She rolled closer to him, both hands against his chest now. "But you saw your mom sometimes?"

"No."

"Never?"

"She was expelled from Saidia." He reached out and caught her hair again, playing with the strand. "I wouldn't see her again for almost twenty years. In fact not until just a few months before your sister Morgan's wedding."

*"What?"*

He let go of the strand. "I couldn't see her after she left, and then, I wouldn't see her."

Jemma just stared at him, eyes wide, her expression shocked. "You punished her for the divorce."

He shrugged. "I had a hard time forgiving her for divorcing my father. Because yes, she knew that by divorcing my father, she'd lose me. He made it clear he wouldn't let me leave with her. But she divorced him anyway. She chose to leave Saidia and leave me behind." Mikael abruptly pulled away, rolling from the low cushions to stand up, and offered her his hand. "It's hot. We talked. I think it's time to cool off with a swim."

They swam and splashed for a half hour until their lunch was brought to them. They sat in their wet swimsuits beneath the shade of a palm tree eating lunch.

As Jemma nibbled on her salad she watched Mikael from beneath her lashes.

She was still processing everything he'd told her in the pavilion about his parents' marriage and divorce. Knowing that his mother was an American made it worse as Jemma found it so easy to identify with the woman, and how she must have felt in this Arab country with her powerful royal husband. And yet, even though his mother was an American and unhappy here, how could she leave her child behind?

How could she adore her son but then walk away from him?

"Do you look like your father?" she asked Mikael as they finished their meal.

Mikael ran his hand through his short black hair. "I wish I hadn't told you about the divorce."

"Why?"

"I'm not comfortable with it. Or proud of my father. Or myself. Or of any of the decisions made."

Jemma understood, more than he knew. She'd wanted to go live with her mother when her parents divorced, but she hadn't wanted to lose her father. And for years after the divorce, she'd still looked forward to seeing him, and she'd cherished the gifts he'd sent in the early years after the divorce—the dolls, the pretty clothes, the hot pink bike for her twelfth birthday—but then her parents quarreled again when she was thirteen, and all contact stopped. Her father disappeared from her life completely.

She hated him, and yet she loved him. She missed him and needed him. She went to London to start over, to get away from her past and herself, and she thought she had. Until the news broke that he'd stolen hundreds of millions of dollars of his clients' money.

Jemma looked at Mikael. "I sometimes think that if my parents hadn't divorced, and my father had been more involved in our lives, he would have made different choices. I think that if maybe we'd stayed close, he would have realized how much we loved him and needed him."

Mikael's expression was incredulous. "You blame yourself?"

"I try to understand what happened."

"He was selfish."

She flinched. "You're right."

"He was the worst sort of man because he pretended to care, pretended to understand what vulnerable people needed, and then he destroyed them."

Jemma closed her eyes.

"Who befriends older women and then robs them?" he demanded.

Eyes closed, she shook her head.

"Your father told my mother to refinance her house and give him the money to invest, promising her amazing returns, but didn't invest any of it. He just put it into his own account. He drained her account for himself." Mikael's voice vibrated with contempt and fury. "It disgusts me." He drew a rough breath. "We should not talk about this."

She nodded, sick, flattened.

Silence stretched, heavy and suffocating.

Mikael left his chair and paced the length of the pool. Jemma's eyes burned and she had to work very hard not to cry.

She was so ashamed. She felt raw and exposed. In the Arab world, she represented her family. She was an extension of her family, an extension of her father. Here in Saidia his shame attached to her. His shame would always taint her.

Silently Jemma left the pool, returning to the Chamber of Innocence to shower in the white marble bath, and shampoo her hair to wash the chlorine out. As she worked the suds in, she gritted her teeth, holding all the emotion in.

She wasn't sad. She wasn't scared. She wasn't lonely. She wasn't miserable in any way.

No, miserable would be living in Connecticut, trying to find a place to stay, wondering who might take her in, if maybe one of her mother's few remaining friends might allow her to crash on a couch or in a guest bedroom.

Rinsing her hair, she lifted her face to the spray. It was so hard to believe that her family had once had everything. Hard to believe they'd been placed on a pedestal. Their beautiful, lavish lifestyle had been envied and much discussed. Magazines featured their Caribbean home, their sprawling shingle house in Connecticut, the log cabin in Sun Valley. They had money for trips, money for clothes, money for dinners out.

Jemma turned the shower off, wrung the excess water from her hair wondering if any of it had been real.

Had any of it been their money to spend?

How long had her father taken advantage of his clients?

Bundled in a towel, she left the bathroom, crawled into the white and silver bed and pulled the soft Egyptian sheet all the way over her, to the top of her head.

It was hard being a Copeland. Hard living with so much shame. Work had been the only thing that kept her going, especially after Damien walked away from her. Work gave her something to do, something to think about. Working allowed her—even if briefly—to be someone else.

Now she just needed to get home and back to work. Work was still the answer. She simply had to get through these next seven days. And seven nights.

Jemma drew a big breath for courage, aware that the night would soon be here.

## CHAPTER TEN

SHE WAS TO dress for dinner.

That's what the card attached to the garment bag instructed: *Dress for dinner. I will collect you at nine.*

Jemma unzipped the bag, and pushed away tissue to discover a sumptuous silk gown the color of ripe peaches. Ornate gold beading wrapped the hem and the long sleeve of the asymmetrical gown. The gown gathered over one shoulder creating a full flowing sleeve, while leaving the other shoulder and arm bare.

It was beautiful. Exotic. A dress for a desert princess.

There was a jewelry box in the bottom of the garment bag containing gold chandelier earrings studded with diamonds and pearls. They looked old, and very valuable.

She lifted an earring, holding it to her ear and looked in the mirror. The delicate gold and diamond earring was stunning against her dark loose hair. She'd wear her hair down tonight, dress like a desert princess. She hoped Mikael would not be angry this evening. The morning had been fun. He'd been a great companion. For a couple hours she'd forgotten why she was here.

He arrived at her door promptly at nine. Jemma had been ready for almost an hour. Opening the door she discovered he was dressed in his traditional robe again and she felt a stab of disappointment, preferring him in Western clothes. She felt more comfortable when he looked familiar, and not like the foreign sheikh he was.

"You look stunning," he said.

She smiled, hiding her nervousness. "Thank you."

"Do you know what we are doing for dinner?" he asked, leading her from the room, and down the outer corridor.

"No."

He smiled down at her. "Good."

He escorted her all the way to the front of the Kasbah, and out through the grand wooden doors. A car and driver waited for them.

The driver opened the back door of the black sedan. Jemma glanced at Mikael before climbing in. But he said nothing and his expression gave nothing away.

With Mikael seated next to her, the driver left the walled Kasbah. Soon they were driving through the desert, the car flying down the ribbon of asphalt. Moonlight bathed the miles of undulating sand.

Mikael pointed to the landscape beyond the tinted window. "This, my queen, is all yours."

She looked out the window, at the vast desert, and then back at Mikael, struggling to keep a straight face. "It is truly lovely sand."

"Are you making fun of my desert?"

"Absolutely not."

"Good." His eyes gleamed. "Because I value every single grain in this desert."

She smiled, and he smiled back and then his smile faded. He reached out and lightly touched the ornate gold chandelier dangling from her lobe. "These look beautiful on you."

"They are exquisite," she agreed.

"But you said you do not value jewels."

She looked at him warily. "Not as much as some women, no."

"But you value…*talking*."

He sounded so pained that her lips curved and her heart turned over. "Sharing," she explained.

"How do you feel about apologies?"

She lifted her brows. "In my experience, women love them. Men tend to hate them."

He smiled faintly. "That seems true in my experience as well." He hesitated. "And as difficult as it is for me to say I'm sorry, I owe you an apology. I was curt with you earlier, at the pool, and I focused my anger on you, when it's your father I am angry with."

She shifted uncomfortably. "You don't have to apologize. Every word you said was true. Your mother was treated terribly—"

"Yes," he interrupted quietly. "But that doesn't excuse how I spoke to you. And it doesn't make my behavior acceptable. You were reaching out to me, and sharing your experiences, and your feelings, and I lashed out, hurtfully. I am sorry for that. I take no pride in my faults, and as you have seen, I've many."

For a long moment Jemma could think of nothing to say. It was hard to speak when her eyes burned and her throat ached. She was surprised, and touched, by his honesty, never mind the humility. "Of course I forgive you. We all have things that hurt us."

His dark head inclined. "I am sensitive with regards to my mother, because my father mistreated her, and then I mistreated her, too."

"You were just a boy at the time of their divorce."

His features tightened. "I hated her for getting the divorce." The words were said bluntly, sharply. "Was her pride so important? Was her pride more important than me? She knew when the divorce was finalized, she'd leave the country, without me." He extended his legs as much as he could. "I'd be lying if I said that I understand now. Because I don't. Maybe I won't ever. But it was terrible then, being eleven, and knowing my mother chose to leave me."

Jemma reached to him, put her hand on his arm. "Perhaps she didn't think she'd really lose you. Maybe she thought things would turn out differently."

"How?"

"Maybe she thought your father would back down, change his mind, not move forward and marry a second wife. Or maybe she had worked out some sort of alternative custody arrangement. Maybe your father had agreed to share you…or even grant her custody while you were a child." Jemma leaned toward him, the delicate gold and diamond earring tinkling. "If your father had deceived her about the marriage contract, who knows what he might have said to her? Or promised her?"

He glanced at her. "But I didn't know that as a boy. I didn't know he was to blame. That he was the one who'd lied. So I blamed her."

"You were angry with her."

"I hated her."

"And then as an adult you learned the truth."

"Yes." His lips curved but the smile didn't reach his eyes. "And I hated him."

"You told him that?"

"No, not then."

"But you did go to your mother? You tried to make amends?"

He sat still, expression blank. "I waited a long time. I waited too long. If I'd gone to her earlier, and tried to help her earlier, she might not have relied so much on others. On outsiders."

"Like my father."

He nodded. "I should have been there for her sooner." His expression turned mocking. "You can see why I don't like talking about the past. I was not a good person. I was a very destructive person, and that is why I'm so driven to redeem the Karims and restore honor to our family and Saidia. I cannot let my mother's death be in vain."

"I think you judge yourself too harshly," she said gently.

"Power is never to be abused."

"I have yet to see you abuse your power. If anything, you appear determined to be fair, even if your idea of justice is very different from how we, in the West, would view it."

"Then perhaps I have begun to make amends." He smiled at

her, but his smile failed to light his dark eyes, then he glanced out the window, and nodded. "See those lights in the distance? That's where we are having dinner tonight, my queen."

Jemma gazed out at the swathe of darkness with the pinpricks of light. "Is that a restaurant?"

"No." Amusement warmed his voice. "Not a restaurant. At least not the way you'd think of it. But it is where we're eating."

## CHAPTER ELEVEN

JEMMA WAS SPEECHLESS as Mikael escorted her into the tent. Plush crimson carpets covered the sand. Rustic copper lanterns hung from the tent's wooden poles. More lanterns and candles glowed on low tables. From the fire pit outside the tent she caught a whiff of roasted lamb. As if on cue, her stomach growled.

Mikael looked at her. "Ready to eat?"

"Starving," she admitted.

"You're in luck. Our first course is ready."

The grilled vegetables and meat were served with a couscous flavored with slivered almonds and currants. They scooped up the couscous and meat with chunks of warm sesame bread and Mikael was fascinating company, as always.

Jemma welcomed his stories about Saidia's history and tribal lore, understanding now why he'd worn his robes tonight. This was his desert. His world.

Just then the evening breeze played with the sheer silk panels lining the tent, parting the material, giving her a glimpse of the white moon and the deep purple black sky.

The night sky was so bright and the stars dazzled. The sky never looked like this in London or New York. But in the vastness of the desert, with darkness stretching in every direction, the sky literally glowed with light.

"Beautiful night," Mikael said, following her gaze.

She nodded. "Amazing. I feel like I'm in a fairy tale."

He hesitated a moment. "I think after the honeymoon, we

should go visit your mother. I don't want her to worry about you. She has enough worries already."

"You'd let me travel with you?"

"With me, and without me. Marriage isn't a prison, and I'd never keep you from your family, or opportunities, provided you were able to fulfill your duties as my wife and queen." He paused, studying her. "I have a house in London. It's large, and comfortable. Well located. It needs you. Someone to fill it with people and parties."

Jemma looked away, emotion making her chest ache. "Now you're just teasing me. Tempting me with possibilities that are…impossible."

"How so?"

"You shouldn't dangle things before me. Or opportunities. I'm strong, but not that strong. If I stayed here, it shouldn't be for things." She turned to look at him again, her gaze locking with his. "It should be for the right reasons. It should be for you."

For a moment there was just silence. And then Mikael leaned forward, captured her face in his hands and kissed her lightly on the lips before releasing her.

Jemma's heart turned over. Her lips tingled. She nearly pressed her fingers to her mouth to stop the throbbing.

"Next time I see Sheikh Azizzi I must thank him," Mikael said, his deep voice pitched even lower. "I was angry with him in Haslam. I was angry that he'd try to saddle me with you, but obviously he knew something I didn't."

"Saddle doesn't sound very complimentary."

"You weren't happy about it, either."

No, that was true. She was shocked, angry, desperate. But happy? No.

But she almost felt happy right now. For the first time in months and months she felt calm. She felt content. She felt as if she could breathe.

Which is why she had to be careful. She needed to keep her guard up. It was vital she not let Mikael get too much closer.

While they'd talked a servant had removed the dishes, replacing the platters and bowls with trays of delicate biscuits and dried fruits.

"You really like London?" Mikael asked her, taking one of the dates stuffed with cheese and rolling it between his fingers. "It was never a culture shock?"

"I liked it from the start. No one paid me any attention. I felt free there." She selected one of the flaky almond cookies and broke it in half. "It's different now. I'm known, and more alone than ever."

"You're lonely?"

She nodded. "Yes. I miss what I had. Not the things, but the friends, the activities, the energy. I used to wake up every day, excited to see what the day would bring. Now I just get by. Push through."

"Once we return to Ketama, once everyone knows of our marriage, you will discover that doors presently closed to you, will open. As my wife, you will be welcome everywhere. As my wife, no one would dare to shame you, or exclude you."

Jemma popped half the cookie in her mouth and chewed, but her mouth had gone dry, and the cookie tasted like sawdust. "I don't want to be accepted because people are afraid of alienating you. I want to be accepted because people like me." Her eyes suddenly burned and she took a sip from her golden goblet. "It hurts to be scorned."

"Which is why you need my protection. I do not want you to suffer more than you have."

His gaze met hers and held. His dark eyes burned into her. She felt her pulse quicken, and butterflies flit wildly in her middle, her body humming with awareness.

Mikael would be a protective husband. He would probably be generous to a fault. He'd already showered her with gifts and trinkets, and was good at paying her compliments.

She wondered what marriage to him would be like. Not the honeymoon part, but the *ever after* part.

What kind of husband would he be?

Would he have expectations for his wife's behavior? Rules for the relationship? What would he not permit, or tolerate?

Mikael's eyes met hers, and held. "You have something on your mind."

"You can read me too easily. Have you always been so attentive to women?"

"No. Never." He leaned over and refilled her goblet. "I'm usually accused of being insensitive and self-absorbed."

"Are you different with me?"

"It would seem so."

"Because I am your wife?"

"Because I can't help but pay you attention. You command it."

"I *command* it. Interesting."

"You are a queen now. You are in a position of significance."

"Careful. The power might go to my head." But she was laughing as she said it, and from his lazy smile, she knew he was amused. "Do you enjoy your power?"

He thought about the question for a moment and then nodded. "Sheikhs are allowed to be as demanding as they like. It is the benefit of being royal. But power carries responsibility to provide for one's family, and people, and protect them as well. This is where my father failed. This is where I cannot fail."

"I do not think you will. You have the right mindset. You are focused on the right goals."

"I am less focused now that you are here," he admitted. "With you here I find I only want to think about you."

"It is your honeymoon."

"*Our* honeymoon," he corrected, reaching out to stroke her cheek, and then press his thumb to her lips.

Heat raced through her, followed by a frisson of sensation that made her breasts tingle and her legs quiver. She felt so aware of him and the awareness was a bittersweet tension, her body humming in response. She ached inside, at the place where her thighs joined, and she hated wanting…needing…

Jemma squeezed her thighs together, denying the need, and

struggling to ignore the way her skin tingled, sending fresh darts of sensation from her breasts to her belly.

His gaze met hers and held, and he couldn't know what she was thinking or feeling, but she blushed anyway, heat racing through her, making her hot and cold.

She was attracted to him. She was responding to him. It crossed her mind that she just might be in over her head.

"Yes, *laeela*?" he asked, reclining against the cushions. "What are you thinking?"

She shouldn't have agreed to this. She shouldn't have played this game. It was a game she could lose. "You…your government," she stuttered, thinking she could never admit that sex was on her brain. Sex, seduction, sensual lovemaking…no, better to keep the conversation away from the personal.

"Our government?" he repeated, eyes crinkling. "Politics intrigue you?"

*No, but you intrigue me. You make me wonder about everything I do not yet know.* Instead she crossed her legs and tried to calm herself. "Did you inherit your power?"

"Yes."

"Because you were first born, of the first wife?"

"Yes."

"Do you have brothers and sisters?"

"Yes. Many."

Interesting. "Are any of them in a government position?"

"There are three that have inherited significant tribal power and wealth, but so far these half brothers prefer to avoid work and responsibility."

"They are the sons of your father's second wife?"

"She had three boys in quick succession. They are handsome, popular, and quite headstrong."

"You like them?"

"I love them." He hesitated, smiling wryly. "And I imagine I will like them even better once they begin to grow up."

She grimaced. "It's easy to be self-indulgent when you're given everything. I grew up in a wealthy family, surrounded by peers from equally wealthy families. It's not the real world. As difficult as it's been this past year, I'm glad to be living in the real world. I know now who my true friends are. I know what matters."

"I hope one day my brothers discover what's true, and real."

"Perhaps they need an incentive to mature. Perhaps it's too easy for them…being young, handsome, and wealthy."

"They do have it too easy. Nothing is worse than a spoiled, billionaire prince."

"Were you ever like that? A spoiled, billionaire prince?"

"It was different for me. I've always known I would be king. And I've always been conscious that I was the son from the bad first wife, the American wife. I've tried hard to do the right thing, to avoid additional scrutiny and criticism."

She studied him, still warm, still so fascinated by this man and how he made her feel things and want things. But she had to be careful. She needed to remain in control. "We don't hear much about Saidia in the news in the US."

"That's because we try to stay out of the news, and we are a stable country. Historically, the Karims have gone to great lengths to ensure our people's happiness."

"So people are happy?"

"Yes. We have excellent schools and health care. Girls are actively encouraged to attend school, even pursue higher education. Marriage is forbidden under the age of eighteen, without parental consent." His dark eyes glowed. "Does that answer all of your questions? Or is there something else you'd like to know?"

The gleam in his eye was dangerous. It made her pulse leap, and her stomach lurch. Just like that, she felt him…near her, around her, as if they were connected. One. Which was ludicrous. She barely knew him and they weren't touching. He was reclining four or five feet away.

And yet her skin tingled and her insides felt strange, her nerve endings wound too tightly.

The desert wasn't safe. Not with Mikael in it.

"And what are you thinking of now?" he asked, his deep voice pitched low, making her think of dark sensual things that she shouldn't be thinking, not when alone with him.

"What is your seduction plan?" she asked. "What's supposed to happen tonight?"

He didn't smile, but she could have sworn he was laughing at her.

"What do you think is going to happen?"

She hated it when he answered her question with another question. "No idea. That's why I asked."

"I have an idea of how I think the evening will go," he said, watching her with that lazy interest, which she knew now wasn't lazy at all.

He was paying close attention to her, listening attentively to everything she said, observing everything she did.

He, too, was aware of the energy between them. Something was happening. She felt the heat and tension, the prickling awareness. It was sexual. And tangible. Her gown which had been so comfortable earlier now felt hot and tight, constricting.

"You are impossible," she whispered, breathless. He made her breathless.

Did he know the effect he had on her? Did he know that he made her curious? Weak?

She felt weak now, and hot, so hot, as tiny tongues of desire made her nipples tighten inside the delicate fabric of her dress.

"Yesterday was touch," he said. "I gave you a massage."

"Yes," she agreed. "It was an incredible massage, too."

"Today…what have we done so far?"

"Kissed," she whispered.

"Exactly. Today I can only kiss you."

"Oh." She tried to stifle the stab of disappointment.

"Fortunately, there are many different ways I can kiss you."

He stood up and walked around the perimeter of the tent, dropping the heavy panels, making the soft sheer silk curtains flutter in as the outside covers fell. "Different places I can kiss you."

Jemma held her breath as he continued to walk around the tent, closing them off from the night, and his staff, tying the cords on the inner panels, sealing them into a private world.

Soon the tent was a cocoon, and darker, with the loss of moonlight.

Mikael reached for a lantern and moved it, hanging it a little behind her. "Different places you might want me to kiss you." He moved another lamp, bringing it closer to the table next to her. "The lamps are so I can see you," he said. "I want to see you."

Her insides wobbled. She bit down on the inside of her lip to hide her flurry of nerves.

"I want to see you as I make you come," he added.

Her lips parted, shocked. She sat up taller, her hands going to her knees.

She shouldn't like it when he talked to her like this, but she did. He was untamed. "You think I'm joking?" he asked.

She didn't know how to answer, wasn't sure what to do or say, so she simply looked at him, chewing on the inside of her lip, nervous. Anxious. Excited.

This was his night. His game. He held the power.

"I have waited all afternoon for this," he said, prowling around her again, dark eyes burning, emphasizing the high hard lines of his cheekbones, jaw and chin. "Waited to see you naked. Waited to taste your skin."

A funny pang pinched her heart. She struggled to breathe.

He was frightening, arrogant, headstrong.

He was also overwhelmingly powerful, physical, and sexual.

She'd never met another man like him and she shouldn't be drawn to him, but she was.

For some reason she responded to him, to his edges and complexity. She was intrigued by his harsh justice, as well as his sensual nature.

She craved the sensual side of him. She wanted the sensation and pleasure of being bedded by him. She wanted to sleep with him. Wanted him naked against her, wanted his bare hands on her breasts and his mouth on her body. Wanted to be pinned beneath him and feel him thrust hard and deep, burying his body inside hers.

He moved in front of her, crouching before her, and tilted her chin up to look into her eyes. "I want you," he said, his deep voice velvety soft. "But I want your pleasure more."

And then he kissed her, deeply, the kiss so slow and so erotic that it immediately torched her senses, making her head spin.

He pressed her back against the soft carpet, and stretched out over her. She could still feel the press of his arousal through his robes. He was long and thick and hard.

His hand found her breast through her thin gown, his fingers rubbing and pinching and kneading her taut nipple. She trembled and sighed as he focused on one breast, and then the other.

She was hot and wet and aching for more.

Jemma pressed her thighs together, craving satisfaction.

"Don't come," he murmured against her mouth. "Relax. Let me enjoy your beautiful body."

"You're turning me on," she answered.

He shifted his weight, his hips grinding against hers.

The head of his arousal pressed against her pubic bone. His warmth made her want to open to him. She wanted him inside her, not on her. "This is torture," she whispered.

"Good torture," he said, drawing away, and placing a kiss on her chin, and then her neck, and he kissed his way down to her breastbone, and then lower, over the fabric of her gown covering her belly and then lower still, kissing the V of her thighs, his breath heating her skin, making the silk gown warm and damp. Making her warmer, damper.

She groaned as his teeth lightly nipped her. "Please," she whispered. "Be nice."

"I'm being very nice," he said.

And then he shifted his weight off her completely, and he reached for the hem of her gown.

Her heart slammed into her rib cage as he pushed her skirt

up, and carefully tugged her lace panties down, sliding them off her ankles, over each of her jeweled shoes. Then he parted her thighs, pushing them wide, and settled between them to kiss the inside of her knee, and then continued kissing her inner thigh, slowly working his way to her most intimate place.

Jemma gasped as his warm mouth settled on her, his tongue sliding up and down, stroking her.

She shuddered with pleasure, overwhelmed by the intense sensation. His mouth and touch made her feel so many different and disorienting emotions and sensations, filling her head with pictures and colors, all intense and vivid, electric and erotic.

The eroticism exposed her. The eroticism challenged her.

Who was she? What was she? What was true?

Jemma cried out as his tongue pushed deeper, his mouth cool where she felt so warm, his tongue circling provocatively across her taut, sensitive nub. At the sound of her cry, his hands pushed her thighs wider, his thumbs pressing against her bottom, holding her open.

It was shocking. Shocking because it was *him*, doing this to *her*.

She'd been raised to think for herself, raised to be independent, successful, and her brain told her she shouldn't enjoy this...being handled, managed, seduced. But her body liked it, and she was beginning to realize there was another side of her, a side she found rather frightening.

It was darkly sensual, and wanton. Illicit, too.

It was almost like an erotic dream...sexy, and sensual, and intense...

So intense, especially when he sucked and there was no holding back. The tension and pressure grew, electric sensation shooting through her. She couldn't resist it, couldn't resist him. With a cry she climaxed, shattering from his expert tongue and the intimate kiss.

For a moment after, Jemma didn't know who she was, or where she was. For a moment, she was just part of the night and the diamond studded sky. She felt endless, and open and free.

And then little by little she returned to herself, and him.

Opening her eyes, she looked at him, unsure as to what his reaction would be.

His dark eyes were hooded, his expression watchful. But protective. Maybe even a little possessive.

"Say something," she whispered.

"You're beautiful."

Her cheeks burned. "I don't even know how…or why…." She licked her upper lip, her mouth dry, her heart hammering. "Or what happened."

"I do." He crouched next to her, lifting a strand of hair from her warm, flushed face. "I wanted you to feel good. Did I make you feel good?"

"Yes."

"Then I feel good."

# CHAPTER TWELVE

AN HOUR AND a half later, back at the Kasbah, Jemma lay in the center of the enormous bronze jeweled bed in the Topaz Chamber, and watched the blades of the fan turn overhead, hearing but not listening to the hum of the fan, seeing the orange silk panels at the window stir. The cool air felt good against her heated skin.

The soft whir of the fan's blades and the caress of cool air soothed her.

She was panicking. But there was no need to panic. Everything would be okay. Nothing terrible had happened, nothing life changing. He'd kissed her. Touched her. Brought her to an orgasm. It wasn't the end of the world, and it was not as if she hadn't ever indulged in oral sex before. Damien hadn't loved to do it, but that didn't mean she couldn't enjoy it.

And yet it was all so confusing. Her feelings. Her desire. And that rush of guilty pleasure, after he'd brought her to a climax.

Why had she felt guilty? Why should she feel bad for feeling pleasure? Was it because his lovemaking lacked love? Was it because his lovemaking had been so erotic?

She wished she knew. She wished she understood. She wished she wasn't alone now, in the bed, feeling this way.

Mikael had said he'd return soon. He'd told her after he escorted her back to the chamber, that he needed to make a phone call, and promised to come back as soon as he could, but it'd been an hour. She was still waiting.

"What's wrong?" Mikael's voice sounded in the doorway.

She sat up quickly, startled, and yet also relieved.

"You're back," she said, drawing the sheet closer to her breasts. She'd changed from the evening gown into the peach satin nightgown with the gold straps that had been left out for her.

"Yes. Disappointed?" he drawled.

"No. I'm glad."

"Are you?"

She nodded, feeling strangely undone. Her throat ached. She swallowed around the lump. "I…missed…you."

He turned on a small golden lantern in the corner; the soft light illuminated the wide gold and orange stripes on the walls, this room as exotic as the tent earlier in the desert.

He'd showered and changed into black silk pajama pants and a black robe that he'd left open over his bare chest. His skin gleamed, gold. "I was gone longer than I intended," he said, reaching into the pocket of his robe. "But I've come bearing gifts."

"You know how I feel about presents," she said, as he took a seat next to her on the bed.

"Yes, but you should know by now how much I like giving them." He drew a wide jeweled gold cuff from the pocket of the robe, the thick cuff inlaid with pink diamonds, rubies, and topaz and fastened the bangle around her wrist

She glanced down at the heavy gold bangle, thickly studded with jewels. It had to be worth hundreds of thousands of dollars. "Are these all real gems?"

"Yes."

"It's old."

"At least one hundred and fifty years."

The ornate bracelet on her wrist slid forward, exquisite pink and ruby stones catching the light, casting prisms on the wall. A jeweled bed. A jeweled wrist. But jewels wouldn't keep her here. Jewels sparkled but they couldn't keep her warm. They wouldn't make her feel needed, loved. And that was what she wanted most. Love.

"Thank you," she said, giving her hand another light shake, admiring the enormous stones in the thick gold, using the time to divert his attention so he wouldn't see the tears in her eyes.

Things were becoming more complicated. She'd begun to feel things and if she wasn't careful, she'd make a mistake. A terrible mistake. And enough mistakes had been made.

"My pleasure," he answered.

She glanced up at him, hoping he wouldn't see her chaotic emotions. "Did you just return to give me this?"

"No." He took off his robe, and tossed it onto a low chair in the corner. "I forgot something."

"You did?"

"Yes. You." He went to the gold lantern and turned off the light before returning to the bed. "Scoot over. And don't worry. You can relax. You are safe. Nothing is happening tonight. I just want to sleep near my beautiful wife."

In bed, he drew her close to him, his arm loose around her waist, his hand resting on her hip.

For a moment she couldn't breathe. For a moment she waited, wondering if panic would hit. If she'd become nervous or uncomfortable.

If she'd dislike being held by him, held close to him.

None of those things happened.

He felt good. He felt warm. She felt safe.

Jemma woke up alone.

She told herself she didn't mind. Told herself she was glad. She needed space. She liked her independence. But it'd felt good having Mikael near her last night. She'd slept deeply for a change and she woke rested, and anxious to see him.

But Mikael didn't put in an appearance that morning. Instead there was a purple bikini and delicate violet silk cover-up waiting for her, along with a note telling her that tonight she'd sleep in the Amethyst Chamber.

Jemma changed into the pretty purple bikini and slipped the delicate silk cover up over her head, letting the light fabric settle against her tummy and thighs.

Purple was a good color for her. It flattered her skin. She wondered if Mikael would have a gift made from amethyst gems for her tonight. A necklace, a ring, or possibly earrings. She didn't want it, or need it, but it gave her something to think about, rather than her emotions.

She missed Mikael.

She didn't want to be alone.

But she had breakfast outside and then paced the courtyard, swimming when she grew too hot.

Lunch came and went, with her again eating by herself inside one of the air conditioned pavilions, needing the shade.

It was a long day waiting. She grew restless and angry. She peeled off the filmy violet cover up and swam again, and then stretched facedown on a lounge chair, the high desert temperature drying her purple suit almost instantly.

She buried her face in the crook of her arm, telling herself to relax, and calm down. She was getting herself worked up over nothing. Mikael would join her when he could. He'd be there as soon as he could manage it. There was no reason to feel so desperate, or lonely…

And then he was there.

Just like that.

His shadow stretched over her lounge chair, blocking the sun, and she turned over onto her back and looked up at him.

He gazed down at her with dark, smoky eyes. He was dressed in his robes. She suspected he'd had business earlier. But she didn't ask and he didn't tell her.

She raised a hand to shield her eyes and she let her gaze wander over him, up over his chest, to his neck, his hard jaw, the chiseled cheek and then to his eyes. He had ridiculously beautiful eyes. She'd kill for his lashes. It would save her a fortune in eyeliner and mascara.

"You smile." Mikael's deep husky voice vibrated between them, coloring the air, filling the space around them.

Heat danced through her, little sparklers lighting nerve endings beneath her skin. She flexed her feet, feeling her toes curl.

Amazing how little it took for him to turn her on.

Just a long glance from his dark eyes.

A word from his lips.

A certain pitch in his voice.

That's all it took and everything within her melted, wanting. Wanting him and what he did to her, and what he could make her feel.

Jemma drew a slow breath, and then exhaled just as slowly, trying to calm the frantic beating of her heart. "You have the longest, darkest eyelashes," she said, hating the slightly breathless note in her voice, knowing he'd notice. He always did. "I should steal them. You don't need them. I'm the model, not you."

The edge of his mouth lifted. He sat down on the edge of her lounge chair, his hand settling on her knees and then sliding up a couple inches on her thigh. "No Saidian queen has ever held a job."

"Are you saying I can't work if I am your queen?"

"You *are* my queen, and I haven't made any decisions with regard to your career. Although truthfully, it would be very unusual in Saidia, and would probably create a great deal of controversy, if you did continue working."

"So we know what that means."

He tapped the tip of her nose. "We don't know what that means, Miss Smarty Pants." He moved his hand to her thigh, his palm warm against her skin. "Would you miss modeling?"

"I would miss working."

"But not modeling specifically?"

She shrugged, and struggled to focus, which wasn't easy with the warmth of his hand stealing into her thigh. "I enjoyed my job until recently…when everyone dropped me."

"Could you be happy doing other things?"

He'd begun to draw invisible circles on her thigh, setting the nerve endings on fire.

"Such as?" she asked, her voice growing husky.

"Making public appearances. Talking to girls and advocating literacy. Making love to me. Having babies."

Every word he spoke was accompanied by another swoop of his finger across her bare skin, flaming the nerve endings all the while moving closer to her tiny purple bikini bottoms.

She was tempted to press her knees together to stop his fingers and yet she loved his touch, wanted more, wanted him to strip the bottoms off of her and part her thighs and settle between them again, and put his mouth on her, using his tongue and fingers to trace the shape of her soft folds and the tight sensitive clit—

"You're distracted," Mikael said, leaning in to kiss her, even as his palm slid over her thigh to her hip.

She shivered at the caress and the brush of his lips over hers. He pushed her heavy damp hair from her face and kissed her again, more deeply.

She sighed, as he lifted his head. She wanted more, not less. "Maybe a little," she agreed. "Where have you been?"

"I had some business to attend to."

"Out here?" she asked glancing around. "In the middle of the desert?"

"There is technology." He dipped his head, kissed her again, another tingling, soul-stirring kiss that made shivers race through her.

She reached up to touch his face. "When can I use your technology?"

"When the honeymoon is over."

"Is this tradition, or your rule?"

"Both. I want you to myself, and tradition says I have eight days to do just that…keep you hidden from the world during my attempt to win your heart."

"Are you trying to win my heart?" she asked, as his hand

stroked up her waist to brush the curve of her breast. “Or win my body?”

“I think I’ve already done that.”

“You sound so sure of yourself,” she said, gasping as his hand slipped beneath the fabric of her bikini top to cup her breast.

“I am.” His head dropped and he kissed her again, even as he kneaded her breast and teased her sensitive nipple.

Desire surged through her, a hot, insatiable current that scalded her skin and made her melt on the inside. She leaned into his hand, her body aching, straining for more contact.

“You’re starting it again,” she whispered against his mouth. “You’re wreaking havoc on my defenses.”

His dark gaze held hers, the irises dark, mysterious. “You don’t need defenses against me.”

“Oh, I absolutely do. If I lose control, all bets are off.”

“If you lose control, you’re still safe with me.” He kissed her again, and then caressed her lower lip, and the hollow beneath. “You will always be safe with me.”

“I don’t know, because this feels pretty dangerous.”

He smiled a wicked smile which made her breath catch and her pulse race, making her heart pound and hum with the rest of her body.

His dark gaze settled on her mouth, and the quiver of her lower lip. “Good. Because this is desire.”

The quiver of her lip intensified, along with the reckless rhythm of her heart. Blood drummed through her veins, warming her, making her skin hot and sensitive.

“And desire is important,” he added, drawing his fingertip from her lower lip, down the middle of her chin, and lower still, down her neck to the base of her throat, and then on to her breastbone. It was such a light stroke, but slow, and long, and he lit every nerve ending he touched. “Desire makes us feel alive.”

“It’s so sexual.”

“Mmm,” he murmured, the corner of his mouth curving, and yet it wasn’t a smile. It looked like hunger. “Is that a problem?”

She shivered, and would have looked away if he hadn't caught her chin, and forced her gaze to meet his. Her mouth dried. She licked her lips, blood roaring in her ears. "Sex without emotion is empty," she said.

"Is it? Even when you have this intense chemistry?" he asked, stroking the curve of her breasts, avoiding the taut, straining nipple. "How can this be empty?"

Her thoughts slowed, became tangled, her senses taking over, smothering reason. Was this empty? Was this connection bad?

Mikael's fingertip drew slow, lazy circles down the slope of her breast to the valley between, and then down across her flat belly to gently press against her through the material of her bikini bottoms.

She sighed as her head lit up with color and lights and pleasure.

"We enjoy each other," he added, tracing her softness, his knuckle brushing against her where she was so very sensitive. "We've been affectionate. We both feel a strong physical connection. What is missing?"

Love.

She wanted more than sex, more than pleasure. She wanted love. But it was so hard to say when he was touching her so intimately, making her head spin, and her senses pop and explode.

It was hard to focus, even harder for her to speak. "A relationship can't just be about sex," she said. "And I want more than pleasure."

"You don't think pleasure can lead to more?" His fingers slipped beneath the material to caress her intimately. She was hot and slick and he teased her, making her gasp and squeeze her thighs together to ignore what was happening inside of her.

"Can't pleasure generate love?" he persisted, before leaning over her and kissing one taut nipple through her top.

"I don't...think...so," she said, sucking in a breath as he

sucked her, drawing on her hard enough to create sharp pinches of sensation, the pleasure so intense it was almost like pain.

As he worked her breast he pressed his fingers into her, stroking her deep and rhythmically, matching the draw on her nipple.

Fire streaked from her breast to her womb. She felt her inner muscles clench him, her body already so hot and wet she knew she wouldn't last, knew she couldn't hold back. He had magic in his hands, and he knew just how to touch her, just how to seduce her. He could make her his slave with just a kiss and a touch…

"But you don't know for sure," he said, stroking deep, creating a maddening friction. His dark eyes sparked. "Pleasure happens in the mind. Love happens there, too." He leaned close, his lips grazing hers. "Why can't one lead to the other?"

She leaned in to the kiss, kissing him with desperation and hunger, as the tease of desire became a fierce consuming need. She hummed with tension. It coiled inside of her, throbbing, insisting, making her feel wild for release. "I need you," she choked. "Need you to make love to me."

"I am," he said, as his fingers pressed deep.

She bucked against his hand, frantic, and frustrated. "Not like this. I want you, your body, your skin, in bed, on me." She'd go mad if she didn't have him soon. "Let's go inside," she whispered, licking her lip, her mouth dry, heart hammering. "Now."

"And what shall we do there?" he asked.

She gave her head a shake, dizzy, dazed. "Everything."

The corner of his mouth lifted. "This is only day three, *laeela*. We're to draw the pleasure out…make you wait."

"I waited all day for you!" she protested.

"Pleasure can't be rushed."

"Oh, I think it can. You've already made me half mad." She sat up, and pulled him forward to kiss him deeply, drawing his breath into her, opening her mouth to him, welcoming the tip of his tongue, sucking on the tip even as he thrust his fingers into her. She was so close to shattering, so close that she was afraid he'd stop, and walk away, and leave her aching. "I need you," she whispered against his mouth, frantic for him, frantic for release.

"You have me," he answered, his hands where she needed them, his mouth on hers, his tongue answering hers.

Her fingers curled into his crisp hair. Her nails pressed against his scalp. She leaned into him, pressing her breasts to his chest, letting her hips move, grinding against his hand. She was wanton but he felt good and tasted good and right now, she felt alive, and hungry for life, which was so different from how she'd felt this past year.

To go from dead to life…

To feel beautiful, and powerful…

He brought her to a climax, and she cried out as she shattered against him. She tipped her head against his, panting in release.

She should be horrified. Instead she felt strong. Hopeful. Jemma opened her eyes, looked into his. "What have you done to me?" she whispered.

"I'm just making sure you're satisfied," he said, kissing her.

"I'm satisfied," she said, still breathless. "But what about you?"

"I'm good."

"Yes," she agreed. "You are." And he did feel good. He felt solid and real and permanent in the best sort of way. "Can we now go to the bedroom?"

He kissed her again, and smoothed her hair back from her face. "I wish I could. Unfortunately, I have another conference call and this one is going to take a while. The staff knows to serve you dinner when you're hungry. Don't wait for me."

"Not again!"

"I know it's frustrating but it's important. Trust me." His dark eyes held hers, searching hers. "Do you believe me?"

She sighed, and nodded, because she did believe him. She couldn't imagine him lying to her. Not now. Not ever. "Yes."

"Just know that I will come to you tonight in the Amethyst Chamber, as soon as I can."

"I don't want to go there without you."

"But I will be there, *laeela*. I promise. Soon."

She ate dinner alone in the Amethyst Chamber, the walls painted a deep plum, and then stenciled in gold. The low wooden bed was framed with long embroidered silk curtains in shades of purple and plum, with violet hued pillows and a silk coverlet decorating the bed.

She didn't belong here, she thought, finishing her dinner, and returning the dishes to the tray by the door.

She didn't belong in Saidia and she didn't belong in Mikael's life. When she was with him, he distracted her from reality, making her forget what was true and important.

Like her work, and her family.

Like getting back to London and to those who did love her.

It was good to be away from him this evening. It was good to have time to herself, to find herself, and most of all, to remember how she'd come to be here, at the Bridal Palace, in the first place.

She'd been forced here. She'd been forced into this marriage. And she'd been forced to surrender to Sheikh Karim.

She had to remember that. Had to remember the facts, and reality, next time Mikael showed up, and touched her, and kissed her and made her want nothing but him.

She fell asleep, with the light on, determined to be strong when he arrived. She would resist him this time. She wouldn't melt for him. She wouldn't ache or need or shatter in his hands. Not anymore. Never again.

As her eyes closed she counted the days and nights she'd been here. Tonight was the third night. That meant there were just five more and then she'd be free.

Jemma woke up, blinked. It was morning. She looked around, pushing her long hair back from her face, and tugging the strap of her filmy purple nightgown back up onto her shoulder.

She was alone.

Good.

*Good*, she silently insisted. She'd gone to bed alone so it shouldn't surprise her that she was the only person in the bed, but she'd dreamed about Mikael all night, dreamed of Mikael kissing her, making love to her, and it'd felt so real. She woke up feeling as if he had been there, with her.

But he wasn't. It was a figment of her imagination. A dream.

She stretched her arm out across the empty bed, suddenly terribly homesick.

Day four, she told herself. Just four more days, and four more nights, and she'd be home.

The thought should have pleased her, reassured her, instead her heart fell, and her eyes burned. She missed Mikael. She shouldn't miss him. She should hate him.

The wooden door to the en suite bath creaked. Jemma sat up, startled.

Mikael appeared in the doorway, wearing nothing but loose cotton pajama pants that hung deliciously low on his hip bones. He raked a hand through his dark hair, making muscles ripple in his arms and chest.

She stared at his lean flat abdomen, each muscle hard and distinct.

"You're awake," he said, walking toward her and giving her the most devastatingly wicked smile.

Her heart lurched. "Where did you come from?"

"The bathroom."

Her heart did another funny little tumble. Just looking at him made her feel a pang. She didn't understand why he did that to her. She frowned. "How?"

"I walked."

She made a face, rolling her eyes. "Yes, but when?"

"Just a few minutes ago."

Her mouth dried. Her pulse was doing crazy, wild things. "But you weren't here. I fell asleep waiting for you."

"You might have fallen asleep before I arrived, but I did

come to you last night. I slept with you last night. I promised you I'd be here, and I am." He drew back the covers and slid in next to her. "You don't remember last night?"

"No." She frowned. "Did we…do…things?"

He reached across the bed for her, dragged her toward him, tangling her bare legs in the covers. "No. Regretfully not. I just held you. And spent the night with an endless hard-on."

She laughed as he pulled her under him but her laughter died as he lowered his powerful body onto hers. He was hard now. His length pressed against her belly.

"It's back," she whispered breathlessly.

"That's because it never went away." He dipped his head and kissed the side of her neck.

She sighed and arched against him. His hips ground against hers. She pressed her hips up, rubbing against the tip of his thick shaft, wanting it, wanting him.

"You want me," he said, his voice a rasp in her ear.

She nodded as his mouth covered hers, and she wrapped her legs around his hips. She did want him. All of him. And not just the things he did to her, but the things he made her feel. "Yes," she said, because she needed this, needed to feel. It had been a year of so much sadness and confusion that she needed to feel something warm and good again.

Mikael was making her feel very warm and good.

"What shall I do to you?" he murmured, kissing her jaw, and then her chin, before brushing her mouth with his.

She reached up, and wound her arms around his neck, drawing his head down. "Everything."

They kissed for hours, kissing until they were both panting and damp and tangled in sheets. Jemma wanted more, but she also loved this, the intense need, the desire, the fierce pleasure of just wanting and being wanted.

Her body ached and throbbed, even as her heart ached and throbbed. And as Mikael kissed her, touched her, his hands lighting her on fire and keeping the flames burning, glowing, she began to think that this might not just be lust anymore.

This wasn't about sex, either. It was more than sex. More than desire. Something else was stirring to life but what it was, she didn't know, and wasn't ready to face. Wasn't sure she could.

"I have news for you," he murmured against her mouth, his hands tangled in her hair. He kissed her once more. "We should talk."

Jemma went still. "What is it?"

"Your mother." He shifted his weight and moved away from her, rolling onto his back. He grabbed a pillow and placed it under his head. "And she's not sick, so you don't need to look at me like that."

"Like what?" Jemma demanded, sitting up, and tugging her sheer nightgown down, hoping she was adequately covered.

"Like something terrible has happened to her. Nothing terrible has happened. What's happened is good."

"What's happened?"

"It isn't good for your mother to have so much stress. A woman of her age needs to have her own home. I think she will do better if she has her own place again."

"Of course she would. We would all like that for her. But it's a dream at this point."

"There's a turn of the century shore colonial in Keofferam in Old Greenwich that I think would suit her. It has a big wraparound porch, and a small caretaker's apartment over a detached garage for a housekeeper or nurse, should your mother one day require one. It's recently been renovated so your mother wouldn't have to do anything."

"Yes, that all sounds very lovely, but you can't buy property in that area for less than two million, and a home such as the one you describe would easily be upward of three million—"

"Almost four," he agreed, "but it's in pristine condition and has the high ceilings and elegant formal rooms she would enjoy."

Jemma reached for a pillow and drew it to her chest. "You sound as if you know her."

"I did meet her at your sister's wedding, but you forget, your mother and mine were very similar in background. It's not difficult to imagine the kind of home she would be comfortable in, so I can tell you now that the house is in escrow, and I've been assured it will close at the end of today, as the wired funds have already reached the bank. I had my Realtor purchase the house in your mother's maiden name, which apparently is her legal name again. No one can take it from her."

Jemma stared at him. "I don't understand."

"I think she's suffered enough, don't you?"

Jemma struggled to speak around the lump filling her throat. "But you hate the Copelands."

"I hate your father, but your mother shouldn't be punished for his crimes." He hesitated. "Nor should you. So I did what I thought was best. It is my gift to you—"

"It's too much. I can't accept—"

"You don't have to. The gift is in your mother's name. There's nothing you can do about it."

"She won't accept it."

"She has."

"What?"

"I have been communicating with your brother, Branson. He has assisted me with a few financial details."

"He would never do that!"

Mikael sat up, muscles tightening across his chest, rippling down the length of his bare, lean torso. "You don't think a son wants his mother safe? Protected?"

"I know Branson. He wouldn't allow you to do such a thing."

"He would, if he understood we had done it together."

Jemma grew still. "You told him about…us?"

"I told him you were here with me, and that I intended to make you my queen."

"And he was okay with that?"

Mikael nodded and lay back down, arms folding behind his head. "Better than okay. He was very pleased for both of us and offered to throw us a party in London, as soon as we could visit. I told him we'd be there soon, probably before the end of the month."

She squeezed the pillow tighter. "You sound so smug."

"You should be happy I helped her, not angry."

"You can't do these things, though."

"Why not? I am your husband. It's my duty to provide for you and your family."

"A family you hate."

"Things have changed. You are my wife, and my family now, and I seek to honor you, and your family—"

"But what happens when I leave here in four days? What happens when you send me back? You promised you would, if I wasn't happy—"

"Are you unhappy?"

Her mouth opened but no sound came out. Was she unhappy?

It was strange to be asked that question now, so bluntly, because no, she wasn't unhappy. She was actually happier than she'd been in months, maybe even years.

"That's not the point," she said, sliding off the bed to pace the room.

"It's not?"

"No." She paced back toward him, confused, frustrated, no longer sure of anything.

"Then what is the point? Because I thought I had eight days to prove to you that I could make you happy, and I am making you happy, so what is the problem?"

She threw out her hands. "This!" she cried, gesturing at the purple walls with gold stencil. "This," she added, plucking at the silk nightgown. "This," she said, pointing to the bed, where he lay so supremely confident and comfortable, looking every bit a king. "None of this is real. None of this is my real life. It's just a dream. It's surreal. It's not going to last!"

"Says who?" he asked tersely, revealing the first hint of impatience.

"Me!"

"And you are an expert on reality? You, with the model for a boyfriend and the plan to enter Saidia on a stolen passport?"

"It wasn't stolen, it was my sister's, and you're hateful to throw Damien in my face. You know I loved him, and you know he hurt me. And you're just jealous because you can bombard me with expensive gifts but you know deep down, you'll never be able to buy my love."

Jemma walked out, pushing through the doors to the central courtyard, and then on to the other side, through a door to the Chamber of Innocence. She grabbed an ivory robe from the bathroom, wrapped it around her, and then walked out, leaving the Bridal Palace in search of her own wing. Her rooms, the ones she'd been brought to on arriving at the Kasbah.

She was done with this stupid honeymoon game. Done being kept locked up like a kidnapped bride. She wanted out. She wanted to go home.

"Where do you think you're going?" Mikael's deep voice rang out behind her. "We're not done, *laeela*."

"I am."

"It doesn't work that way."

"Maybe not for you!"

"Or you," he retorted, scooping her up into his arms and dropping her over his shoulder. "You owe me eight days and nights, and we're only halfway through. I get four more, and I will take all four."

"I don't want to do this anymore!"

"Too bad." He was carrying her back the way she'd just come, walking swiftly, his arm anchored across the back of her legs, holding her in place. "This isn't a game. You don't get to run away when you're tired or your feelings are hurt. This is real, you and me. This is reality."

He'd kicked open a door down the hall and then kicked it closed behind him. The room was dark and yet he knew where he was going, crossing the floor with long sure strides to drop her unceremoniously on the bed.

She scrambled into a sitting position. "Get out."

"That's not happening."

"I want to be alone."

"That's not happening, either." He untied the sash at her waist, peeled the robe off her shoulders and reached for the hem of her nightgown.

She slapped at his hands. "Don't touch me!"

"That, my dear wife, *is* happening."

# CHAPTER THIRTEEN

MIKAEL REACHED PAST Jemma and turned on the small glass lamp on the bedside table, flooding the room with soft ruby light. The bed beneath Jemma gleamed with luxurious red satin, while the large jeweled mirror on the ceiling reflected the silk-covered walls and the decadent satin sheets.

With an irritated flick, he yanked the hem of Jemma's violet nightgown up, pulling it over her head and then tossing the scrap of violet silk onto the floor, before kicking off his own pajama bottoms. "We don't need these anymore," he said flatly, "now that we're in the Crimson Chamber."

Jemma scrambled back on the bed. "You've lost your mind."

"Maybe. Or maybe I've lost all patience. I'm not sure which right now," he said, grabbing her ankle and pulling her back toward him.

Jemma sprawled back on the bed, her long dark hair spilling across the crimson satin, her green eyes flashing. She'd never looked more beautiful. He would have her now. No more games. She was his. He'd chosen her. Married her. She was his queen.

He stretched out over her, and settled his weight between her thighs, his arousal pressing against her core.

She was hot, wet and his length rubbed against her slick heat. It would be so easy to thrust into her, and take her.

So easy to prove to her how much she wanted him.

He knew she craved him physically.

He knew he could make her scream and climax. He could draw out the orgasm and make it last for hours, too.

But that wasn't the point. His expertise as a lover wasn't in question. His future as a husband was. His father might have failed as a husband, but Mikael wouldn't.

Mikael dropped his head, and kissed her neck just above her collarbone, and then kissed higher on her neck, at the spot beneath her ear. He kissed the hollow and then the earlobe. He caught her earlobe in his teeth, his teeth lightly scraping, his breath lightly blowing in her ear.

He felt her nipples pucker and harden against his chest. He released her wrists and stroked her arms, moving in toward her ribs to cup the sides of her breasts, her skin soft and warm and then he stroked out again until his hands covered hers, his fingers linking with hers.

He kissed the side of her jaw, kissed the pulse beating frantically in the hollow beneath her ear and then he covered her mouth with his and kissed her, deeply, his tongue thrusting into her mouth, probing, possessing.

Her thighs parted wider for him. Her hips arched, her body rocking up against him.

"You aren't really angry because I helped your mother," he said, lifting his head to look down into her face. The paleness in her face was gone. Her cheeks flushed pink. She wanted him. "You're angry because you're afraid. You're angry because you're afraid these gifts—particularly this gift to your mother—will trap you in Saidia, with me."

Her eyes widened and she bit down into her lower lip.

He was right. That was her fear.

His chest grew tight. He felt an unaccountable pang, the pang eerily reminiscent of the ache and loss he'd felt after his mother left Saidia all those years ago. "*Laeela*, I made you a promise. You give me eight days and nights, and I will not keep you here against your will—"

"It's not you I'm afraid of," she interrupted. "It's me. I believe you will let me go. I believe you will put me on a plane should I request it. But I'm afraid that I might not request it, might not insist on it, and then everything that is uniquely me and mine, everything that I have worked so hard for all these years, will be gone."

"But if you remain here, you gain a new identity and a new life."

"As *your* wife. But I won't be anyone without you, and I vowed years ago to never be dependent on a man, much less a powerful man, and here in Saidia, I will be completely dependent on you."

"Is that such a bad thing if the powerful man is a just man?"

Her eyes turned liquid and she swallowed hard. "You already make my heart ache."

"I think we would make a good team, *laeela.*"

She struggled to smile. "Maybe you should just make love to me."

He dipped his head, kissed her lips. "Good idea. So what do you want, my beautiful bride? How can I please you today?"

"You," she said. "I just want you."

Jemma saw heat flare in Mikael's eyes and felt him harden against her.

She rocked her hips up, savoring the sensation of him against her. He was hard and warm, so warm, and she couldn't remember ever wanting anyone like this. "Make love to me, Mikael," she added, wrapping her arms around his neck and sinking her fingers into his crisp hair. "I need you."

His mouth covered hers, his tongue parting her lips to take her mouth even as he thrust smoothly, deeply into her body, filling her, stretching her.

He felt unbelievable.

*She* felt unbelievable.

Jemma's eyes burned and her chest ached, emotion bubbling up inside of her. Her arms slid down around his shoulders to hold him tighter. He was big and powerful and yet he fit her, and felt perfect to her.

Mikael kissed her, drawing her tongue into his mouth, sucking the tip even as he buried himself deeper into her body. She welcomed his weight and the fullness that stole her breath, and then he began to move. His lean sculpted hips dipped and he pressed deeper, then withdrew, only to stroke deep into her again.

She sighed and arched as he hit a spot inside her that tingled with pleasure. "More," she said, pressing up against him as he drove into her.

"I don't want to hurt you."

"It doesn't hurt. It feels so good." And it was true. It felt delicious everywhere. She felt delicious. Everything inside her was warm and sweet and bright. She felt like sunshine and honey, orange and spice and each stroke made her sigh a little deeper, and press against him a little harder.

"Don't stop," she whispered, meeting each of his thrusts, needing the friction, feeling the tension build. Each stroke of his body made her nerve endings tense, tighten, tingle.

He drove into her faster, increasing the rhythm. She loved the rhythm, the deep hard thrusts, the slickness of their bodies together, the warmth of his chest against hers. She could smell the scent of him, and them together, and it smelled right, felt right, more right than anything she'd ever felt before.

It didn't make sense, but then, none of this made sense and maybe passion never did.

The teasing tension within her quickened, sharpened, becoming bigger, and more powerful.

She panted and strained against him, wanting to come, not sure she could come and then he slipped his hand between them, stroking her even as he thrust hard into her wet tight body.

She wasn't prepared for the intensity of the orgasm and she screamed his name as he continued to stroke her, pushing her over the edge, her control shattering, her body climaxing, convulsively tightening around him.

He tensed, strained, his big powerful body arching as he buried himself deep inside her. She was still convulsing around him, her body squeezing him. With a guttural cry, he pulled out, making sure he spilled his seed into the sheets and not her.

She rolled over on the bed, on to her back, eyes closed, still struggling to catch her breath. He followed, lying on his side, next to her, his hand settling low on her hip.

She floated, feeling blissfully relaxed, and yet also very aware of Mikael at her side. She could feel the pressure of his hand, the warmth of his skin, smell his masculine spicy scent, practically hear his steady heartbeat. He was more real to her right now than she was.

He'd become her world in four days. It was exactly as she'd feared.

Jemma opened her eyes to find Mikael looking at her, his dark eyes so beautiful but so impossible to read. "Yes?" she whispered, dazzled, dazed.

"How do you feel?"

She let out a soft laugh and she turned to him, moving into his arms to rest her face on his chest. She could hear his heartbeat, smell his scent.

He smelled good. He felt good. He felt perfect, really.

"Good," she said softly, smiling unsteadily, because her emotions were bubbling up high and fast. "Very, very good."

They slept for an hour like that and Jemma woke first, sleepily stirring but couldn't move as Mikael's arms were around her and his muscular thigh was tucked between hers.

She lifted her head, looked down at him. He was still asleep, his thick black lashes beautiful onyx crescents against the gold of his cheek.

He looked different asleep. Younger. Boyish. Just a man, not a sheikh.

She put her head back down and nestled closer, liking the weight of his arm, the texture of his skin. He felt right. Perfect.

Did other women feel this way after making love? She'd had sex before but it hadn't felt like this. Like something important had happened. Something significant.

Even now she felt the rippling of emotion, like aftershocks. Something inside her felt aware, awake. Stirred.

Was this love? It couldn't be. She had to be feeling merely the side effect of seduction, and passion, all the result of his expert lovemaking.

If that was the case, then why did her very heartbeat seem to repeat his name? *Mik-ael. Mik-ael. Mik-ael.*

A moment later, he shifted, rolling on to his back, carrying her on top of him. His hand tangled in her long hair, and he parted her thighs, pushing her down against his hips. He was hard again, his erection rubbing against her. "Are you too sore to let me love you again?" he asked, his deep voice as husky and smoky as his dark eyes.

"No."

He lifted her, drawing her down on him, and with his hands on her hips, he helped her ride him, slow and deep, and then faster as the pleasure built.

After they both came, she tumbled forward onto his chest, and he held her. Her eyes closed. She listened to the thud of his heart and breathed him in.

He felt so good. He made her feel safe. *Happy.*

She was happy. This was the best place she'd been in months, emotionally, physically. In years.

Silence stretched between them, silence and a tingling awareness that everything had changed.

Mikael breathed in, out, and she traveled with his breath, his chest lifting her, carrying her.

That's how it'd been when they were joined. She'd felt lifted, carried, supported.

It had been so intimate, and yet it wasn't just sex. It felt like so much more, maybe because it had been so intense, and so physical, it'd demanded all of her, and she'd surrendered.

Making love to him, she gave herself up to him, offering him everything—her body, her mind, her emotions…her heart.

Why her heart? It made no sense. Jemma protected her heart. She'd learned it was necessary for survival. And yet in one morning of lovemaking, she'd dropped her defenses, lost her boundaries and become someone else. Or something else.

*Changed.*

There was that word again. She couldn't help going back to it. Changed. Altered. Shattered.

*Confused.*

How could sex do that? How could sensation be so powerful? She didn't understand and yet everything inside her felt open. Her heart felt open.

She pressed her palm to his chest, savoring the steady thud of his heart. "Did you really buy my mother a house?" she asked huskily.

His fingers played with her hair, twisting the long strands. "I will go check and see if the escrow has closed. I expect it will have."

"And then it will be hers?"

"And hers alone," he agreed.

Jemma hesitated. "Even if I leave here in four days?"

"No one can take it from her."

Jemma was profoundly moved, but also troubled. "I don't know what to say. I know I should thank you—"

"You don't need to thank me. I didn't buy it for you. I did it for her."

"You don't even know her."

"I met her at Morgan's wedding. She was kind to me. I liked her. She reminded me of my mother."

Mikael left her to check on the status of the house and Jemma showered and dressed, slipping into the long ruby beaded skirt and matching ruby top laid out on the bed. Breakfast was served in the courtyard. She'd just sat down and had her first coffee when Mikael returned.

"Escrow closed. The paperwork has been signed. The house is hers," he said, taking the chair opposite Jemma's.

"Thank you," Jemma said. "Thank you for caring for her. Thank you for wanting the best for her."

"I do for her what I should have done for my mother." His brow furrowed, and his voice dropped, cracking. "I was not good to my mother. I failed her, and I will carry that pain, and that shame, with me forever."

She reached across the table, and covered his hand with hers. "How did you fail her? What did you do?"

"Nothing. That is what I did. Absolutely nothing."

"I don't understand."

"When I explain, you'll be appalled. And you should be. My behavior was selfish and it still disgusts me, but it's too late to fix things. Too late to make amends."

Jemma winced at his sharp tone, his voice laced with self-loathing and scorn. "Explain to me."

"I was twenty-two when I learned the truth about my father and mother, that my father had lied to her, and had destroyed their wedding contract so he could take another wife. I was furious with my father," he said, "but I'd lost my mother years ago, when I was just a boy, eleven, and I was terrified of losing my father, too. He had so many other children, so many other sons he could admire and love, and so I pretended I didn't know the truth about the divorce. I pretended that I didn't know who my father was—a liar, a cheat—and I acted as if my father was this wonderful man."

"You were his son," she said. "You were showing him respect."

"My father had turned his back on my mother. I understood he expected me to do the same. And so I did, even when she came to me on my twenty-fifth birthday, asking for help. She was nervous about her future. She wanted financial assistance, and advice. She was worried she wasn't managing her money well. She was worried she'd run out if she didn't have the right investments."

"Did you help her?"

"No."

"No?"

His jaw tightened. "I took her to coffee and told her I couldn't help her, that she'd created this situation by leaving my father. I told her there was nothing I could do." Mikael averted his face, staring off across the courtyard, his features set. "She didn't cry. She didn't beg. She just folded up her papers and slipped them back into her purse, then kissed me, and left."

Jemma's eyes burned. "You were young."

"I wasn't young. I was angry." He turned to look at her, expression fierce. "I wanted to punish her for leaving me all those years ago, for leaving me with a father who barely remembered me because he had so many wives and sons and daughters, all clamoring for his attention. So I rejected her, wanting her to hurt as I had hurt."

Silence stretched.

He drew a deep, rough breath. "I never did help her with her investments, even though I had degrees in finance and economics. Even though I worked in London as an institutional investor until I was nearly thirty." Mikael shifted restlessly. "I knew money. I knew how to make money. And I could have aided her, protected her, but I didn't. So she went to your father and trusted him, and we all know how that turned out."

"But she didn't go to my father until after Morgan's wedding. At least, that's what I thought you said."

"Yes. But she went to him because she'd made some bad investments earlier, and your father promised he could do impossible things with what capital she had left. He could get her an incredible return on her investment with him, and so she gave him everything. Everything. And he stole it all."

Jemma winced, sickened all over again by her father's betrayal. "That's on his head, not yours."

Mikael turned his head, looked at her from beneath his dense black lashes. "My mother should have died of old age, comfortable in her American home. But she lost her home, along with her nest egg. Heartbroken, and terrified, she took her life. Hung herself in the hall of her home the day she was to be evicted."

Jemma stared at him, aghast. "She killed herself?"

He nodded. His jaw worked, and he ran a hand down his throat, as if trying to find the words. "She was just fifty-four," he said when he could finally speak again. "But she'd lost her home…again. She knew she couldn't go to my father. She was afraid to come to me. We were still rebuilding our relationship and she was afraid I'd be disappointed in her, so she panicked. She did what she thought was the best answer for all."

"I'm so sorry."

"I still have that last note, the note she left, saying she was sorry, and begging me to forgive her for being stupid and weak."

He turned his head abruptly but not before Jemma saw the suffering in his eyes.

For several moments there was just silence, an endless, impossible silence heavy with grief.

Jemma reached out and placed her hand over his. "People make mistakes," she whispered.

"It's my fault she died," he said. "At first I blamed my father, and your father, but I am the one responsible for this. I did this to her. I rejected her. Refused her. I left her no hope—"

"Would you have helped her if she came to you about her house, Mikael?" she interrupted, leaving her seat and moving around the table to kneel before him. "If she'd told you her situation, that she had nowhere to go, and no way to pay her bills, would you have taken care of her?"

"*Yes.*"

"Are you sure? Or is that what you say now?"

He stiffened, shoulders squaring. His dark eyes burned down at her. "You don't think I would?"

"*I* know you would," she said, taking his hands, holding them tightly. "But do you? That's the important question. Because until you believe you would have helped her, you won't be able to forgive…you, her, or your father."

# CHAPTER FOURTEEN

MIKAEL WAS DONE talking. He'd said far more than he'd intended to say but he was glad he'd told Jemma the truth. Glad she knew now who he was, and what he was. Better for her to know on the fourth day than the eighth. Better to give her all the facts up front, instead of blindsiding her at the end.

He rose from the table, drew her up to her feet. "I cannot think anymore, or talk anymore. I am talked out. I need diversion. What about you?"

"What do you have in mind?"

"You'll see."

She followed him back into the Crimson Chamber. The satin sheets had been changed, and freshly made, the bed lined with stacks of ruby-hued pillows.

A bright white light shone from the ceiling, onto a screen attached to the far wall.

He saw Jemma glance up at the light, and then saw the moment she realized it was actually a projector. "Is that what I think it is?" she asked, turning to him.

"Do you like movies?"

"Yes."

"I do, too. I thought maybe you could use a break from the pool and the sun and would enjoy a good film."

"I'd love it. But only if you stay with me. Otherwise I wouldn't enjoy it at all."

Jemma loved their afternoon at the movies in the Crimson Chamber. The dark red walls and rich burgundy and ruby pillows and cushions made the room feel like an elegant, and exotic, movie theatre. Staff brought them food during a break between the two films, a break Jemma laughingly called the "intermission," and then curled back up in Mikael's arms when the second film began.

He had to leave at the end of the second movie to check in with his staff. He kissed her before he left and promised to meet her for dinner in the courtyard. They were to dine outside tonight, inside the pink and turquoise tiled pavilion. "We'll go to the Turquoise Chamber tonight. You'll enjoy tonight," he told her, kissing her again.

"I've enjoyed every night," she answered truthfully, smiling up at him.

She arrived in the courtyard that evening before he did, dressed in the filmy turquoise kaftan that had been laid out for her.

The kaftan was long, reaching her ankles and it swished as she walked, clinging to her stomach, hips and thighs.

Jemma wandered around the grand courtyard, admiring the large blue tiled pool lit by blue and pink lights, and pausing to smell the sweet fragrant lilies and roses that grew in clusters in enormous glazed pots.

She was glad she'd arrived in the courtyard before Mikael. She enjoyed having this moment to herself, liked the excitement bubbling within her, and the sense of anticipation.

She'd enjoyed this afternoon with Mikael. She'd found it hard to concentrate on the movies, though, with him there, at her side. She'd wanted him to make love to her, but he hadn't. He'd held her, and kissed her several times, but he'd otherwise shown admirable restraint.

She, on the other hand, wanted to be touched. She'd curled at his side, pretending to watch the movie when all she really wanted was touch. She was beginning to feel addicted to pleasure. Or was she addicted to him? She didn't know, wasn't sure how she could know.

Jemma felt a tingle down her spine. She wasn't alone anymore. She knew Mikael had arrived even before she turned to see him.

Slowly she faced him. He was standing at the far end of the pool, watching her. "That color suits you," he said.

Suddenly the courtyard hummed with energy. She felt the same electric surge in her veins, her heart racing, too.

He was wearing black trousers and a white linen shirt and he looked handsome and virile and confident.

Her husband. Her king.

She smiled, amused by the thought, but the thought took hold. He might very well be a good husband for her. He seemed to be a good king.

A servant appeared with a tray of cocktails and together Jemma and Mikael walked around the courtyard, with Mikael pointing out various plants that had significance, whether due to age, or relationship to the Kasbah.

"The date palms were for a great-grandmother, and the citrus trees were for my grandmother. The trees are replaced every ten to fifteen years, depending on their maturity and fruit production. My mother loved pink roses, so those were for her." Mikael smiled at her. "What shall we plant in your honor? What is your favorite flower?"

She shook her head. "I think it's all perfect just the way it is. I wouldn't change anything."

"You don't want to be immortalized in the Bridal Palace's garden?" he asked.

She knew he was teasing her. She could see it in his eyes and the quirk of his mouth and she felt a bubble of warmth inside her.

She was happy.

That's why she felt different…why everything seemed different. The happiness explained the bright sparks in her head and in her eyes. The happiness made her tingle, and her insides fizz.

It wasn't the desert heat temperatures heating her, warming her, but happiness. And she was happy because of him. Happy because she cared about him. And cared maybe more than she should.

They made love in the Turquoise Chamber and fell asleep tangled together, skin damp, limbs intertwined.

Jemma woke first, it was early.

Day five, she thought. She would be here for only three more days.

She counted the nights in her head, remembering the colors…

White the first night in the Chamber of Innocence, and then Topaz, Amethyst, Ruby or Crimson, and then last night was Turquoise.

Where would they go tonight? To the Emerald Chamber? Sapphire?

Did it even matter?

She had to leave. Had to return to London. Didn't she?

Confused by her conflicting thoughts, Jemma quietly left the bed and stepped outside to the courtyard. It was still early. The sun was just rising and the temperature felt cool, the early morning painted the palest pink and yellow.

Jemma's maid appeared in the courtyard with coffee and a tray of breakfast pastries. Jemma refused the pastries but sipped the coffee in a chair near the tranquil pool, listening to the chirp of birds nesting high above in the palm fronds.

Mikael appeared in the doorway a half hour later. He'd showered and dressed and was wearing his robes. "I need to go to Ketama," he said, approaching her to drop a kiss on the top of her head. "I will be back tonight. I wouldn't leave if I didn't have to."

She tipped her face up to him, frowning at the amount of time he'd be traveling, first by camel, and then by car. "Won't it take you all day to get there?"

He kissed her again, this time on her brow. "I have a helicopter here. The pilot's ready. If we leave now, I'll be back this evening."

"And you have to go?"

"Yes," he said, sounding very decisive.

"Be careful," she said.

He kissed her one last time, this time on the lips. "Always."

It seemed as if it would be a long day with Mikael gone, but Jemma's maid led her to the Emerald Chamber, with the wall of antique leather-bound books.

Jemma studied the spines, delighted to discover that many were in English, and many were written by her favorite English authors. Charles Dickens, Thomas Hardy, Jane Austen, the Bronte sisters, E.M. Forster, and more.

Jemma selected *Mansfield Park* by Jane Austen and curled up in bed to read. She read the afternoon away and was still reading when the maid appeared to help Jemma dress for dinner.

"Is His Highness back?" Jemma asked, reluctantly putting the book down.

The maid shook her head. "No."

"Then why do I need to dress for dinner? Can't I have dinner here, in bed?"

Jemma finished the novel over dessert and promptly began *Sense and Sensibility* but ended up falling asleep over it.

She was still asleep, holding the novel, when Mikael arrived at midnight.

He stood over the bed for a moment watching her before carefully plucking the book from her hand, drawing the covers up to her shoulder, and turning the lamp out next to the bed.

He showered in the marble bathroom and then after drying off, joined her in bed. He was naked. But then, so was she.

Jemma woke up in the night and reached out to her side, relieved and delighted to discover Mikael there.

She moved toward him, and he opened his arms to her, drawing her close.

She pressed her face to his warm chest, breathing in his scent. He was back and he felt good and smelled good and she lifted her face to his, offering her lips. He kissed her, taking her mouth and then rolling her onto her back, to thrust deep inside her.

She wrapped her legs around his hips, taking all of him, wanting to hold him as close as possible, aware that things were changing. She was changing.

She…loved…him.

She loved him.

All of a sudden it made sense. She was happy because she was in love.

They fell back asleep and then woke up sometime in the morning to make love again. This time Jemma didn't fall back asleep but slipped from bed to head to the bathroom to shower.

Mikael watched Jemma cross the bedroom, naked, her beautiful body so familiar to him now.

Maybe that's why his chest felt heavy and tight as he watched her disappear into the bathroom.

Maybe that's why sex had felt different last night and this morning.

Maybe it's because she was familiar to him. Important to him.

But she was different, too, he thought. She hadn't merely been in his arms, but with him…in him…which didn't make sense, as it was his body filling hers, but somehow she'd gotten inside of him. He had felt *her*, feeling her not just with his body but his heart.

The emotions and sensations had made the sex more intense.

She'd felt so alive beneath him, so fierce and fragile, so beautiful that he couldn't get close enough to her, and he'd tried, God knew he'd tried.

Slow, deep strokes, hands holding her down, and still so he could kiss her, ravish her, draw her all the way into him.

And it hadn't been enough. He couldn't get enough. Even after one, two orgasms…hers, his.

Before, when he'd pleasured her, he'd wanted to blow her mind, enslave her through passion, make her yield to him. Belong to him. If she was going to be his, she should be happy with him.

But today it'd been something else.

There had been more heat than ever before but the heat wasn't about skin or erotic zones. It wasn't about the orgasm, either.

It was her. Wanting her. Holding her. Being with her.

And he could have sworn she'd been into him. Not the act. Not the friction and tension, not the positions, either.

Somehow the game of seduction had changed and become something more. More real, more honest, more raw. Suddenly, the stakes seemed higher than ever. Could he make Jemma happy? Could he keep her here with him in Saidia?

And if he could, was it fair to her? Or to those in her family?

Mikael threw back the covers, and headed for the bathroom where he could hear Jemma showering.

Hot steam filled the white marble bath, thick fragrant clouds hanging in the air.

He could just make her out through the wisps, her long hair piled high on her head, her hands on her breasts, spreading the bath gel across her lovely pale skin. He hardened, wanting her, craving her again.

He should be sated by now. He should have had his fill.

How many times did a man need a woman?

And yet watching her dark head dip, as she looked down her long, slim torso, to the suds running from her breasts to her belly, his body tightened, his arousal surging upright.

He couldn't stay away. He needed her. Again. He'd have her, too.

Mikael pushed open the glass door to the sunken shower, steam rising, embracing him.

Jemma turned toward him, startled, her lips parting in surprise.

Her eyes, those lips, her face…

Hunger raced through him. Hunger and the need to have her, hold her, keep her. He reached for her, and pushing her back against the wet marble wall, pressed his chest to hers, feeling the slippery film of soap suds between them, skin slick, enticing.

He rubbed his chest across her soft breasts and felt her nipples pebble. He inhaled sharply, as something wrenched in his chest.

This was new, this need. He didn't understand it. Didn't understand this desire. It was bigger than before, fiercer, wild in a way that baffled him, knocking him off balance.

Sex did not confuse him.

Women did not confuse him.

But he was confused now.

Confused by Jemma with the green eyes and soft lips and sweetness that pierced his heart and made him want to please her and protect her, keeping her safe, keeping her from harm's way.

With the water coursing down she lifted her face to his and he couldn't resist her lips. His head dropped, his mouth slanting across hers, hands framing her face.

Beautiful Jemma.

Beautiful woman.

Beautiful heart.

His chest burned. His eyes stung. He leaned in, crowding her, trying to take the upper hand. He was the master here. He was in control. He would prove this was just sex.

He broke off the kiss and turned her around, pressing her breasts to the warm slick marble even as he pulled her bottom toward him. His hand reached between her legs, finding her softness, and heat. He pushed up against her bottom, stroking her, feeling her legs quiver as his body strained against her.

She was so hot, so wet. He wanted to bury himself in her,

wanted to have her surround him, hot and tight, but he was too rough right now, and he couldn't hurt her. Couldn't force her. She'd given him so much earlier, it would be wrong to just take her now—

"I'm waiting," she said, her voice husky, her hips rocking against him. "Stop teasing me. You know I want you."

The sex was hot and Jemma left the shower satisfied, but Mikael did not.

That wasn't right, taking her like that. But was bringing her to the Kasbah in the first place right? He'd kidnapped a foreign woman. Forced her to marry him.

He toweled off slowly, guilt beginning to eat at him, even as a little voice in his head whispered, *you are wrong. This is wrong.*

He didn't like the little voice, didn't want the little voice. The voice represented the past, and weakness. But Karims must be strong. Karims must be above the law.

Mikael spent several hours at his desk on phone calls and in meetings before changing into comfortable clothes to meet Jemma for dinner in the grand courtyard. The pavilions and pools had been lit with sapphire and pink lights.

Jemma wore a long deep blue kaftan with silver and gold embroidery. The inky color of her dress made her green eyes even more brilliant. He sat across from her at dinner to see her, but the table between them meant he couldn't touch her too easily.

Instead he watched her face and her eyes as she talked during their meal. Her green eyes shimmered when she laughed. She laughed easily, her expression dancing.

She was so warm. And good. She deserved good things, and good people.

He was not a good person.

Powerful, yes. Wealthy, exceptionally so. But good? No.

During dessert and coffee he remembered he had a gift for her, and he pulled the velvet box from the pocket in his robe.

"For you," he said, handing her the box.

She looked up at him, dark winged eyebrows lifting higher. "You have to stop."

"Never."

She laughed, eyes dancing. "Fine. I tried. I won't fight you anymore because a gift now and then is rather nice." Then she opened the box, lifted the stunning sapphire earrings out, jaw dropping in awe. "Oh," she whispered, giving one earring a slight shake. "These, my husband, are absolutely stunning."

Mikael's lips curved, and yet on the inside he grew very still.

*My husband*, she'd said. Not sarcastically, or angrily. But kindly. Warmly.

It made his chest tighten and ache. He tried very hard to be a good king, but that didn't make him deserving of a woman like Jemma.

"Be careful," he said to her, leaning across the table and kissing her gently. "Be careful of wolves in sheep's clothing."

She smiled into his eyes as her hand reached up to cup his face. "I know of no sheep. Just wolves. And hawks. And scary desert scorpions and snakes."

He stared into her eyes an extra moment, taking her in, feeling the impact of her beauty and warmth. "I could very well be one of those poisonous scorpions or snakes."

"You could." She rubbed his jaw, fingernails scratching lightly along his stubble before sitting back. "But I don't think so. I've seen who you are. You're a man determined to restore honor to your country, and preserve tradition. You are protective of women, just look at how you've treated me, and provided for my mother."

"Because I failed to provide for mine."

"You're making amends."

"Too late, though, for her."

He rose abruptly from the table, unable to sit another moment, and extended his hand to her. "Come with me."

He led her to the enormous bed in the Sapphire Chamber, and stripped her of her gown and delicate silk bra and thong before kissing her and making love to her. The lovemaking was slow, sensual, lasting for hours.

Satiated, Jemma remained in Mikael's arms. He held her closely and Jemma sighed, feeling secure.

He felt right to her. Being with him felt good. The humiliation and shame of the past year couldn't hurt her when she was in his arms. Damien's rejection no longer mattered. Damien wasn't anything but a lousy model, a spineless man. She smiled to herself, feeling safe…content…loved.

Mikael had somehow made her feel whole again, and strong.

Saidia wasn't home, but Mikael could be. And while he hadn't said words of love, he'd given her something else. His commitment. His promise.

She trusted his word. She cherished his vows because he was a man of his word, and a man who took his commitments seriously.

This, she thought, wrapping her arms over his, this is what she needed. This is who she wanted. This was her future.

In the morning, Jemma woke slowly, feeling deliciously lazy, and deeply rested. Eyes still closed, she let herself breathe and float. At least, it felt as if she were floating. Everything inside her was warmth and light. Easy.

The world was good.

Life was better.

Her lashes fluttered, a butterfly kiss, and she opened her eyes, and saw Mikael lying next to her. She smiled with pleasure. She loved sleeping with him, loved having him there with her all night.

She was quite attracted to this man.

"Good morning, *laeela*," Mikael said, eyes still closed, his voice deep and husky with sleep.

"You're awake," she said, pleased.

"No. I'm still sleeping," he said, his voice still with that lovely gravelly growl she found enormously sexy. "My eyes are shut."

"Then how did you know I was awake?" she asked, amused, propping her head on her hand.

"I could feel you watching me."

"Then you are awake."

He sighed. His beautiful dark eyes opened, and he looked at her, black eyebrow lifting. "*Now* I am."

She grinned. "Hi."

He sighed again, heavily, but his eyes glinted. "Hello."

Jemma laughed softly. He was acting put out but he wasn't really. "How did you sleep?" she asked him.

"Well. And you?"

"Exceedingly well."

"You like our fresh desert air."

"No, I like you. Being held by you." She felt bold, but she didn't care. How could she be shy around him when he made her feel so beautiful and strong? "That's three nights you've stayed with me, all through the night."

"I am committed to your pleasure."

"You most certainly are," she agreed, hiding her smile as she studied his hard, handsome features. Such a striking face. All strong lines and edges and then that soft curve of lip… lower, upper. He was so nice to look at. "I appreciate your commitment."

A deep groove formed next to his mouth. His lips quirked. "You are shameless."

"You've only yourself to blame, Your Highness. You've made me shameless."

He reached out to brush long strands of hair from her brow, gently pushing them back from her face, his thumb easing across her forehead in a soft caress. "Have I? How?"

Just that light touch sent shivers through her, and darts of pleasure to her breasts and between her thighs. Senses stirred, she exhaled slowly, carefully, her thoughts tangling. It was hard to think when Mikael touched her. "How can I feel shame when everything we do together makes me feel wonderful, and powerful?"

"Sex makes you feel powerful?"

She frowned. It didn't sound right, not phrased like that. "I'm sure great sex makes lots of people feel powerful, but I wasn't referring to sex in general, but sex with you." She frowned again. Because that didn't sound right, either. She wasn't having sex with Mikael. She was making love with Mikael. She was loving Mikael.

She was most definitely *in love* with Mikael. She wished she could tell him. Wished she knew how to tell him that the pleasure she felt with him wasn't merely sexual. It wasn't just physical. Her pleasure was in her heart, and soul.

She looked into his eyes, and she flashed back to that first day on the desert dunes when she'd been melting inside the fur coat and high boots. He'd had the same intense expression in his dark eyes and she'd been afraid…

Now she was afraid again, but for a different reason. She couldn't imagine being happy without him.

"Kiss me," she whispered, reaching up to his face, placing her hand against his hard, high cheekbone as she pressed her lips to his. "Possess me. Remind me that I'm your wife and queen."

*His wife and queen.*

Mikael stared blindly out through the glass doors, seeing nothing of his courtyard, and seeing only Jemma's face.

He, who was so good at creating order, structure, and discipline, hadn't planned on falling in love with her. He hadn't planned on wanting her, or needing her, not the way he wanted her and needed her.

He'd married her out of duty and responsibility but suddenly his marriage was one of love. Trust. *Respect.*

He'd known he was growing fond of her these past few days. He'd known he was getting attached, too. It hadn't troubled him. At least, he hadn't let it trouble him. He would only allow himself to think of one thing—doing what was right for Saidia. But now he felt a wash of shame. This was wrong chaining her here, to him. He couldn't trap her in Saidia. He couldn't do it to her. She deserved so much better than this.

Jemma was in her sapphire room, sitting on the floor, painting her toenails when Mikael entered a half hour later.

He didn't knock. But then, he hadn't knocked on the door in days, taking it for granted that her room was his. That she was his. He was right. It hadn't even taken eight days to fall in love with him. She'd given him her heart far earlier...maybe even that first day they'd met, when she'd been modeling on the sand dunes.

He silently watched her paint her pinky toe a foamy mint green. She glanced up at him, smiling. "I remember how much you like the color green."

"I don't remember that at all."

"You said you loved my eyes."

"Yes, your eyes. Not green toenails."

Jemma laughed and dipped the brush into the bottle for more polish. "Are you sure that's what you said? I worry about your memory."

"I worry about you and facts."

She grinned, happy. Ridiculously happy. Everything inside her bubbled up warm, and hopeful. Her heart felt good. Mikael made her feel good. And safe. *Loved.* He might not say the words the way she wanted to hear them, but she felt his love in his actions. She felt his affection and love in the way he touched her, and the warmth and passion with which he kissed her. She saw it in the amusement in his eyes as they talked, teasing, bantering. The fact that he would banter with her, and laugh with her, said it all.

Lips curving, she added a second coat to the pinky toe, before capping the bottle of polish and setting it aside. She tipped her head back to look up into his beautiful face, with those dark, mysterious and oh so sexy eyes. "What can I do for you this beautiful day, my love?"

The hint of amusement died from his eyes, his expression

shuttering, his jaw hardening. It was a subtle shift. Someone else might not have picked up on the change, but she did. Jemma had spent so much time studying him these past eight days that even the narrowing of his eyes didn't go unnoticed.

"There is nothing you need to do. It's all been done," he said.

"It can't *all* be done," she said, noting the change, but trying to tease him. "The Kama Sutra refers to hundreds of positions, and we've only tried—" she scrunched her eyes closed, as if thinking very hard "Four or five?"

"I think you've practiced plenty."

She feigned shock. "You're sick of sex?"

His smile was crooked. "No, but I think we need to get out. Go and do something. I've a picnic packed. Get your suit. We're heading to the beach."

"Camels to the beach? Now that would be interesting."

His mouth quirked, reluctantly amused. "We'll take the helicopter to Truka, and then my car to the beach town of Tagadir."

In the helicopter, on the way to Truka, Mikael explained that the Karim family owned miles of a beautiful private beach in the ancient resort town of Tagadir. There had once been an elegant nineteenth century villa in Tagadir, but the villa had been torn down by Mikael's father who planned to build a new one, but the new one was never constructed. However, the beach was still there, with its soft white sand and beautiful warm water.

They reached the entrance to the Karim estate just after noon, passing through tall black, wrought iron gates. The long driveway toward the water was bordered with blooming hibiscus hedges in pinks and bright corals, but on reaching the end of the drive, right where one would expect to see a grand building, there was nothing but the ruins of a cement foundation, with stone steps leading down to the beach.

The driver delivered the picnic basket and blankets to the beach and then returned to the car. Jemma stood on the last step and surveyed the private cove. A small, but elegant stone pavilion rose from the sand. Otherwise there was nothing. The beach truly was lovely, and private.

After lunch, Mikael and Jemma swam. They dried out on their blanket and then returned to the water to cool off when the sun became too fierce. Mikael was back on the blanket now, watching Jemma float and splash.

Her skin glowed golden after these past few days lounging at the Kasbah pool. The touch of gold in her skin brought out the green of her eyes. In her white bikini she was beyond stunning.

He watched as she waded in, stepping from the surf to wring the water from her long dark hair.

He loved looking at her and talking to her and making love to her. He loved her company and enjoyed her laughter. The laughter was good, and needed. He had a tendency to be silent and stern but she brought out a more playful side in him. He hadn't always been hard.

Loving Jemma had opened him up, softened his heart.

He needed to send her home, back to her family, back to those who loved her and wanted what was best for her like her mother, and Branson, her brother, and the sisters who all adored Jemma.

Mikael wasn't sure that Jemma would understand. He hoped she wouldn't take his decision as a rejection. He wasn't rejecting her, but protecting her.

This was the time he could return her to her people, without shame or stigma. After the eight days and nights, before the official sixteen days of honeymoon ended.

He couldn't wait, either. He didn't want her to become too attached. He didn't want her to confuse lust and love. She was dazzled by pleasure, seduced by endorphins and chemicals. Orgasm tricked women's brains, flooding them with chemicals that made them attach…feel…need.

There was a reason Saidia men made love to their captive brides for eight days without ceasing. The sex, the pleasure, it was a drug. The frequent and intense orgasms helped the woman bond to her man so by the end of the honeymoon, the bride didn't want to leave her groom. The bride had become attached, even addicted to her groom, craving his scent, his touch, his feel, and each coupling would reinforce the attachment, and aid in procreation.

Mikael knew all this. Jemma didn't.

It was time he told her.

She dashed across the hot sand to join him on the blanket. She was laughing as she tumbled down onto the blanket, dripping water on him, making him wet.

"Wicked girl," he said, reaching for her.

She wrinkled her nose at him, making fun of him. His chest grew hot and tight. He had to have her, needed to touch her. He slid his hand into the long damp strands of her hair, the sea making her hair gritty, and he rolled her onto her back, and settled over her, kissing her, drinking her in.

He could taste the salt water on her lips and the cool ocean on her breath and it heated his blood, making him hungry. He deepened the kiss, his tongue parting her lips. Mikael teased her tongue, stroking it, stroking her mouth, delving into it until he felt her shudder and arch against him.

He shifted, and leaned back on the blanket, and drew her on top of him, settling her slim hips between his thighs, so that his arousal pressed thickly against her.

Jemma sighed against his mouth, and he felt her yield to him, her body softening, shaping to his, her lovely full breasts crushed to his chest, her nipples peaked, hard, and he reached around to cup her bottom. She sighed again as he palmed her buttocks, his fingers kneading the smooth muscle. She groaned deep in her throat as he pressed her down against him, rubbing her pelvis against him, feeling her softness cup him. He nearly groaned, too.

She felt so good. He stroked her hips, her rounded bottom, her inner thighs, all while driving his tongue into her, an insistent rhythm that made her writhe helplessly against him, her body trembling in anticipation.

She strained to get even closer, her breath coming faster.

His hands slid up her thighs, until his fingers brushed the fabric of her bikini bottoms. She was hot, wet, and her heat scorched him. He rubbed across her, feeling her softness through the fabric, finding her sensitive spot.

Her eyes widened and she panted. He loved the way she did that…gasp, shudder, pant. She was so beautiful and sensual. He loved that she could forget her inhibitions and lose herself in him. In them.

He caressed her between her thighs again and again, feeling her grow hotter, wetter. She jerked, nerve endings exquisitely sensitized, and flung her head back, her eyes emerald, cheeks flushed. With her dark hair still wet and the halo of sun above them, she looked like a goddess from the sea and he had to have her, now.

He rolled her over onto her back, and tugged her damp bikini bottoms off of her. His thighs parted hers and he sank into the cradle of her hips, nudging her soft folds, eager to be inside her. His tip stroked her smooth, secret places, her creamy heat calling to him, drawing him in.

Mikael entered her with a thrust, slipping deeply inside her tight body.

He loved her the way he knew she liked to be loved—deep, slow, hard—and with his body he tried to say all the things he'd never be able to say in words.

That she mattered too much.

That she was too valuable.

That she deserved so much more than he could give.

# CHAPTER FIFTEEN

JEMMA LAY IN his arms on the blanket in the sand, resting comfortably, happily. There was no place she'd rather be than here, in his arms, against his chest. "What day is this?" she asked, lifting her chin, to look at him.

"I think I've lost count," he said, smoothing her hair back from her brow.

She lifted a brow. "Really? I don't believe that for a minute."

"So what day is it?"

"Day eight. The last day and night of your half of our honeymoon."

She waited for him to say something. He didn't.

"Tonight you are still in control," she added, blushing a little. "But tomorrow I take over. Tomorrow I'm in charge for the next eight days and nights."

She smiled into his eyes, waiting impatiently for him to say something, something warm and sexy. Something encouraging. Something.

But he didn't speak. He just looked at her, his dark eyes somber, expression grave.

Her heart did a funny double beat. Nervous and uncomfortable, she chewed the inside of her lower lip. "You've gone awfully quiet," she murmured.

His jaw shifted, his lids dropping, hooding his eyes. "I have been thinking a great deal about tonight."

"So have I. I think it's time you let me pleasure you."

"I don't think there is going to be a tonight."

Jemma froze. Blinked.

"There is just…today," he added quietly.

For a second she couldn't breathe. She couldn't think. Couldn't do anything at all.

"I married you so you wouldn't have to remain in Haslam under house arrest for seven years. But the eight days are up. I have fulfilled my responsibility as a groom, and I can now return you to London, without losing face."

She still couldn't take it all in. She took his words apart, bit by bit, processing them. Digesting them.

He didn't want an eighth night. He didn't want to be married to her. He intended to put her on a plane for London.

She licked her lips, her mouth dry. Parched. "I'm confused," she whispered.

"I did what needed to be done," he said carefully, after an endless moment, a moment where the silence cut, wounded.

Jemma slowly pulled away, and then scooted away, and sat up. She crossed her legs, hiding herself. "You never intended to keep me as your wife?"

"It's not feasible. Nor realistic. My mother wasn't happy in Saidia. You wouldn't be happy here, not long term. You'd be better marrying an American or a European man. Someone Western with Western thought processes and beliefs."

"So all this time…these eight days and the past seven nights…what was it about? Just sex?"

He shrugged. "Please."

"But you said pleasure could lead to more. You said pleasure could lead to love."

"I was wrong."

She looked at him, then away, trying to ignore the panic in her head and the sickening rush of hurt and pain through her veins.

This wasn't happening, not now. She'd fallen in love with him and she'd given herself to him.

"Why?" she whispered, staring out at the white sandy beach

and the sea beyond. "Why do this to me? Why go through all the motions and seduce me and pleasure me and pretend to care? Pretend to want me?"

"I do care about you. I never had to pretend to want you. I still want you. I still desire you. But I've realized I care too much about you, to trap you here in Saidia. You need more than this desert and my palaces. You need the world you grew up in."

"This isn't about me," she said, interrupting him. "This is about your mother. It's about her relationship with your father, not about you and me." Jemma drew a rough, unsteady breath. "I am not your mother. I am not sheltered. I am not a naive young American girl thinking she's being swept off by Valentino. I've experienced hard things and known tremendous pressure, and public criticism, and personal shame. So don't think for me, and don't make decisions for me, at least, not without consulting me, because, Mikael, I know what I want and need, and I want and need *you*."

"You don't know me."

"I don't know who you were in the past. I never knew you as a boy or a young man, but I know who you are now. You're smart, courageous, honest. *Brave*. You have strong morals and values, and a fierce desire to do the right thing. I love that about you. In fact, I love you."

"You don't love me. You love the pleasure, you love the sensation."

"That's ridiculous!"

"It's not. I've seduced you with pleasure. I bonded you to me with all the hormones from sex and orgasm."

"Stop talking," she said, springing to her feet. "Your words are killing me. They're poisonous. Toxic. Just get rid of me now. Drop me off at the airport. But don't say another awful, hateful word."

He rose, towering over her. "You're being irrational."

"I am? Really? You spent eight days seducing me. Eight days making love to me in every conceivable position, showering me with gifts, assuring me that as your wife I'd be protected, safe, *secure*. Well, your idea of security is very different from mine, Sheikh Karim!"

"I'm sending you home to protect you."

"From what? *Whom*? The paparazzi? The media? The bloodthirsty public? Who are you protecting me from?"

"Me," he ground out, his voice low and hoarse.

She flung her head back, stared into his eyes, furious. "Maybe it's time you let go of the past, and your self-loathing and hatred. Maybe it's time to forgive. Because you are so determined to be fair to your country and your people but, Mikael Karim, you are not fair to yourself, and you're screwing up royally right now. You had me. You had my heart. And you've just thrown it all away."

They didn't speak on the walk back to the car.

They didn't speak, either, as the car traveled the long private driveway lined with hibiscus and palms to the enormous black and gold iron gates that marked the entrance to the Karim family's private beach.

The gates opened and then closed behind them. Jemma turned her head as if to get a last look at the brilliant blue coastline before it disappeared and swiftly wiped away a tear. The sun shone down on the water, and the ocean sparkled. She turned back to face the front, and wiped away another tear, seeing how the red gold sand stretched before them, reminding her of the Kasbah and the Bridal Palace and how Jemma and Mikael had spent the past eight days there.

All the experiences. The sensation. The pleasure. The emotion.

The car picked up speed on the empty highway. There was so little traffic in this part of Saidia that the driver could fly down the black ribbon of asphalt. He did, too.

Mikael stared out the window, lost in thought, and Jemma left him to his thoughts.

One minute all was quiet and the next they were smashed

sideways, slammed off the road in a screech of screaming brakes, screeching metal and shattering glass.

The impact knocked Mikael's car sideways, and the two cars, hit again, and once more, before the red sports car went sailing overhead to land off the road in the sand.

The heavy black sedan spun the opposite direction, until it finally crashed on the other side.

For a moment inside the car there was no sound.

Mikael shook his head, dazed.

"Jemma?" Mikael's hard voice cut through the stillness as he turned toward her.

She lay crumpled against the door, her face turned away from him.

"Jemma," he repeated more urgently, reaching for her, touching the side of her face. It was wet. He looked at his hand. It was covered in blood.

She was flown by helicopter to the royal hospital in Ketama. Mikael traveled with her, holding her hand. Mikael's chauffeur walked away with cuts and bruises like Mikael, while the driver of the other car didn't need a helicopter. He'd died at the scene.

Jemma spent hours in surgery as the doctors set bones and dealt with internal bleeding. She then spent the next few days heavily sedated.

Mikael refused to leave her side. Fortunately, he was the king, and this was the royal hospital named after the Karim family, so no one dared to tell him to leave her, either.

The doctors and specialists had all said she'd be okay. She was simply sedated to help reduce the swelling. She would mend better, and be in less pain, if she were sedated, and resting.

Mikael wanted her to rest, but he needed to know that she was okay.

So for three days he slept next to her bed. Nurses brought

coffee to him. His valet brought him clean clothes daily. Mikael used Jemma's hospital room shower when needed.

He struggled with that last day, the beach trip to Tagadir, her reaction when he told her he was sending her away, and then the silent car ride before the sports car slammed into them.

Was the accident karma?

Was this his fault, again?

He leaned over the bed, gently stroked her cheek, the bit of cheek he could reach between all the bandages. The shattered window had cut her head badly. They'd picked glass out for hours before finally getting the side of her head stitched and stapled closed.

He'd been furious that they shaved part of her hair, but the doctors insisted they had to. Now he just wanted to see her eyes open. He wanted to hear her voice. He needed to apologize and tell her he loved her and it wasn't lack of love that made him send her away, but the need to protect her, and do the right thing for her.

She didn't understand how much she meant to him. She was laughter and light and life.

She was his soul mate.

His other half, his better half. Yes, his queen.

That afternoon on the beach, she'd said hard things to him, but she'd also spoken the truth.

Mikael's battle wasn't with her. His battle was with himself.

He didn't like himself. Didn't love himself. Couldn't imagine her, her of all people, loving him.

And so he was sending her back to a world he wasn't part of, sending her to people who were more deserving.

Mikael closed his eyes, his fist pressed to his forehead, pushing against the thoughts and recriminations, as well as the memories tormenting him.

He should have been a better son to his mother. He should have denounced his father once he realized his father had lied, that his father had broken his promise to his mother. He should have given his mother the assistance, advice, and support she'd needed.

But he hadn't. And she'd died alone, in terrible emotional pain. And he couldn't forgive himself for his part in her suffering.

How could he?

He squeezed his fist tighter, pressed harder against his forehead, disgusted. Heartsick.

She'd be alive now if he'd given her help. She'd be alive if he'd acted when he should have. It would have been easy. Asking forgiveness was not that complicated. It was simply a matter of pride.

His eyes burned and he squeezed them shut, trying to hold the burning tears back. *Forgive me*, he thought, sending a silent prayer up to his mother.

And not that he deserved any help, or protection, but Jemma did. Jemma deserved so much, and maybe his mother could pull a few strings up there. Maybe his mother could do something on Jemma's behalf.

*Help her, Mother. Help my Jemma. Help her heal, if you can.*

And then gently, carefully he lifted Jemma's hands to his lips, pressed a kiss to her skin.

He didn't know how long he sat there, holding her hands, his lips pressed to her skin, but he wouldn't let her go. He refused to let her go. He needed her.

He loved her.

He couldn't be the man he wanted to be without her.

She had to survive and forgive him. She had to survive to be his friend, his lover, his companion. She had to survive so he could make things right with her.

"Forgive me, *laeela*," he whispered, exhausted by the vigil by her side, but not wanting to be anywhere else, either. He wouldn't leave her. Not now. Not ever.

Her eyes fluttered. Mikael sat forward. He stroked her brow, where her delicate, dark eyebrows arched. "Forgive me," he repeated. "I need you to come back. I need you with me."

"Forgive…" Jemma whispered, her eyes fluttering again, and slowly opening. Her brows tugged. Her gaze was unfocused. "Mikael?"

"You're awake."

"Where am I?"

"Ketama. The royal hospital."

"Why?"

"There was an accident." He stood, and gazed down intently into her eyes. "You were hurt."

It seemed hard for her to focus, but otherwise her eyes looked the same, clear and cool and green.

She blinked, and licked her lips, her mouth dry. "Do you have any water?"

"I'll ring the nurse." He pushed the button on the side of the bed. "Do you hurt?"

"A little. Not bad." She frowned. "I don't remember an accident."

"That's all right. You don't need to. It was bad. It's a miracle you're here."

She was silent a long moment. "What day is it?"

"Monday."

"No, what day? Of the eight days?"

He leaned over, kissed her gently on the cheek. "Day eleven, or twelve. I forget. It's been a blur."

"Oh." And then her expression changed, her brows knitting, tightening. "You're sending me home. You don't want me."

"Let's not talk about that right now."

"You don't love me."

"Jemma. *Laeela*," he said roughly, sounding agonized.

She turned her face away from him, closed her eyes. "It's fine. I want to go home. I want to go now."

A knot filled his throat. His chest ached with bottled emotion. "You can't go anywhere until you're better."

She tried to sit up. She winced at the effort.

"Lie down, be still—"

"I won't have you making decisions for me," she interrupted hoarsely. "I won't have you commanding me or dictating to me, because you're just like the others. You're just the same, making promises you never intended to keep—"

"That's not true," he interrupted fiercely, before lowering his voice. "I love you. I do. I don't know how it happened, but it happened. I didn't want a love match, but love found me anyway in you, and the only reason I was sending you home was to give you your freedom and future back."

"But my future is with you! My home is with you. And you, you—" She broke off and squeezed her eyes closed even as tears seeped beneath her lashes. "You don't even care."

"I care," he said, leaning over her, and kissing her carefully on the forehead, between bandages. "I care so much that I only want what's best for you, and I am not sure Saidia is best for you. It wasn't good for my mother. She was lonely here."

"But I'm not your mother," Jemma answered, opening her eyes. "And you're not your father. We can have our own marriage, and we can do it all differently. We can do it right. But you have to believe that, too. You have to fight for us, too."

"I'm fighting," he murmured, stroking her cheek gently, tenderly. She was all bruises, scrapes and stitches and more beautiful than any woman in the world. "I'm fighting for us, fighting for you. I haven't been able to leave your side, afraid that if I left, you'd disappear."

She struggled to smile even as tears fell, slipping from the corners of her eyes. "I'm here."

He smiled down at her, and caught a tear before it slid into her hair. "Yes, you are, my wife, my heart, my queen."

Jemma's lower lip trembled. "You can't ever threaten to send me away again."

"I won't. Not ever. We are going to make this work, and we will have hard days and arguments and hurt feelings, but

I promise you, I am here for you and with you. You and I are meant to be together."

"Not because it's your duty," she whispered.

He smiled. "No, it's not because of duty. We are together because you are my love, and the queen of my heart."

* * * * *

**'I won't let you take my baby, Nadir.' Imogen hated it that her voice rang with fear. 'If that's your plan.' She'd never even considered it before, but now that she had she couldn't push it from her mind.**

He glanced at her impatiently. 'If I wanted that then you couldn't stop me.'

'I could. I'd…' Panic clawed inside her throat. 'I'll…'

'But I *don't* want that.' He made an impatient gesture with his hands. 'I am not so callous that I don't realise a baby needs its mother. That is why I plan to marry you.'

*Marry her!*

She shook her head, biting back a rising sense of hysteria. She needed time to make sense of everything that was happening, and she couldn't because her mind didn't know which way to turn.

'Breathe, Imogen.'

Nadir went to put his hands on her shoulders and she jerked back, wondering how he had got so close to her without her being aware of it.

Imogen shook her head. 'You're crazy to think that I'd marry you after the way you treated me.'

Nadir's mouth thinned and he stepped closer to her, contained anger emanating from every taut line of his body. 'I can assure you that I'm not. This is non-negotiable.'

# ONE NIGHT WITH CONSEQUENCES

*When one night…leads to pregnancy!*

When succumbing to a night of unbridled desire it's impossible to think past the morning after!

But, with the sheets barely settled, that little blue line appears on the pregnancy test and it doesn't take long to realise that one night of white-hot passion has turned into a lifetime of consequences!

Only one question remains:

How do you tell a man you've just met that you're about to share more than just his bed?

Find out in:

*Nine Months to Redeem Him* by Jennie Lucas
January 2015

*Prince Nadir's Secret Heir* by Michelle Conder
March 2015

*Carrying the Greek's Heir* by Sharon Kendrick
April 2015

More stories in the ***One Night with Consequences*** series can be found at millsandboon.co.uk

# PRINCE NADIR'S SECRET HEIR

BY

MICHELLE CONDER

Published in Great Britain 2015
by Mills & Boon, an imprint of Harlequin (UK) Limited,
Eton House, 18-24 Paradise Road, Richmond, Surrey, TW9 1SR



ISBN: 978-0-263-25054-1

Harlequin (UK) Limited's policy is to use papers that are natural, renewable and recyclable products and made from wood grown in sustainable forests. The logging and manufacturing processes conform to the legal environmental regulations of the country of origin.

Printed and bound in Spain
by CPI, Barcelona

With two university degrees and a variety of false career starts under her belt, **Michelle Conder** decided to satisfy her lifelong desire to write and finally found her dream job. She currently lives in Melbourne, Australia, with one super-indulgent husband, three self-indulgent (but exquisite) children, a menagerie of over-indulged pets, and the intention of doing some form of exercise daily. She loves to hear from her readers at www.michelleconder.com

**Books by Michelle Conder**

***Dark, Demanding and Delicious***

*His Last Chance at Redemption*

***Scandal in the Spotlight***

*Girl Behind the Scandalous Reputation*

*The Most Expensive Lie of All*
*Duty at What Cost?*
*Living the Charade*

**Visit the author profile page at millsandboon.co.uk for more titles**

For Pam Austin, who planned the most wonderful holiday while I wrote this book. Meeting you on that train ride to Paris was one of life's little gifts.

And for Paul for always being there.

# CHAPTER ONE

SOME DAYS STARTED out well and stayed that way. Others started out well and rapidly deteriorated.

This day, Nadir Zaman Al-Darkhan, Crown Prince of Bakaan, decided as he stared at a very large and very ugly statue squatting in the corner of his London office, was rapidly sliding towards the latter. 'What the hell is that?'

He glanced over his shoulder at his new PA, who blinked back at him like a newly hatched owl transfixed by a wicked wolf. She'd been recommended by his old PA, whose recently acquired husband had taken offence at the seventeen-hour work-days Nadir habitually kept, and he wasn't sure how she was going to work out.

In general people either treated him with deference or fear. According to his brother, it had something to do with the vibe he gave off. Apparently he emanated an aura of power and ruthless determination that didn't bode well for his personal relationships, which was why he didn't have many. Nadir had merely shrugged when Zach had delivered that piece of news. Personal relationships ranked well down below work, exercise, sex and sleep.

*Not always*, a sneaky voice whispered in his ear and he frowned as that voice conjured up an image of a woman he had once briefly dated over a year ago and had never seen since.

'I believe it's a golden stag, sir,' his PA all but stuttered, definitely falling into the fearful category.

Applying some of that ruthlessness his brother had mentioned, Nadir banished the image of the blonde dancer from his mind and turned back to the statue. He could see it was a stag and he only hoped it hadn't once been alive. 'I got that, Miss Fenton. What I should have said is—what the hell is it doing in my office?'

'It's a gift from the Sultan of Astiv.'

Ah, just what he needed—another gift from some world leader he didn't know, offering commiserations over the death of his father two weeks ago. He'd only been back in Europe a day since the funeral and he was, frankly, tired of the reminders which always brought up the fact that he felt nothing for the man who had sired him.

Annoyed, he strode across to his desk and sat down. His PA stopped in his doorway with her iPad clutched to her chest.

'Tell me, Miss Fenton. Should a person feel badly that their father has just passed away?'

His PA's eyes slowly widened as if he'd just raised a gun to her head. 'I couldn't quite say, sir.'

Meaning she didn't want to say. Which didn't surprise him. It wasn't as if he was known for seeking out the personal opinion of those who worked for him. Not on private matters anyway.

Still, he couldn't quite contain his frustration as his PA shuffled into his office and perched on the edge of an office chair. Between fear and awe he'd go with awe every time but his new PA looked as if she was waiting for him to attack her with a blunt instrument, which could have something to do with the whole host of unwanted emotions and memories his father's death had stirred up in him. He knew a shrink would tell him that was a good thing. As far as Nadir was concerned, long buried emotions and memories were long buried for a very good reason.

'What else have you got for me, Miss Fenton?'

She flashed him a relieved look that he had turned his mind to work. 'Miss Orla Kincaid left a message.'

Nadir already regretted calling up an old mistress to see if she was free for dinner. Earlier, when it had crossed his mind, he'd been bored by a group of business executives who couldn't give away a cold beer to a dying man in the desert let alone convince him to shell out millions to invest in a product they were trying to manufacture on the cheap. 'Let's have it.'

His PA shifted uncomfortably. 'She said—and I quote—"I'm only interested if he's going to take our relationship seriously this time"—unquote.'

Rolling his eyes, Nadir told her to strike that one. 'What else?'

'Your brother rang and wants you to call him ASAP.'

Maybe Zachim had received a giant stag as well. But more likely he wanted to know how Nadir was going with his plan to help haul their Arabic homeland into the twenty-first century. With a spaceship, Nadir thought wryly, or maybe a really big front-end loader. His father had ruled Bakaan with an iron fist and now that he was dead it was supposed to be Nadir's job to lead the country into the future. Something he had no intention of doing.

Years ago he had made a promise to his father that he would never return to rule Bakaan and Nadir always kept his promises. Fortunately, Zachim had been groomed in his stead and had agreed to take on the position as the next King of Bakaan. Poor bastard. 'Get him on the phone.'

'I have other messages,' she said, balancing her iPad with one hand.

'Email them to my palm pilot.'

Moments later his palm pilot beeped right after his landline. His new PA was efficient; he'd give her that at least.

'If you're going to hassle me over the business proposal to reinvent the Bakaani banking system I'd like to remind you that I do have an international business to run,' Nadir grouched good-naturedly. Despite the fact that they were only half-brothers, Zachim was the only person Nadir would call a true friend and they caught up whenever their work paths crossed.

'I wish it was only that.' His brother's tone was grim. 'You need to get back here right away.'

'Ten hours in that place was ten hours too long,' Nadir drawled. Before that he hadn't been back to Bakaan for twenty years and he'd be happy to make it another twenty. The memories his homeland conjured up in him were better left buried and it had been more of a battle to keep them at bay yesterday than he'd be willing to share with anyone. In fact the only way he'd succeeded was to call up images of that exotic dancer and he hadn't much liked thinking about her either. Especially with the way things had ended between them. And here he was thinking about her again. He scrubbed a hand across his freshly shaven jaw.

'Yeah, well, you hotfooted it out of here before you heard the news,' his brother said.

Nadir lounged in his seat with a relaxed feline grace and propped his feet on his desk. 'What news?'

'Father named you the next in line to the throne. You're to be King and you better get your sorry arse back here quick smart. Some of the insurgent mountain tribes are making moves to cause instability in the region and Bakaan needs a show of leadership.'

'Hold up.' Nadir's chair slammed forward as his feet dropped to the floor. 'Father named you the heir.'

'Verbally.' The frustration in Zach's voice was clear. 'It seems that doesn't hold much sway with the council.'

'That's ridiculous.'

'That's what happens when you die of a heart attack without putting the paperwork in order.'

Nadir forced himself to relax and sucked in a deep

breath. 'You know it makes sense that you become the next Sultan. Not only do you run the army but you've lived there most of your life.'

He heard his brother's weary sigh and hoped another lecture wasn't coming about how Nadir was the oldest and how it was his birthright. They'd discussed this ad nauseam for years but it was only yesterday that he'd realised Zach had always believed that he'd one day return to Bakaan and take over. 'I think you're making a mistake but you'll need to officially renounce your position to the council.'

'Fine. I'll send them an email.'

'In person.'

Nadir swore. 'That's ridiculous. This is the twenty-first century.'

'And, as you know, Bakaan is labouring somewhere around the mid-nineteenth.'

Nadir ground his jaw and picked up the stress ball on his desk, tossing it through the basketball hoop set up beside the Matisse on his wall. His father might not have planned to die when he had but he would have known the succession protocol. Was this his way of trying to control him from the grave? If it was, it wouldn't work. Once, when Nadir was a child, they might have had a close relationship but that had ended when Nadir realised how manipulative and self-centred his father was. 'Set it up for tomorrow.'

'Will do.'

He rang off and stared into space. That was what you got for not tying up loose ends at the right time. Twenty years ago he'd left Bakaan after his father had refused to give his mother and twin sister a state funeral after a fatal car accident. They had shamed him, his father had said, when they had tried to flee the country to start a new life. It didn't matter to his father that they had not lived as man and wife for years or that his mother and sister were desperately unhappy with their exiled life in Bakaan. It only mattered that they continued to live where his father had placed them. When Nadir had stood up for their honour his father had basically said it was either his way or the highway.

So Nadir had chosen the highway and his father had disowned him. It was one of his old man's specialities—turning his back on anyone who displeased him—and Nadir had said *sayonara* and left to make his own way in the world. And it had been a relief because it helped him forget the role he'd inadvertently played in his mother and sister's deaths. It was also the last time he'd let his father manipulate him. Nadir had no doubt that not changing his will to reflect Zachim as the next leader had been a deliberate move on his father's part. But he wouldn't win.

Memories surged and Nadir cursed and rocked to his feet. He stared out of the window as a stream of sunlight broke through the clouds, casting a golden hue on the Houses of Parliament. The colour reminded him of Imogen Reid's long silky hair and his mood headed further south as he thought of her once more. She was another loose end he had yet to tie up, but at least with that one he had tried.

Frustrated with the way the day was turning out, Nadir thumbed through the messages his PA had sent to his palm pilot, his eyes snagging on one from his head of security.

A sixth sense—or more a *sick* sense—told him his day was not about to take an upward swing just yet.

'Bjorn.'

'Boss-man.' His head of security spoke in a soft Bostonian drawl. 'You know that woman you asked me to track down fourteen months ago?'

Damn, he'd been right and every muscle in his body tensed. 'Yes.'

'I'm pretty sure we found her. I've just sent through an image to your handheld for you to check.'

Gut churning, Nadir pulled the phone from his ear and watched as the face of the beautiful Australian dancer who had haunted his thoughts for fourteen long months materialised on the screen. Fifteen months ago he'd met her at the Moulin Rouge after he and Zach had found themselves in Paris at the same time.

His brother had claimed he could do with seeing something pretty so they'd headed to the famous dance hall as a lark. Nadir had taken one look at the statuesque dancer with hair the colour of wheat and eyes the colour of a freshly mown lawn on a summer day and four hours later he'd had her up against the wall in his Parisian apartment with her incredible legs tightly wrapped around his lean hips. Then he'd had her on his dining room table, under his shower, and eventually in his bed. Their affair had been as hot as the Bakaani sun in August. Passionate. Intense. *All-consuming.*

He'd never felt such a strong pull to a woman before and even though his brain had warned him to back away he'd still made four consecutive unscheduled weekend trips to Paris just to be with her. Right then he should have known that she was trouble. That their affair was unlikely to end well. Little had he known it would end with him finding out she was pregnant and her claiming the child was his. Little did he know that she would then disappear before he'd have a chance to do anything about it.

Likely she'd disappeared because she *hadn't* been carrying his baby at all but still, the thought that he had fathered a child somewhere out in the world and didn't know about it ate away at him. A flush of heat stole over him. He didn't know what her game had been back then but there was no question that she had played him. He just wanted to know how much—and why. 'That's her. Where is she?' he bit out harshly.

'Turns out she's in London. Been here the whole time.'

'Any sign of a child?'

'None. Should I ask? I'm sitting inside the café she works at now.'

'No.' A welcome shot of rage pumped through Nadir's bloodstream, priming his muscles. It looked as if today was the day he was being given a chance to rid himself of all the irritating issues in his life and now that he thought about it that could only be a positive thing. A faint smile twisted his lips. 'That pleasure will be mine. Text me your location.'

'That guy looking at you is giving me the creeps.'

Tired from lack of sleep due to her teething five-month-old daughter, Imogen stifled a yawn and didn't bother turning towards the back of the room even though she knew who Jenny was referring to. He was giving her the creeps as well and not just because of his hard looks. She recognised him from somewhere but couldn't think where.

She folded a paper napkin at her station at the bar and darted another quick glance outside the café window to see if her housemate Minh had turned up. Her shift had already ended but she'd stayed back to help tidy up until he arrived.

Jenny elbowed her. 'I think he wants to ask you out.'

'It's the blonde hair. He probably thinks I'm easy.' Fifteen months ago she'd had an equally imposing male think the same thing of her but he'd been wearing a three-thousand-dollar suit and had completely charmed her. He'd also been a billionaire playboy with the attention span of a single-celled amoeba. She wasn't so gullible when it came to men now. And, anyway, this guy looked as if he belonged to the secret service or something. Which only made her feel more uneasy. The little retro café where she waitressed didn't usually attract the kind of clientele who required personal security, and she knew that the playboy in the three-thousand-dollar suit used to have his own detail. Was that where she had seen this guy before? With Nadir? It seemed impossible but, before she could dart another quick glance his way, Jenny nudged her.

'No need to worry now. I think I spot your boyfriend outside.'

Heat shot through Imogen's face and her head came up as for a split second she thought Jenny was referring to the playboy she'd never be able to forget, no matter how much she tried.

When she caught sight of Minh waving to her through the café window a whoosh of air left her lungs in relief. Boy, but she was jittery all of a sudden.

'I've never seen him before,' Jenny continued. 'And he looks so gorgeous carrying your little girl in that sling.' She sighed. 'I wish I could meet a man who was a looker and also a caring dad.'

Heart still pumping, Imogen waved to her friend and infant daughter. She guessed Minh was a looker with his exotic Eurasian tanned features and he was certainly one of the nicest men she had ever met in her life but she'd never seen him as anything other than a friend. And not just because he was gay but because Prince Nadir Zaman Al-Darkhan had not only left her with a baby to take care of but he'd also left her with a phobia about falling in love.

Well, maybe not a phobia, exactly. More a deep resolve to never let a man take advantage of her again. Her own father had taken advantage of her mother's inherent goodness and it had devastated Imogen to watch her mother make excuse after excuse as to why her father hardly ever spent any time with them.

'*Your father works so hard, baby girl—he just needs time to relax, that's all.*'

Relaxing with another woman and eventually leaving his wife for her? Imogen would never let that happen to her. If she ever attempted another relationship in the future she'd do so with eyes wide open and it would be on her terms and her terms only. A picture of Nadir's handsome face materialised in her mind and she pushed it away.

'Unfortunately, he's not my boyfriend.' Or her baby's father.

She threw Jenny a smile and wished her a fab Friday night out on the town before heading towards the back of the bar to grab her handbag and head out to meet her makeshift family.

Minh had been a godsend in more ways than one this past year. When she'd discovered she was pregnant her roommate, Minh's sister, had told her that her big brother was heading to America for six months and was looking for someone to housesit. With the lease coming up on their flat in Paris anyway, it had seemed like an opportunity straight out of the heavens and she'd jumped at the opportunity to look after his swanky Knightsbridge pad. But then she probably would have gone to Siberia if it meant getting out of Paris at that time.

With no close family to fall back on in Australia, she'd anticipated having time in London to lie low and sort herself out before the baby arrived. Unfortunately she hadn't reckoned on being so sick she could barely move from Minh's sofa the whole time. When Minh had returned home he'd taken her under his wing and told her she could stay for as long as she needed. He'd even visited her in the hospital right after her precious daughter had come into the world, while no doubt her baby's father had been wining and dining some supermodel on a tropical island or some such.

Imogen grimaced. She'd known about Nadir's reputation as a handsome rebel bad boy from the start and as far as she was concerned you could add irresponsible bastard to that list of seedy qualities as well. And maybe add stupidity to her own because at the time she'd imagined she had fallen in love with him. *Fool.*

To say she owed Minh a lot was an understatement. She especially owed him a chance to have his boyfriend move in with him without her and Nadeena cramping their style and she gratefully accepted the tips the barman passed to her on her way out. In another week or two she should have enough to look for her own place but she knew Minh wouldn't push. He had a heart as big as a mountain.

'Hey, gorgeous,' he said, kissing her cheek. 'How was work?'

'Fine.' She grabbed her smiling daughter out of his arms and planted kisses all over her upturned face. Nadeena stared up at her with Nadir's striking blue-grey eyes and ebony lashes. His smooth olive complexion. 'What have you two been up to?'

'I took her to the park and the outdoor café. I hope she's not smelly,' Minh said as he untied the baby sling. 'It's like holding a hot brick against you in this weather. And they complain London summers are tepid.'

Imogen laughed. 'One twenty-eight-degree day and you English are ready to call it quits. The trouble is that you don't know how to handle the heat.'

Minh gave her a droll look. 'The trouble is we don't *want* to handle it.'

Grinning, Imogen took the sling and slid it over her shoulders and settled Nadeena against her, all her earlier feelings of unease completely gone. She linked her arm through Minh's. 'You know how much I appreciate your help, right? I mean I can't thank you enough for babysitting today. Yesterday.' She made a face. 'Last week.'

'She's a darling child and the dodgy film I'm editing is still in the can. Until they call me back I'm a free man.'

'Don't let David hear you say you're a free man,' she teased.

About to give her some spunky reply, Minh's jaw fell open and nearly hit the pavement. 'Hold that thought,' he breathed in a stage whisper. 'The archangel of heaven has just landed and he's wearing Armani and a terrific scowl.'

Laughing at the theatrics he picked up from working with film stars, Imogen turned and her jaw not only hit the pavement, it continued all the way to Australia.

The ruthless, heartless bastard who had left her pregnant and alone in Paris was heading towards her, his long, loose-limbed strides eating up the pavement and scattering startled pedestrians like a shark mowing down a school of tuna.

Imogen's arms instinctively came up to wrap around a sleepy Nadeena, her mind completely blank.

Nadir stopped directly in front of her. 'Hello, Imogen.' As tall as she was, she still had to tilt her head back to look into his eyes that were currently shielded by aviator sunglasses reflecting her own stunned expression back at her. 'Remember me?'

Imogen was in such a state of shock at seeing him after only just thinking about him so vividly all her addled brain could come up with was how impossibly good-looking he was in his black suit. How tousled his midnight hair looked—no doubt from where he had run his fingers through it a hundred times already. Her own immediately itched to do the same thing and she curled them into the soft fabric of Nadeena's sling, disconcerted by the immediate and compelling effect he still had on her.

'I…of course.'

She swallowed heavily as his eyes dropped to Nadeena. The glint from his sunglasses made him look like a steely-eyed predator eyeing succulent prey. 'You had the baby.'

Something in the way he said that in his deep, smooth baritone that defied geographical distinction made the hairs stand up on the back of Imogen's neck.

It was the underlying anger, she decided. Maybe even fury. And for the life of her she couldn't imagine why he should be so upset. *He* had left *her* fourteen months ago so didn't that mean she had the jump on anger right now? Unfortunately all she could conjure up was paralysed shock.

Sensing her unease, Minh shifted defensively beside her and Imogen took a deep breath, rallying her scattered senses. 'Yes.' She cleared her throat.

'That's nice.' Nadir's smile was all even white teeth and completely lethal. Then he slowly drew off his sunglasses and his shockingly beautiful blue-grey eyes drilled into hers with all the warmth of a glacier. 'Who's the father?'

# CHAPTER TWO

*WHO'S THE FATHER?*

Imogen stared at Nadir, slowly digesting his snarled words. She'd only heard him use that tone once before and it was on the phone to some poor sod in his home country and the shock of it kick-started her brain into a usable gear. Steadying her trembling knees, she forced a smile to her lips and thought that of course he would want to know about the baby. Why wouldn't he? It was his doctor, after all, who had confirmed her pregnancy that fateful night in his Paris apartment all those months ago.

God, if she'd only left work five minutes earlier or later this whole situation might have been avoided. She swallowed heavily and forced herself to meet his hard stare, his raised eyebrow that could make him look either wickedly seductive or incredibly foreboding. Today it was definitely foreboding, which didn't help to explain the electrodes of excitement pulsing through her body, making her both shivery and hot at the same time.

No, not *excitement*, she corrected; it was *adrenaline*. Her fight or flight system was on overload; her reaction could hardly be considered excitement after the way he had treated her. The reminder of that helped calm her down and she gave him a tight smile, a deep sense of self-preservation warning her not to answer his question just yet. 'It's a surprise to see you like this.'

'I'm sure it is, *habibi*. Now answer my question.'

Swallowing heavily, she raised her chin. He used to whisper that term of endearment to her when he was about to seduce her and God, she wished it wasn't such an effort to hold those erotic memories of their fleeting time together at bay but it was. 'Why do you ask?'

'Don't play games with me, Imogen. I'm not in the mood.'

A ripple of unease slid down her spine and Minh, obviously sensing Nadir's ire as much as she could, half stepped in front of her. 'Ease up there, chief. There's no need to be aggressive.'

Nadir slowly turned his razor-sharp gaze to Minh and, although Minh didn't flinch, Imogen did. Unfortunately Minh had no idea that the infamous rebel prince was Nadeena's father. Imogen hadn't told anyone.

'And you are?' Nadir's question came out as if he'd just asked Minh if he had any last requests.

'Imogen's friend.'

'I suggest you back off, *Imogen's friend*.' Nadir's lip curled into a sneer. 'This is not your business.' Then he turned the full force of his attention back to her and Imogen really wished that he hadn't. 'Well?'

How could he make one word sound so powerful?

'Sorry, but I don't like your attitude, chief.' Minh puffed out his chest and Imogen groaned. 'You need to dial it down a little.'

'It's okay, Minh.' She gave his arm a squeeze, only just realising that her arm was still linked with his. 'I know him.'

Nadir pinned her with a patronising look. 'That's putting it mildly, *habibi*.'

His meaning was clear and Imogen felt a flush rise up her neck.

'I don't like him,' Minh said softly.

Neither did she but she drew on all her training as a performer and gave him a smile worthy of an award. 'It's okay. Really. Why don't you head home? I can take care of this.'

'You're sure?' Minh looked dubious.

'She just said she was, didn't she?'

Imogen only just managed to prevent Minh from trying to stand up to Nadir again and patted a sleepy Nadeena, who had grown restless. 'Go. Really. We'll be fine.'

'Call me if you need me,' Minh ordered, reluctantly heading towards Green Park tube station.

As soon as he was out of sight she let out a relieved breath. One hardcore male was better than two, wasn't it?

Reluctantly turning back, she calmed her breathing and faced Nadir. 'What's this about, Nadir?'

'What do you think?'

She tried to pull off a nonchalant shrug but her movements felt stiff and disjointed. He'd walked away from her fourteen months ago so she had no idea. 'If I knew I wouldn't ask,' she countered, slightly annoyed herself now.

His silvery gaze transmitted how unimpressed he was with her response. 'How old is she?'

'How do you know she's a she?' Imogen hedged.

'I don't think it's customary to dress a boy in a pink sunhat.'

'Maybe I'm just bucking the trend.'

His hissed breath held a wealth of reaching-the-end-of-his-tether impatience. 'How. Old. Is. She?'

Completely unprepared for both his anger and his relentless questioning, Imogen was at a loss as to how to follow the advice of her inner voice that warned her to tread cautiously and found herself blurting out the truth. 'Five months.'

He rocked back on his heels, his hands going to his waist and pushing his jacket back to reveal his broad chest. 'Then our affair did result in a child.'

*Their affair?* Talk about clarifying how he had felt about her back then… 'I didn't say that,' she retorted forcefully.

The words came out rushed and his eyebrows shot up. 'Then you *were* sleeping with someone else while we were together.' His voice held the tenor of a wounded bull, which didn't impress her at all.

'Trust you to take that line of thinking,' she said scathingly, remembering how he had basically accused her of the same thing their last night together in Paris. 'And it's none of your business.'

'If she's not mine then whose is she?' His gaze once again narrowed in on Nadeena.

'Mine,' she countered evenly.

Nadir's lips turned up into a snarl. 'Do you really think you can fob me off with semantics?'

Imogen felt a dull pain tweak behind her right eyebrow. After the way he had treated the news of her pregnancy, she wanted to know his current motivation before blurting out any more home truths. 'Look, Nadir—'

He said something in Arabic, cutting her off, and stepped closer to her, his wide shoulders blocking out all the natural light behind him. Imogen felt the cool glass of the shop window at her back and briefly closed her eyes to try and steady her racing heartbeat, only to snap them open again when Nadir's voice sounded way too close to her ear. 'Dammit, you're not going to faint, are you?'

*Faint? Faint?* She stared up at him and then darted her eyes to the side. No, she wasn't going to faint. But she did want to run. Fast.

'Uh-uh.' As if reading her thoughts, Nadir shook his head. 'You're not going to run again, Imogen, my sweet.'

*Again?* What was he talking about—*again?*

'I have no idea what you're talking about but I really need to go. I'm working another shift tonight.'

His eyes narrowed. 'Just so we're clear, *habibi*,' he

grated silkily, 'I have not searched for you for the past fourteen months to be given the runaround now.'

Imogen immediately felt hot and cold and then hot again and, just like the first time she had laid eyes on him, all the oxygen went out of the air—something that had almost been disastrous at the time as she'd been in the middle of performing the can-can in front of a full house. She'd noticed Nadir watching her almost straight away. He'd been sitting at a small front table with his brother—she'd later found out—but she had only had eyes for Nadir. And he for her, right up until the moment he'd found out she was *enceinte*.

As if sensing her distress, Nadeena stirred and shifted against her chest and Imogen tried to calm her nerves, if for no other reason than to keep Nadeena asleep.

Her first priority was to keep her daughter safe.

Secure.

Not that she expected Nadir to hurt her physically. No, what she feared was his power to hurt her emotionally, which was often much worse because most bruises healed while mental scars remained for ever. Imogen knew because she had spent many years trying, and failing, to win her father's love and she wasn't about to condemn Nadeena to the same fate.

A picture of the secret service type in the café came to her on a rush just as she caught sight of him standing a little way off to the side. Had Nadir been looking for her all this time? It seemed impossible.

Her troubled eyes flew to Nadir and her ripple of unease ratcheted up to dread. 'Fourteen months? What are you talking about?'

Noting the deep groove between Imogen's beautiful green eyes, Nadir instantly regretted his emotionally ragged outburst. What he needed to be right now was cool and controlled. Finding her with a child strapped to her body challenged that considerably. As did her evasive attitude, which implied that she had something to hide.

'We will not discuss this any further on the street,' he decided. Apart from the fact that Imogen looked uncomfortably hot, it was also far too public a place for this type of discussion. 'Come.'

'No.'

Haughty as ever, Nadir noted as he turned back to her. He'd been attracted to that regal aspect of her nature when they'd met. Now the trait annoyed him. As did her wide-eyed ingénue look.

Back when he'd first noticed her she'd seemed different from the other women who had adorned his life from time to time. Less artificial. More sincere. More genuine. Hell, he could laugh at that now. Imogen Reid had turned out to be as genuine as a whore with a hundred euros in her hand.

He glanced at the baby sleeping in her arms. Everything inside him said that she was his child and he wondered how much longer Imogen would have waited before turning up 'ta-da' style on his doorstep and demanding maintenance payments worthy of a queen. Not that it mattered. *He* had found *her* and that definitely gave him the upper hand.

And it mattered even less that her complexion had leached of all colour. These past months of not knowing if she had given birth to the child she had claimed was his, if she was okay, if the baby was okay, hell, if either one of them was even *alive* had eaten away at him. When she'd sent him a text telling him she had 'taken care of everything' he'd assumed she'd terminated the pregnancy. He'd felt sick at the thought but then knowing he'd got her pregnant in the first place hadn't exactly made him feel like dancing around a room.

Fatherhood wasn't something he'd ever contemplated before. Now it seemed that the fates had other ideas and if this woman had kept his child from him…deliberately… Callously…

He glanced at her. He didn't think he could like a person less if he tried.

'Nadir, please, if I…' She moistened her lips with the tip of her tongue. 'If I tell you that you're the father can we just leave it at that? Can we just…can we just part as friends?'

Nadir reeled. Was she serious? Because she couldn't possibly expect him to walk away from her after basically admitting the child was his with little more than *Have a nice life*. In fact, if he discovered that this child really was his then he wouldn't be walking away at all.

He stared down at her and noticed she had the look of a frightened mouse that had just been caught in a very large inescapable trap.

*Apt*, he thought—*very apt*. From the minute he'd laid eyes on her, his first instinct had been primal. He'd wanted to wrap her up and keep her. He'd wanted to brand her as his own. Disconcertingly, that urge was just as strong as ever.

He tugged on the collar of his shirt. Somehow, in the time between meeting her and now, he had lost his equilibrium and he wanted it back. Not even the thought of having to renounce the throne tomorrow affected him as deeply. Or maybe it was the combination of the two. 'I don't think you could have ever called us *friends*, Imogen.' Bed partners. Lovers. Now those fitted. Friends, not so much.

She looked up at him as if he'd just kicked a puppy. 'Good to know,' she said flatly, her ponytail swinging around her shoulders as she made to move past him. 'Frankly, I don't know why you're even here.'

It was supposed to be her parting shot but Nadir moved so that once again he was directly in front of her.

'Come now, *habibi*. I know you're smarter than that.'

'Look, Nadir, the stand-over tactics are very intimidating. Well done you. But you can't stop me from walking away.'

He blew out a frustrated breath. 'If you'd cooperate and tell me what I want to know I wouldn't need to use any *tactics*. Now, my car is waiting at the corner.' He arched his arm towards a low-slung black beast of a Mercedes. 'Shall we?'

'No,' she bit out, 'we shall not. Not until I understand what this is about.'

The line between her brows reappeared as she stared at him and a pulse point beat frantically in the base of her throat. A pulse point he still had an inexplicable urge to cover with his lips. His tongue.

He muttered an old Arabian curse and realised what he'd just done. What was it about this woman that made him unconsciously regress to his native language? *By Allah…* He cursed again. Jerked his eyes back to hers. 'What this is about,' he began with a calmness that belied the heated blood pounding through his veins, 'is that it looks very much like you had my child and didn't tell me.'

If possible, the line between her brows deepened and he had the stupidest notion to place the pad of his finger against it and smooth it away. 'What's her name?' he asked gruffly.

Emerald eyes darkened almost to black before dropping from his. 'This is pointless, Nadir.' Her soft, desperate plea fell between them as insignificant as one of her gauzy dance costumes and he savoured the defeat in it.

'Pointless for you, perhaps,' he agreed pleasantly.

A soft moan broke from her lips and his body registered it as one she used to make in bed and it appalled him that he could be so angry one minute and so aroused the next. It was those damned memories of having her spread out naked on his bed that were the problem.

During his more unguarded moments those memories

crept up on him like the flu and reminded him that once—once—he had thought he'd found something special with a woman.

A low growl filled the base of his throat. This, he would have said, was not an unguarded moment and yet his control over his body felt tenuous, tangled up in the silken awareness of the female in front of him, who was dressed in nothing more provocative than denim jeans and a red T-shirt.

'Please, Nadir…'

'Please what, Imogen?' he rasped, hating the sound of his name on her treacherous lips and welcoming another shot of anger as it jetted through him. 'Please forgive you for keeping the birth of my child from me? Because she is mine, isn't she?'

He didn't know if it was his words or his tone that brought her chin up but her beautiful eyes glittered angrily. 'I did not keep her birth from you. You knew I was pregnant and you didn't want anything to do with her.'

Her voice had grown shrill and a couple of shoppers hesitated before passing them by.

'I don't think so. Now come.'

'You didn't even believe it was your baby. God,' she exclaimed, 'can't you just forget that we ever saw each other again?'

'Like you want to?'

She didn't answer, to her credit, which was just as well because his control was heading in the same direction as his day. 'Tell me,' he began silkily. 'Do you believe in fate, Imogen?'

'No.'

'Then you'll just have to put this meeting down to luck, won't you?'

She glared at him and pulled her bottom lip between her teeth, which meant she was thinking hard. Not that it mattered. He stepped closer to her, inhaling her wonderful, sweet scent that was somehow the same and yet different. He swallowed against a sudden rush of conscience. He had nothing to feel guilty about here. 'You're coming with me,' he said quietly. 'Even if I have to put you into that car myself.'

Her brows shot up at that. 'Not even you would do something so heinous.'

Nadir gave a sharp bark of laughter. If only she knew how close he was to doing *exactly* that.

'Then what are you afraid of, *habibi*?'

'I'm not afraid. I'm confused,' she said with bald honesty. 'What do you want?'

'To talk.' He had a lot of questions to clear up; not least of all was how she had hidden herself away so effectively his security team hadn't been able to find her until now. And then there was the small matter that he wanted to be a part of his child's life. A permanent part. But he had no doubt she'd welcome that. It would mean money and status and he hadn't met many people who wouldn't put that ahead of integrity and self-respect.

# CHAPTER THREE

IMOGEN SLICKED HER tongue across her dry lips, her heart pounding towards a heart attack as Nadir led her towards the car.

*To talk*, he said. But was that really what he wanted? And why was he so angry with her about Nadeena?

Every instinct in her body warned her that she shouldn't go with him but really she wasn't afraid of Nadir. And, despite his hostile manner, it wasn't as if he would want to have anything to do with Nadeena in the long run.

In truth, he probably just wanted to make sure she wasn't going to go to the press with news of his indiscretion. Her stomach turned. That was the most likely scenario here. That and to ensure that she wasn't going to make any financial demands on him in the future. Maybe he'd even offer to set up a trust fund for Nadeena. If he did, she wouldn't take it. She would provide for her daughter herself. Nadeena need never know that her father hadn't loved her enough to want her in his life.

Unable to stop herself, her eyes ran over his face. He was still the most ruggedly attractive man she had ever laid eyes on, with thick black hair that fell in long layers, olive skin and an aquiline nose that perfectly offset a square jaw that always looked as if it was in need of a shave. And his mouth. Surely that had been fashioned by Ishtar because it could look either surly or sexy depending on his mood.

Currently, he wasn't in a good one. But okay, she would

be rational. Talk to him. Answer his banal questions. Reassure him that she wanted nothing from him. 'Fine. I can give you a few minutes.'

He didn't answer and warning bells clanged loudly inside her head again as the car door was smoothly opened by a burly chauffer. Then a waft of deliciously cool air hit her and she bent her head and manoeuvred inside as best she could with Nadeena still strapped to her chest.

'Wouldn't you be better taking that thing off?'

His gruff question came from the opposite seat and Imogen momentarily lost her train of thought as his masculine scent enveloped her. 'That *thing* is a sling and no, I can't. Not without waking her.'

'So wake her.'

'Not a good idea. Don't you know you should never wake a sleeping baby?'

His slight hesitation was loaded. 'How would I?'

Cold censure laced every word and she had to force her eyes to remain connected to his. Nadeena really did have his eyes, she thought absurdly. Lucky her. 'So I'm here.' She let out a pent-up breath. 'So talk.'

'This is not a conversation for a limousine.' Nadir made a motion with his hand and said something in rapid-fire… Italian? Greek? Before Imogen knew it, the car was in motion.

'Wait. Where are we going?'

Nadir's eyes snagged with hers and the heat from his gaze made her go still all over. His eyes drifted over her face with insolent slowness and sexual awareness turned her mouth as dry as dust.

Determined not to be so weakened by him again that she turned into a puppet on a string, she forced air in and out of her lungs in a steady stream. But the act took up every ounce of her concentration so when he informed her that they were going to his apartment it took longer than it should have for his words to take hold.

'Your apartment? No.' She shook her head. 'You've misunderstood me. I meant a few minutes *here*. In the car. And it's illegal to drive with an infant not strapped into a proper baby carrier.'

Nadir leaned forward and spoke to his driver again and instantly the big car slowed.

'My apartment is close by. And it is you who has misunderstood me, Imogen. We have to talk and a few minutes isn't even going to cover the first topic.'

Imogen narrowed her eyes. 'I don't see why. I did what you wanted fourteen months ago and disappeared from your sight so I don't understand what you want with me now.'

His sculptured lips thinned into a grim line. 'You did disappear, I'll give you that. And you still haven't told me her name.'

*Her name?* Imogen lowered her gaze to the safety of her daughter's head. No way could she reveal her name. No way did she want to see this man who had once meant so much to her mock her for her sentimentality. Maybe even pity her. At the time she'd named her she'd been feeling particularly sorry for herself and hopelessly alone. The three-day blues they called the come down from the emotional high some women experienced after giving birth. Now she wished she'd named her Meredith or Jessica—or any name other than the one she had.

Fortunately the car pulled up at the kerb before she had to answer and, feeling sick, she followed Nadir as he strode through the large foyer of his building with a bronzed water feature at one end and a smartly dressed concierge at the other.

'When did you move to London?' she asked, suddenly

wondering if they had been living in the same city the whole time.

'I didn't.' He stabbed at the button to call the lift and she remembered that of course he had apartments in most of the major financial centres in the world.

Casting a quick glance around his beautifully appointed living room, she inwardly shook her head at the absurd difference in their lifestyles. Of course she'd known that he was wealthy when she'd met him—her fellow dancers had informed her as to whom he was—but, apart from his outrageously divine apartment on the Île Saint-Louis, their time together had been incredibly normal. Nights in bed, mornings at the local patisserie, afternoons strolling or jogging along the Seine. More time in bed.

Shaking off the rush of memories, she headed straight for a set of plush sofas and laid Nadeena on one. Glancing back at Nadir, she asked him to hand her the baby bag he'd carried up and checked Nadeena's nappy while he stood beside her.

Of course Nadeena went quiet in that moment. Her big, curious eyes riveted to Nadir, as most other females were when they first clapped eyes on him. She blinked as if trying to clear her vision and a small frown formed between her round silvery-blue eyes.

'She has my eyes,' he said hoarsely.

The sense of awe in his voice was hard to miss and an unexpected swell of emotions surged inside Imogen's chest. Emotions that were so twisted together they were too difficult to define.

'Here you go, little one.' She lifted Nadeena into her arms and settled her back in the crook of her shoulder, silently willing her not to complain. Then she glanced at Nadir. 'I need to feed her.'

Nadir waved his hand negligently. 'Go ahead.'

Imogen moistened her lips. 'I'd like some privacy.'

He paused and Imogen was sure her cheeks turned scarlet.

'You breastfeed?'

Even though she had breastfed in cafés and parks and not blinked an eye before, this moment, in a quiet living room with a man she had once believed she had fallen in love with felt far too intimate. His continued perusal sent another frisson of unwelcome awareness zipping through her. 'Yes.'

She knew her voice sounded husky and when her eyes met his she couldn't hold his stare. What was she doing here in this room with him? More importantly, what was he doing in this room with her and Nadeena? She felt self-conscious and it was all too easy to remember how it felt to have him at her breast, drawing her aching nipple deep into his mouth. All too easy to recall the pleasure that had turned her into an incoherent puppet for him to master at his will.

When she continued to hesitate and Nadeena grew restless Nadir pivoted on his foot and stalked to the long windows overlooking some sort of dense green park that most likely belonged to him as well. Imogen quickly arranged her T-shirt and Nadeena latched on like a baby that had never fed before.

'When were you going to tell me I had fathered a child, Imogen?' His quiet question held a wealth of judgement and loathing behind it and Imogen felt as if someone had just dropped an icy blanket around her shoulders.

She didn't look at him. She couldn't because all of a sudden she felt horribly guilty about the fact that she had never intended to tell him. And hot on the heels of her unexpected guilt rode anger. Anger she welcomed with open arms. *He* was the one who had run away when he'd learned she was pregnant, not *her*. *He* was the one who had made it clear that he didn't want a baby in his life when she had felt such a rush of elation at the time she had almost grinned at him like a loon. Then she'd seen his stricken face and her world had fallen apart.

A sound like a low growl came from deep in Nadir's throat and he towered over her. 'Never? Is that the word that is at this moment stuck in your throat, *habibi*?'

'Don't call me that,' Imogen growled back, unable to contain her rioting emotions.

'It's preferable to what I want to call you, believe me.'

Imogen had never seen Nadir angry before and he was magnificent with it. Fierce and proud and so *powerful*.

She swallowed, hating that she still found him so utterly attractive. 'How dare you come over like the injured party in this scenario?' she snapped. She was the one who had been as sick as a dog carrying Nadeena. She was the one who had been all alone in the birthing suite as Nadeena had come into the world. She was the one who struggled day to day with the demands of motherhood and putting food in their mouths. And she had asked for nothing from him. Absolutely nothing. 'I have done very well for myself since you left my life,' she said, her body vibrating with tension. 'I have survived very well on my own. I've eked out a life for myself and Nadeena is healthy. She's happy and—'

'Nadeena?'

Imogen's eyes squeezed shut and her temper deflated when he repeated the baby's name. His irreverent tone somehow made her remember how lonely she had felt when Nadir had walked away from her. She'd felt lonely before, of course, but with Nadir she had felt as if she had got a glimpse—a *taste*—of paradise, only to have it snatched away when she was least prepared.

Powerful memories surged again and she couldn't look at him. 'Why am I here, Nadir?'

He didn't say anything, his eyes troubled as they made contact with her own. He leant against the cherry wood dining table, his gaze riveted to Nadeena, kneading her T-shirt like a contented cat, his silence drawing out the moment. Drawing out her nerves until they lay just beneath the fine layer of her skin like freshly tuned guitar strings. 'Why is there no public record of her birth?'

Bewildered by both the flat tenor of his voice and the unexpected question, Imogen frowned. 'There is.'

His gaze sharpened and she could see his agile mind turning. 'Under what name?'

Imogen stared at him. At the time of Nadeena's birth she had only put her own name down on the birth certificate. She hadn't known what to put in place of the father's and a kindly registrar had told her that it wasn't essential information. That she could fill that part out later. So far, that section was still blank because she'd been so busy and so tired learning how to care for an infant she hadn't even thought about putting Nadir's name on it. Sensing that this was a loaded question, she raised her chin. 'Mine.'

'Imogen Reid.'

His earlier words—*'I have not searched for you for the past fourteen months to be given the runaround now'*—and his personal bodyguard waiting for his arrival came back to her and clicked into place in her mind and confused her even more. 'Benson.'

There was only the briefest of pauses before he roared, 'You gave me a false name!'

Imogen pressed back against the seat of the sofa. 'No.' Well, not intentionally. 'Reid was my mother's maiden name and…' She swallowed, hating herself for explaining but compelled to do so by the fury she read in his eyes. 'It wasn't deliberate. The girls suggested that I use a stage name because they sometimes had trouble with the clientele and you only asked me my name one time.' She took a quick breath. 'At the beginning.'

He stabbed a hand through his hair and paced across the

room like an animal trapped in a too-narrow cage. 'And your mobile phone number?'

'What about it?'

'You changed it.'

'I lost it…well, it was stolen my first day in London. I just use a pay-as-you-go now.'

He swore under his breath, a ferocious sound.

'What's this about, Nadir? As I recall you were the one who left town the morning after you found out I was pregnant. Are you now saying you tried to contact me?' She tried to stifle a small thrill inside, wondering if perhaps he had been worried about her. That perhaps he had cared for her after all… Another more skeptical voice reminded her of the horrible text he'd sent her but still some deeply buried hope wriggled its way to the surface.

'I had an emergency in New York and by the time I got back to Paris you had disappeared as if you'd never existed,' Nadir grated. 'The Ottoman Empire would have benefited from your stealth.'

Resenting his sarcasm, she stiffened. 'I did not disappear. I left.'

'Without a trace. No one had any idea where you had gone.'

That was most likely because the only person who knew had been Minh's sister, Caro, and she had been leaving to go travelling at the same time. Imogen had meant to keep in touch with some of the other girls but she hadn't counted on feeling sick and sorry for herself during her pregnancy and she hadn't had time since then.

'Nor did you give your employer a forwarding address or email.'

'I didn't?' She blinked. 'I wasn't exactly thinking straight at the time.' And since her pay went directly into her bank account, she hadn't even realised. 'I'm surprised you didn't check my bank records.'

His look said that he had. 'False names tend to hinder that kind of search.'

'I told you that wasn't deliberate.' She took a deep breath and tried to keep a lid on her emotions so she could think rationally. 'Why were you looking for me, anyway?'

'Because before you ran you were supposedly pregnant with my child.'

'I did not *run*,' she bit out tensely. 'Why would I when you had made it abundantly clear you didn't want anything to do with me any more?'

She heard the challenge in her voice and knew it was because some part of her was hoping he would refute her statement.

'I texted you from New York.'

Her top lip curled with distaste. That horrible text was still etched into her brain as if it had been carved there. 'Oh, please,' she scoffed, 'let's not talk about your lovely text.'

'Or your response,' he grated. 'Telling me that you had *taken care of everything*.'

Imogen tossed her ponytail over her shoulder, careful not to awaken Nadeena, who had dropped into another exhausted sleep. 'I did take care of it,' she said softly, her arms tightening around Nadeena.

'Yes, but not in the way I expected.'

*Hoped*, his tone seemed to imply. And there was the reason he'd been looking for her. He'd wanted to make sure she'd done what he expected.

Imogen felt that small spark of hope that she'd been wrong about him completely wither and die and she felt angry with herself for succumbing to it in the first place. Had she not learned anything from his treatment of her in the past?

Caro's words of warning came back to her. *'Be careful, Imogen. Any man who takes off like that without a word and accuses you of sleeping around is likely to insist on an abortion if he ever comes back.'* At the time Imogen had thought her friend had been overreacting. Now she knew that she hadn't been and she felt physically ill.

'And now you'll have to deal with the consequences,' he grated, staring at her as if she was somehow to blame for everything that was wrong in the world.

# CHAPTER FOUR

IMOGEN LAPSED INTO a horrified silence, focusing on her daughter instead of the sick feeling swirling in the pit of her stomach.

Quite honestly she had never expected to see Nadir again and she really wished she hadn't. But at least he'd well and truly put paid to those times she'd wondered if she shouldn't contact him and let him know that his child had been born. Put paid to those silly girlish fantasies that he would one day ride in on a big white horse and offer her undying love.

Yeah, right. Probably she'd listened to way too many love songs while she had been incapacitated on Minh's sofa and possibly watched way too much day time TV.

But at least that whole time hadn't been a complete waste. She'd used it to plan out her and her baby's future and decided to follow a long-held dream and teach dance. She'd even taken a short online business course. She had a vision that when she had enough money she and Nadeena would move to a mid-sized town where she could open a studio. Nadeena would rush home after school and if she wanted to she could dance; if not, she could sit and do homework or read. Then they would go home together and chat while Imogen cooked dinner and at night…at night… she hadn't really thought about the nights. Her imagination had only gone so far as to envision her and Nadeena as a tight-knit unit.

The two of them happy and contented.

And when Nadeena asked about her father, as she surely would one day, Imogen hadn't quite worked out what she was going to tell her. She didn't want to lie to her but nor did she want Nadeena to know that her father had never wanted her. She glanced at Nadir standing by the window, his broad back to her as if he couldn't stand to look at her. Well, that was fine with her. She couldn't stand to look at him either.

Careful not to waken Nadeena, she eased herself off the sofa, not as easy as it looked since it was one of those squishy ones designed for long afternoons lazing about, and cradled Nadeena in her arms.

Hearing her, Nadir turned towards her and she hastily pulled her T-shirt back into place.

'Where do you think you're going?'

Imogen raised her chin at his surly tone. 'Home.'

'To that buffoon you were with earlier?'

It took her a beat to realise he was referring to Minh but she wasn't about to get into another lengthy discussion with him and, although it was illogical, her gut warned her that if she answered his question honestly he'd never let her leave. And that was exactly what she was about to do. 'You have no right to ask me that. But I am curious as to why you brought me up here. It seems like a waste of your time and mine.'

His eyes held hers and he continued as if she hadn't spoken. 'Is he your current lover?'

Chilled, Imogen cuddled Nadeena closer. 'You answer my questions and I'll answer yours.'

'I'm sorry.' Nadir's voice, his stance—heck, his very demeanour—had turned alert with predatory intent. 'Did you assume you were in a position to bargain with me?'

Imogen rubbed the space between her eyes, her arms starting to ache from holding Nadeena.

'What I assumed,' she said as she laid her daughter on the sofa and fixed cushions around her, 'was that you weren't interested in anything about me and what I do, or where I live.'

'You are the mother of my child,' he said as if that answered everything.

And then she remembered why she was here and could have laughed at her own stupidity. This wasn't about some romantic reunion of past lovers. This was about a man with self-preservation on his mind. 'We've already established that you don't care about that.'

'I care.'

Imogen curled her lip. What he meant was that he cared about how much cash she was going to hit him up for.

'I get it,' she said tonelessly. 'And while I think it's incredibly selfish of you not to want to provide for your own flesh and blood you'll no doubt be relieved to know that I don't want anything from you and I never will.'

'Excuse me?'

'Nor do I expect that you will want to see her and that's more than okay with me as well.'

He started to laugh and she felt even more disgusted with him. 'I don't see what's so amusing. It's a travesty if you really think about it too much. Which I try not to do.'

'You're serious.'

'I certainly don't think abandoning your own child is something to laugh about, but maybe that's just me.'

'Except I didn't abandon her—you took her.'

'Are we back to that again?'

His eyebrow rose. 'Did we ever leave it?'

'I want to go home, Nadir.'

'That's not possible,' he said briskly. 'I should have already left for Bakaan by now.'

*His homeland?*

'Please don't let me stop you.'

One corner of his mouth quirked in a parody of a smile. 'I don't intend to. But unfortunately we have run out of time to get things you might need from your house. If you write me a list I'll make sure you have everything on hand when we arrive. We shouldn't be gone long. A day at the most.'

Imogen blinked. 'We?'

'That's what I said.'

'You must be mad.'

He pulled his phone out of his pocket and started dialling as if he hadn't heard her.

'Nadir, what are you doing?'

He looked up at her. 'Claiming what is mine.'

Imogen waited a beat before responding. Waited for the punchline. When he stared back with all the confidence of a man used to getting his own way she felt dizzy.

'I am not yours and I never was!'

He raised an eyebrow. 'I meant Nadeena.'

*Sanctimonious bastard.*

Embarrassed at her gaffe, Imogen hauled the baby bag over her shoulder. 'Didn't you just hear me? I said I don't want anything from you.'

'I heard you.'

She shook her head. 'I'm going.'

Before she had time to reach Nadeena, Nadir abandoned his call and yanked the bag off her shoulder, spinning her around to face him. 'You've stolen the first five months of my daughter's life from me.' His voice seemed to harden with every word even though its tenor didn't change. 'You won't be stealing any more.'

*Stolen?* Imogen's knees started to shake and the sense of dread from earlier returned with force. 'I haven't stolen anything. And how do you know she's even really yours?'

A grim smile crooked the corner of his mouth. 'She has my eyes.'

'Lots of people have silvery-blue eyes,' she said on a rush. 'They're as common as mice.' Rats.

One dark eyebrow rose. 'You gave her an Arabic name.'

'Nadeena was a great-aunt of mine.'

'And you're proving to be a terrible liar. Which is in your favour.'

'I don't understand this at all.' She threw her arms up in front of her. 'You don't even want children. Why would you want us to go with you?'

He widened his stance and her eyes couldn't help but notice his strong legs and lean torso. God, did he have to be quite so damned virile?

'How do you know that?'

Gossip, mainly. She lifted her chin and focused on his hard face, which wasn't much better. 'Well, do you?' she asked coolly.

'I'd say that's a moot point now, wouldn't you?'

'No, I most definitely would not. I'd say it's very relevant considering the way you're behaving.'

'Sometimes, Imogen, life throws us curve balls but that doesn't mean we have to drop them. I don't need a DNA test to confirm that I have a child.'

Frustration made her voice sharper than usual. 'Of course you need to do a DNA test. What kind of crazy talk is that? No rich man in his right mind would take on a child as his own without doing a DNA test.'

Nadir laughed and this time it rang with genuine amusement. 'You always were just that little bit different from the pack, *habibi*.' His voice, so gentle and deep, brought a rush of memories back into her dizzy brain. 'But you need not worry. I plan to do my duty by her.'

*His duty?*

A sense of terror entered her heart. Was that what he meant by saying he'd be claiming what was his? She didn't want to know. Not right now. 'I don't need you to do the right thing by Nadeena.' She'd been looking out for herself for a long time now and she could look out for her child as well.

Nadir raked an impatient hand through his hair. 'Nevertheless, I will.' His striking eyes narrowed. 'Now quit arguing and give me a list of things you will need for our flight to Bakaan.'

Striving for calm, Imogen tried to slow down her heart that was banging away inside her chest so loudly he must surely be able to hear it. Right now she felt as if she was trying to survive a fierce gale that was corralling her towards the edge of a very high cliff. Then a horrible thought froze the blood inside her veins. 'I won't let you take my baby, Nadir.' She hated that her voice rang with fear. 'If that's your plan.' She'd never even considered it before but now that she had she couldn't push it from her mind.

He glanced at her impatiently. 'If I wanted that then you couldn't stop me.'

'I could. I'd…' Panic clawed inside her throat. 'I'll…'

'But I don't want that.' He made an impatient gesture with his hands. 'I am not so callous that I don't realise that a baby needs its mother. That is why I plan to marry you.'

*Marry her!*

She shook her head, biting back a rising sense of hysteria. She needed time to make sense of everything that was happening and she couldn't because her mind didn't know which way to turn.

'Breathe, Imogen.' Nadir went to put his hands on her shoulders and she jerked back, wondering how he had got so close to her without her being aware of it.

Imogen shook her head, fear spiking inside her like a flash of lightning. 'You're crazy to think that I'd marry you after the way you treated me.'

Nadir's mouth thinned and he stepped closer to her, contained anger emanating from every taut line of his body. 'I can assure you that I'm not. I've had a lot of time to review my options while you were in hiding and this is non-negotiable.'

Imogen tried to still the trembling inside her body. 'I was not hiding.'

'It's irrelevant now.'

She laughed. What else could she do? 'You can't just come back into my life and think you can do whatever you want.' Her father had behaved that way. Coming and going as he pleased with little concern for either her or her mother. As if she'd shackle her and her daughter to a man cut from the same cloth. 'I'll fight you.'

'What with?' She hadn't realised that her hands had balled into tight white fists until Nadir's mocking gaze drew hers to them. He reached out and raised them in front of her, enclosing them inside his much larger grip. 'With these, hmm? I have to confess that, as aggressive as you can be in bed, I didn't take you for the violent type.'

She wouldn't have before today either. 'Nadir, we had an affair,' she cried, throwing his earlier words back in his face and tugging at his implacable hold. 'We only had sex a…a…a couple of times.'

He resisted her feeble attempts to break free with embarrassing ease and hauled her closer. 'Let's see,' he said with a snarl. 'Four weekends, around three times a day, more at night.' His eyes dropped to her mouth and lingered before returning to hers. 'You don't have to be Einstein to know that comes to more than *a couple of times*, *habibi*. And it was good sex.'

His words and his tone combined to set off a wildfire reaction inside her body.

'It meant nothing,' she choked out, still trying to free her hands from within the prison of his. Wishing that his grip was hurting her to distract her from the riot of sensations being this close to him was setting off inside her.

She couldn't seem to focus her thoughts when she became enshrouded in his earthy male scent, the sensitive tips of her breasts rising against the lace of her bra and the deep achy feeling between her thighs reminding her of how it had once been between them.

'Nothing?' His soft question had a lethal undertone that had her raising her eyes to his, but she only reached his mouth, which seemed so close to her own that if she held still long enough she was sure she could feel his breath against her lips. 'Nothing, Imogen? I don't think so.'

'I'll get a lawyer,' she said breathlessly, yanking harder on her hands, only to find that they were now trapped against his hard chest.

He laughed. 'From what I know of your finances, you can't afford a decent babysitter.'

'Bastard!'

His eyes bored holes into hers. 'And what court of law is going to side with a mother who kept a child's existence from its father? Who leaves her baby with friends while she works?'

'Lots of mothers do that.'

'Yes, but lots of mothers do not have a child of royal blood. Nadeena is a Bakaani princess.'

'I don't think of her like that.'

'Right.'

'I don't!' she exclaimed at his cynical tone. 'She's just an innocent baby to me, not a commodity. And no court in the world would favour a father who thinks like that.'

Nadir arched a brow. 'You're not that naïve, surely.'

'Nadir, stop this, I beg you.'

'Do you?'

She flushed, remembering the last time she'd said those words to him. It might as well have been five minutes ago for the response of her body. The feeling of being helpless beneath him, her hands held above her head as he'd nudged her thighs wider with his knees, the feel of his silken hardness at that first moment he pushed himself inside her body, that feeling of her softness giving way to all that male strength in inexorable pleasure.

Her body clenched and mortification filled her. She tried to twist away from him now but somehow that only made her more aware of the press of his hips, forcing the hard ridge of his erection into her belly.

*Erection!*

Imogen's eyes flew to his. 'No.'

He gave a hollow laugh. 'Oh, yes, Imogen, you still turn me on,' he said thickly. 'Despite your treachery.'

His head descended towards hers and she shoved against his chest. She didn't want him—not again. He'd accused her of sleeping with someone else while seeing him—had probably done so himself while he was seeing her—he'd thought they were having an affair that he'd had no trouble ending while she had nearly died inside when he'd walked away from her. She didn't want him. She couldn't!

But she did and none of that mattered to her wounded heart when his lips touched hers in a searing kiss that narrowed the time they had been apart to nothing. Still, she attempted to resist him, clamping her lips into a straight line that, in the end, was no defence at all.

Certainly no defence against her own raging need to touch him and be touched by him and when he took advantage of her confusion and drove his tongue into her mouth Imogen was lost. He just felt too good, tasted too good, and it had been so long for her. So long since she had felt the press of a man's lips. The press of *his* lips.

All of a sudden she was no longer pushing him away, but drawing him closer. Her hands flattening over the hard muscles of his chest to snake up around his neck, her mouth moving beneath his in an age-old request for more.

And he gave it to her. Eagerly. Impatiently. Thrusting his tongue into her mouth and drinking in her very essence.

His other hand came up to cup her jaw, holding her steady. A low groan, more like the growl of a hungry wolf, worked its way out of his throat as he angled his mouth over hers and ravaged her lips as if he was as desperate for her as she was for him.

Nothing else seemed to matter in that moment. The room disappeared. The world. It was just the two of them. As it always had been when they'd come together. Like magic.

'Nadir,' she whispered, shuddering against him as his strong fingers followed the line of her spine, spanning her waist before dropping lower to cup her bottom and bring her even closer. Unbearably close. Imogen squirmed and forked her hands into his hair to anchor herself to him, one leg already rising to rest over his lean hip.

And then suddenly she was free and he had stepped back from her, reaching out to steady her as she stumbled without his body weight to hold her up. 'It seems I still turn you on as well, hmm, *habibi*?'

*What?*

Dazed, she blinked up at him and then his condescending words hit her and she was instantly appalled at her behaviour.

Had he just kissed her to prove a point? To prove how weak she was when it came to him? To prove how much power he still had over her? Her face flamed and she was so angry she wanted to punch him.

Realising just how close she was to hitting someone for the first time in her life, she lowered her bunched fists to her sides. 'Don't ever touch me again.' *Was she hyperventilating?* She placed a hand against her chest. It felt as if she was hyperventilating. 'I hate you, Nadir. I *really* hate you.'

'Don't be stupid about this, Imogen,' he rasped, pulling

his phone from his pocket again. 'You can't provide everything our daughter needs and I want her to grow up secure.'

'I want that too. Which is why I would *never* marry you.'

From the stiffening of his spine she could see that he didn't like that. 'Be serious,' she continued desperately, trying to appeal to his rational side. 'You never *wanted* Nadeena.'

'I may not have *planned* Nadeena.' His expression grew fierce. 'But she is here and this is the best solution.'

Imogen's nostrils flared as if she was a lioness sensing danger. Nadeena's emotional welfare was on the line and Imogen had vowed a long time ago that she would rather be a single mother than have her child raised by a parent who didn't want her. Especially the autocratic tyrant Nadir had turned into. But then maybe he had always been that way. She had never challenged him before, had she? 'This is the *worst* solution.'

Nadir put the phone to his ear. 'Bjorn, tell Vince we'll be at the airport within the hour.'

He rang off and Imogen felt icy-cold with dread. 'You selfish bastard,' she raged raggedly. 'You won't even consider my needs.'

'Actually, I would say I was considering them very well.'

'Ha!' she scorned. 'You're nothing but a bully.'

His eyes flashed a warning she was in no mood to heed. 'Careful, Imogen. I will only tolerate so much from you.'

'Like I care,' she fumed, restless energy making her muscles vibrate. 'You can't do this, you know. I have rights.'

She stared at him as if she really knew what she was talking about but inside she was quaking. Not that she'd let him see that. The stakes were far too high for him to think that he had the upper hand. For him to assume that she was a pushover.

'What you have,' he said in a carefully modulated tone, his face a cold mask, 'is my child.'

A discreet knock at the door interrupted the stark silence that followed that statement and Nadir turned to answer it.

'And Imogen?' She glanced at him, hoping he was about to tell her this had all been a joke. 'You *will* marry me.'

It was a great parting shot, she thought as she sagged against the arm of the sofa and speared wishful daggers into his broad back. But she would have the last word because she would never marry a man she didn't love.

## CHAPTER FIVE

THE PLANE TOOK off into the air and Nadir wondered if he needed to have his head examined for bringing Imogen and Nadeena to Bakaan with him.

He could have easily had Bjorn or any one of his men watch her. And what was with the announcement that he was going to marry her?

He scowled. He hadn't intended to blurt it out like that but hell, that woman could make him do things he'd never intended to do. She always could.

Back in Paris it had been her coy smiles to get him to play tourist or to laze around reading the Sunday papers over brunch. Who had time for that, anyway? Not him. And the fact that he'd done it still rankled.

He'd been so overcome with lust back then he'd let her call the shots. He wouldn't do that again. Not that he was planning to be an asshole about it. He wasn't. But nor was he going to be hoodwinked by her nice girl persona either. Hoodwinked by her innocent sexuality.

No. She'd run once. He wouldn't give her the chance to do it again.

Still, he could have waited until he returned tomorrow afternoon before revealing his plan and he had no ready answer as to why he hadn't.

Probably he'd still been shocked from finding her with his child. That had to be it. He gulped down a mouthful of water from the bottle his staff had handed him upon boarding. He noticed that Imogen hadn't accepted one and he frowned.

She hadn't said boo to him since they'd left his apartment and that was fine with him. All except for the way she made him feel that she was being some sort of martyr in coming with him. And why would she be?

It didn't make sense. Was she still playing him in some way? Acting hard to get to whet his appetite? Not that it had worked. That kiss… He scrubbed a hand across his face, gulped down more water. He hadn't meant to kiss her before, let alone back her against the wall. And he didn't like to admit that he'd got lost in that kiss. Only the fact that she had as well had salved his pride.

Damn, but she tasted sweet. Exactly as he'd remembered. Even now his body throbbed with an inexplicable urge to have her. It was like a driving need. All-consuming. It had always bothered him. The extent of his need. Needing people led to emotional weakness, which led to mistakes being made. He knew that better than anyone and yet fifteen months ago he'd let himself be drawn into her silken web anyway.

Of its own accord, his mind returned to the Sunday afternoon he had found out she was pregnant—an extraordinary blue-sky summer day in Paris. Not wanting to think about his later flight home to New York, they had wandered around Paname—as the Parisians affectionately called their city. He had shown Imogen some of his favourite haunts and she'd dragged him around what felt like every flea market in the known universe. That was where he'd learned she adored Aubergine Provençal and that she was a hoarder of ancient postcards and scarves. The afternoon had ended with her vomiting over his toilet bowl and a doctor announcing her condition with a happy flourish that had floored him.

And okay, he hadn't taken the news that well. What contented bachelor would? So he'd flown back to New York and called his thousand-dollar-an-hour lawyer.

'First, establish the kid is yours.'

When Nadir had told him that was going to be a nine-month wait, his lawyer had shaken his head. 'Not so,' he'd said. 'Modern medicine has moved right along. There's a test, see. It's called some amnio thing. I had to arrange one for a client a few months back. Boy, was he relieved when the results came back negative. The lady had been sleeping around. Tried to pin him with someone else's kid.'

His lawyer had *tsk*ed in disgust and Nadir had murmured some agreement. Asking Imogen to take the test had made sense. So he'd texted her with the request. Perfectly reasonable in his view.

Finding her gone without a trace when he'd flown back to Paris hadn't been reasonable at all.

A dream he'd often had over the last fourteen months winged into his consciousness. It had always been about a child of indiscriminate gender. But the eyes had always been emerald-green and ringed with brown curly lashes. Usually the baby then became the woman, which was when he usually woke up. Usually sweating. Usually cursing.

He thought about her claim that she hadn't run away from him. The different surname. His gut tightened. Was he being played for a fool? And what was up with the buffoon who had tried to defend her? The one who had trod off like a trained seal at her bidding.

Seeing Imogen with her arm linked through his, that sweet smile on her face that could fell an army of warriors…another screw in his gut turned.

She lived with him. He knew that and the water turned sour in his mouth. He'd nearly decked the guy when he'd tried to keep him from her. As if he'd had a chance. On some level he knew his reaction wasn't logical, but logic had never been his firm friend when she was around.

He glanced over as she laughed at something Nadeena had done. He had always loved her laugh. Deep and throaty and redolent of all the pent-up passion of her personality. She had laughed a lot when they had been together. Laughed and teased him as no one else ever had. And she had done it right away, something he'd found as sexy as hell. As sexy as he found her now in faded denims and a simple cotton T-shirt. As sexy as he found her—

*Breathing?* a mocking voice in his head suggested.

*No,* Nadir silently snarled back.

And why was he even thinking like this? Brooding over things he couldn't change wouldn't make this whole situation any easier. It didn't matter that he had never met a woman who affected him as strongly—or as quickly—as Imogen. It didn't matter that she made him angry or frustrated or horny or hell—guilty. What mattered was that they get married and make the best of the situation.

What mattered was that he was a father.

*A father.*

Hell. The thought rocked him. But he knew it was true. He had known the minute the kid had looked up at him with his twin sister's soulful eyes staring back at him. His eyes. And Imogen had given her an Arabic name as if she'd been racked with guilt over knowing she was never going to tell him about his child. Anger rolled through his blood, thick and renewed, and he recalled how she'd called him a bully. Did she just expect him to give up on his daughter without a fight? Whether she liked it or not, he had a hundred options up his sleeve. And he didn't give a damn how Imogen felt about that because he wanted his daughter.

He had wanted Nadeena—truly wanted her—from the moment he had looked at her with her chubby hands fisted on Imogen's soft breast and her wide eyes staring up at him as if she was trying to learn everything about him, as if she was looking directly into his soul. He swallowed heavily. He'd taken one look at her and he'd been…he'd been smitten.

It had been the same the first time he had looked at Imogen and felt that his life would never be the same again.

Hell. What was he thinking?

His life hadn't changed when he'd first laid eyes on Imogen. They had only been having an affair.

No, his life had changed when she had become pregnant with his baby. And now hers was about to change and he had no doubt that she would acquiesce when she got down from her high horse and realised how much he could provide for her. He nearly laughed. As if she hadn't already thought of that.

But that was okay. He could live with her wanting him for his money. It would be a small price to pay to know that his daughter was safe and well.

He signalled the hostess waiting to serve them. This was going to be okay.

'Yes, sir.'

'Coffee, please and…' he glanced at Imogen '…food for Miss Reid—Benson. I haven't noticed her eating anything yet.'

'Miss Benson said she's not hungry, sir.'

Nadir checked out the thin outline of her once curvy body. 'Give her something anyway. Have the chef cook up Aubergine Provençal.'

'I'm sorry, sir. What was that?'

*Yeah, what* was *that?* He scowled. 'An omelette, then. Something. Anything. Just as long as it's vegetarian.'

'Of course, sir.'

Nadir flipped open his laptop, determined to focus on work for the rest of the trip. Once he renounced the throne tomorrow and married Imogen his life could get back to normal. Or as normal as it would be with a wife and a child and why didn't that notion bother him half as much as it had fourteen months ago?

*Marriage?*

The word clunked around in Imogen's brain for the millionth time like a giant-sized anvil and she hoped to God Nadir was at this very minute coming to his senses and seeing how ridiculous the idea was.

*The best solution...*

Of course there were other solutions, and she'd looked some up on her phone as she'd waited for his plane to take off. Not that she wanted to head down the shared custody route and she was sure—once he had calmed down and thought rationally—that neither would he. What rich playboy would? Especially once he learned how detrimental having a child would be to his bachelor lifestyle and she had every intention of pointing it out to him. Because, although she didn't think those things, she knew that once the reality of parenthood set in Nadir would never take his responsibilities seriously. Not with his reputation as a serial dater. No, he wasn't the faithful type and she'd been serious when she'd told him she wouldn't marry him.

And he couldn't force her. No one could do that in this day and age. The worst he could do was to take her to court and fight for custody of Nadeena. And that was… She swallowed heavily, her eyes darting across the aisle to where he was ensconced in work. Could he win? Would a court of law side with his sob story that she had run away with Nadeena?

Not that she had run; she'd simply taken charge of her life. Taken charge without him in it. And he hadn't wanted to be in it. Or at least that was the message she had taken from his acerbic text.

She still remembered with embarrassing clarity the

burst of happiness she had felt when it had pinged into her phone. It had sat there for a full five minutes before she had clicked on it and by then her heart had constructed a full-on fairy tale around what it would say. She had imagined that the text would confirm that he'd had time to think about things and he missed her. That he wanted her in his life. That he wanted their baby. In fact the foolishly sentimental organ in her body had imagined every possible thing he could have written except for what he had.

Imogen, there is a DNA test that can be done while the child is in utero. I have organised an appointment for you at a specialist. If the child is mine I will be in contact.

Devastated by his callousness and influenced by Caro's dire warnings, Imogen had left. And really, what had been the alternative? To write back to him and plead? *Are you sure you don't want our baby? Are you sure you don't want me?* She did have *some* pride.

A delicious smell wafted into the cabin and Imogen's stomach growled as a flight attendant stopped beside her.

'The chef has prepared an omelette for you, Miss Benson. It's vegetarian.'

'Oh.' How had the chef known she was vegetarian? 'I'm sorry. I didn't order this.'

'Prince Nadir ordered it for you.'

Imogen glanced across at the man she was trying hard to think about rationally. Objectively. Something that was almost impossible, given his startling demands and that kiss…

Kiss? She felt a blush heat her cheeks. That kiss had shattered her equilibrium. As had her response. Given his hateful, overbearing behaviour, she'd like to have been left cold when he had touched her. She'd like to have been able to say she was over her sexual infatuation for him and was completely unmoved. She'd also like to be able to say there was no poverty or no ugly wars in the world either.

She sighed and rubbed the back of her neck. It didn't make sense that he could still make her heart jump just by looking at her and her body throb for more with one touch. How could a man who was a veritable stranger and who totally disregarded her needs and desires still affect her so intensely?

He shouldn't be able to. That was the logical answer. Back in Paris, yes. Back then her mother had just died and her absent father had remarried a month later and Imogen had been looking for a change. She'd been looking for excitement and adventure. She'd been looking for passion.

She pulled a rueful face.

Maybe this was just a case of being careful what you wished for.

Because she'd got it, hadn't she. The excitement. The adventure. The *passion.* She'd got it in the form of a man who had awakened a hunger in her she hadn't even realised she'd possessed and who had given her a child. The child she loved. The child she could deal with. The man not so much. Especially not when he kissed her. When he touched her.

So she'd just have to be ready the next time and make sure he didn't get that close. And maybe he wouldn't try and touch her again because, although he had been as aroused as she had been, he hadn't wanted to desire her any more than she did him.

She watched her daughter stacking wooden blocks together on the floor in front of her and tried not to feel so anxious. She had to trust that even now Nadir was reconsidering his outrageous proposition—because surely no one would call 'You *will* marry me' a proposal. That even now he was trying to come up with a way to bow out of it gracefully.

And if he wasn't, well, Imogen had a plan. She would sit down with him over a cup of tea and she would go over all the information she had downloaded in a calm and rational manner. She'd point out, in the nicest possible way, that if his actions were motivated by some sort of guilt—or attack of conscience—then he could rest easy because she didn't need him in her life and she certainly didn't want to trap him.

She smiled. That word ought to put the fear of God into him. No man wanted to feel trapped, did they?

'Ma'am? Did you want the omelette?'

Yes, yes, she did. She just didn't want to have anything to do with the man who had ordered it for her. But that wasn't the hostess's fault and Imogen smiled up at her. 'Yes. Thank you.'

Her upbeat thoughts lasted right up until they landed and Imogen found herself in a small airport that made Tullamarine look like LAX. For some reason she'd thought Bakaan would be like Dubai—or the pictures she'd seen of Dubai. It wasn't. But, even so, it was immediately apparent from the few people milling around in traditional garments and the warm dry air that smelled faintly of vanilla and spice that she had entered an ancient realm full of mystique and promise. Much like her impression of Nadir had been that first night.

A shudder ran through her as the car raced through the night dark city and headed up an incline that led to an impressive well-lit palace that sat just above the ancient city like a golden mirage. As much as she hated to admit it, she was a little unsettled and a lot intimidated by the formality of the palace and the very real sense that she was the one who was trapped instead of Nadir.

'My Lord, it is so good to see you again.'

Imogen looked past Nadir to where a small white-haired servant in white robes knelt on the polished stone steps of the palace, his sombre tone increasing Imogen's sense of unease.

'Staph—' Nadir pulled the old servant to his feet '—I told you not to do that the other day.'

*He'd been here recently?*

The servant's mouth quirked but the solemn note didn't leave his voice. 'We are glad of your return, My Lord.'

'I wish I was.' He switched to Arabic then and the old man bowed at her feet and beamed at her, speaking in rapid-fire Bakaani. She smiled hesitantly, wondering what it was that Nadir had just told him.

'My Lord, Mistress Imogen, Princess Nadeena.'

Shocked at the label he had given her, Imogen shook her head. 'I am not his mistress,' she corrected a little more sharply than she'd intended. Had Nadir told him she was?

The little man dropped to his knees again and started spouting effusively in Bakaani but there was no smile this time.

Confused, Imogen shot Nadir a helpless glance and he sighed. 'Staph meant you no discourtesy, Imogen. The word does not mean the same in our country as it does in the West.'

'Oh, well…please tell him to get up. The ground must be really hard on his knees.'

She felt awful and smiled warmly at the man to show him she hadn't meant to hurt his feelings. 'I'm sorry, I—'

'Leave it, Imogen.'

Nadir's face softened as his eyes fell on his daughter, half asleep in her arms. 'Do you want me to take her?'

'No!' Nadir had offered to take her as they had boarded his plane earlier but she hadn't been ready for that. She still wasn't, even though her reluctance made her feel totally selfish. There was just too much unfinished business between them. 'No. I've got her.'

His eyes narrowed but he didn't push and she was grateful. 'Come then. I will show you to our suite.'

*Their suite?*

She hurried after him.

'I hope you know I'm not sleeping with you!'

Nadir turned halfway up the steps and the servant cast her a worried look.

Shaking his head, Nadir lowered his voice so he wouldn't be overheard. 'Bakaan is a conservative country, Imogen, and Staph does understand some English. Please keep your discussions about our situation private.'

'I just want you to know that I'm not sleeping in the same bed as you in case you need to organise another room for us,' she half whispered.

'There are many bedrooms in the suite we will be using.'

'Well, good.' She felt her cheeks redden when she realised that he'd just confirmed her earlier suspicion that he didn't want to sleep with her any more than she wanted to sleep with him.

*Or any more than she wanted to want to sleep with him*, she amended to herself. 'At least we're on the same page about that.'

The look he gave her was a mixture of exasperation and something darker that she couldn't define. 'Imogen, I doubt at this point that we're even in the same book, let alone on the same page. But the steps of the Shomar Palace are not the place to discuss it.'

Silently agreeing, Imogen followed him through a wide doorway into an atrium with high coved ceilings and delicate mosaic-covered walls. The champagne marble tiles that lined the floors and the ornate brickwork dated back to what she thought might be the Moorish period, the surrounding artwork and centuries-old statues recording a history that was both dark and wondrous.

'Has Prince Zachim been notified of our arrival?'

'Yes, My Lord. Will you be needing anything else?'

'Not tonight. Thank you, Staph.'

The man nodded. 'I will bid you goodnight then.' His English was stilted but Imogen appreciated the effort. 'And may I say congratulations, My Lady.'

This time Imogen waited for the servant to retreat before questioning Nadir. 'What is he congratulating me for, exactly?'

'Our marriage. This is your room.' He opened one of the doors inside and waited for her to precede him.

Imogen didn't move, incredulous that Nadir would say such a thing when she had not agreed. 'You told him we were getting married after I distinctly told you we wouldn't be?'

'Not exactly.'

'What does "not exactly" mean?'

'It means he believes we are already married.'

Imogen's brows rose to her hairline. 'I hope you relieved him of that erroneous view,' she said primly.

When he sighed she knew that he hadn't. 'As I said, Bakaan is a conservative nation.'

'You lied to him. That's why he bowed at my feet.'

'I didn't lie. He assumed we were married.'

'And you let him believe it.'

Nadir's eyes flashed his frustration. 'It was better than the alternative.'

'What? That I was your mistress and had your baby out of wedlock?'

A muscle ticked in his jaw. 'You might not care how Nadeena is perceived in the future, but I do.'

'Of course I care. You're just twisting my words to suit yourself but as soon as I see that man again I'm going to correct him.'

'No, you won't. I won't have Nadeena's name smeared because you can't see reason.'

'I can't see reason?' So much for her hope that he would use the time on the plane to reconsider his proposition.

He stopped directly in front of her. 'And, to all intents and purposes, we are married.'

Imogen coughed out a protest. 'We most certainly are not.'

'Signing a piece of paper isn't going to make it any more real, Imogen. You're going to have to get over whatever reservations you have and get used to it. But we can talk about this later, hmm? It is not a conversation we should be having in front of our daughter.'

'She doesn't understand,' Imogen snapped, fuming because she knew he was right and she should have thought of the same thing herself. Because, although Nadeena couldn't understand their words, she was soaking up the heightened emotions in the room and that wasn't good.

Sweeping past Nadir, she gasped as she entered a beautifully appointed bedroom with vast ceilings and long ornate keyhole-shaped windows lined with pale floaty curtains. Deep pink fabric was draped over the elaborate king-sized bed but, other than that, the furnishings wouldn't have been out of place in any five-star hotel. A freshly made up cot stood beside the bed.

'I thought you might like to keep Nadeena close.'

She hadn't expected him to show her that level of thoughtfulness.

'Thank you,' she said stiltedly, rubbing her arms against the chill in the air. 'Is it usually so cold?'

'Always.'

Startled by the gravity of his tone, Imogen stared across at him. His hands were shoved into his pockets and the hard planes of his face seemed even more austere, the grimness of his expression making her think he was talking about more than just the air temperature.

'I'll have the thermostat adjusted. Get some sleep. You look tired.'

Excellent. She looked exactly how she felt.

'I have organised clothing and baby-related items for you which should be through the dressing room. If there's anything the staff has missed just let me know.'

'How could you arrange this so quickly?'

'Bakaan might be somewhat of a backwater compared to the Western world, but it does have retail outlets. And Dubai is an hour away by plane. Anything we didn't have they would have.'

'It seems you've thought of everything.'

His eyes were shuttered as he looked at her. 'Let's hope so.'

With a brief glance at Nadeena, who was wide awake and taking in her new surroundings with open curiosity, Nadir left and closed the door softly behind him.

So civilised, she thought, feeling anything but civilised herself.

'Okay, baby girl. What now?'

Deciding to check out the items Nadir had supplied in the dressing room, she was shocked when she saw just how much he had bought.

She lay Nadeena on her tummy on the floor, watching as she slowly pulled herself towards a row of shoe boxes. Curious herself, Imogen lifted the lid on the first box and gasped at the sight of an exquisite pair of designer shoes nestled amongst the tissue paper. They were her size and she wondered how he had known and then she remembered the day he had taken her shopping in Paris. Did he still remember? Probably not. Probably, it had just been a good guess. He did know women, after all.

Not wanting to dwell on that disagreeable topic, she next checked the clothing hanging on the rack. Most of them were Western, with a few traditional-looking dresses amongst them.

There were more clothes on the hangers than in her own wardrobe and she felt uneasy at why he would have supplied so many. Not that she'd wear them. But she would need to change Nadeena and she couldn't suppress her delight at each of the baby outfits his staff had provided. Gorgeous soft cottons and silks, the like of which she hadn't been able to afford herself.

'All this for one day,' she said to Nadeena. 'The man has clearly never had to work to a realistic budget in his life.'

Nadeena answered with a litany of ga-ga noises and upended a box of shoes. Saving the shoes and confiscating the tissue paper, Imogen let her have the empty box, which she immediately started banging on the floor.

Feeling suddenly weary and lost, she changed Nadeena into a soft cotton sleeping suit and fed her. Then she laid her in the cot and grimaced when she saw how wired she was. Sleep looked like a long time coming. Deciding it would be a waste of energy to try to sing her to sleep, she rang Minh instead.

'I was beginning to get worried when I didn't hear from you after your brief text. How are you? How's our darling girl?' he asked.

'Nadeena is fine.' She'd particularly enjoyed Nadir's private jet. 'And I feel like I've been put through a spin dryer ten times. He wants to see her,' she added softly.

She heard Minh settle into his leather sofa and wished she was there with him with a nice bottle of red between them and a rom com on the TV.

'I've already guessed he's the father or you wouldn't be in Bakaan so you know, he does have a right to see her,' he said.

'I know that.' Imogen watched Nadeena stuff the ear of a soft teddy bear into her mouth and chew. 'At least logically I know that.' Emotionally, she wasn't ready to concede the parenting of Nadeena to anyone else but herself and a couple of trusted friends. 'I just never thought he'd be interested in her.'

'Well, he clearly is. And maybe that's a good thing.'

Imogen pulled a face. 'I don't see how.'

'He's a very powerful man. He can provide for her, you know.' Minh's voice grew soft down the end of the phone. 'And no doubt for you as well.'

'I don't want his money.'

'I know that. But you could use someone to take care of you.'

That had been her mother's mistake. It wouldn't be hers. 'And what about love?' She picked Nadeena up when she saw her yawn and laid her head on her shoulder.

'Are we talking about for Nadeena or for you?'

'Nadeena. The way he looked at me today…' She felt heaviness inside her chest and it was hard to get the words out. 'Believe me, there's no love lost between us.' And she would never want Nadir's love for herself again. She'd got over that unrealistic desire a long time ago.

'Try to look on the bright side,' he said. 'It might not be so bad.'

Imogen released a pent-up breath. Looking on the bright side wasn't exactly her forte. She was more a planning for the worst case scenario kind of girl. It was her safety blanket. It kept her from making mistakes—or being surprised by things. If her own mother had crossed every *t* and dotted every *i* maybe she wouldn't have been so shocked when her father had left them and never came back. Maybe she would have been more prepared.

'He left me when I needed him the most,' she said, wondering why that still had the capacity to hurt. She'd got over that as well, hadn't she? 'How could I ever trust him with Nadeena? With me?'

'That's definitely a black mark against him. But you have to think of what's best for Nadeena now.'

Imogen chewed on her lower lip so hard she tasted blood. '*I'm* what is best for Nadeena. He's nothing more than a playboy prince who comes and goes as he pleases and gets whatever he wants.' Imogen steeled her heart, more resolved than ever to resist him. 'I won't let Nadeena have my childhood and that's all Nadir can offer.'

They talked for a few minutes more, with Minh promising to call her boss and tell him that she wouldn't be in over the next couple of days, and then Imogen focused on getting Nadeena to sleep.

Her conversation with Minh had unsettled her. She'd wanted him to tell her that Nadir was a rat bastard but all he'd done was say things that had flashed across her own mind, which left her more conflicted than ever.

She knew giving in to his demand that she marry him would ultimately end in tears. Most likely Nadeena's. And quite possibly her own. In frustration, if nothing else!

## CHAPTER SIX

In the end it took her an hour to put Nadeena to sleep and when she went looking for Nadir she wasn't expecting to find him barefoot and shirtless with a dark-haired woman bending over his lap.

The sight shocked her and suddenly a long-lost memory of her fifteen-year-old self flew into her mind. She'd been with a bunch of friends on a school excursion when they had come across her father in a passionate embrace with a woman who wasn't her mother. The woman's hands had been in her father's hair, his hand close to her breast, his mouth devouring hers. Imogen had been stunned. Sickened. The girls with her had giggled nervously and her father hadn't even looked contrite. He'd scowled at her and asked her why she wasn't in school. God, she hadn't remembered that in years.

The woman in the white *abaya* straightened and Imogen saw she was holding an empty silver tray and a tumbler of Scotch sat on the low table beside the sofa.

Imogen did a double-take when she realised that the woman was a servant who was now retreating from the room. Her mind had put two and two together and come up with ten. Maybe she was more tired than she'd realised…

'You must be Imogen?'

Whirling around at the sound of a deep male voice, Imogen saw a man bearing a striking resemblance to Nadir standing over by the keyhole windows. He looked tall and imposing in his traditional white robes and matching headdress and Imogen knew that there was no way she would have missed him if she hadn't been so riveted by the sight of Nadir's impressive chest.

'Imogen, this is my brother, Zachim. Zach, this is Imogen.'

Zachim nodded, his eyes glinting amber-gold in the softly lit room as he regarded her. 'I remember you from the dance hall and it's a pleasure to finally meet you.'

Feeling trapped by her pent-up emotions and unsure what Nadir had told him, Imogen was uncertain as to how to proceed. It seemed highly improper to let rip with the frustration and angst clawing at the inside of her throat and yet she didn't want to wait till morning to discuss things with Nadir. It seemed important to do so now. 'I'm sorry; I didn't mean to interrupt. Perhaps you can let me know when you're free.'

'I thought you were going to bed?'

The easy familiarity with which Nadir spoke to her in front of his brother made her instantly defensive. 'Why—because you told me to?'

'No. Because you look like you're about to fall over with exhaustion.'

Imogen glared at Nadir and felt even worse when his brother cleared his throat discreetly from behind her. 'I think I should leave you both alone.'

'No, please.' She was horrified at what he must think of her. 'I didn't mean to interrupt you.'

Prince Zachim smiled but it was weary. 'You didn't. My brother is being his usual obstinate self. Maybe you can talk some sense into him. He won't listen to me.'

Imogen was about to say that Nadir didn't listen to her either when he rose from the sofa and the sight of all those hard muscles rippling across his abdomen as he moved made the words fly out of her head.

'I'm not going to change my mind, Zach.'

'It's your birthright.'

'If you're feeling guilty about taking something from me then don't. I don't want anything to do with Bakaan.'

'Nadir, I know you're still angry about the past but—'

Nadir made a motion with his hand that cut his brother off. 'Goodnight, Zach.'

Zachim scowled. 'All right, Nadir, You win this round.'

'Hallelujah.' Nadir's voice held no enthusiasm and Imogen wondered what it was Nadir was still angry about and what exactly Zach was taking from him.

'I have to fly to the mountains early tomorrow,' Zachim said as he turned to go. 'But I'll be back by noon.'

'I'll be waiting.'

Zachim gave her a weary smile. 'Lovely to meet you, Imogen. I'm not sure if I should congratulate you on your impending marriage to my brother or offer commiserations.' His smile held a touch of irony. 'But I definitely look forward to getting to know you and to meeting my niece over lunch tomorrow.'

Imogen smiled warmly. As handsome and dashing as he was, this brother didn't tie her insides up in knots like Nadir did. 'I look forward to it.'

Zach looked back at Nadir as if he wanted to say more but Nadir gave him a faint smile. 'Give it up, Zach. You're perfect for the role and you know it. And stop flirting with my fiancé.'

'Nadir!'

His name left her lips in an appalled reprimand but Zach just laughed heartily.

'You might not like being back in Bakaan, brother, but I like you being here'

Nadir watched his brother give him a mocking salute and stride out of the room and knew that he was doing the right thing in giving Zach the leadership role. They had different mothers and therefore vastly different experiences of their father and their homeland. And it wasn't just anger or resentment at the past that stopped Nadir wanting to be the next King; it was also the painful memories that haunted him every time he was here. It was the sense of guilt his brother would never understand because Nadir had never told him of the cowardly role he'd played in his mother and sister's deaths. The feelings of shame and ineptitude. A feeling of emptiness.

If he'd thought the people of Bakaan really needed him, if he thought he could add some value Zach couldn't as leader then he might do it. But the fact was Zach was a capable military leader and was perfect for the job.

'I apologise if I ruined your conversation with your brother. It wasn't my intention.'

He eyed Imogen still standing in the middle of the room and picked up his Scotch, hoping it would distract him from his bleak thoughts. He knew a way she could distract him as well but he didn't think she'd be as biddable as the Scotch. Unfortunately. 'You didn't; he was leaving anyway.'

She chewed the inside of her lower lip and he couldn't take his eyes off the little movement.

'Are you okay?'

Her soft question made him gulp a mouthful of the fiery liquid and he relished the burn of it down his throat. No, he wasn't okay. 'Concerned for my welfare, *habibi*? I'm touched.'

He saw her posture stiffen and regretted taking his frustration out on her. But hell, she was partly to blame. Sorting out the leadership issue would be over and done within a matter of hours. Sorting out the rest of his life with a wife and child… He didn't want to contemplate how long that would take. Particularly given the light of defiance burning hotly in Imogen's eyes. A defiance he had yet to fully understand.

'Don't be,' she responded smartly. 'It was an aberration that won't happen again.'

He smiled. He hadn't realised she was so feisty when they'd been together back in Paris. Back then she'd always been thrilled to see him, delight written all over her expressive face. And it had been catching. For those all too brief weekends he'd been happy too. Perhaps that had been her allure. That and the red-hot chemistry between them. 'Whatever you've got to say can wait until morning.'

'Really?' Her eyebrows arched skyward. 'Because you decreed it, *My Lord*?'

No, she definitely hadn't been this feisty in Paris but part of him—the part that turned caveman every time she was around—liked it a little too much for comfort. 'Yes. That and the dark circles under your eyes which suggest you need sleep more than conversation.'

'I'm sorry you don't approve of the way I look.' She dipped into a mocking curtsy. 'I'll try to do better next time, *My Lord*.'

'I wouldn't use that term too often,' he advised softly, tossing back another finger of Scotch. 'I might like it.'

She scowled at him but her eyes followed his hand as he rubbed it across his chest and his blood surged as he saw the breath catch in her throat. He'd forgotten Zach had interrupted his shower. Did the sight of him bother her? He'd sure as hell be bothered if she was standing before him half naked. Hell, he was bothered anyway and she still had on her crumpled clothes from earlier.

A spike of conscience needled him. She might still be as beautiful as ever but she really did look worn to the bone. His eyes scanned over her body and came to rest on her chest. And she was braless.

'So, anyway…' She cleared her throat and his eyes rose

from her round, full breasts to the pulse point beating like a small trapped bird inside her creamy throat. 'I've looked up some options I'd like to go through with you.'

With his instincts pulling at him to go to her and haul her up against him and tame that defiant look in her eyes until she softened and became once again pliant and wanton in his arms, Nadir forced his mind to recall her words. 'Options' was the only word that had stuck but he knew she wouldn't want to discuss the options he was presently interested in. 'Now is not a good time.'

'I disagree.'

Of course she did. 'You had ample opportunity to talk on the plane. You chose not to.'

She perched on the edge of the sectional sofa and faced him. 'Nadeena was awake the whole time. I didn't want her to realise how tense I was. At this age babies feel everything the mother feels.'

He gave a short laugh. 'If that's true you wouldn't have fooled her. Even a blind man could see you were about ready to snap in half.'

'And whose fault is that?'

'Mine, no doubt. Did she go to sleep easily?'

Her lips tightened. 'Yes, thank you.'

'Thank you?'

'For asking, I suppose.' Frustration flashed in her green eyes. 'I...can we just stay on topic?'

'By all means. But you can stop treating me like a stranger. I'm not.'

'You are.' She rubbed the back of her neck as if it ached and rolled her slender shoulders. 'But I didn't come out here to argue with you.'

Nadir took another swallow of Scotch. 'What did you come out here for?'

The air between them thickened and he nearly said to

hell with arguing; it was time to relieve some of the tension between them.

'To talk.'

'I've got a better idea.'

She frowned and he saw the moment the meaning behind his rough words became clear because her gorgeous eyes widened in shock. 'I hope you don't mean what I think you mean.'

'Oh, I definitely mean exactly what you think I mean.'

She gasped softly. 'How can you think about sex at a time like this?'

He thought about sex with her all the time. 'Too soon for you, *habibi*? That's okay. I'm a patient man. I can wait.'

'Look, Nadir—'

'Look, Imogen.' He scrubbed a weary hand across his face. 'I'm not in the mood for a discussion. We can talk tomorrow after one o'clock.'

'Why? What happens at one o'clock?'

At one o'clock one of his pesky loose ends would be resolved. 'It's not important.'

Her eyes narrowed. 'Does it have to do with what your brother was talking about before?'

'It doesn't matter.'

'It seemed to matter to him.'

'He'll get over it.'

Her lashes fluttered down to hide her frustrated gaze. 'Keep your secrets. I don't want to know them anyway.'

'It's not a secret. I have business to sort out in Bakaan that doesn't concern you.'

'Fine.' Her tone implied it was anything but fine. 'Let's stay on topic and discuss something that does concern me.'

'By all means let's stay on topic. Tomorrow.'

Imogen didn't like the way his gaze swept over her and wished she'd kept her bra on after Nadeena had gone to sleep because every time his eyes dropped to her chest her nipples peaked. She just hoped that the lighting from the lamps was low enough that he wouldn't notice. Not that she couldn't see every muscle shifting on his torso. He raised his hand to rub at the smattering of hair on his chest again and Imogen barely resisted the urge to fan herself. *Stay on topic yourself,* she admonished silently.

The last thing she needed right now was to think about the offer he'd just made. Which only reinforced his playboy mentality.

*I'm a patient man. I can wait.*

So much for her earlier assumption that he didn't want to sleep with her. The man would obviously sleep with anyone but he'd be waiting a long time if he thought he could use her to slake his hunger for a night. Been there, done that and now had the baby to prove it! A baby who didn't need him.

Deciding that starting with that statement would be like waving a red flag at an irritated bull, she went straight to the second half of her plan instead.

'So.' She cleared her throat yet again. 'Given that you said that you wanted to be part of Nadeena's life, I looked up some alternative options for us that don't include marriage.'

'Good for you.'

His response was frosty but at least it cooled the air between them and she wouldn't let it put her off. She narrowed her eyes as he crossed his ankle over his knee and then she calmly folded her hands in her lap. 'So it's obviously not an in-depth analysis, but from what I can tell there's legal custody and physical custody and they're quite different from each other.'

'Are they?'

His laconic response reeked of disinterest and Imogen did her best to cap her irritation. 'Yes. They are. Legal custody is about who makes decisions for the child and can be sole or joint and physical custody is about seeing the child. Again, that can be either sole or joint and that breaks down into supervised and unsupervised and even virtual visits nowadays.' She took a deep breath and rushed on before he could interject. 'There's also the issue of how to split the time and it seems that the most popular is for the father to visit the child every second weekend and on public holidays. Unless you want to go the virtual route, of course.'

'Of course.'

Imogen waited for him to say more. When he just smiled and curved his hands behind his head she suspected he was toying with her. 'Well?' she prompted stiffly.

'I can see you've put quite a bit of effort into this.'

Imogen sucked in a litre of air and released it slowly. Perhaps she'd been wrong and he wasn't toying with her. Perhaps he was going to be cooperative and let her go. 'Not really.' She gave him a small smile that seemed to stretch her dry lips to the point of cracking. 'But it's a start.'

And, perversely, the possibility that he might agree with her didn't thrill her the way she had imagined it would. Instead, she felt unaccountably disappointed and realised just how much she still wished that their relationship in Paris could have progressed like so many other happy couples did. Couples like Minh and David, who loved each other so much they would do anything for the other person.

She sighed. What had her mother always said? *If wishes were horses, beggars would ride.* Such an old-fashioned saying, passed down through the generations. Would she pass it on to Nadeena with that same air of inevitability?

'Tell me,' he began conversationally, 'did the Internet mention the custody arrangements for a woman who kept her child's birth a secret from its father?'

No, he was not going to be cooperative and icy shivers tripped down her spine as she saw that she had angered him again 'No,' she bit out tersely.

'Then you're right—' his smile was even tighter than hers '—when you say that your analysis isn't very complete. And furthermore,' he drawled with icy control, 'while you might be happy sharing custody of our daughter, I am not.'

'I'm not either,' she replied hotly. 'But you're not giving me any other choice.'

'On the contrary; I've given you the best choice there is,' he drawled arrogantly.

'Marrying you?'

She could see instantly that he'd taken offence to her contemptuous tone from the stillness of his big body but dammit, he didn't love her. If he did…if he did then things might be different…

'This is all something you should have thought about before you ran away,' he bit out contemptuously.

'I did not run away,' she retorted. 'I left.'

He made a low noise in the base of his throat that startled her. 'I told you I would return and we'd talk about options.' His eyes glittered dangerously. 'You weren't there.'

'Like abortion?' she spat, remembering how cold she had felt reading his missive. How icy she had felt in his apartment when he had confirmed that yes, he'd have preferred not to be an expectant father.

'No, not that.'

He lost colour and tugged a hand through his hair as if the thought truly horrified him.

'Well, it probably would have happened if you had pushed for that horrible paternity test you told me I had to take.'

His brows drew together. 'A paternity test made sense.'

'Do you have any idea how dangerous those tests are?'

'No, I—'

'About one in three hundred amniocenteses end in miscarriage and I would have needed the earlier test. With the CVS you can double the chance of a miscarriage. But then that would have worked a lot better for you than this, wouldn't it?'

Nadir jumped to his feet, his movements lacking their usual grace. 'For the love of all things holy, Imogen, I would never have put you or our baby's life at risk. You must know that.'

Imogen wrapped her arms around her stomach, all the anger leaching out of her as he stood before her all ferocious and earnest as if he meant what he was saying.

Did he?

She didn't know. What she did know was that she didn't want to be forced to do something stupid that they would both later regret because Nadeena would be the one to pay the ultimate price when things turned bad. Still, a twinge of regret spiked inside her chest. The way he'd said 'our baby', as if he really felt something for Nadeena already. 'And you would have just accepted that I not take the test, I suppose,' she scoffed.

'Of course I would have accepted it.' He settled his hands on his hips. 'At what stage in our relationship did I ever show you that I was unreasonable?'

Imogen tapped her foot and wanted to say *all the time.* But the truth was that he had never been unreasonable towards her. Ever. He had always been thoughtful and kind. Loving. A lie she couldn't afford to be swayed by again. 'Now. You're being unreasonable now.'

'That's a matter of opinion.'

'Damn it, Nadir.' A flash of renewed irritation surged inside her. 'You can't keep me here against my will.'

'Actually, I can,' he said with all the arrogance of a man born to privilege. 'But I won't.' He paused, ran his hand across his stubbled jaw. 'I will, however, stop you from taking Nadeena away from me again.'

Imogen's insides seized and she knew her face went

pale, her breathing laboured. 'I hate you.' Because he'd just effectively narrowed her choices down to marriage to him or give up her child.

He nodded as if this was normal. As if she hadn't dreamt of him and wished in her darkest moments that he wouldn't come for her. Tell her that he missed her. Tell her that he loved her. Tell her that he couldn't live without her. Dreams not worth the sleep they had interrupted.

'A child deserves to be raised by both parents.' He regarded her steadily. 'Or are you going to argue with me about that too?'

'Only if both parents love and want her.'

'I agree.'

Imogen clamped her mouth mutinously closed and turned her attention to the intricate patterns on the Persian rug at her feet before she said something she'd truly regret.

Nadir sighed. 'Believe it or not, Imogen, I only have Nadeena's best interests at heart.'

'Do you?'

'Yes.' She heard a hardness enter his voice at her scepticism.

She looked at him and all the fight left her and a great sense of doom pervaded her limbs. 'And what if a marriage between us is the worst thing for her?'

He looked genuinely perplexed by her question. 'I don't see how it could be.'

'Because it would be nothing but a marriage of convenience.'

'I don't see it that way.'

She blew out a frustrated breath. 'How can you not?'

He stepped in front of her, breathing as hard as she was. 'Because there's nothing remotely convenient about marriage and ours will be real.'

*Real?* Imogen swallowed heavily and lost her breath. 'I hope you don't mean what I think you mean.'

'We will be man and wife in every sense of the word, *habibi,'* he said softly with the same confidence she had once loved.

Imogen's chin jutted forward. 'I didn't think you were into force.'

She knew that if she revealed just how badly he affected her it would be akin to lying down and waving a white flag. So she held her breath as his eyes ran over her face and down over her throat and willed herself not to move, silently urging her racing heartbeat to slow to a moderate gallop.

As if he couldn't help himself, he raised his hand and brushed his thumb across her lips in a whisper-soft caress that made every one of her nerve endings tingle. For a long moment they just stared at each other and then he ruined the moment by speaking. 'Force, *habibi*?'

The gentle words mocked her and she jerked back and stepped away from him, doing her best to ignore the way the blood pounded heavily through her body and highlighted her inability to control her attraction to him. No man had ever affected her so deeply that she forgot who she was and where she was and she refused to give him that kind of power over her again. It made her feel helpless to follow her own will. It made her hungry to taste him. It made her willing to risk everything. Almost…

Forcing herself to take another slow step backwards, she banked her confused emotions as best she could and reached down deep for reason. 'Be serious, Nadir. A child will completely cramp your lifestyle. They're inconvenient and messy and exhausting and…and…' *Wonderful and joyous and funny and loving...* She swallowed. 'And smelly. Really smelly at times.'

Nadir paced away from her and then turned sharply on his heel. 'I don't understand you. Most women would be jumping for joy at the prospect of having a rich man take care of her and her child.'

'Except I'm not most women and I *know* this is a mistake. My parents married because my mother was pregnant with me and it was a miserable affair for everyone. They stayed together even though my father was seeing another woman because my mother believed a child should be raised by two parents. My father resented being tied to us and after a while I stopped wishing he would pay me attention.'

'I won't resent you.'

Embarrassed at having revealed her deepest wounds to him, Imogen scoffed. 'How can you say that? You have a reputation of being the unobtainable playboy that spans continents.'

His lips thinned into a flat line. 'People see what they want to see. But if you think love is some sort of guarantee of a happy union, it isn't. My parents were the poster children for that particular misconception and they didn't last.'

Imogen frowned. 'I find that hard to believe if it was true love,' she said huskily.

'Believe it. They separated when my father took a second wife and—'

'Took a second wife!'

'Yes, it is the custom that men in Bakaan can take more than one wife.'

'You can definitely forget marriage then.'

He smiled wearily. 'Don't worry. I am not a masochist.'

'Is that supposed to be funny? I think it's appalling that men are allowed to have more than one wife. I bet the women aren't allowed more than one husband.'

'No. And it bothered my mother just as much. In the end they hated each other so much there was never any joy in visiting either one of them. My mother was always trying to get us to prove our love by feeding her information about our father and our father was constantly derogatory about her and wanting to know what she was up to behind his back. It was as if they couldn't let each other go and frankly it was exhausting.'

And no doubt emotionally crippling, Imogen thought. Which was so unlike the picture she had formed in her mind about his childhood. For some reason she had assumed that his life had been full of opulence and fun and the security of belonging to an ancient dynasty. It seemed she had been wrong. At least about the fun and security.

Curiosity made her pause and she wanted to ask him more but he got in first.

'Forget it.' His flinty gaze seemed to penetrate deep into her mind. 'And forget shared custody, Imogen.'

At the reminder of their earlier argument Imogen's spine straightened. 'You're impossible to reason with.'

'That's because you know I'm right.'

Shaking her head, she would have turned away from him then—anything to put some distance between herself and his half-naked body that seemed to beckon her to reach out and touch it—but his hands came down on her shoulders and held her immobile.

Imogen trembled and knew he felt it by the satisfied gleam that seemed to soften his gaze. 'I've never stopped wanting you, Imogen, and that kiss back in my apartment proves we share an incredibly strong chemistry. Why fight it?'

Realising with a pang that she was held captive under his unwanted spell, Imogen wrenched herself out of his hold and swung away from him. Embarrassed at how easily she became enthralled by him, how easily she succumbed to his words, his touch, she let anger at him, at herself, at the whole world take hold. 'You want to know why?' She squared off in front of him. 'Because, no matter what happens, I have no intention of marrying you and because, despite what you believe, a marriage based on sex will always be weak.'

'Perhaps. But you're a smart girl and you must realise that a marriage based on mutual chemistry and shared interests has strength.'

Imogen didn't feel very smart right now. She felt wrung out and beaten. 'And what do you think that we *share*, Nadir?' she all but spat at him, desperate to lash out at him in any way that she could. Desperate to alleviate the giant ball of emotion welling up inside her and threatening to burst right out of her. 'That could possibly hold a marriage between us together?'

She slapped her hands on her hips and waited for his response but she should have known that he'd have an answer poised on his lips that would floor her. She should have known that a man whose negotiation skills in the business world were second to none would have something up his sleeve to make her feel as big as a thimble.

'Nadeena.' He paused to let his words sink in. 'We have Nadeena.'

# CHAPTER SEVEN

AFTER WAITING FOR Zach inside the council chambers for nearly an hour it was safe to say that Nadir was now extremely irritated. Yes, he'd managed to field a few important work calls while he waited but there was only so much he could get done from a country with limited Internet resources.

He also needed to sort things out with Imogen but she'd steadfastly avoided him all morning and frankly he hadn't tried that hard to challenge her on it. Last night's discussion—hell, argument—had played heavily on his mind and made sleep impossible.

Before picking her up yesterday he'd expected to find that she'd aborted his baby, mainly, it had to be said, because she hadn't approached him for a truckload of money and for a while yesterday he'd continued to think that maybe she was somehow playing him for a fool. He'd continued to believe that she had run from him because she'd had something to hide.

He didn't think that now. She was too earnest in her attempts to get him to change his mind about their marriage. Too earnest in her belief that he had been the one to do the wrong thing by her and not the other way around.

He recalled her fierce expression when she'd mentioned his text. At the time he hadn't contemplated the possibility that she would be upset by it. He hadn't contemplated the possibility that she would feel abandoned by his return to New York and feel as if she had to deal with her pregnancy alone. Guilt knifed through him.

He supposed, if he was honest, he'd been mostly to blame because he hadn't communicated his feelings to her, but how the hell was he supposed to have done that when he didn't know how he had been feeling?

Dealing with emotions had never been his strong suit, even before his mother and sister had died.

He remembered his mother encouraging him to embrace that side of his nature and his father telling him it was dangerous and it had been his father who had been proved right.

Nadir sighed. He'd never seen the benefit of rehashing the past and he still didn't. A man either took action or he bowed out of the game. Nadir had no intention of bowing out. Not with Imogen at any rate.

He glanced at the admiral's chair his father used to occupy at the end of the room during council meetings. As heir to the throne he had always been encouraged to sit in on those meetings and he'd loved them. He'd loved listening to his father taking charge and issuing orders. Watching him handle political issues.

His father had openly shared this side of himself and it wasn't until Nadir had left Bakaan that he'd realised how isolated and increasingly paranoid his father had become. How only a select few were ever allowed into his inner sanctum and then only if those select few agreed with him. From the age of twelve Nadir had started to do that less and less and that was when the rot had set in. That was when his father had started trying to keep him from his mother and sister, explaining that the ties he found the hardest to cut were the ones that needed to be cut most of all.

He rubbed a hand across his face. One of the issues between him and Imogen was that she was, at heart, an emotional and sensual woman who didn't hold back. It was both a draw and a deterrent—although right now he was honest enough to admit that the draw side was definitely winning out. Probably it had been too long since he'd had a woman. It wasn't natural for a healthy male to go without sex for fourteen months.

Hell.

Did he owe Imogen an apology for his behaviour back then? It wasn't a position he had found himself in for years and the last two people he'd needed to apologise to were dead.

Out of the corner of his eye he noticed one of his father's senior council members break away from the group and, like a drowning man grasping for a life raft, he welcomed the interruption to his thoughts.

Old and set in his ways, Omar had never been on Nadir's list of favourite people but he was knowledgeable and, as far as he was aware, loyal to a fault.

'Well?'

'We don't know where he is, Your Highness. He's not answering his phone.'

Nadir gritted his teeth. His brother had said he needed to go into the mountains on some business or other. He'd flown the helicopter himself. Now he was nowhere to be seen and the helicopter was still at the airfield. There was no sign of foul play or anything amiss. 'Fine—we'll proceed without him.'

'I'm afraid that's not possible, Your Highness.'

'Why not?'

'In order for you to renounce your position as King, we need to have your successor present.'

'Well, he's not here and I have a business to run.'

'The council understand, Your Highness,' he said in a way that let Nadir know they didn't understand at all. 'But you are still our acting King and there is a UAE dinner tonight that has been planned for months. It is too late to cancel. Many of the heads of state have already flown into Bakaan. It was quite a coup for Prince Zachim to arrange it. Many will be staying all week on official business.'

'Then Zachim should be here to run it,' Nadir bit out.

'Indeed, Your Highness.' Omar nodded deferentially.

Aware that he was being manipulated but knowing that he was boxed in until Zachim returned, Nadir muttered a curse. 'Okay, I'll do it.

'Very good, Your Highness. And shall I set a place for your wife?'

Nadir's gaze sharpened on the older man. 'Why would you do that?'

'Because spouses have been invited to the dinner. As everyone has heard about your wife, they will expect to see her there.'

Nadir had a good idea how Imogen was going to take that news. 'Try calling my brother again.'

'Of course, Your Highness.'

Nadir paced again while Omar dialled his phone. Most likely it wouldn't work, given the rudimentary telecom system his father had installed in the country. That was another possible reason why no one could reach Zachim. Either that or his brother was hiding out in some attempt to get him to step into the role as leader.

Nadir stilled. Was that it? Was Zach forcing his hand? He frowned as the idea sprouted roots and leaves. As a child, Zachim had often run away and hidden when he was in trouble, waiting for their father's wrath to subside before coming out again. By then Nadir had usually copped Zach's share of the punishment as well as his own so it wasn't a bad strategy—one Nadir had been too proud to ever try himself—but it was quite possible that Zach was right now holed up somewhere with a woman and a case of wine. If he was…Nadir shook his head. If he was, he'd beat him to a pulp when he returned.

'No luck, Your Highness.'

'Fine. Set a place for Imogen.' Nadir turned to leave the room, already thinking about what needed to be done before the evening dinner when Omar's next words stopped him cold.

'And your wedding?'

'Excuse me?'

'Your wedding? You may have forgotten but a Western marriage is not recognised as legal for a member of the royal family. It would be best, Your Highness, if you formalised the marriage in a traditional ceremony as soon as possible.'

Hoping that the issue of his legal ties to Imogen wouldn't have arisen in the small amount of time he was supposed to be in Bakaan, Nadir sighed. 'I suppose you have a perfect date available, Omar?'

'As soon as possible, Your Highness. There is some unrest in the northern part of the country and some who would wish to destabilise the throne. It is important that the people observe their crown prince behaving in a way befitting the leadership.'

'You know I do not intend to become the next leader of Bakaan, Omar, so the timing doesn't matter,' Nadir said tightly.

'As you wish, Your Highness.'

Realising that he was being obstinate and the council members had no idea why he didn't want the damned leadership role, Nadir softened his position. 'I know you're worried, Omar, but don't be. Zachim will most likely be back before the evening meal is served. In the meantime, if you think that formalising my marriage is absolutely necessary then organise the ceremony for a week from today.'

That would give Zach plenty of time to stop playing his

games—if he was actually staying away on purpose—and get back here. And on the off-chance he was still holding out on him in a week then they would marry. It wasn't any big deal because it was going to happen, one way or another.

'I'm sorry—who did you say you were?'

Imogen placed Nadeena in the baby recliner beside the beautifully paved swimming pool and fastened the safety catch, the fronds of the palm trees overhead keeping the scorching sun from burning her. When she was done she turned to the two women standing in the open doorway. One was young and striking-looking in the traditional cream-coloured outfit that denoted the palace servants and the other woman was much older and dressed in faded black garments. And her eyes were transfixed by Nadeena.

'My name is Tasnim and this is Maab,' the younger one said with a wide smile 'We are your servants, My Lady.'

'Oh.' Imogen smiled kindly. Used to fending for herself and preferring it that way, she had no need for servants. 'Thank you, but—'

Before she could say anything, Maab had moved closer to Nadeena and was crooning something in Arabic. As if sensing Imogen's regard, she turned and bowed her head, speaking in rapid Bakaani.

'I'm sorry,' Imogen said, 'I don't understand.'

'Please excuse Maab, My Lady. She does not speak very much English but she is excellent with babies and helped raise the royal siblings when they were little. She is asking if she might approach the little princess.'

'Well, of course she can.' Imogen smiled encouragingly and the old woman knelt down in front of Nadeena and gasped in surprise. She started spouting the name Sheena and smiling broadly.

Confused, Imogen turned to Tasnim for clarification.

'Maab says that the little princess looks just like Sheena.'

'Sheena?'

'The King's sister, My Lady.'

'Oh, Nadir's aunt? That's nice.'

Tasnim gave her a funny look. 'No, My Lady, she means King Nadir's sister.'

Imogen was silent for a moment as she processed that piece of information. She'd never heard of Nadir having a sister but that wasn't surprising, really. Their short relationship in Paris hadn't progressed past the intensely sexual phase and, whether by accident or design, neither of them had wasted their time talking about family or personal history. For Imogen that had been deliberate. She hadn't wanted to talk about her mother's recent death and her father's remarriage a month later. Had Nadir chosen not to speak about his past because he was upset by it as well?

'The King has asked me to help you prepare for the evening ahead. Would you like to do that now, My Lady?'

*The evening ahead?* Feeling as if her life was once again spinning out of her control and not wanting to look like a complete dill, Imogen kept her expression bland. 'By King you mean…Nadir?'

'*Na'am*, My Lady. Yes.'

A sudden sense of unease fluttered up from her stomach. Nadir couldn't be King because if he was that would mean they were going to be here for a *little* longer than a day, but if he wasn't then why were these women even here?

'I think there must be some mistake,' she began slowly and then Zach's words jumped into her head from the night before.

*It's your birthright.*

Was Nadir here to discuss some sort of succession planning? She hadn't contemplated that and perhaps he would expect her to meet his father. She nearly grimaced. It was one thing to meet his brother but if his father was anything like her own then he was unlikely to approve of her.

Maab started saying something again in Arabic and there was a hint of pride in her voice.

'Maab says that we are delighted that he has come back, My Lady. That King Nadir will be a great king because he was a great boy. Kind and loyal and very strong.'

Imogen had no doubt that Nadir had been strong but she wasn't so sure about the kind and loyal part. *Ruthless and self-serving?* Now that she would have believed in an instant and she wasn't sure how she felt hearing this woman's hero worship of a man she was convinced was set on doing the right thing because of a *guilty* conscience rather than a *good* one.

'That's lovely,' she murmured.

Tasnim nodded. 'She was very sad to think that Nadir would not return after the death of his father.'

*'The death of his father?'*

Tasnim gave her another funny look and Imogen's pride kicked in. 'Oh, yes, the death of his father.'

*What the heck was going on here?*

'It has been a troubling two weeks for those of us working in the palace,' Tasnim continued. 'And not knowing what would happen…but I'm sorry, My Lady, you don't want to hear all this.'

*Not want to hear it?* Imogen wanted to hear that and more. She could hardly believe what Tasnim had said so far. Had Nadir's father truly died two weeks ago? And what did that mean? Was Nadir going to be King? Did he expect Imogen to move to Bakaan? The whole concept was totally implausible and she could feel panic threatening. She needed to speak to Nadir to sort this out. Right now.

Giving Tasnim what she hoped was a benign smile,

she said, 'Thank you, Tasnim. Would you mind telling *my husband* that I don't need any help and I'd really like to see him?'

'Your wish is my command, *habibi*.'

Swinging around at the sound of Nadir's voice, Imogen's jaw nearly hit the floor at the sight of him dressed in flowing black robes that made him look like a pirate. Absurd excitement gripped her and rational thought was whisked away on the light, hot breeze.

And she wasn't the only female affected by the sight of him because Maab rushed to her feet with the agility of a woman half her age and threw herself on the ground in front of him.

'Maab.' Nadir raised the woman and hugged her tightly, speaking to her in his native language, his tone warm and deep. Tears sparkled in the old woman's eyes and, seeing it, Imogen felt tears as well; her emotions much closer to the surface since her daughter had been born.

She wasn't sure what Nadir had said to the women but moments later they had bowed low to them both and disappeared as quickly as they had arrived.

Nadir's gaze swept over her and a small frown of disapproval immediately knitted his brow. 'Why aren't you wearing the clothing I provided?'

Tense and uncertain after what she'd just heard, Imogen was in no mood to talk about fashion. 'Forget the clothing. Why did you lie to me?'

'I did not lie to you. I have never lied to you.'

'You told me we would be leaving today and I've just heard that I'm supposed to be attending a dinner. And that you're the King.' She peered at him, looking for signs that something had changed. 'You're not really the King, are you?'

'No, I'm not the King,' he said in a way that didn't convince her at all.

'Then why do those two women call you the King?'

'Because they believe that I soon will be, I suppose.'

'But why would they think that?'

His face turned grim and Imogen felt worry spike inside her. 'A glitch.'

'A glitch?'

'Nobody is King until the coronation but in the meantime the country needs someone to lead it. I am acting head of state until Zachim returns.'

'So, it's true that your father died recently.'

He shoved his hands into the pockets of his robe. 'It's true.'

Imogen didn't know what to say in the face of his implacable regard. 'I'm sorry for your loss.'

'Don't be.' He drew a weary hand across his jaw. 'The whole purpose of my return to Bakaan was not to take over the throne but to cede it to Zachim.'

'Oh.' Didn't he want to be King? And if not, why not? 'I suppose, given that women aren't allowed multiple husbands in Bakaan, your sister isn't allowed to take over the throne instead.'

'My sister?' A muscle flickered in his jaw. Once. Twice. 'Who told you about my sister?'

Not wanting to get the young servant into trouble, Imogen hesitated. 'Tasnim. But don't blame her. I pushed for the information.'

'Then you didn't push hard enough.' His expression made her feel chilled. 'My sister is no longer alive either.'

'Oh, God, I'm so sorry.' Imogen felt stricken as she saw a mask of pain briefly cross his face. 'Did she die with your father?'

'No.' Nadir expelled a harsh breath, his emotions hidden behind the screen of his impossibly long eyelashes. 'But you are right. She would not have been allowed to be a sheikha.' His lashes raised and she could see that his emotions were now firmly under control. 'Now, since Zachim has disappeared for the moment, I must attend a state dinner tonight and I need you to accompany me.'

'But what about our return to London?'

'It has been delayed.'

'It can't be delayed. I have a job I need to get back to and we're really short-staffed at the café.'

Nadir gave her a dry look. 'You will no longer need that job, Imogen, so you might as well quit.'

Imogen shoved her hands onto her hips. 'I will not quit.'

Nadir let out a long sigh. 'I hope to Allah that not every conversation we have is going to feel like I'm pulling out hen's teeth. If you go into your dressing room you will find an evening gown for the dinner and Tasnim will help you prepare. If you need anything else—'

'Nadir, every conversation feels like a struggle because you won't listen. And I'm not going anywhere with you tonight when nothing has been resolved between us.'

'Of course it has. We resolved everything last night.'

As far as Imogen was concerned, they had resolved nothing last night. 'When?'

'When we talked.'

She shook her head, frustrated that he could be so obtuse. 'You might have resolved something last night but I didn't.'

His sigh was one of aggravated patience. 'Okay, tell me what you need to make this work for you.'

Was he serious? 'Time.' *For one thing.* 'You listening to what I want would help.'

Nadir pulled a wry face. 'I promise to try and listen to you but unfortunately I can't do anything about your first request because time is something I seem to be in short supply of right now. And I have never seen the point in stalling when the outcome is not in question.'

His high-handedness was one of the things that had attracted her to him so she really only had herself to blame. 'I take it you mean the outcome of us marrying and if you do then the outcome is only not in question for you.'

'For us.'

'This is what I would call not listening,' she said with exasperation. 'Because at this point there is no us. There is you and me and a baby. I mean—what about where we're going to live? What about what school Nadeena will go to? What about her emotional well-being?'

His crooked grin made her breath catch and she wondered if that wasn't exactly the outcome he'd been trying to achieve. 'You will live where I live. Nadeena will go to a good school and we both want what is best for her.'

'You're simplifying.'

'And you're making it complicated.' It was he who sounded exasperated now.

'It *is* complicated.'

'It doesn't have to be.'

Imogen's eyes shot to his as the tenor in his voice roughened and, just like that, sex was in the room again. Or at least in her thoughts. 'Be serious, Nadir—we don't even like each other any more.'

'I like you.'

About to tell him that what he thought of her was inconsequential anyway, she found the words dissolving on her tongue as she watched him hunker down and start trickling water over Nadeena's feet. Nadeena reached forward and grabbed one of his thick fingers in her chubby hand. Imogen closed her eyes and then opened them again when Nadeena giggled and splashed the water with her feet.

Nadir smiled. That smile that had melted a thousand hearts, including her own.

They looked so beautiful together. Her daughter and the man who had once made her so impossibly happy she'd thought she would burst. Both dark-haired and with goofy smiles. Nadir started saying something softly to Nadeena in Arabic and Imogen felt that strange tug in her chest she knew was a type of longing. A type of longing that she really didn't want to feel again.

'Don't you want more?' The words were out of her mouth before she knew she was even about to say them and when Nadir looked up her heart stuttered at how incredibly virile he looked.

His eyes skimmed over her and if she wasn't mistaken lingered on her lips. Heat suffused her cheeks. 'More what?'

Imogen didn't want to say it but it was as if someone else was directing her mouth. 'Love. Don't you want to marry for love?'

His grimace spoke volumes. 'Love is for greeting cards and grandmothers, not for marriage.'

'Which shows you how wrong we are for each other because I only want to marry for love.'

'I already told you my parents married for love. It caused nothing but grief.'

She could tell by his tone that he was deadly serious. 'You really believe that, don't you?'

'No, I know it. Otherwise you would not still be arguing with me and resisting this marriage. You would be embracing the fact that I can give you a life few others can.' His mouth tilted mockingly at the corners. 'Including your *friend* back in London.'

Ignoring his last comment, Imogen was shocked by his view. 'You would prefer that I marry you for your money? That's so cold and…empty.'

'It's honest.' He gave a frustrated shake of his head, keeping his face soft for Nadeena's sake. 'And tonight is important, Imogen. Or I wouldn't ask.'

She swallowed and lifted her eyes to his. 'Why?' she

asked bleakly. 'I got the impression that Bakaan doesn't mean anything to you.'

'That's complicated too.'

'How?'

His face closed down and she knew he wouldn't answer her.

'Let's just say that it is and leave it at that.'

'So much for listening,' she muttered.

He looked at her. 'I have answered every question you've asked.'

'You think?'

He rubbed a hand across his jaw. He needed a shave, she thought absently, and how was it possible for his mouth to be such a perfect bow? He caught her staring and awareness pulsed between them.

The kiss they had shared the day before jumped into her mind and by the way his eyes had now dropped to her own mouth she suspected it had jumped into his as well.

His silent scrutiny unnerved her and she moved sideways to get around him and hoped to heaven that he didn't touch her because she wasn't sure how she'd react if he did. Or at least she *was* sure but she didn't want to have that reaction. She had a horrible way of mixing sex up with love when it came to this man and given his miserable views on love it would be emotional suicide for her to risk her heart—and Nadeena's—on him again.

'My country suffered a great deal because of my father's reign. I will not worsen that by ignoring my current duties. Now, as much as I *enjoy* arguing with you, we are out of time. Will you come with me tonight?'

It wasn't really a question. 'Do you always have to be so pushy?' she complained.

A cloud came across his face and, just like that, he was a stranger again. 'I will watch Nadeena while you get ready.'

Frustrated at the way he just seemed to corral her into

a corner as if she was a rogue horse, she tried to think of some way out. 'She needs a bath.'

'Then I will give her one.'

'By yourself?'

'Don't look so surprised. I doubt it's rocket science but if it makes you feel better I will have Maab present so that Nadeena can bond with her.'

Outdone by his logic, Imogen gnashed her teeth. 'It will be a mistake taking me.'

'Why do you say that?'

Because she had no experience of dealing with world leaders and dignitaries and she'd likely embarrass them both. 'I'm a dancer. I danced at the Moulin Rouge. Surely everyone will think I'm unsuitable to be the wife of a king.'

'No doubt some will.'

That stung and his ready agreement was like the flick of a knife across a wound that hadn't quite healed.

He glanced at her impatiently. 'But I won't be King so it doesn't matter.'

'Why not? Too much responsibility for you?'

He shoved his hand through his hair and turned it into a sexy mess. 'Are you trying to annoy me to get me to change my mind about our union?'

'Would it work?'

'No.' His brow quirked with a mixture of frustration and humour. 'Now, stop with the delaying tactics. Nadeena will be fine and, as beautiful as you undoubtedly are, yesterday's jeans and T-shirt aren't going to work tonight.'

'I hate you,' she said, but the words lacked the heat they had carried the day before and by the way he smiled he knew it.

'I got that memo last night. Now, let's get this duty over and done with, hmm?'

Yes, Nadir was all about duty but Imogen knew that

duty was a poor motivator that led to anger and neglect and resentment unless it was backed up by something deeper and she feared that was exactly where they were headed if she conceded to his demands.

# CHAPTER EIGHT

'KID, THAT'S SOME pitching arm you've got on you.' Nadir leant down and picked up the ball Nadeena had lobbed from her high chair for the millionth time. It was a game she never seemed to tire of. 'I can see you being a softball star when you're older.'

She babbled gleefully when he placed the soft fabric ball back in front of her but, instead of throwing it straight away, she reached towards him with a big grin and tried to grab his *keffiyeh*. 'Not that.' He grinned down at her and pushed his headdress back over his shoulder. 'I've explained that it doesn't look so good scrunched up by grubby baby hands.' Redirecting her attention to the ball, he checked his Rolex again and spied the empty doorway.

If Imogen didn't show up soon they wouldn't have time to stop for him to give her the ring that was burning a hole in his pocket and he didn't want her facing a room full of dignitaries and gossips without it. And somehow it seemed important to solidify things between them. Important to remind her that she was with him now and always would be.

Their earlier conversation and her look of surprise when she'd asked him if he wanted more—and he'd said no—replayed in his head. For a moment she'd looked so vulnerable that he'd wanted to snatch the words back but there had been enough misunderstanding between them and he didn't want there to be any more. But he supposed he should have realised that she was a romantic. That she would want love. It still irked him that she had said she didn't want to marry without it because clearly she didn't love him and he didn't love her.

Which did not mean that their marriage was doomed. He had feelings for her and she might not think great sex was any reason to get married but it was a start and he knew she wasn't as immune to him as she tried to pretend to be. Hell, that kiss had been proof enough of that, as was the way she held herself so carefully whenever he got close to her.

Nadeena clapped her chubby hands together with delight when he returned the ball to her yet again. 'If only your mother was so easily pleased,' he said softly.

She blew him a raspberry and he stroked his hand over her silky head. His daughter was a revelation to him—as was the depth of his feelings for her. Which only made him more determined to forge ahead with this marriage. Nadeena would not suffer the division of two parents' expectations for her the way he and his sister had.

As she babbled at the ball again as if she might direct it from sheer will alone, Nadir grinned and felt his heart clench at her trusting gaze. He dropped a kiss on top of her head, turning when he heard the swish of fabric behind him.

Only to have his heart clench all over again.

Imogen stood framed in the doorway wearing a blue silk floor-length gown that on the hanger had looked beautiful. On her it looked extraordinary. Her slender dancer's arms and the graceful line of her neck was exposed to his gaze, her hair a soft fall of golden waves around her shoulders. She looked every bit a royal princess. Every bit a woman any man would want on his arm. In his bed.

'I think this is going to be too much for Nadeena. She didn't sleep well last night.'

Nadir couldn't take his eyes off her. 'Do you mean you didn't?'

Imogen's mouth tightened. Her face looked pale and he could see the pulse in her throat going crazy. It bobbed as she swallowed and he couldn't control the wave of tenderness that overcame him in that moment. Imogen—fearless Imogen who took him on at every turn—seemed truly daunted by the prospect of the evening ahead. Or was it something else? Him, perhaps?

It annoyed him that she was so set on ignoring the chemistry between them that pulled tight every time they were together. As far as he was concerned, that was the *only* thing really working for them right now and he'd happily embrace it if she would.

'I've never left Nadeena with a stranger before.' She gripped her hands together tightly. 'She's always had the neighbour across the street or Minh.'

The mention of her ex-lover seemed to wipe any rational thought from his brain. In fact imagining her with any other man did that… 'She will be fine.'

'My daughter *needs* me.'

'*Our* daughter,' he said impatiently. 'And she's just had two hours to get used to Maab and she seems genuinely happy with her.'

'Two hours! It takes more than that to feel comfortable with someone.'

It hadn't taken him five minutes to feel comfortable with her. 'The grand ballroom is in the west wing, only a few minutes from here.'

'I think I feel sick.'

Sympathy replaced irritation. This was all new for her; he had to remember that. 'I will be by your side, *habibi*.'

She threw him a pithy glance. 'Is that supposed to be of comfort?'

Yes, it had been. 'Should I have told you that you will

be on your own and if you make a mistake you'll receive a thousand lashes?'

'I might have believed that.'

Her dry sense of humour had drawn him from the start and right now he wanted to laugh, shake her and kiss her all at the same time. 'Come.'

She stood stock-still. 'I am not a dog, Nadir.'

'No, you are a stunning woman who is trying her best to rile me,' he said softly. 'Fortunately for you, I have infinite control.' Usually, he amended. Usually, when she wasn't in the room, shredding it. He watched her wide, kohl-lined green eyes sparkle and then drop behind a veil of ebony lashes. Did she have any idea how incredibly beautiful she was to him? How much he wanted to possess her? How much he wanted to haul her into his arms and eat that pink gloss right off her lips? Having his old nanny and his daughter in the same room helped prevent it. But only just. 'We need to go.'

If possible, she angled her chin higher. 'To London?'

'Not quite. But I admire your humour.' He opened the door and beckoned for her to precede him.

She walked over to kiss their daughter before speaking to Maab. 'If she cries at all then you'll come and get me?'

'*Na'am*, My Lady.'

'Immediately?'

'*Na'am*, My Lady.'

Her gaze looked troubled when she neared him. 'I notice they say that a lot,' she whispered. 'Can I trust her?'

God, she was breathtaking. 'Nothing will happen to Nadeena. Relax.'

*Relax?* Impossible. She was too acutely aware of the way Nadir's regal robes brushed against the skirt of the amazing dress he had provided for her and the sense of power he effortlessly exuded. Walking beside him, it was hard to remember that none of this was real and that she didn't want it to be real.

Or did she?

The moment Nadir had leant forward and kissed the top of Nadeena's head as he played with her jumped into her consciousness and her heart lurched inside her chest. It had been identical to the thousands of kisses she had deposited on her daughter's head herself—an instinctive and unconscious gesture of love. Was it possible she was wrong about Nadir? Was it possible he might one day love their daughter as deeply as she did?

Feeling confused and out of her depth, her steps faltered as they entered a grand atrium with exquisite inlaid arabesque carvings on the ceilings and walls and highly polished bronze flooring. Six elaborately dressed Bakaani guards stood to attention with guns strapped to their hips. One of the men glanced briefly at Nadir and stepped forward, his hand poised on a gilt-edged doorknob.

Imogen swallowed heavily, aware that she had no experience of this kind of thing, and insecurity and a deep sense of inadequacy fought it out for top position in her mind.

Stopping beside her, Nadir delved into a hidden pocket in his robe, muttering something about 'earlier' under his breath. Then he turned towards her and held out a ring with a stone the size of a small grapefruit—an oval-shaped diamond grapefruit that was exquisitely hand-crafted and the most divine piece of jewellery Imogen had ever seen. Both her heart and her mind did a double-take.

'Before we go in you'll need to put this on.'

Momentarily blank, she stared at it.

'It's an engagement ring.'

She knew what it was. Sometimes as a young girl she had imagined receiving one from a man she loved. She and her friends had even gone engagement ring shopping once when they had been bored after school. They had then dreamed up elaborate ways their future beaus might pop what had felt like the biggest question of their lives back then. At no time had any of them come up with the man of their dreams saying, 'You'll need to put this on.'

And how many times was she going to get her hopes up over this man only to have them dashed by the reality that he was here because she was the mother of his baby and for no other reason?

'That's not necessary,' she said huskily, instinctively snatching her hands behind her back.

A frown drew down his brows as if her reluctance hadn't occurred to him. 'Of course it is. Many of the guests at the dinner are Western. They will expect to see you wearing my ring.'

A sickening sense of inevitability crept over Imogen and made her feel incredibly vulnerable. Incredibly exposed. 'I can say I lost it if anyone asks.'

His frown turned into a scowl. 'If it's the fact that you didn't choose it yourself that's the problem you can swap it at a later date.'

That wasn't the problem. The problem was that she didn't want to swap it. The problem was that the ring was exactly what she would have chosen had he given her the choice. But he never would. The ruthless way he kept sweeping aside her insistence that she would not marry him as if it was nothing more than an empty spider's web dangling in a doorway was evidence of that alone.

'You have no idea, do you?' she tossed at him, wanting to somehow hurt him the way he was currently hurting her. 'I don't want to wear your ring because it will ruin it when someone who really loves me wants to give me one.'

Swearing under his breath, Nadir's expression grew stormy. 'Damn it, Imogen, there won't be anyone else putting a ring on your finger. So you can get that out of your mind right now.'

She shook her head, aware that they were studiously *not* being watched by the guards who stood to attention around them. As if sensing her discomfort, or uncomfortable himself, Nadir drew her to the side of the room in what probably looked like a loving gesture.

'I thought I had explained how important tonight was.'

'You don't explain things, Nadir, you talk until you get what you want.'

'I *have* explained.' His tone was marked with frustration. 'I was supposed to renounce the throne today but Zach didn't show up. Now I have to host a dinner.'

'But why don't you want to be King? Zach said it was your birthright.'

He shut down. She saw it instantly in the set of his jaw. 'The why is not important. It's the intention that counts. I don't want the job. Zach does. I suppose you intend to be difficult about this as well.'

Hurt by the implication that she was being difficult just for the sake of it, she flinched. 'I'd like to understand it.'

'Do you want to be Queen—is that it?'

'No, that's not it. I didn't even think about that until just then.'

He looked at her.

'I didn't. Why would I when I haven't even agreed to marry you?'

She'd be flattered at his insistence on marrying her if she thought there was any deep sentiment behind it. Basically, it was because of Nadeena with great sex thrown in as a side order.

Without warning, Nadir reached out and raised her chin so that her eyes met his. Instead of looking fierce and commanding he looked frustrated and weary and her heart lurched.

'I need you to cut me some slack here, Imogen. I feel like I'm holding on by a thread.'

The raw words and his pained expression gave her pause but she was loath to let her heart soften towards him because he'd likely trample on it without even noticing.

Of course the traitorous organ didn't listen to her head. It never did when he was around. When he was this close to her that his scent wound its way inside her and made her ache to lean in and press her face into his neck.

'What is it, Imogen?' His thumb drew light circles across her chin, the gesture more comforting than sexual. 'What are you thinking?'

The width of his broad shoulders blocking the soldiers from her view established a feeling of intense intimacy between them and it was as if the dinner guests on the other side of the large doorway didn't exist. 'Honestly, Nadir, I don't know what to think.' She looked up at him and knew that her expression was troubled. 'I don't know what to feel or what to do any more. This is all so confusing and unexpected. One minute I'm alone with Nadeena and then… And what we had in Paris.' She swallowed heavily and his frown deepened. 'It was so…so…' She couldn't say it. She couldn't say that it was so special. That she had counted the minutes from Monday to Friday during that month they had been together and prayed that he would fly in and rap on her front door and kiss her even before he said hello. 'And now I'm scared because everything feels so broken.'

Broken like her own home life had been. Like her heart had been after he had left Paris and like she feared it would be again if she let her guard down and agreed to marry him.

Nadir cupped her face, gently smoothing his fingers along her jaw line, stroking the velvety skin beneath her earlobes.

'Imogen, look at me.' The whispered words were fierce and oh, so close to her ear she could feel his warm breath stirring her hair. She could feel the tips of her breasts pressed lightly against the front of his robes. She stopped breathing as his voice washed over her in deep, melodic waves, her eyes riveted to his as her emotions surged to the surface. 'Do not be scared. I promise you that I will take care of everything. You...Nadeena. I will protect you and provide for you.' He tilted her chin up with the tip of his finger when her eyes fell away from his. 'You will want for nothing, *habibi*. Not clothing or food or shelter.' He searched her face. 'Not diamonds or holidays or palaces. Whatever your heart desires I will give to you. What more is there?'

*Love*, Imogen thought achingly. Trust. Companionship. *Friendship.* And while she could see that he meant what he said, she knew that he was unlikely to feel those things for her and she was so afraid that she already did for him.

Imogen looked up and found that his silvery-blue eyes had turned stormy with emotion, dark with desire. His nostrils flared. She felt the change in the taut lines of his body and an answering response immediately swept through her own and made her feel soft and weak.

*Force majeure*, the French dancers had called him and they weren't wrong. He was an irresistible power, a force of nature, and Imogen was like a house of straw caught up in the devastating storm of his masculinity. The devastating storm of his self-assurance.

The hand at her hip moved to the small of her back, pressing her so close it was bordering on indecent. Her gaze shifted to his mouth. His lips parted and hers did the same. Would he kiss her? Here? Now?

'What do you say, Imogen? Will you give us a chance? For Nadeena.'

Imogen felt as if a lead weight had landed inside her chest. He wanted this for their daughter, who bound them together and divided them at the same time. She knew that if she continued to say no it would be beyond selfish because Minh had been right. Nadir did have a right to their daughter and she could either dwell on the past or try to embrace the future.

Feeling as if she was standing on the edge of a precipice with no clear landing over the side, she held out her left hand. 'Okay, Nadir.' She swallowed heavily. 'For Nadeena.'

With only the briefest of hesitations, Nadir took her hand in his and slid the ring into place. Imogen stared at it, cold and heavy on her finger, and willed her heart to stay uninvolved this time.

# CHAPTER NINE

NADIR DISMISSED MAAB after she gave him a full report on Nadeena's well-being at the end of the evening and circled the living room waiting for Imogen to return from checking on her.

In many ways they were just like any other couple returning home at the end of an evening out. One saw to the sitter, the other checked on the baby.

He glanced towards the drinks cabinet and thought about pouring them a glass of brandy. If they really were just like any other couple they would take advantage of the fact that the baby was sleeping and maybe have a nightcap before falling all over each other as soon as possible.

Nadir's eyes tracked down over Imogen as she stepped into the room, the evening gown flowing around her svelte frame and clinging to her hips. Images of her in his king-sized bed fogged his brain. Her long, toned, flexible legs wrapped around his hips, her supple back arched in passion as she rode him, her small, high breasts jutting forward, begging for his mouth. If they were just like any other couple he'd have her in that position pronto.

And why not? She had agreed to marry him. Or, rather, she had acquiesced—because that was what her strained little *For Nadeena* had sounded like to his ears. Even so, he should be feeling relieved right now to have that sorted. Triumphant, even. But he didn't. If anything, he felt as if it was a Pyrrhic victory because, while he might have gained her agreement, he could see by the wall she had erected between them that he had gained very little else.

And right now he wanted to tear that wall down. Right now he wanted more from her than shy, covert glances that only served to heighten his awareness of her as a woman. His awareness of her as *his* woman.

All night she'd been giving them to him as she worked the room like a pro. At first he'd thought her nervousness stemmed from some sort of insecurity but he'd soon discounted that. She'd handled herself beautifully. Talking to the Sultan of Astiv about his love of antique glassware while those around him nearly fainted with boredom and then recounting war stories about the trials and tribulations of competitive waterskiing with the Prince of Mana.

He'd hated the prince knowing something about her that he hadn't had a clue about and he'd liked even less the way the Prince had looked at her. But then he pretty much didn't like the way any man looked at her and that possessive feeling wasn't something he'd ever had to deal with before.

She gripped her hands together as if she didn't know what to do with them. 'Nadeena is asleep.'

'Good. Maab said she had most of the milk you expressed at eleven o clock.'

'Oh, okay. In that case I'm glad I didn't wake her to change her nappy because she should sleep for a few more hours now.'

'Good.' Nadir wondered how it was he could stand in the middle of the room having a stilted conversation about Nadeena when all he wanted to do was strip Imogen naked and bury himself deep inside her lush body. 'How long do you think we've got before she wakes up?'

He watched her eyes widen as comprehension dawned and thought, *Oh, yes, my sweet, I have exactly that in mind.*

If he was going to be breaking down walls tonight he didn't plan on doing it with a sledgehammer.

'Not long.'

He smiled. Her 'no' couldn't have been more transparent.

Realising that he still wore his *keffiyeh,* he reached up and yanked it from his head, ruffling his hair. He felt her eyes on him but when he glanced over her gaze flitted away and she shifted like a mare scenting the approach of an overly randy stallion.

She cleared her throat and lifted her chin and he knew she was about to try and call an end to the evening. 'Well, I hope the night was okay from your point of view but—'

'The night was excellent. You were brilliant.'

'Oh. Well, thank you.'

He studied her. 'Why were you nervous tonight?'

'Who said I was nervous?'

He felt a small smile touch his lips. 'I could tell. But I don't know why.'

'Because I knew everyone would be looking at me.'

'But you're a dancer—you must be used to being on show in front of people.'

'Being in a performance is totally different from being myself.'

So he'd been right about the insecurity. He frowned, wanting to reassure her. 'People like you. You're a natural. And a waterskier, I understand. How was it that the Prince of Mana knew that you had once won the Australian championships and I had no idea?'

'Maybe because he asked and you didn't.'

Nadir scowled. 'I'm asking now.'

She shrugged. 'It wasn't that big a deal. My mother was into waterskiing, which is how I came to do it, but when I was sixteen my ballet teacher told me that I needed to give up all dangerous sports if I was to take the dance seriously and I stopped.'

'But you loved it,' he guessed.

Her eyes glowed with an inner light that made them sparkle. 'The speed was pretty exhilarating.'

He grinned. 'Something we have in common.'

In Paris he'd been too obsessed with touching her to get to know her properly. Now he realised he wanted both. 'Have a nightcap with me.'

'I don't think that's a good idea.'

Nadir walked over to the wet bar and smiled. 'Have one anyway.'

Imogen knew that smile. He'd used it often when they'd been out and he'd come up and wrap his arms around her and tell her something, like how tired his feet were from walking or how cold he was and how he really thought they should head indoors. What he'd meant was that they should be in bed. Usually she'd melt against him at that point and he'd hail a cab, her need for him just as overpowering as his was for her.

Even that first night her need for him had eradicated her natural cautiousness around men and overshadowed her commonsense. She closed her eyes in the vain hope that the memories would go away but instead she felt as if she was back in Paris inside his elegant apartment.

The only reason they'd even shut the main door that first night was so he could crush her up against it. After her show he had prowled into the backstage area, his eyes hot with intent. Imogen had quivered with raw excitement, a deep feminine instinct having already warned her that he would come for her. And he had. He'd told her his name and asked her how long it would take her to change. When she'd told him ten minutes to scrub off the stage make-up he'd said, 'I'll wait.'

He'd made it sound as if he'd wait for ever. One of the other girls had rushed to lend her a short black dress since she'd only brought her jeans and a T-shirt to change back into and had sighed as if she wished she'd been the chosen one. Heels had materialised and the girls had tittered around her and told her who he was. Imogen hadn't really taken any notice, her mind buzzing with a sexual excitement she'd never felt before. He had taken her to one of Paris's exclusive supper clubs in his black Ferrari and been the perfect gentleman while they ate.

Not that she remembered much of the food. Or the conversation, for that matter, but she remembered how his hands had cradled his glass of Scotch as he'd watched her then he'd led her back to his car, his hand hot on the small of her back. He'd asked if she would like to go to his place for coffee. She'd said yes even though she hated coffee; a fact they had laughed at the following morning.

Imogen remembered feeling immeasurably shy and nervous seeing as how it was her first time going home with a man. Her only other lover had been a self-centred dancer who had come on to her after a sweaty but exhilarating rehearsal in her late teens and the rehearsal had been so much better.

Not that she'd told Nadir any of that. She hadn't known how. To tell him in the car ride to his apartment that she was pretty new to all this would have seemed presumptuous in the extreme and then when they had taken the lift—the very tiny and interminably slow lift—to his floor he hadn't touched her. He hadn't said a word to her in fact and nor had she to him, but her body had hummed with a life of its own and a hollow ache had risen up between her thighs with every floor that flashed past.

Finally they'd arrived. Nadir had pushed the door open, Imogen had made to move past him and accidently brushed her bare arm against his. That was all it had taken. One touch of his skin against hers and she had been lost. Gone up in a fireball of heat and need and powerful yearnings that had driven out all sense and caution. She remembered that the door had slammed shut and then thankfully she was up against it as her body had grown too heavy for her legs to hold her up.

Nadir had groaned against her neck, told her how much he wanted her. He'd cupped her face and pushed her hair behind her shoulders. Then he'd taken her mouth with his, ran his hands all over her body, pulled up her too-short dress and ripped her silky panties away. Awestruck, Imogen had been unable to do anything but grab onto his broad shoulders and kiss him back as he'd filled her. His body hot and hard and so powerful as he'd thrust into her. She'd had a moment's discomfort, which he'd sensed because he'd slowed and the change in pace had pushed her over the edge embarrassingly quickly. She'd cried out. He'd cried out and then they had been meshed together, both panting in the silent, dark hallway. He'd given a self-deprecating laugh, told her it had never been like that for him before and carried her into the bedroom. Ran the tub. Made love to her what felt like a hundred times more throughout the night.

'What are you thinking about, *habibi*?' His deep voice broke into her reverie and she started, her hands pleating the sides of her dress.

She took a deep careful breath in and eased it out. She wasn't stupid, she knew what he'd been suggesting before and she knew she wasn't emotionally ready to take that step. Not after a night of having his focus on her as if she was the most important person in the world to him. 'Nothing.'

He stepped in front of her. His eyes were dark and intense on hers. She wanted to look away because she knew her own must mirror the hunger she saw there but she couldn't. She was trapped by a desire that was becoming harder and harder to ignore the more time they spent together.

His eyes slid down her body, warming her from the inside out until they stopped on her hands.

'Where's your ring?'

All night he'd been at her about the ring, telling her not to fidget with it because then everyone would know that it was new.

'Everyone would be right,' she had whispered irritably at the start of the night. 'And it feels wrong on my finger.'

Of course he'd been annoyed by that. 'Before you know it you'll forget it's even there.'

Just as he would one day forget her and Nadeena were even there? 'What did you do with it?' he asked now.

'I took it off,' she said with a touch more defiance than she'd meant.

A muscle ticked in his jaw. 'So you can keep pretending this is not happening, *habibi*?'

When she didn't answer, because yes, in some way it was easier to pretend this wasn't happening, he stalked past her and straight through the doorway into her bedroom.

'Nadir!'

Worried that he would wake the baby, she ran after him and nearly collided with him in the doorway. Grim-faced, he reached for her left hand and jammed the ring back on her finger. 'That stays on.'

Supremely irritated with his overbearing attitude, Imogen wrestled with the ring, not sure what she intended to do with it once she got it off, but Nadir grabbed her hands and shoved them behind her back, bringing her body into full contact with his own.

Time seemed to stop as they stared at each other, both breathing hard. She wanted to tell him to let her go and perversely to hold her tighter at the same time.

She stared up at him, slightly dazed. Perhaps she was losing her mind…

'Dammit, Imogen, you would try the patience of a saint and I'm definitely not a saint.'

She'd had every intention of resisting his kiss but every moment seemed to converge with her wanting his mouth on her. His hands. It was madness. It was glorious and when his mouth came down over hers and his hand rose to palm her breast Imogen moaned and gave herself over to the mindless pleasure of being close to him again. This—touching him, tasting him—was thrilling and she wasn't sure how far she would have gone or when she would have called a halt to things when fate stepped in—or was it luck?—and they both broke apart as the high-pitched wail of a baby's cry rent the air.

Panting and shocked at the sheer wantonness of her own response, Imogen nearly fell out of Nadir's arms in her haste to put some space between them, her mind spinning, her body sluggish with arousal.

Nadir stared at her, his own chest heaving, and beneath his heated gaze and Nadeena's sharp cries her breasts started to tingle and leak milk all over the front of the exquisite silk dress. Mortified, she cupped her hands over her breasts and fled next door to her daughter.

Trying to slow her breathing, she reached for the baby and cradled her against her chest before easing into the corner chair to feed her. 'It's okay, angel. Mummy's here.' She closed her eyes, her face hot with embarrassment at how easily she had slipped back into Nadir's arms without thought or care of the consequences. Yesterday she had been trying to convince him that marriage was a mistake and now she had agreed to it. She had his ring on her finger and she still wasn't sure she wasn't about to make the biggest mistake of her life.

As if conjured by her thoughts, Nadir materialised in

the doorway, his hair askew where her fingers had tangled in it, his features drawn tight with unfulfilled desire.

'Do you need anything?' His deep voice rumbled through her and momentarily distracted Nadeena. She glanced down to find her daughter's eyes open and staring, trying to find her father and feed at the same time.

'I'm fine.' Imogen stroked her hand over Nadeena's head, settling her. She wasn't fine, of course—she was flustered, confused, *unsatisfied*.

'Water? Can I get you water?' For the first time he looked out of his depth and her heart clenched. 'I read that breastfeeding mothers need to drink lots of water.'

*He had?* Her surprise must have shown on her face because he ran a hand through his hair and his jaw set hard.

'Water would be nice,' she said softly, her mind struggling to adapt to the return to normality between them. She shook her head at that. It struggled to adapt to what passed as normality between them since Nadir had stepped back into her life. A normality that was still defined by past hurts and an uncertain future.

'Here.'

She blinked as a glass of water was thrust in front of her.

'Thank you.'

'You're welcome.' He nodded and took it back when she'd drained the glass. 'Can I get you anything else?'

'No, no.' She placed Nadeena on her shoulder to burp her. 'No, everything should be—oh!' Imogen squirmed as she felt warm baby spew slide down over her bare shoulder and the top half of her dress. 'Oh.'

She heard Nadir chuckle. '"Oh" is right.'

The look on his face made her suddenly feel like laughing and groaning at the same time with embarrassment. Then Nadeena grew fussy and started crying, jamming her tiny fists into her mouth.

'What's wrong with her?'

'I suspect it's her teeth.' She touched her hand to Nadeena's forehead. 'She's not overly hot so…' She scrunched her brow. 'It could be that she's just tired and out of sorts because it's late. It's hard to figure out what's wrong with babies sometimes.'

'Not just babies.'

His rueful comment hung between them and just when she might have asked what he meant by it he held out his arms. 'Here, give her to me.'

'No, no…it's fine, I can—'

'I know you can, Imogen,' he agreed flatly. 'But you need to go clean up and I can settle her while you do it.'

'Oh, right.' Clean up. She'd completely forgotten about the sour milk on her shoulder and dress. She handed Nadeena to him and watched as he confidently tucked her into the crook of his muscular arms. 'Come on, *habibti*,' he crooned, 'let's get you settled.'

Again Imogen was momentarily struck dumb by the sight of them together but unfortunately Nadeena didn't stop crying and it made her hurry into the shower, where she quickly rinsed her hair and washed herself.

Pulling on the oversized T-shirt she had used the night before, she hurried back to her room to find Nadir pacing back and forth and singing what sounded like an Arabic lullaby in his soft baritone.

'She's nearly asleep. Should I put her in the cot?'

'I need to change her first.'

'I've done it already.'

Imogen stared at him. 'You have?'

'I'm not completely useless, Imogen. I can change a baby's nappy.'

Given that Nadir was the most capable man she had ever met, she didn't know why she had ever doubted he could. Maybe because her father had never shown much interest in his duties as a parent. It made her realise just how low her expectations had been on the night that Nadir had walked out after discovering that she was pregnant. Maybe they had been low all along.

The thought stunned her.

Had she been waiting for him to disappoint her? Fail her? Because he had. Spectacularly so. Which didn't fit with why he was being so helpful now. Was it to garner her cooperation with his dogged plan for them to marry or because he genuinely cared?

Too many questions and too few answers but Imogen suspected that maybe he wouldn't change his mind about marrying her and, worse, part of her didn't want him to. This…she swallowed back a ball of emotion rising inside her chest…this was nice. Sharing the care of Nadeena with him, working together as a team. It was every woman's wish to have her lover—her partner—around to talk with and iron out the kinks of parenthood. To journey through life hand in hand with someone there to help field the knocks it inevitably handed out. Someone who would care.

But Nadir wasn't her lover or her partner at this point and her mother's dating advice had been to warn her that a man could put on a good show for thirty, even forty, days before the cracks started appearing. If you added up their time together in Paris and the last couple of days, Nadir fell smack bang in the middle of her mother's bell curve. Would he revert to his playboy ways after that and start ignoring them both?

'Imogen?'

Realising she had spaced out and that she was extremely tired after all the emotion of the last couple of days, she glanced up at him holding Nadeena. She looked so tiny and perfect in his arms.

'Just…' She had no idea what she was going to say. 'She might need a top-up.'

'A top-up?'

'A bit more milk.' Her face flooded with colour as he understood and she thought how ridiculous that she should be embarrassed after all they had shared but she was. 'I'll do it in bed. It's sometimes easier.'

'But is it safe? What if you fall asleep?'

'Of course it's safe,' Imogen said sharply. 'I wouldn't put her at risk, Nadir.'

'I wasn't questioning your mothering skills, Imogen, I…oh, hell.' He rubbed his jaw. 'This is all new to me. I want you to be safe.'

Imogen's heart gave a little leap. *Not you*, she derided the foolish muscle in her chest; he means he wants Nadeena to be safe. 'I won't fall asleep,' she said wearily. 'You can go.'

Their eyes connected in the dim light and Imogen saw a look come over his face that she couldn't quite define. If she had to guess she'd say it was as if he was trying to work something out but, whatever it was, it seemed to elude him.

She lay on the bed and waited almost breathlessly as he leant over and laid Nadeena in the crook of her arm, sleepiness invading her limbs as her daughter latched onto her nipple once again.

'Your hair is wet,' he said gruffly.

'I know.' Imogen lifted her hand to smooth the damp, irritating strands away from her shoulder and tried not to show her surprise when Nadir's hands took over the task, smoothing the long strands out on the pillow behind her.

'It's fine,' she said, her breaths shallow and hurried at the intimacy of the moment. 'You don't have to do that.'

'Stop trying to shut me out, Imogen. If you leave your hair like this it will be all tangled in the morning.'

He continued working out the kinks and Imogen decided it was better if she just let him do it. And it felt good. So good.

'Go to sleep,' he said gruffly as he perched on the bed behind her. 'I'll transfer Nadeena to the cot when she's finished.'

'I can…' Imogen yawned. She wanted to say she could do it but she didn't. Instead she did something she hadn't done for months. She fell into a contented sleep before her baby had fully settled.

# CHAPTER TEN

NADIR LOOKED DOWN at the woman sleeping on the bed so soundly, her deep breaths even and relaxed. He remembered that she had always slept like the dead and he had often teased her about how hard he'd had to work to wake her through the night. Sometimes he'd even been in the process of kissing her soft body, teasing her awake with caresses that had tortured him and woken her panting. Always when she came awake like that she had wrapped her arms and legs around him and pulled him closer. Always she had moved with him and he'd angled his body in such a way that he knew would bring her to orgasm in no time. She'd groan in his ear, clasp him tighter, urge him on and then afterwards she'd sigh and curl herself around him, pretty much like she was doing to their daughter right now, and Nadir had the strongest urge to get into bed behind them and do the same thing.

Only he didn't.

They both looked too peaceful. His heart clenched and he took a step back. He wondered how life had brought him to this point. To this woman and child. Fate?

It certainly wasn't planned. All his adult life he'd assumed he'd walk his path alone and he'd been okay with that. After the rigid childhood he'd had where his father's word was law he had made sure that he had plenty of choices in life that had all been about taking care of himself. It was a selfish existence for sure but it was also safe because he didn't need anyone and no one needed him in return.

But that had changed now. Now he had a child and a woman he was responsible for and he was determined that they would make a better family unit than his had been. Nothing would make him turn away from them.

Careful not to wake either female, he carefully lifted Nadeena into his arms and marvelled at how small and how fragile she was. He nuzzled her downy dark hair and breathed in her sweet baby smell.

A smile curved his lips as he recalled how Imogen had tried to put him off marrying her by telling him that babies were smelly. They were but in a good way.

They were also a lot cuter than he'd ever noticed before and he grinned when he placed Nadeena into the cot and she promptly sprawled onto her back with her arms flung out to the sides, her tiny mouth moving as she resettled into sleep.

Feeling comfortable that she wasn't about to wake up, he turned towards Imogen. She had shifted more onto her stomach, her leg hitched high on the bed. If he'd been lying beside her that leg would have been draped over his hips and his groin hardened predictably. He wanted her and he didn't mind admitting it. Sex was normal. Healthy. But deep down he knew what he felt for her went beyond sex. For once he didn't try and stop his mind from drifting back to the way things had been between them in Paris. Carefree and passionate. Relaxed and somehow contented. *Contented?*

His mind processed the thought. Had he really been contented when he'd been with her in Paris? When they'd been strolling together arm in arm around the city just like any other couple in the world? He remembered ignoring those feelings at the time and putting them down to sex. Lust. Passion. But, looking back, he could see that he'd felt completely at ease in her company. Relaxed and, yes, contented. And then another startling thought gripped him. He didn't want her to endure their marriage. He wanted her to want it. He wanted her to want to make it work as much as he did. He wanted her to want him.

He rubbed his eyes and for the first time he wondered if he was doing the right thing by forcing this marriage onto her. But what else could he do?

She made a sound, almost as if she was having a bad dream, and called out his name. Nadir stilled. In his mind's eye he saw her rising from the bed, her short T-shirt riding high on those shapely legs before she reached him and wound her arms around his neck and pulled his mouth down to hers as she had done so many times in the past.

Naturally enough, she didn't do that but she did call out again and Nadir found himself crossing the floor to her side.

'Imogen?' He reached down and placed his hand lightly on her shoulder. 'You're dreaming, *habibi*.'

He thought he'd spoken softly enough not to really disturb her but her eyes flew open and she blinked and the little frown line appeared as she stared up at him.

'Where am I?'

Despite the warning in his head telling him she was tired and needed sleep, he didn't stop himself from reaching down and placing his finger against the frown line. 'It's okay. You're in Bakaan.'

She made a small sound and pushed up into a sitting position. She wasn't wearing a bra and he couldn't keep his eyes off the gentle sway of her breasts. 'Imogen.' Her name was more like a groan on his lips when he caught her staring at his mouth.

By Allah, he wanted her. Wanted her more than he'd wanted any other woman in his life. More than he'd wanted anything at all for a long time and, as if in slow motion, he reached out and took hold of her hand and tugged her up onto her knees.

She rose to him, all sleepy and pliant, and his mouth swooped down to capture hers in a sweet, lingering kiss. He felt her hands flutter close to his jaw and snag on the stubble of his beard growth. He'd need a shave if he was going to stop himself from marring her pale skin but more than that he needed her and for the first time ever he didn't feel concerned by that driving need.

Something had been slowly changing within him since he'd found her again. He didn't know what it was but it was almost as if a piece of his life had slotted into place. Impossible really, given how out of synch his life was right now but still…the feeling persisted.

Not wanting to disturb Nadeena, he broke their kiss and tugged her towards him. When she clung to his shoulders he swept her into his arms and strode out of the bedroom.

'Nadir?' She wriggled and he let her slide down the length of his body until she found her feet. But he didn't immediately let her go.

'I want to make love to you, Imogen. I want to take you to my bed and show you how well this can work between us. How good it can be again.'

The words were raw, his voice almost hoarse with need. Her eyes widened and even in the low-lit hallway he could see colour rising high on her lovely cheekbones.

She swallowed and pushed the tumble of her hair back from her face and he just wanted to bury his hands in it. He just wanted to kiss her. So he did.

As soon as his mouth touched hers, Imogen felt her body catch fire and soften against him and all thoughts of the past and the future dissolved. How was it possible to feel so much for one person? To want so much from one person? And then she couldn't think any more. Just feel—her heart ruling her actions.

Moaning, she gripped his hair in her hands, letting her body melt against his. This was what she had craved for so long. This aching pleasure only he could give her. And like this they were equals with no past and no future. Just the present.

Pressing closer, she felt Nadir fall against the wall, his laugh husky as his hungry mouth worked its way down her throat. Imogen arched and rose onto tiptoe, her lower body aching to join with his.

Driven by a deep yearning, she clawed at the yards of fabric that made up his robe and felt him turn them both and press her against the wall, his hands pushing up the hem of her T-shirt and hastily dragging her panties down her legs and then finally, blissfully she felt him cup her and she almost dissolved as he parted her slick flesh and delved between her legs, his fingers and thumb gliding over her and into her and stroking her in all the right places.

'Nadir, you—'

'Imogen, *habibi*, you drive me—'

She shifted and he grunted, wedging his knee between her thighs to hold her upright while he parted his robes singlehandedly.

Imogen tried to bring her hands down to help him but he effortlessly held her high against the wall, his upper body powerfully hard beneath her fingertips and then he brought her down over the top of him and she heard a loud keening sound as his smooth, thick hardness opened her up and penetrated deep inside her body.

He swore. Maybe she did too and for a minute they were both completely still, suspended between two worlds, both adjusting to the exquisite sensation of being joined together.

Then he tangled one hand in her hair and tugged until

her dazed eyes met his. The skin on his face was pulled tight, his eyes glittering with a hunger that sent shivers racing down her spine. Those eyes said that this time together would not be gentle or slow. That it would be fierce and urgent and uncontrolled. That she would feel him plunge into her with every fibre of her being and her body pulsed in anticipation.

'Is this okay?' His question was a panting growl and tinged with desperation as if he was having trouble holding himself back. 'I mean you had a baby not long ago and—'

Imogen wound her legs around his waist and hugged him tight. Now that she had given herself over to this it was all she could do not to let the fire inside burn her up. 'It's fine. Please, Nadir—'

He crashed his mouth down over hers again, his tongue thrusting deep as he gave her what she craved and moved powerfully inside her. In no time at all Imogen felt her orgasm building and writhed against him, forcing him to press one hand against the wall to hold them both upright and then she was there, on the pinnacle of that exquisite release she had only ever experienced in his arms, their mouths fused together as if their lives depended on it. Imogen opened her eyes at that moment to find him watching her and the connection was so elemental it hurtled her over the edge into a place filled with bright lights and dizzying heights. And then it was all too much and she threw her head back and let her release rush through her on long exquisite pulses. Seconds later Nadir's grip on her hips tightened to the point of pain and his thrusts grew brutal just before he threw his own head back and bellowed her name into the still night air.

The comedown from the desperate rush to orgasm was slow and noisy, both of them panting hard to catch their breaths.

Nadir raised his head from where it was now buried against her neck. 'Are you okay?'

'Yes. Out of shape, but good.'

Nadir gripped the underside of her thighs and hoisted her legs higher around his waist while he remained buried deep inside her. 'You're not out of shape, *habibi.* You're perfect.'

'Where are we going?' she asked quickly as he carried her down the hall.

'My bed.'

'What about Nadeena?'

'I'll leave the door open.' He strode inside the room and didn't even bother with the light as he collapsed with her onto the bed.

Imogen tilted her head back and felt the silky fabric of the comforter against the sensitised skin of her back. Part of her knew that she should get up but her body felt as if it was on fire, renewed desire coiling through every cell, and all she wanted to do was wrap herself around Nadir and not think about anything right now. Not the future that seemed so insurmountable and not the past which was tinged with the bittersweet memories of first love and then the utter despair of rejection. Right now her body just wanted his, *needed* his, and she was powerless to resist.

Not that Nadir was exactly giving her time to question his demands as he kissed and licked his way down over her collarbone towards her breasts.

Before she could object, he raised her T-shirt over her head and tossed it onto the floor.

'This time we do it a little slower,' he said gruffly. 'And I might even throw in a little finesse for good measure.'

Imogen laughed at his playful words and then suddenly felt self-conscious as she realised where his mouth was headed. 'Nadir, stop. My breasts aren't the same any more and I'm feeding.'

He batted her hands away and rose up on one powerful arm to peer down at her, his other hand drawing lazy circles around the outer swells of each breast before cupping each one in turn. She felt her nipples peak and rise up eagerly for his touch. 'I don't care. You're beautiful, Imogen.' He lowered his head and laved one nipple lightly with his tongue, making her gasp with pleasure. Nadir grinned. 'I love that you can feed our child. I love that your nipples are slightly darker than before.' His head bent again and he blew across one straining tip. 'I love your taste. The way you feel.'

Lost in his words and his touch, Imogen's arms rose up again to mould his sinewy shoulders and cling to the taut wall of muscle at his back. It was that untamed, unrefined side of him, encapsulated within sleek, sophisticated masculinity that had always drawn her to him. Had always drawn every woman to him.

Forgetting about the past, she inhaled, pulling the wonderful scent of sweat and man deep into her body. 'I love the way you taste too. Take off your robe. I want to feel you against me.'

Nadir didn't need any further urging and within seconds he had come down over the top of her again. Naked. A gloriously prowling male in his prime. Imogen's breath caught at the sight of his thick length jutting hard up against his ridged abdomen. He was so potently virile. So unselfconsciously male he took her breath away.

'Like what you see, *habibi*?' he drawled lazily.

*'Comme ci, comme ça.'* She pretended to yawn.

He growled at her cheekiness and pushed her thighs wider with his knees. 'I'll give you *comme ci, comme ça*,' he whispered roughly, reaching beneath her to angle her bottom up better for his penetration.

He groaned as he sank into her warm, willing flesh. 'I was going to take this slow but now…' he thrust forward and Imogen clung to his arms, her fingernails digging into his hard biceps to anchor herself against him '…now I just want to plough into you and make you scream. How's that for finesse?'

'Finesse is so terribly overrated.' She gasped out each word as he did exactly what he said.

He grunted his pleasure, his gaze hungry as it raked over her face. 'Tell me if I'm too rough?'

Imogen shook her head and brought her hands up to cup the hard planes of his face, her fingers stroking over the rough bristle on his jaw. 'No. Give me more. I want more.'

'Ah, hell, Imogen. *Habibi.*' His words of praise became more urgent and mixed with Arabic as he drove into her over and over and over until they both fell apart with the extent of another mind-blowing orgasm.

Finally sated, Nadir bent down and kissed her sweetly on the mouth. Then he rolled onto his back and took her with him, tucking her head into the crook of his shoulder and it was as if no time had passed at all. She could almost hear the sounds of Parisians dining and chatting and going about their business from the open window of his apartment. But time had passed and it had created a chasm and her chest tightened as she thought about getting up and going back to her own room. If only she wasn't feeling so weak, ripples of her release still coursing through her lax body.

'What?' he asked as if he sensed her tension.

'I should go back to Nadeena.'

He gently tugged her still damp hair out from under his arm and stroked it back against the pillow. 'Stay. I've missed holding you like this.'

His admission startled her and set off a warm glow as if a cluster of fireflies had set up house inside her chest. 'Me too.'

She felt him place a light kiss against her hair and turned her face into his throat.

'Then sleep. I'll check on Nadeena in a minute.'

She wanted to protest, she wanted to say that she needed to do it because she always had and Nadeena's safety was her responsibility but Nadir rolled her onto her side and spooned her, his big body swamping hers and cocooning her in the most delicious warmth and a deep lassitude invaded her already weakened limbs and turned her limp. It was blissful, this feeling of being utterly taken care of, and no doubt—if she let it—highly addictive.

# CHAPTER ELEVEN

OR IT COULD have been highly addictive if it had continued. But of course it had not, Imogen thought glumly as she stretched to place her nose against her knee, her groin muscles protesting the once effortless stretch.

They had made love twice more during the night, once fast and another time slow and indulgent, his fingers drifting and stroking over every inch of her body as if he couldn't get enough of her and then in the morning she'd woken up to find him gone.

At first she'd not minded, stretching her overused muscles and indulging in sensual recall. Then she'd realised that she couldn't hear anything and that she'd overslept for the first time since she'd become pregnant and had raced out of bed, pulling on her T-shirt that had been wedged half under his giant bed and set off down the hallway to find Nadeena's cot empty.

Slightly panicked, she'd then rushed into the living area to find Tasnim and Maab taking care of Nadeena at the outdoor table. Relieved, she'd pulled up, taken her smiling daughter into her arms and hugged her, the rush of relief bringing with it the subtle aches and pains in her body that brought her awareness back to how well loved she had been the night before. Then she'd glanced around for Nadir. Tasnim said that he had given Nadeena the small amount of milk left over from when Imogen had expressed the night before and told them not to wake her unless it was absolutely necessary.

As if on cue, her breasts had tingled and she'd sat in a shaded lounge chair and fed her daughter. And waited for Nadir to return.

She'd sat there with a secret smile on her face and thought that maybe she'd been wrong to leave Paris so hastily fourteen months ago. That maybe she'd been wrong not to have realised that he would want what was best for her and the baby.

That had been yesterday morning's thoughts. Now, another day and a half later, Imogen was wishing that she had run further fourteen months ago and that he'd never found her because, apart from a note sent to inform her that he would be in late last night, she hadn't seen or heard from him since.

It would have been the classical wham-bam-thank-you-ma'am scenario except for the fact that she still had an enormous ring on her finger that she was sure someone would hack off to obtain if she ever ventured out into a public place with it on.

She glanced at it now, wondering why she still wore it.

It wasn't because she was under any illusion that the man who had given it to her genuinely cared about her. And it definitely wasn't because she thought he craved her company as much as she stupidly craved his. Not that he'd ever know that was how she felt. No, she might have felt her heart crack open a little when he was touching her, kissing her, *making love to her,* but his behaviour over the last two days had sealed it back up with more precision than a blowtorch. And to think she'd imagined that she was falling for him all over again. Thank goodness she'd disabused herself of that errant notion.

And yes, on some level she knew she was being unfair to him because of his current issues in Bakaan but she knew he had a reputation for working hard. Working hard and playing hard. So she knew this was just a sign of her life to come and she didn't like it. He made her feel like an afterthought while she found herself wanting so much more from their relationship. More than he clearly did.

The realisation was emotionally debilitating and if he thought that giving her a couple of extraordinary orgasms would be enough to make her comply with his every wish then he had another thing coming. Especially since she'd had at least a day now to stew over the news that they were to be married at the end of the week.

She doubted she would have taken the news that well if it had come from Nadir, but since it had come from Tasnim asking what style of dress she would like to wear she felt like telling Nadir to go to hell. That she'd been right all along and this was nothing but an enormous mistake they would both live to regret.

A slight noise from behind her had her hackles rising as she recognised the subtle shift in the air that told her it was him. Pride kicked in and fortified her spine. There was no way she would let him know that his actions had hurt her. Determined to be cool and dignified despite her racing heartbeat, she finished off a leisurely stretch and then stood up as if she didn't have a care in the world.

He walked towards her, his eyes raking over the casual clothing she had found in amongst the clothes he had provided for her. She hadn't wanted to wear them but then she hadn't really had any choice. Nadir was garbed in traditional white robes that emphasised his regal bearing and sun-bronzed skin. How a man could make robes look sexy was beyond her, but unfortunately they only seemed to enhance Nadir's physical perfection rather than detract from it.

He ran a hand through his hair and she realised that he looked tired beneath his natural tan. 'Where's Nadeena?'

Of course he would ask after their daughter first. It was why she was even here after all. Stupidly, it hurt.

'Having a late afternoon nap.'

He nodded. 'Has she been okay?'

'Great.'

'Okay then it's you.' His eyes narrowed. 'What's wrong?'

She kept her expression bland. 'What could possibly be wrong?'

Nadir didn't know, but something was. He'd spent the last two days meeting with members of the UAE to determine Bakaan's future membership into the federation and he was exhausted. It had been a frustrating endeavour because his father had never been interested in political or economic alliances and instead had treated Bakaan as a lone wolf. Naturally enough that made some of the members of the federation highly suspicious of what Bakaan's intentions were and what the benefit was in including them into the federation at all. When he had explained his and Zach's vision of the future—drawn up and refined over many years and many lagers—he'd had a breakthrough and all but one had signed the new treaty.

Reform would be slow, he knew, and arduous but intensely satisfying once it started to take effect. And it was also supposed to be Zach's job—not his. Zach, who had still not returned any of his phone calls.

Now Nadir was supposed to travel to Sur, a Northern city, and present the terms of the agreement to the outer tribal elders who still held a lot of influence in certain sectors of Bakaan.

First, though, he'd wanted to stop off and see Imogen and Nadeena. He'd been frustrated the past two days that he hadn't been able to see them at all but the federation members had been due to leave and Nadir had needed to strike while the iron was hot. When he'd returned to his suite late last night, even though he'd sent a note telling Imogen when he would finish up, he'd been disappointed to find her already in bed. And not his. After their love-making two nights ago he'd assumed that things between them would improve. Seeing the look on her face now, he knew that had been an erroneous assumption.

He stepped closer to her and she stepped back. His smile turned wry and he deliberately kept his gaze above her neck or he knew he wouldn't give a damn about finding out what was wrong and fix it in his own way. 'I don't know, Imogen. But something is.'

She shrugged and he gritted his teeth. The wall was back up between them and she'd added a couple of bricks for good measure. Did she really find the idea of being tied to him so hateful? Or was it something else? Her London lover, perhaps?

He tried to cap his instant irritation at the thought of them living together and reminded himself that the buffoon was part of her past and she was as entitled to one as much as he was. Unfortunately, it didn't help. 'Did you get my message last night?'

She tossed her head in a feminine challenge and her wheat-blonde braid swished over her shoulder like the tail of an angry cat. 'I did.'

'But you ignored it.'

'I was tired.'

Not much he could say to that since the reason she was most likely tired was because he'd kept her up most of the previous night making love to her.

'And what would have been the point in waiting up anyway?'

Now there was a lot he could say to that and he barely resisted the urge to just pull her into his arms and show her. 'I would have thought after the night we spent together you wouldn't need to ask that.'

She shrugged again. 'We were two people letting off steam. It meant—'

'Do not say *nothing*, Imogen.' His jaw clenched tight. 'Not unless you want me to set about proving just how much it did mean.'

Her eyes flashed and it looked like she bit her tongue. 'Did you come here for a reason? Has your brother returned?'

He drew his hand across his lower jaw. 'No. Unfortunately not. And something about his lack of contact no longer rings true. I've sent a convoy out to check on his whereabouts. In the meantime I have to convince our tribal leaders in the north that this union will be for the good of Bakaan.'

'Sounds busy. You'd better go.'

A muscle ticked in his jaw.

Imogen turned dismissively as if she had a hundred better things to do and Nadir's frustration and tiredness tripped over into anger. 'You could show a little more interest than that.'

She seemed unconcerned by his outburst. 'What would you like me to say?' She was formal, polite. *Reserved.* The warmth from their lovemaking had gone as if it had never existed. 'Break a leg?'

It took three steps to reach her and when he clamped his hands around her slender arms she went as rigid as a poker. He gentled his touch. 'What's wrong, *habibi*? Has someone upset you?'

She tried to shake him off. 'You don't talk to me about anything—why should I talk to you? I'm just an additional problem you don't want. Nadeena and I both.'

'That's not true. I don't have a lot of time right now.'

'When will you?' She lifted her chin. 'Never, that's when. If this marriage goes ahead—'

'It will.'

'So I heard.' She lifted her chin. 'In five days' time, *apparently*. It would have been nice of you to tell me. What if I wanted to invite some of my friends for support?'

'Invite whomever you want.' His brow furrowed. 'And I thought I had told you. It's been decreed by the council.'

'I don't care if it's been decreed by the Queen of England. The last thing I want is a husband who is off having a good time without his family. I tell you, Nadir, if Nadeena ever hears of any affairs you've had I will unman you.'

'There will be no affairs.'

'Right.' Her green eyes flashed sceptically. 'All that travel and long hours at work…I know how it goes.'

'I do not operate that way and I never have.'

'And if you fall in love one day?' Her delicate brows arched in challenge. 'What then?'

Nadir gritted his teeth. 'That won't happen.'

Instead of being relieved by his reassuring words, she looked achingly vulnerable and he was beyond frustrated because he had no idea how to please her. No idea how to win her over.

'Go away, Nadir. I understand you have important people waiting for you.'

Her words stuck in his head. There was no doubt the emirs waiting for him were important. But so was she and he didn't want to spend another night away from her. 'Actually, I don't. I've cancelled all my other obligations.'

Her eyes narrowed warily. 'You have?'

No, but he would. It was only a white lie and what was he doing telling white lies anyway? He hated lies and liars and had never seen any excuse for those who did so. And yet here he was, telling one because he knew if he didn't he'd somehow hurt her again.

Anyway, Omar could travel north with the emirs. He was equipped for the job and Nadir could use the time to take stock of all that was happening in Bakaan. Take stock of the fact that he'd relished the challenge of the last couple of days. And why wouldn't he? It was what he did for a living after all. Bought companies experts said were dogs and turned them into cash cows.

If it was part of Zach's plan to disappear so that he'd have no choice but to get involved in Bakaani business then it had worked. To a degree because he still wouldn't take on the leadership role, no matter how sly Zach was. But right now all that was second to putting things right with Imogen.

He felt her try to pull away again but he slid his hands down her arms and felt goose bumps rise up on her flesh. His muscles hardened as he registered what the shiver beneath her skin betrayed and the need to stamp his claim on her became paramount. Forcing his hold to remain gentle, he sipped at her lips, took her bottom lip between his teeth and suckled it rhythmically until he heard the small hitch in her breath that said she was his. That little sound always undid him and he drew her closer and groaned as her soft curves yielded to his hardness.

'And I'm taking you out for dinner,' he found himself saying. 'There's a dance troupe in the city showcasing some of Bakaan's tribal dances. They're performing tonight.' He was sure he'd seen it on the list of possible excursions for the emirs because he'd immediately thought of her. 'There might be some other leaders present but I booked a private table.' Another white lie that would only be so until he got onto Staph.

# CHAPTER TWELVE

NADIR WAITED FOR Imogen to return from the restaurant bathroom and thought that if one more person stopped at their table to suck up to him he'd have them locked up for making a nuisance of themselves.

Of course it wasn't just him they were interested in. With her blonde hair and natural grace, Imogen would no doubt become the Jackie Kennedy of Bakaan if he were to become King. Something everyone assumed was already the case.

He sighed and was thankfully distracted from heading down that line of thought as Imogen wove her way through the crowd, Bjorn keeping a discreet but alert distance. She'd chosen to wear a traditional *abaya* for their night out and the thoughtfulness of the gesture wasn't lost on him. She could just as easily have worn something shockingly skimpy to embarrass him but it wasn't in her nature. He didn't know why he hadn't seen from the start that she wasn't manipulative or two-faced, as many of the other women he had dated in the past had turned out to be. Women who would simper and preen and bend any which way he asked them to. He smiled as his memories of the other night came back on a rush. He was already looking forward to the end of this evening and bending Imogen to his will again.

'Wow—this looks delicious.'

Nadir followed her gaze to the table. He'd forgotten all about the food.

'I hope you didn't wait for me to start.'

'Of course I did.'

'Oh, thanks.' She leant forward and sniffed appreciatively. Her eyes closed and a look of total bliss swept across her face and he very nearly called for his car.

'Is that cardamom and cinnamon I can smell?'

'And vanilla and honey,' he said roughly. Like her skin.

'What's this dish?'

Shelving his sexual appetites for now, Nadir turned his attention to the food. For the next hour they ate and talked and when it was time for the music to start the tables were cleared to make room for the dancers to take the floor. Of course he and Imogen were given a central position and moments later a lute started playing. Then a flute joined in along with a *riqq*. Imogen started swaying in time with the music.

She leant closer to him so that she could be heard above the music and revelry of the excited audience, her lips so close to his ear he could feel her warm breath. 'What's that instrument?'

Nadir turned his head, his gaze snagging with hers, their mouths inches apart. He thought about kissing her but knew he couldn't. Public displays of affection were currently considered a crime in Bakaan. Instead he inhaled her fragrance and reminded himself that he was a man reputed to have wonderful self-control. 'Which one?'

She swivelled her head and pointed towards a group of musicians and he breathed in her tantalising scent.

'The one across that man's lap that looks like a harp.'

'A *qanun*.'

She smiled up at him. 'It's beautiful.'

No, she was beautiful and he wondered how it was possible for his heart to feel so light when Zach's continued lack of contact was starting to worry him and insurgents were right now threatening to disrupt industry in the north.

She tapped her feet in time with the music and the lead dancer noticed. With a smile on her face she headed their way and Nadir knew what was coming.

'Would the new Sheikha like to join in the line-up?'

Imogen's face lit up and she said, *'Shukran,'* which impressed everyone within earshot, and joined them.

The audience cheered when they realised what was going on and the female dancers surrounded Imogen, much to Bjorn's consternation, and wound shimmering skeins of fabric around her to match their own costumes.

She stood with her feet together, toes turned out and he grinned as he remembered the time he had teased her about looking like a duck. She'd quacked and told him that after years of dancing she couldn't help it. He'd kissed her and told her he loved it. He still did.

Missing a step, she laughed and delighted the other dancers with her unaffected nature and he tensed as he wondered how any man looking at her could fail to want her as much as he did. Immediately following that thought was the one that said he should bundle her up right now and take her back to the palace. Back to his bed.

Only the dance had started and he couldn't turn away from her as she mastered the routine. His gut tightened and then the dance changed and the men joined in.

They looked at him with an air of hope rather than expectancy because, of course, his father had never mixed with his people like this, preferring to rule from the lofty heights of the palace walls. If he were to take the job he wouldn't rule that way and neither would Zach.

And then he realised what dance they were about to perform. It was the dance a man did when he was courting a woman and his instinct was to beg off but then he caught Imogen's eyes, her swaying figure. To hell with it. He moved to stand opposite her. He had never performed it before but he had seen it done many times as a boy. She looked up at him with a shy expression. Did she know what this performance represented? That it signified undying love?

His steps faltered as he circled her. Was that what he was feeling? Love? He immediately discarded the idea. He'd never wanted to find love in his life because—as he'd learned from first-hand experience—deep emotion brought even deeper mistakes and he liked his mind clear and sharp. Not that it was exactly clear or sharp right now but that was just lust and lust could be sated.

Imogen's words about how she only wanted to marry for love came back to him. What would it be like to have hers? Something tightened in his chest. He didn't want that from her. It was enough that they were compatible in bed. That they enjoyed each other's company. He stepped closer to her than he should have. 'Let's get out of here,' he growled in her ear.

She looked up at him with big eyes and he thought to hell with it and kissed her before dragging her off the dance floor amidst the shocked gasps of his countrymen. Things would be changing soon enough in Bakaan. He'd just add PDAs to that long list of improvements.

Imogen could feel the tension radiating from Nadir's big body in the car and desire made her blood grow sluggish in her veins. That dance they had performed back at the restaurant had been highly erotic even though they'd never actually touched. And Nadir had performed it like a professional. She'd guessed that it was some sort of mating ritual and she wondered if Nadir had ever danced it with another woman before. She wanted to ask, but she wouldn't.

Instead she thought about how much his people had loved it when he'd joined in and she wondered yet again why he didn't want to be King. He would be exceptional in the role. Was it because of his father? His sister who she didn't feel comfortable enough asking him about? And when would she start to feel comfortable enough with him to be able to freely discuss what was on her mind?

'Did you have a good time?'

'Yes.'

His eyes narrowed. 'You're biting your bottom lip. What's wrong?'

Imogen glanced at the driver of the car. 'Nothing.'

'By now I understand that *nothing* inevitably meant *something*.'

'You're not that clever,' she said, smiling in spite of her misgivings. But he was and it was a bit disconcerting to think that he knew her so well already.

Fortunately he let it drop as the car swung through the palace gates and stopped at the front steps. They both got out and Nadir didn't try to talk to her until he'd closed the door to his suite.

After finding out Nadeena was okay, Imogen once again found herself standing awkwardly before Nadir when what she'd love to do was go up to him and wrap her arms around his neck and kiss him.

With masculine grace he moved to lounge on the sectional sofa. 'You want to talk about nothing yet?'

Imogen sighed. 'Okay, fine. I was wondering why it is you don't want to be the next leader of Bakaan.'

She saw the minute the shutters came down over his eyes and shook her head. 'And why it is that as soon as I ask you something personal you refuse to talk.'

'I run a large organisation that is already showing the strains of my absence. I don't have time to run Bakaan as well.'

'You told me once that you love to take companies that are on the verge of collapse and turn them into something wonderful and, from what I can tell, Bakaan is in an identical situation.' She studied the way he rigidly held himself.

'If it helps, you are clearly a natural born leader, Nadir, and the people love you. You could do this job with your eyes closed.'

'It's not a question of capability. It's…' He sprang from the sofa as if he had too much energy coursing through his system. 'I never expected to do it. And what about you? That would make you my queen. Given that you're struggling with the whole concept of wife I can't imagine you'd be thrilled with the role.'

Surprised that he was even asking for her opinion, Imogen thought carefully before answering. 'I honestly don't know. I always thought I would one day open a dance studio and teach dance and…women seem to be very much held back here.'

'In some ways, yes, but equal opportunity for women is one of the key reforms Zach and I have discussed, along with better social infrastructure that would turn Bakaan into a competitive and vibrant place people would want to visit and invest in.' He stopped as if he realised how impassioned he sounded. 'Zach will make a great leader. And you should definitely open a studio. You're a beautiful dancer.'

*Was he serious?*

'You'd accept having a wife who danced for a living?'

'Why not?'

'I don't know…' Imogen felt at a loss. 'Maybe because you're a prince who has a Harvard education and speaks nine languages.'

The way he studied her unnerved her. 'Why should that matter?'

'I don't know but it does.'

'Not to me.' He frowned. 'Who made you feel bad about your profession? About yourself? Was it your father?'

His shrewd comment startled her. 'Why would you say that?'

'My head of security spoke with him when I was trying to find you and, as far as I'm concerned, a man who doesn't know the whereabouts of his daughter can't be much of a father.'

'He wasn't. And no, he never approved of my occupation. He was quite tyrannical at times and really remote at others. It was very confusing when I was little.'

'Ah, don't tell me—his affection was conditional on how well you toed the line.'

'Your father too?'

Nadir raised an eyebrow. 'My father's idea of giving someone a choice was to tell them how he wanted it.' A shadow came across his face as clear as a puff of smoke being brought in on the breeze. 'I left home at fifteen and headed to the Caribbean, where I took up bartending at a strip club.'

Her eyes widened with shock. 'You did not!'

He laughed. 'I can mix a Slow, Comfortable Screw with the best of them, I promise.'

'Nadir!' Imogen covered her mouth to stop a giggle from breaking out. 'Seriously?'

'It wasn't the most salubrious establishment on the street. After that I joined a building crew in the States and made money playing online poker.'

'I…I'm shocked.' And he made her Moulin Rouge career look like Disney. 'I take it you and your father weren't close,' she said ruefully.

'Actually, we were in the beginning. I was the heir. The golden child. As far as my father was concerned I could do no wrong.' He paused and stared into the middle distance for so long she started to think he'd finished but he hadn't. 'And then I did.'

His blue-grey gaze fixed on hers as if challenging her to ask him what he'd done that was so bad he'd lost the position as the favourite son, his face a mask of dark shadows.

The moment seemed distinctly brittle compared to their earlier camaraderie and she didn't know what to say. Ever since he'd come back into her life she'd wanted him to open up to her like this and share more of himself but now she felt that it would be invasive to ask him to continue because it was obvious these memories were incredibly painful.

He regarded her from beneath his long lashes, a look of self-disgust etched across his face. 'You don't want to know what I did?'

The quietly spoken question was savage and underscored by deep pain. Imogen swallowed heavily. She wanted to go to him and offer comfort but she had no idea how he'd respond to that kind of overture other than to disconnect from her again and it pained her to feel so awkward at a time when she felt he needed her the most. 'Only if you want to tell me,' she said, deciding that the decision had to be his alone without any real prompting from her.

He scrubbed a hand across his face in a gesture she knew meant that he was stressed and her heart went out to him.

'If we stay here for any length of time you'll find out anyway.' The words were toneless, as if he'd locked all emotion about what he was about to reveal in a place he could no longer access. 'When I was fifteen my mother and twin sister were killed in a car accident because my father's soldiers were chasing after them.'

*His twin sister?*

'Oh, Nadir, that's horrible.' She knew words were inadequate in the face of losing someone special because she still remembered how it had felt to lose her mother but she said it anyway because she wanted him to know that she was there for him. 'Why would they do that?'

'My sister suffered from Tourette's syndrome and my father never accepted her condition.' His tone was layered with resentment and contempt. 'As she got older my mother saw how detrimental life was for her in Bakaan and she wanted to move to somewhere in Europe.' His expression hardened. 'My father refused her request even though they were divorced and so she decided to do it in secret. I was supposed to go with them but I knew my father would be angry and I didn't trust what he would do once he found out.'

Almost afraid to ask the obvious question, she did anyway. 'And did you? Go with them?'

He walked away from her towards the windows and leant his arms against the frame as he gazed out at the darkness. 'No.'

If Imogen had ever heard a more bleak word she couldn't remember it and she waited for him to continue, suspecting that whatever he revealed next cut right to the core of who he was as a man. 'Selfishly, I didn't want them to leave either and so I told my father the plan.' He gave a brittle laugh. 'He set his men onto them; my mother panicked during the chase and rolled the car down a steep incline. They died instantly, so I was told. A small comfort, wouldn't you say?'

Imogen sat so perfectly still she wasn't even breathing—she didn't know what to say. It was clear that he blamed himself for their accident and she wasn't sure words alone would be sufficient to ever relieve his guilt. And in a way she understood how he felt because she was sure if their situations were reversed she'd feel just as awful as he did about it. But she also knew that he had to deal with his guilt and let it go because it really hadn't been his fault.

She remembered what he'd said to her on her first night at the palace about how his parents had dragged him and his sister through their marital problems and suddenly she saw him as the eldest child who had been torn between his love and loyalty to both parents and who was damned if he did and damned if he didn't. At least in her own situation she'd had her mother's unconditional love. Nadir had only had his brother…and his sister, who he no doubt felt he had to protect and whose life he felt he had cut short, and she could only imagine how horrible he must feel.

Wanting to at least close the physical distance between them, she went to stand beside him. She stared at his austere profile and she knew she had tears in her eyes because she just felt for him so much and wanted to rip the pain from his body with her bare hands.

'Afterwards my father refused to give either one of them an honourable funeral.'

Imogen's brow scrunched as she absorbed that piece of information. She shook her head. 'Why not?'

Nadir sucked in a deep breath and she knew he was containing his emotions and locking them down tight. 'He said that they had dishonoured and disrespected him and so to this day they don't have headstones on their graves.'

Without thinking, she reached out and covered the hand he rested on the windowsill with her own. His was much larger than hers and sprinkled with dark hair that stroked across her senses. It also felt cold. 'Was that why you left Bakaan when you were fifteen?'

'Yes.' He watched her fingers lightly stroke over the back of his knuckles. 'We argued about it and because I had challenged him once too often he disowned me so I left.'

And closed himself off from everyone ever since. 'Nadir, you know you can't blame yourself for what happened. You were only a child.'

He carefully shifted his hand out from underneath hers. 'I was fifteen. Old enough to know better,' he said bitterly.

'No, not old enough to know better,' she denied hotly and she knew that first-hand because at fifteen she had witnessed her father's affair with another woman and she'd had no idea what to do about it. In the end she hadn't told her mother because she'd known it would break her heart but her father assumed that she had and it had led to him leaving anyway.

He moved away from her and she heard the give of the cushions as he dropped back onto the sofa.

'I don't even know why I told you any of that so please if you're going to patronise me by trying to make me feel better then don't. Nothing will ever do that.'

Imogen crossed to stand behind the opposite sofa and gripped the backrest. 'I'm not being patronising, Nadir, but it's not rational to think that you caused their deaths.'

'I was a selfish idiot.'

'You were a *normal* teenager who was trying to keep his world intact.'

'Imogen—'

'No, I'm serious. I know you're hurting over this but how long are you going to punish yourself for the actions of a man who was an adult and should have behaved better?'

'You don't understand—I knew he would go after them.' His voice sounded as if it was wrenched from a place that was deep and dark.

Rounding the sofa, Imogen stopped directly in front of him. 'Nadir, you loved them and it sounds like your loyalty was completely divided. That's not a nice thing for parents to do to kids of any age.'

'There's no excuse for selfishness.'

'Maybe it wasn't you who was the selfish one. Maybe it was your parents.'

He looked at her as if he'd never contemplated that before and she knew that was probably because instead of processing what had happened he'd just tried to completely forget about it. 'Did you happen to get counselling at all?'

Her question brought a surprised bark of laughter. 'Sure I did. The place was called The Painted Pony.'

Imogen put her hands on her hips and felt the air between them become charged as his gaze drifted over her. 'I'm not talking about the strip place you worked at, although I'm sure there were many ladies ready to offer you a shoulder to cry on.'

'Unfortunately, I don't cry.'

'What a surprise. But, seriously, Nadir. I hate to think that you still blame yourself for something that really wasn't your fault.'

'And I hate to think that we're going to waste a whole evening while Nadeena is asleep rehashing an event that is best forgotten.'

Deciding to ignore that, she continued as if he hadn't spoken. 'Tell me this,' she began quietly. 'If this was Nadeena and she had made a mistake like the one you feel you made would you want her to punish herself for it for ever?'

He pushed himself up from the sofa and paced away from her, holding himself rigid. 'That's unfair.'

The fact that he'd even shared this side of himself with her made Imogen glow. It meant that he trusted her. And maybe it was time for her to start trusting him a little as well. 'Maybe you're the one who is being unfair. To yourself.'

Without thinking too much about it, she went to him and wrapped her arms around his broad back.

He stiffened but didn't move away from her and she could feel the heat of his body through the thin cotton of his *dish-dasha*. 'I think your mother and sister want you to be happy, don't you?'

He made a low sound in his throat that sounded like it came from a wounded animal and her heart felt as if it had been squeezed by a giant fist.

Acting purely on instinct, she ran her hands across his

broad shoulders and pressed herself closer. He didn't move a muscle but she knew she'd got to him because his breathing quickened just a little. Circling around, she stopped directly in front of him and smoothed her hands over his chest.

Emboldened by the fierce glitter in his eyes, she reached up and pulled his head down to hers. He yielded but she knew his mind was still in another place. A bad place.

About to pull back and give him time, she groaned with pleasure as he plunged his hands into her hair and took her mouth in a hungry kiss that completely immobilised her. Dazed at the swift rise of arousal, she pulled at his robe and moaned in frustration when she could find no way into it. 'These things are not fashioned for easy access, are they?' she complained.

Nadir growled and reefed the garment over his head and she heard one of the seams give in his haste to get it off.

Trembling with excitement, Imogen dug her fingers into the waistband of the cotton pants he habitually wore beneath the *dish-dasha* but his hands shoved hers out of the way so he could pull at her own clothing.

Hampered by the delicate *khaleeji abaya* she had chosen, he cursed in Arabic and she gasped when he grabbed hold of the neckline and ripped it clean down the middle. With her breasts bared to his gaze and his hands, Imogen felt her nipples peak as he bent his head to take one into his mouth. She threaded her fingers through his hair to hold him tight and felt his own skim down over her quivering belly, sucking in a deep breath as he ran the tips of his fingers around the lace between her legs.

'So wet,' he murmured. Imogen moved against him but his hands drifted to her thighs, gripping her hips as he dropped to his knees and kissed a line down her belly.

'Nadir, I—'

She didn't finish her sentence because he hooked his

fingers inside her panties to remove them and widened her stance with one hand while he delved between her legs with the other. Almost sobbing with need, Imogen placed her hands on his shoulders and watched as he pressed his face between her legs and stroked her with his tongue. She cried out as he pleasured her, her long hair swinging around them like a curtain as she almost bent double when her orgasm hit.

'Imogen.' Nadir lifted his head and scattered kisses across her pelvis. 'Your taste drives me wild.'

Gazing down at him with his knees spread wide on the carpet and his chest bare, Imogen swooned. 'I want to taste you too.'

She dropped to her knees as he rose before her and shoved the soft cotton pants down his legs. As always the sight of him aroused and erect gave her pause because he was just so big and imposing, so lethally male.

'Touch me, *habibi*,' he urged in a raw voice husky with need, his hands tangled in her hair, his warm strong fingers massaging her scalp. So she did. Flicking her tongue out to wrap around the head of his shaft as her hands slid rhythmically up and down. He let her have her way with him for what seemed like only seconds before he took over, groaning about self-control and need as he pushed her to the floor. Then he was above her and the only sounds that broke the silence were the mingling of their own harsh breaths.

'Look at me, *habibi*,' he commanded. 'I love to watch your eyes as I come inside you.'

'Nadir, please—' Imogen threw back her head as he shifted his weight and then drove deeply into her slick heat. She couldn't have said if her eyes were open or closed because she was in another world and when he brought his mouth down on hers in a demanding kiss she could hold nothing back as her world coalesced into this moment and then splintered into a trillion tiny pieces. He swore and

Imogen held his head in her hands and wound her tongue around his as her orgasm continued to roll through her.

Unable to contain his own climax, Nadir threw back his head and roared his own relief and Imogen knew she would do anything for this man. That she would follow him anywhere. That she loved him completely and utterly.

*God, did she?* Had she really fallen for him all over again? No, she hadn't fallen all over again because she'd never stopped loving him. She groaned and didn't realise she'd made the sound out loud until Nadir swiftly rolled to the side so he was no longer covering her. 'Are you okay?'

Cold replaced his slick warm skin and she shivered. *Was she okay? Would she ever be again?*

'Imogen, did I hurt you?'

*No, not yet.* 'No.' She cleared her throat and shifted on the silk Persian carpet beneath her. 'I'm fine.' At least she hoped she was.

He leaned over and cradled her cheek in the palm of his hand. 'You're sure? I wasn't too rough?'

God, he was divine. Beautifully rugged and so elementally male. Would he hurt her? Or did knowing that he would never love her mean that he didn't have that power any more? Because it was the hope before that had made the crash-landing so disastrous, wasn't it?

'Imogen, you're scaring me.'

'I'm sorry. I'm fine. I was just thinking…I was thinking that this thing…'

She fluttered her hands between them and he smiled. 'It only gets better. Stronger.'

Was he feeling it too? Was it possible he had fallen for her as well? 'Yes,' she whispered, her heart lodged somewhere near her throat and constricted her breathing. 'I…'

'Yes,' he agreed and pushed her hair back from her face. 'Every time we make love I want you more. I wouldn't have said that was possible. It's certainly never happened to me before.'

'Possible…' And then his meaning became clear and she felt quite ill. 'Sex?' He was talking about sex…

'Not just sex.' His eyebrow rose in a sexy slant. 'Hot sex.' He kissed her. 'Great sex.' Another kiss. '*Phenomenal* sex.' His smile was sinful and Imogen buried her face against his neck.

God, she had nearly made an utter fool of herself by blurting out what was in her heart and he was talking about sex!

'I've made you blush.'

She forced herself to laugh softly because what else could she do?

'You feel the same.' There was a deep satisfaction in his voice and Imogen pushed her feelings aside. She raised a small smile because she knew this wasn't a love match and to his credit he had never pretended it was. And what would telling him how she felt achieve anyway? It would only make her feel awkward around him and probably him around her as well.

No, it was better if this was her secret to deal with alone.

# CHAPTER THIRTEEN

IMOGEN CAME AWAKE slowly and felt the sun on her face before she opened her eyes. She felt blissfully relaxed right up until she realised that she was alone in Nadir's bedroom; the only sound she could hear was a hawk calling periodically outside her window.

Nadir had gone again. He'd woken early and left her. Still unused to having help with Nadeena, she sprinted out of bed and only paused long enough to pull on a robe behind the door on her way out. It was Nadir's robe, of course, and it smelt of his special blend of male and spice. Trying to ignore the way his scent made her tingle all over, she padded quickly down the marble hallway and into the living room.

When that was empty she headed for the outdoor terrace.

Expecting that she would find the same scene as she had the last time, Imogen heard the sound of Nadeena's infectious giggles. She waited for the sight of the devoted Maab playing peekaboo with Nadeena when her heart all but flew into her mouth as she discovered that it wasn't Maab or Tasnim entertaining her daughter, but Nadir—in the pool. The sight of his bronzed torso stopped her in her tracks and she drooled at the way the sun glinted off his skin and turned it to burnished copper.

Pausing in the doorway and half hidden by a massive potted palm, Imogen watched Nadir throwing Nadeena up in the air and catching her just as her toes flittered across the top of the water, his biceps stretching and bulging in a fascinating display while Nadeena squealed with delight and clung to his neck.

She watched quietly for a moment, completely unnoticed as father and daughter frolicked in the sunshine. It seemed impossible that only a few days ago he had been a single-minded playboy who worked and played to excess and she could hardly fathom that he could be just as at home presiding over a boardroom full of world leaders as he was blowing raspberries on a baby's stomach.

His handling of Nadeena as he turned her onto her stomach and floated her across the top of the water, speaking to her softly in his native tongue was gentle and tender. But then she'd always known he had the capacity for that because she'd experienced it herself fifteen months ago in Paris.

And after last night she knew he was a man who felt things deeply and she felt awful. Awful for the tragedy he had endured and for the fact that he believed he had created it and awful because she had kept Nadeena's birth from him and had never planned to tell him. In her defence, she had believed that she was acting in the best interests of her daughter but watching the two of them together over the past few days had shown her that she had been wrong.

It seemed bizarre that a week ago she would have said that he was not father material and yet her own father had been held up as a wonderful family man in the community and she didn't have one memory of him holding her and playing with her as Nadir was doing with their baby now.

A lump formed in her throat. Yes, Minh had played with Nadeena and there was no doubt he was a wonderful male figure whom she hoped would stay in their lives for ever but he wasn't Nadeena's flesh and blood and why would she want to substitute that when Nadir obviously cared for their baby so much already? Yes, he could change his mind one day; yes, he could walk away, but maybe he wouldn't either.

'Imogen! *Habibi*.'

Catching sight of her, Nadir moved towards the edge of the pool and Nadeena bounced in his arms with excitement as she smiled and stepped outside. 'I've been teaching the kid to swim and she's a natural.'

Imogen grinned as he called her *the kid*. 'She's five months old—you can't possibly tell.'

'I can tell. And I read that the earlier you get a child used to water the better they are and she loves it.'

She also loved him, by the look of glee on her chubby face, and it only drove her feeling of guilt deeper. 'Does she need feeding?'

'Maybe.' His gaze swept over her and she realised how dishevelled she looked. 'You come straight from bed, *habibi*?'

The way he said *bed* made her blush and she was constantly surprised by her visceral reaction to this man. All he had to do was look at her like he was now and she would happily let him do whatever he wanted as frequently as he wanted. Was it any wonder she had fallen for him again? She knew she'd been a fool to think that she could spend time with someone so utterly virile and not crave more.

'Are you hungry?' he said, climbing out of the pool with Nadeena lifted high against his shoulder. 'There's pastries and fresh fruit on the table and also a pot of tea, although it might need reheating.'

'Thanks.' About to take Nadeena from him, she was startled when he dropped a sweet lingering kiss on her lips. '*Sabah el kheer*. Good morning, beautiful,' he said with a sexy grin.

Imogen swallowed the lump that hadn't quite disappeared from her throat. 'Good morning to you too.'

She settled into an outdoor chair and put Nadeena to her

breast while Nadir sat beside them and fielded calls on his phone. He hadn't bothered to put anything else on in the heat and she couldn't take her eyes off his long lean form in black swimming trunks and nothing else.

When Nadeena had finished he made a joke about her burping technique and walked Nadeena around until her stomach had settled.

Knowing there was no easy way to say what needed to be said, Imogen decided to just bite the bullet. 'Nadir, I'm sorry I didn't try to contact you when she was born. It was wrong of me. I see that now.'

Nadir stilled as if he hadn't been expecting her apology and why would he? It was only this morning she'd really understood how wrong she had been.

He looked at her. 'I wasn't exactly at my best at the time I found out you were pregnant.' He rubbed his stubbled jaw and gave her a crooked grin. 'And I don't blame you at all for running when you did. Hell, I probably would have as well.'

Imogen hated that he still thought she had run from him but then she realised with a flash of insight that that was exactly what she had done.

She had run.

She had done what she had so often begged her mother to do when she'd found her crying over her father yet again.

'That's nice of you but in hindsight I should have hung around to have at least talked to you.'

'But I wasn't there, *habibi*, and I didn't tell you when I'd be coming back.'

She sighed. 'I know, but…'

He moved closer to her and slipped the arm not holding their daughter around her waist. 'It's I who owe you an apology, Imogen. I was the one who failed you in your time of need.'

'No…' She shook her head and he leaned in and kissed

her. Nadeena clapped her hands and Imogen's smile turned watery.

'Yes.' His voice was rough with emotion. 'I should not have walked out on you. It was cowardly.'

'You were in shock.'

'So must you have been.'

Imogen bit her lip and studied him. 'You don't think I did it deliberately, do you? You don't think I tried to trap you?'

He shook his head. 'At first I thought all types of things like that. But I don't any more. I know you would never do something like that.'

Imogen smiled, wondering how it was that she felt better when she'd wanted to make him feel that way.

'What was her birth like?'

His gruff question surprised her and it took her mind back to what might just be the best and toughest day of her life. 'It was hard,' she admitted. 'I was in labour for twenty-four hours and...well, you've probably heard women talk about pushing out a watermelon?'

Nadir nodded.

'Try a beach ball.' She laughed and picked up a bottle of water from the table and took a gulp. 'A very large and very hard beach ball.' Her eyes misted over. 'And then it was over and she was on my chest and honestly I...' Her throat clogged as she remembered that she had looked around the stark, empty hospital room and wished that Nadir was there. She could feel the heat of his gaze on her and her eyes caught his. 'The midwife said that during the birth I called your name.'

In the process of laying Nadeena on a shaded rug, he stilled and looked at her. Imogen instantly felt self-conscious revealing so much and would have taken another quick gulp of water but Nadir was there and pulling her in against his chest. 'I'm so sorry I let you down.' He drew back and stared into her eyes. Rubbed his thumb gently over the drop of water that clung to her lower lip. 'I'm so sorry you had to go through that alone.'

'I wasn't completely alone.' She sniffed back a rush of tears. 'Minh visited and took care of us afterwards.'

'Great.' The word came out on a snarl. 'Remind me to thank him next time I see him.'

Wondering what was up with him, she frowned. 'He's com—'

Nadir placed a finger over her lips. 'I don't want to talk about him.' His voice was low and fierce. 'You won't ever need him or any other man again, do you understand, Imogen?' He was as intense as he had been when he'd told her he was taking her to Bakaan and wouldn't accept any arguments and Imogen was riveted. 'And if we have more children you will never have to go through that without me again. I promise.'

More children? She hadn't given any thought to more children but they hadn't used contraception the whole time they had been in Bakaan. Silly, but she hadn't even thought of it. Her hand went to her belly and she tried to make sense of the jumbled emotions that assailed her. Happiness, disbelief, anxiety…

'What is it, *habibi?* Don't you want more children?'

Yes, oh, yes. She loved being a mother. 'Yes. Do you?'

His smile was the sweetest thing Imogen had ever seen. 'Many.'

A giddy thrill rushed through her. The only thing that would make this moment more special was if he said that he loved her.

She let out a shaky breath. Oh, what she would give to hear those sweet words come out of his mouth.

'I never thought you wanted children,' she said softly.

He gave a short laugh. 'I didn't. I guess things change. People change.'

Imogen thought about her father and wondered if he had changed. If he was nicer to his new family. Had it just been her and her mother he couldn't love?

'What is it, *habibi*?'

Imogen bit the inside of her lip. She smiled up at him and shook her head. 'Nothing.' Why ruin the moment by thinking about the past? Nadir cared about her, she could see that much in his eyes, and he wanted her. Physically, their relationship was as good as she could wish for. As good as she remembered. She rested her head against his shoulder and tried not to give in to the gremlins inside her head that said this bubble of happiness couldn't last.

'Come—I have organised a surprise.'

'What is it?'

'Sand-boarding.'

Having expected him to say something like spa, or oasis, or beach, Imogen was completely flummoxed when he named something she'd never heard of before and which sounded like something builders did to houses when they repaired them. 'What is it?'

'You'll love it, *habibi*. Trust me. It's just like waterskiing.'

'I trusted you,' she groaned as she stretched her overworked hamstrings. 'And sand-boarding is nothing like waterskiing.'

Nadir lounged in the doorway to her bedroom and grinned. 'It isn't?'

Imogen glared at him. Sand-boarding had been just part of the surprise he had organised. He'd also taken them to an oasis and taken delicious advantage of their time alone together every time Nadeena went down for a nap. They had existed in a blissful bubble and then she'd ruined it by trying to sand-board down a dune as big as a mountain. 'You know it isn't. It's completely insane to throw yourself down a one hundred foot sand dune in the middle of the blazing sun.'

'Ah, but that was your mistake, *habibi*—throwing yourself down. The trick is to actually stay on the board.'

Imogen rubbed her sore bottom she'd used to skate down when the steep incline had petrified her. 'Thanks for the tip.'

'But I was very impressed that you even tried it. I don't know another woman who would.'

Imogen rolled her eyes because she'd slid most of the way down on her bottom. 'Pride,' she said ruefully. 'They say it always comes before a fall and I fell so often my butt is still stinging.

Nadir straightened away from the door and came towards her. 'I can kiss it better if you'd like?' He leaned in and kissed her and Imogen wrapped her arms around his neck. Finally when he drew back he left his arms around her waist and she gazed up at him. 'I've had a wonderful couple of days. Thank you.'

'My pleasure. I hope you enjoyed the oasis. It's one of my favourite spots.'

'It was extraordinary and I don't know why it isn't already on everyone's top ten tourist destinations. Really, Nadir, your ideas for turning it into an eco-resort are second to none.'

'You are second to none, *habibi*. Now, please tell me you have changed your mind about us spending the night before our wedding alone.'

Imogen pulled back and made a face. 'I haven't. You know it's a tradition for the bride and groom to spend the evening apart and I want to start our marriage off on the right foot.' And usually the bride spent it with her friends but Caro and Minh hadn't been able to fly in until tomorrow so it was just going to be her and Nadeena once Nadir left. 'But what about Zachim? I know you're really worried about him now and if you want to postpone the wedding we can.'

'No.' He shook his head. 'The council have turned it into a big deal so it's important that our wedding goes ahead. I'll find Zach.'

'And if you don't?'

'I will.'

He was always so confident. So sure.

'Tell me, are you happy, *habibi*?'

Imogen hesitated. Would she jinx herself by saying yes? Because she was happy. Happier than she had been in a long time. Deciding that was a silly superstition anyway, she nodded. 'Yes, I am.'

He kissed the tip of her nose and went to the cot to kiss his daughter, who lay sprawled asleep on her back, and Imogen wrapped her arms around herself and wondered if she had a right to feel so contented.

'Goodnight.'

Nadir gave her a searing kiss that nearly had her changing her mind about tradition but then he pulled away, briefly rested his forehead against hers and left.

Imogen closed the door behind him and leant against it, which was when she realised that she was still wearing his *keffiyah*.

Pulling it from her head, she clutched it to her chest as she remembered him winding it around her head to keep the sun from burning her. She sighed. Already she felt lonely without him and she told herself it was dangerous to want him so much. Dangerous to rely on him so much. But, try as she might, she couldn't remove the grin from her face.

Her phone beeped a text message and she smiled when she saw it was from Minh, telling her they would be arriving tomorrow around noon. Since the wedding wasn't until the afternoon, that would give them time to catch up beforehand.

When she had invited them she had been feeling as if her world was crashing down around her and she'd desperately needed their support.

It had only been a couple of days ago that she'd felt that way and yet so much had happened since then it felt like months. Now she was glad they were coming, not so much for the support and friendship they would offer but because they would be sharing in what was going to be one of the happiest days of her life.

Nerves fluttered in her stomach but she steadfastly refused to give into them and headed towards the shower.

# CHAPTER FOURTEEN

NADIR HAD NEVER been one to suffer from nerves and yet today, his wedding day, he was as jumpy as a stock trader facing his first day on the floor.

Maybe it had something to do with the overcast sky when normally it was true blue and cloudless this time of year. He gazed at the gathering cloud cover. The wind hadn't picked up enough to trigger a sandstorm so that was something at least. Especially since the convoy Nadir had sent out to find Zach had located the four-wheel drive he had been using overturned and buried in the sand. He hadn't told Imogen but he felt slightly sick at the thought that something sinister had happened to his brother. Fortunately no body had been recovered, which meant that he hadn't been buried along with the vehicle.

He knew he should probably call off the wedding until he knew what had happened but for some reason he couldn't bring himself to do it. He didn't think he'd properly relax until Imogen was truly his, which was ridiculous because she'd already agreed to marry him and she seemed happy about it. Or was she just making the best of a bad situation?

He frowned, recalling her slight hesitation the night before when he'd asked her if she was happy. She'd said yes and he had no reason to believe she was lying but that hesitation… Telling himself he was being paranoid, he counted off the other thing bothering him. The leadership position. For days now his mind had been vacillating over what to do about it and for a man who was used to making quick decisions that was just damned annoying.

His daughter bounced excitedly in his arms and he refocused his attention on the one area of his life he felt he had a handle on.

He had taken her early so that Imogen could relax in a deep scented bath and be prepared for him like so many brides had been prepared for their men in times gone by. He'd looked at her seriously and told her it was a tradition she couldn't refuse. She had laughed and said she was a girl and not only would she not refuse, but she'd revel in it while she was there.

That had set off all sorts of images in his head about her naked and wet and smelling like the sweetest flower. Tasting like the sweetest flower.

Nadeena pointed to something over his shoulder and started babbling. 'What is it, *habibti*?' he asked before his mind wandered any further down the sex route. One night away from Imogen and he felt as randy as a teenager who'd just been given the green light to go all the way.

He turned in the direction of Nadeena's chubby finger and saw a young stable hand grooming a mare outside the stables.

*'Hisaan,'* he told her. 'Horse.'

He strode over to it and stroked its arched neck. His sister had loved horses and suddenly a picture of her materialised in his mind and guilt assailed him, as it always did when he thought of her. As it usually did when he felt happy.

*'If this was Nadeena and she had made a mistake like the one you feel you made would you want her to punish herself for it for ever?'*

She was smart, his Imogen, smart to strike right at the

heart of the issue because of course he wouldn't want that for her. So why did he want it for himself?

He shook his head. As awful as that time had been, perhaps it was time he dealt with it and put it behind him. Of course he would change it if he could but he couldn't. But what he could do was take care of his own family. He could do what was right by them. Do what was right by Imogen.

He watched as his daughter gathered her confidence and reached out to place her hand against the horse's soft muzzle. The horse snorted a breath and she drew back, her wide eyes flying to his for reassurance. He gave it to her. Smiling and putting his hand back on the horse, encouraging her to do the same. 'It's okay, *habibti*. Nothing will happen to you while I have you.' His heart clenched as she followed his lead and then the skin on the back of his neck prickled. He glanced back towards the palace and saw Imogen watching them from the balcony of the temporary suite she had occupied the night before. Time seemed to stop and he couldn't take his eyes off her.

Her hair had been swept into an elaborate updo in preparation for the afternoon ceremony and her eyes were rimmed with kohl, her lips a deep pink. The honking of a car horn reminded him that stately cars had been coming and going all morning, delivering guests who would witness his joining with this woman he cherished above all others.

Cherished?

Loved.

He went dead still.

Was that really what was going on here? His heart pounded inside his chest as the words took root in his mind. He nearly laughed. Of course he loved her. It was as clear as crystal all of a sudden. His obsession with finding her, his uninterest in considering shared custody—and yes, he had strong views about that and he never wanted

Nadeena to suffer as he had—but Nadeena wasn't him and neither he nor Imogen would do that to her.

He wiped a smudge of dirt from Nadeena's cheek. The simple fact was that Imogen completed him. Waking up beside her, holding her in his arms at night, listening to her talk about her dreams, her hopes…wanting to see her fulfil her true potential.

Last night she'd turned him away because she had wanted to start their wedding off on the right foot. Now he wanted to do the same thing. Because he knew she only wanted to marry for love and he wanted to tell her how he felt before the ceremony. He didn't want her going into this wedding thinking that this was nothing but a marriage of convenience for him. Or inconvenience, as he had arrogantly claimed a week ago. He gave his daughter a wry smile. 'Your papa can be an ass.'

She looked at him solemnly and babbled something as if she was in complete agreement.

Laughing, he glanced up at the balcony again only to find it empty. A sudden feeling of vulnerability gripped him hard. What would she say when he told her how he felt? And was now really the right time? Perhaps he should wait, sound her out a little before he dived straight in with the *I love you*s? Hell, how did a man even start a conversation like that?

Deep in thought as he strode into the palace, he didn't see his brother until he almost ran straight into him.

Relief was followed swiftly by absolute fury. 'Where the hell have you been? You have a lot of explaining to do.' He took in Zach's dishevelled state—his wrinkled clothes that were covered in dust and dirt, his beard growth that looked to be at least a week old.

'*I* do?' Zach raised a dust-covered eyebrow. 'Thanks for the concern and the belated rescue team.'

Nadir frowned. 'You look like hell. What happened?'

'The short version is that I had an unfortunate run-in with one of the less welcoming tribes in the mountains.'

'Hell. For a while I thought you were holed up with a woman.'

Zach laughed. 'I suppose technically you could say that I was but it wasn't by choice and she's more like a spitting she-cat than a woman. One who is currently locked in the old harem. Not the most convenient situation on your wedding day, but then I didn't know it was your wedding day until about an hour ago.'

Nadir stared at him. 'You have a woman locked in the harem?'

'Farah Hajjar, to be exact,' he growled, his words laced with disgust.

'Mohamed Hajjar's daughter!'

'One and the same.'

Nadir swore. 'Hajjar will have your head for that.'

Zach's gaze turned wry. 'They both very nearly did.'

'For the love of…' Nadir's gaze narrowed. 'You didn't compromise her, did you?'

His brother gave a sharp bark of laughter. 'A wild boar couldn't compromise that woman and nor would it want to.' His gaze fell on Nadeena. 'I take it this is my niece.'

'You're changing the subject.'

'I am.' He smiled at Nadeena. 'She's beautiful.'

'I know.' Nadir wanted to ask his brother what the hell had happened but there'd be time for that later. It was enough that he was back and in one piece. 'I don't have time to get the details now but you're okay.'

'No thanks to you,' he said without rancour.

'Ever heard of the boy who cried wolf? That will teach you for playing so many tricks as a kid.'

Zach grinned. 'Come chat while I get cleaned up.'

'I can't.'

'Why not? The wedding isn't for hours yet.'

'No, but…' Nadir shook his head. He wanted to see Imogen and it was all he could think about. 'Here, take your niece and get acquainted.'

He handed his daughter over and was surprised when Zach took her so easily.

'Hey, don't look so surprised. I'm okay with babies. They're like women and horses. Handle them with the utmost care and don't do anything to rub them up the wrong way. Isn't that right, *habibti*?'

Waiting just long enough to make sure his daughter wasn't going to start bellowing in protest, Nadir smiled when a little frown line materialised between her eyebrows as she reached up to touch Zach's beard. 'Don't let her cut herself on that and if she cries take her to Maab.'

'Where will you be?'

'With Imogen.'

'Ah.' His brother cocked his head and gave a knowing grin and Nadir took the stairs to Imogen's suite two at a time.

This time Imogen made sure she kept well away from the balcony doors. She shouldn't have gone out there before but the time since she had woken until now had been interminable. And she still had another four hours until the wedding.

Butterflies danced in her stomach and her lips felt dry again. At this rate she would go through the whole tube of Rose Delight Tasnim had given her before the ceremony even started.

She wasn't in her dress yet, just a silk robe that was part of a dowry Nadir had ordered for her. It was gorgeous Parisian silk, as was the underwear she had on. The dress too was beautiful. It had been sewn by twenty local ladies and Tasnim had told her they had worked around the clock to create a dress fit for a queen. Which reminded her that she wanted to pay for her own dowry and she headed back inside and wrote a quick note to herself. It was only a small thing but she had started to wear the clothes Nadir had bought for her and she didn't want him providing everything she needed.

She sighed and tried to find something else to distract herself with because none of her old performance tricks seemed to do anything to settle her pesky nerves.

Or was it anxiety? Was it because everything had turned out so perfectly in the end? Or nearly perfectly. Nadir had not told her that he loved her but he cared for her and she believed that he would always do the right thing by her and their children.

Imogen pressed her hand to her belly. Could they have created another life together this week?

A knock on the door startled her and she knew it was Nadir. She hadn't missed that searing look he had given her from the courtyard or what it had meant. The butterflies in her stomach flexed their wings. He wanted her, that much was obvious, but still a little gremlin of doubt managed to insinuate itself into her mind. *What if he'd changed his mind…? What if—?*

Mentally slapping the negative thoughts away, she marched over to the door. Even though she knew she shouldn't see him again before the ceremony, she didn't care. She needed the reassurance of his touch.

'Minh!'

Imogen burst into tears the minute she opened the door and saw her friend standing on the threshold dressed in a bespoke suit and tie, which he'd always said he would never wear.

'Imogen—' Minh stopped smiling and strode inside '—what's wrong?'

All the pent-up emotion of the last week spilled over

and, even though she told herself not to cry because it would ruin her make-up, she couldn't seem to stop.

'Imogen, tell me what's wrong. If that bastard hurt you I'll deck him.' Minh took her into his arms and she shook her head to say that she was fine and buried her face against his chest. It was stupid to cry like this and she gave a hiccup and lifted her head, her smile tremulous. 'I'm sorry…I don't know what came over me. I've been waiting for you to get here and…oh, Minh, I'm just so—'

'Happy?'

Hearing Nadir's deep voice behind her, Imogen reared back from Minh and stared at Nadir. His face was closed. Hard. He raised an eyebrow. 'Ecstatic, even?'

Well, yes. She wiped beneath her eyes and her finger-tips came away black. Oh, she must look a fright! 'I didn't hear you knock.' It was a stupid thing to say but the tone of his voice had thrown her mind into a spin.

'You left the door open.' His steely gaze scared her and then he cut his eyes to Minh. 'I need to speak with Imogen. Alone.'

'What have you done to her now?'

'Minh, don't.' Imogen had a sense of *déjà vu* but she knew by the expression on Nadir's face that something was very wrong. Had he received bad news about Zachim?

'I don't like this, Im. I told you—'

'Please, Minh. I'm sure this won't take a minute.'

Minh's reluctance to leave was as palpable as it had been back in London.

He threw Nadir a warning glare. 'I'll be right outside.'

Imogen breathed out when he closed the door behind him. She turned back to find Nadir by the arched windows, staring out. 'Nadir, what's wrong? Has something happened? Nadeena—'

'She's fine. I left her with Zach.'

'Oh, then he's back!'

'Yes.'

'That's wonderful news. I thought maybe, but…' She took a deep breath. Started again. 'Is he okay?'

'He's fine.'

She hesitated. 'So that's good. Isn't it?'

'It's very good.'

He turned and stuck his hands in the pockets of his jeans and stared at her.

'You're starting to scare me, Nadir.' She gave a soft laugh as if to alleviate the tension in the room but it just ratcheted it up even more.

'I'm sorry. I don't mean to.' He cleared his throat. 'But we need to clarify some things before the wedding.'

His voice was so devoid of emotion it made Imogen's stomach roil. 'Like?'

'Like the fact that you wouldn't be here if it wasn't for Nadeena.'

Her lashes came down to shield the hurt in her eyes. They both knew that was why he had brought her here. It wasn't news. So why was he mentioning it? Was he afraid she had twisted the reasons for their marriage into something it wasn't? Was he afraid she had fallen in love with him? Taking a deep breath, she tried to tell herself that everything was going to be okay. 'I know that.'

He nodded. 'And the fact that you never wanted this marriage.'

Imogen frowned. She half expected to see a gavel in his hand. 'No. I…' She hesitated, wondering how to answer when he jumped in first.

'Wanted to marry for love? Is that what you were going to say?'

She nodded and then shook her head. No, she hadn't been going to say that; she'd been going to say that in the beginning she had wanted that but now—

'Yes or no, Imogen?'

'Yes, I wanted to marry for love but…' She swallowed, her eyes searching his face for some clue as to what he was thinking or feeling. But this was the stranger Nadir—the man who had picked her up a week ago. The man who had walked out on her in Paris. A terrible premonition raised goose bumps along her arms but she pushed aside her apprehension and answered honestly. 'I've come to terms with that now.'

As if he'd somehow been waiting for that exact answer, he slowly raised guarded eyes to hers. 'Then you're free to go.'

'I'm sorry?'

'I said you're free to go.' He moved towards the door.

'Nadir…wait. I don't understand what you're saying.'

'I'm saying that I agree with you. A marriage of convenience is not a good enough reason to tie two people together for ever. Even for the sake of a child.'

'Hold on.' Imogen felt as if she had to fight to get every word out of her mouth. 'You're saying that you no longer want to marry me?'

'I'm saying you're free. You can leave.'

The room tilted and Imogen put her hand out to grip the back of a chair. Tears of disbelief spiked behind her eyelashes but she refused to let them fall. 'What about Nadeena?'

'My lawyers will be in touch about visitation rights—isn't that what they're called?'

*Isn't that what they're called?*

He was so cool and remote she wanted to scream. 'I meant—what about your desire to be part of her life? *Permanently.*'

Her body started shaking. This couldn't be happening. It just couldn't be happening.

'I still plan to be in her life. I just…' He looked away

as if it was too difficult to look at her. 'I have reconsidered my position.'

He had reconsidered his position? As if they were nothing more than a piece of furniture he had decided he no longer wanted.

'Oh, my God!'

'I still want her,' he rasped harshly. 'But not this way.'

Stunned, Imogen could only stare at him, his words barely registering as her heartbeat raced out of control and her thoughts went along for the ride. All she could think was that he had changed his mind. 'I told you this would happen.' Suddenly she was fifteen again and her father was standing in the doorway and her mother was crying on the sofa. Thank God Nadeena wasn't old enough to witness her own humiliation at the hands of this man. She lifted her chin. 'Where's Nadeena now?'

'I told you she's with Zach.' He swiped a hand across his face but Imogen barely noticed.

'Damn it, Imogen. I thought you'd be happy.'

Imogen felt bile rise up in her throat but she held it back by sheer force of will, determined that he would not see how much he had hurt her again. How much she had *let* him hurt her again. God, she was an *idiot* of the most astonishing proportions. 'I am.'

He nodded. 'Then there's nothing left to say.'

'Nothing,' she assured him and sailed into the en suite bathroom before he saw the utter despair in her eyes.

Nadir sat behind his father's old desk, staring at his computer screen. When the door banged open he looked up and found his brother dressed in celebratory robes with a scowl on his face.

Zach didn't waste any time on niceties. 'What are you doing?'

'Working. You look better.'

'It's amazing what a shower and a shave will do.' Zach parked himself in the chair opposite the desk. 'Why are you working? You're getting married in less than two hours.'

Nadir focused on the email he'd been trying to read. 'Not any more. I've instructed Staph to send the guests home.'

'I know. He came to me.'

'Well, it's good that you're here. We need to discuss who will lead Bakaan and I've reconsidered my position. If you don't want the position then I'll be the next King.'

'Big turnaround.'

Nadir grimaced. 'It's amazing what can happen in a week.'

He'd found his ex-lover and his daughter, he'd fallen in love with them both and he'd lost them both. And taking on the role of leading Bakaan into the twenty-first century would keep him busy enough so that he wouldn't think of any of it.

'Nadir, bro…?' Zach used the kind of placatory tone he might if he was facing a band of militants with only a soup spoon to defend himself. 'I'm not sure that's the most important thing to discuss right now. What's going on?'

Nadir thought of the scene he had interrupted in Imogen's room. Her ex-lover holding her tightly in his arms.

At first he'd been furious, his instinct to grab hold of the smarmy buffoon and pull him off her and beat him to a pulp for daring to touch what was his. Then he'd registered that Imogen wasn't resisting. That she was snuggled against him and that she was weeping. Sobbing, almost.

Those tears had torn at his heart and he'd realised in a flash of unwelcome insight that he was behaving exactly as his father had done in stealing his mother from her tribal village in a fit of passion and then forcing her to bend to his will when he had taken another wife. Of course his circumstances were different from his parents, he knew that, but he also knew that the common denominator wasn't. He was a tyrant who hadn't given her a choice. He now had and she'd very definitely exercised it.

He forcibly shut his emotions down. He knew it had been a mistake to let them out. They had confused things. Made him think that sex was love when the truth was that he and Imogen shared a phenomenal chemistry and a child and he cared enough about her that he couldn't force her to do something she didn't want to do. 'Nothing is going on.'

Zach looked at him. 'Pull the other one—it has bells on it.'

Nadir cut him a brooding glare. 'Fine. I found Imogen in the arms of her ex-lover.'

'Naked!'

'No—' he heaved a sigh '—she was crying.'

Zach frowned. 'Why?'

'Because she wants to marry him, not me.' Nadir surged to his feet in irritation and turned towards the windows. 'How the hell should I know? Suffice it to say, she invited her ex-lover to our wedding and now they're together.'

Zach blew out a breath. 'That's rough. Why'd she do it?'

'I assume because she loves him.'

Zach nodded as if he fully agreed and then started shaking his head. 'No, I meant why did she agree to marry you when she's still in love with someone else?'

'Does it matter?' he asked briskly. 'The fact is she was living with this guy in London and now she's free to go back to him.'

Zach nodded again. 'Which she wants.'

'Right. Now, there's a lot to sort out. I'm hoping you want to stay on in Bakaan if you don't take the leadership role because I'm going to need a right hand and I want that to be you.'

'So, to be clear,' Zach began, completely ignoring his

attempt to change the subject, 'she actually said that she preferred this other guy to your face.'

Nadir swiped a hand across his jaw. 'Can we just forget Imogen?' A muscle knotted in his jaw. 'She's not relevant to this discussion.'

'Sure.' Zach eased back in his chair. 'If you're happy with her bonking another guy then who am I to argue?'

Nadir slammed his portable mouse down on the desktop. 'I told you to forget her.'

'I will if you will.'

'Already done.'

'Nope.' Zach glanced at his feet. 'Must have left the bells in my rooms.'

'Dammit, Zach, I gave her a choice and she chose him. You want to rub my nose in it, you can go to hell.'

'Hang on a minute, buddy.' Zach surged forward in his seat. 'I'm not rubbing your nose in anything. I'm saying you might be wrong.'

'I'm not.'

'Then let me ask you this. Are you currently sleeping with her?'

Nadir stared at him, hard. 'You continue down this line of thinking and I can tell you it won't end well.'

'Just hear me out.' Zach threw up his hands defensively. 'I'm not trying to get a blow-by-blow description of your love life, I'm trying to say that I know women.'

Nadir scoffed.

'Scoff all you like, but I do, and I don't know many that would sleep with one guy while they were in love with another.'

Nadir eyed him coolly. 'They're out there.'

'Okay, sure, so what you're saying is that Imogen is one of those—'

'No, she's not. She would never play with people's emotions like that.'

'Right. So stop being a horse's arse.'

'Look, Zach, I know you're trying to make me feel better but you don't have to concern yourself. I'm good.'

'Bro, I'm not trying to make you feel better; I'm trying to talk you down off a ledge.'

'I'm not on a ledge.' Nadir's jaw hardened. 'The fact is I had no choice but to let her go. I forced her to come here. I forced the idea of marriage onto her and I wouldn't take no for an answer.'

'Like the old man.'

'Yeah.' Nadir blew out a rough breath. 'Just like the old man. Hell.' He stared at Zach bleakly. 'When did I turn into him?'

'You didn't.' Zach frowned. 'Admittedly, you're stubborn and a little on the arrogant side but you don't take advantage of people and you'd never step on someone else for your own gain.'

'That's where you're wrong.' Nadir stared at him bleakly. 'I stepped all over Imogen.'

Zach shook his head. 'I doubt that's true but if you did then go apologise and make nice. Tell her how you feel. See what happens.'

The thought of that made Nadir's gut pitch. He never told anyone how he felt. It was easier and no one got hurt that way. Least of all him. 'Hell. I love her.'

'You think?'

Nadir shook his head. 'I know you think you're pretty clever but frankly I wouldn't wish this sick feeling in my gut on anyone.'

'I would love to care for a woman as much as you do yours. Instead, I have to figure out how to stop myself from being shackled to a living, breathing fire-eater who would as soon run me through with a *kanjhar* than look at me.'

Nadir had forgotten all about Farah Hajjar. 'I doubt her father will push it. He hates our family.'

'It's fine. I can deal with Farah and her insane old man. You just do us both a favour and go get your woman.'

'Prince Zachim!' Both men looked up as Staph knocked and shot through the door like a rocket, his breath heaving. 'You need to come quick. The woman you put in the harem has disappeared.'

'Disappeared?' Zach frowned. 'That's impossible. I've put an experienced guard on the door.'

'Yes, My Lord. He can't find her.'

Zachim rattled off a string of curse words Nadir hadn't heard in a long while. He smiled and came around the desk. 'I'd love to stay and help but...'

His words faded as Zach, his mind already on the disaster that awaited him, strode out of the room.

Nadir headed for the door himself and stopped. 'Staph?'

'Yes, My Lord?'

'What did you tell the wedding guests who have already arrived?'

'Nothing, My Lord.'

Nadir gave him a faint smile. 'You're a sly old dog, Staph. I hope your faith in me isn't misplaced.'

'I would say not, My Lord.'

'And Imogen and my daughter?' He cleared his throat. 'Where are they?'

'In your suite.'

Imogen sorted out what she would need for Nadeena for the plane trip back to London and searched around for some sort of bag to put it into. Nadir had luggage in his dressing room but no way was she going back into his bedroom ever again.

What he had said to her before...she still couldn't digest it because it felt as if he'd ripped a hole in her heart and inserted a stick of dynamite for good measure.

The only thing she was thankful for was that her daughter would never know how it felt to have an absent father because she would be used to having him part-time in her life and Imogen only hoped he would be good to her when he had her. That he wouldn't have a string of stick-thin models parading through his house who— Oh, God. Imogen felt her stomach heave and leant against a chest of drawers to steady herself.

It was so ridiculous to feel like this because she had known all along that once the reality of marriage and parenthood set in then he would run a mile and she'd been proven right. And the prize? She shook her head at her reflection in the mirror. Her prize was a broken heart the size of Asia.

'Imogen? *Habibi*? Are you all right?'

Imogen swung around at the sound of his voice, fire pouring out of her eyes. 'What are you doing here?'

He stopped short and she was thankful that she had wiped all her make-up off after her initial crying fit and dressed in her T-shirt and jeans. She intended to go home exactly the way she had arrived. Well, almost.

'I needed to see you.'

To make sure she was all right? She couldn't fault his manners. 'Well, now you've seen me, please go.'

'*Habibi*, I—'

'Do not call me *habibi*.'

'Okay—fine.' He held up his hands as if she were a wild thing about to pounce on him and maul him to death. What a pity, she thought, that shape-shifting was pure fantasy. 'I know I'm the reason you're upset and I just want to talk.'

'No.' Imogen shook her head for emphasis. 'No more talking. I'm done here, Nadir.'

He looked around the room and frowned when he saw the minuscule amount of clothing on the bed. The empty cot. 'Where's Nadeena? Isn't she due for a sleep?'

'Yes, but since we're leaving, Minh is trying to keep her

awake so that she'll sleep on the—oh, this is not important. Could you please just go?' The last thing she wanted to do was break down and sob in front of him and the longer he stayed the more likely that was to happen. It was too painful to see him. Too painful to be near him.

He cleared his throat and shoved his hands into his pockets. 'It's probably good that we talk about him and get it out of the way.'

'Talk about whom?'

'Your friend, Minh.'

'What about him?'

He looked at her and his throat worked as he swallowed. 'Do you love him?'

*Did she love him*? 'Why are you asking me that?'

'Because I need to make sure I've done the right thing in letting you go.'

'Letting me go?' She shot him a fulminating look. 'You told me to go. You've reconsidered, remember—you don't want to marry me.'

'Of course I still want to marry you. I only reconsidered the reason for our marriage.'

Imogen shook her head. 'You're not making any sense. You cancelled the ceremony.'

'Yes, but I didn't want to.'

'Then why do it?'

'Because you told me the reason you were marrying me was because we had Nadeena and I wanted more.'

'More?'

'Hell.' He swiped a hand across his face. 'I need to start again. What I'm trying to tell you is that I love you.'

'You love me?'

Her shock must have registered on her face because his expression turned grim. 'Yes, but if you prefer Minh then I'll walk away.'

'Nadir, Minh is gay.'

'Gay!' The look on his face was priceless and Imogen would have laughed if she hadn't felt so ill. Had he seriously thought that Minh was her lover? Looking back, she supposed he might have got that impression initially but… 'How could you think that I could be in love with him and make love to you?' she demanded hotly.

'As I explained to our daughter this morning, I'm an ass. Particularly where you're concerned. I can't seem to keep my head on straight when you're in the room and every male who looks at you sideways is a threat.'

'Are you serious?'

'Yes. If you knew how many ways I wanted to hurt them—'

'No.' She gazed up at him, not really daring to believe this was happening. 'The part about loving me.'

Nadir cupped her chin in his hand and kissed her deeply. Imogen moaned and pulled back. 'Stop that—it will only confuse things.'

'On the contrary, our physical relationship is the only thing that's not confused. Imogen, *habibi*, can you ever forgive me for being so stupid this afternoon? My only excuse is that when I saw you crying in the arms of your… friend I assumed it was because you didn't want to marry me and I couldn't bear the thought of hurting you.'

'But why would you think I didn't want to marry you?'

'Because I realised today that I'm more like my father than I would like to think I am and that I was forcing you to bend to my will and I couldn't do it. I wanted to set you free, to give you a choice.'

Imogen dashed at the tears on her face. 'I thought you had decided that you didn't want me. That I wasn't enough for you.'

'Oh, *habibi*, you're too much for me. You're too wonderful, too beautiful, too giving. I'm pretty sure I fell in love with you the minute I saw you in Paris because I haven't been able to stop thinking about you since, only I didn't want to see it because I was so afraid of getting hurt.'

Imogen sniffed back more tears. 'I'm guilty of the same thing and oh, Nadir, I feel exactly the same way. I fell in love with you the minute I saw you and I've never stopped. I love you so much it hurts.' Elation rushed through her until she thought she might burst. 'Pinch me—I can't quite believe this is happening.'

'Believe it,' he growled, pulling her in close against him. 'And mark my words when I tell you that there will be no more misunderstandings between us. No more worrying about how the other person feels. You know that I love you. That I will always love you and whatever children we have. Tell me you believe me.'

'I believe you.' She grinned up at him. 'And not just because you command it to be so.' And then she turned serious because she knew she had to be just as open with him. 'I think part of the blame for today lies with me, though, because in my own way I saw what I expected to see and I didn't fight for you. I didn't fight for us. I won't do that again. I won't doubt either one of us again.'

'And I will never give you a reason to. Now, please, *habibi*, if you wouldn't mind giving me this?' He took her ring from her finger.

Then he got down on bended knee and Imogen didn't think she could love him more but, before he could ask her the question she knew he was about to, there was a noise in the doorway and she looked up to find Minh standing there with Nadeena, his eyes as big as saucers as he took in the scene.

'Ah, I think we'll come back.'

'No.' Nadir rose and swiftly crossed the room. 'I know we haven't formally met but I am Nadir Zaman Al-Darkhan and I would like my daughter, please.'

'Oh, right.' Minh blinked up at Nadir and Imogen thought he might swoon.

Then Nadir was in front of her again and taking up all her attention. He handed her Nadeena and then got down on one knee again. 'I'm glad our daughter is here because I want her to witness how a man should behave when he's in love with a woman so she will be in no doubt as to what to expect from a man in the future.'

'Oh, Nadir—' Imogen's nose tingled as tears formed in her eyes '—I love you so much.'

Nadeena clapped her hands and tried to reach for the ring Nadir held up but he shook his head. 'Sorry, *habibti*, this is for your mother.' Then he lifted his blue-grey gaze to hers. 'Imogen Reid Benson, will you please do me the honour of becoming my wife later this afternoon?'

'This afternoon!'

'Yes. Apparently there is a room full of guests waiting for us.'

'But I'm not ready!'

Nadir gave her a wry smile. 'Can I take that as a yes?'

'Yes, oh, yes. Most definitely yes!' She pulled him to his feet and stepped into his arms, where Nadeena promptly laid her head against his broad chest. Seeing it, Imogen did the same and Nadir cupped the nape of her neck and lifted her mouth to his.

'I think I need a tissue.'

Having forgotten all about Minh in the doorway, Imogen beamed him a wide smile. 'I'm getting married.'

Nadir brought her mouth back to his for one last searing kiss. 'Yes, you are. In an hour. And you should know that I've told Zach that I intend to become King if he doesn't want the position.'

Imogen smiled and finally felt that everything was as it should be in the world. 'He won't. You were born to be King, Nadir.' She reached up and ran her hand across his stubbled jaw, her eyes full of the love she felt for him. The love she would always feel for him. 'You were born to be *my* King.'

Nadir's smile was slow and sexy. 'A king who will be at your service. Always.'

* * * * *